When the
BISHOP NEEDS
an ALIBI

BOOKS BY VANNETTA CHAPMAN

THE AMISH BISHOP MYSTERIES

What the Bishop Saw

When the Bishop Needs an Alibi

PLAIN AND SIMPLE MIRACLES

Brian's Choice
(ebook-only novella prequel)

Anna's Healing

Joshua's Mission

Sarah's Orphans

THE PEBBLE CREEK AMISH SERIES

A Promise for Miriam

A Home for Lydia

A Wedding for Julia

"Home to Pebble Creek"
(free short story e-romance)

"Christmas at Pebble Creek"
(free short story e-romance)

When the
BISHOP NEEDS
an ALIBI

Vannetta Chapman

HARVEST HOUSE PUBLISHERS
EUGENE, OREGON

Scripture quotations are taken from

>The Holy Bible, New International Version®, NIV®. Copyright © 1973, 1978, 1984, 2011 by Biblica, Inc.® Used by permission. All rights reserved worldwide.

>The King James Version of the Bible.

Cover by Bryce Williams

Cover Images © FooTToo, Bodhichita, soleg / iStock

Published in association with the literary agency of the Steve Laube Agency, LLC, 24 W. Camelback Rd. A-635, Phoenix, Arizona 85013

WHEN THE BISHOP NEEDS AN ALIBI
Copyright © 2017 by Vannetta Chapman
Published by Harvest House Publishers
Eugene, Oregon 97402
www.harvesthousepublishers.com

ISBN 978-0-7369-6649-8 (pbk.)
ISBN 978-0-7369-6650-4 (eBook)

Library of Congress Cataloging-in-Publication Data

Names: Chapman, Vannetta, author.
Title: When the bishop needs an alibi / Vannetta Chapman.
Description: Eugene, Oregon : Harvest House Publishers, [2017] | Series: The
  Amish bishop mysteries ; 2 | Description based on print version record and
  CIP data provided by publisher; resource not viewed.
Identifiers: LCCN 2017016467 (print) | LCCN 2017022465 (ebook) | ISBN
  9780736966504 (ebook) | ISBN 9780736966498 (paperback)
Subjects: LCSH: Amish--Fiction. | Clergy--Fiction. |
  Murder--Investigation--Fiction. | BISAC: FICTION / Christian / Suspense. |
  FICTION / Christian / Romance. | GSAFD: Christian fiction. | Mystery
  fiction.
Classification: LCC PS3603.H3744 (ebook) | LCC PS3603.H3744 W49 2017 (print)
  | DDC 813/.6--dc23
LC record available at https://lccn.loc.gov/2017016467

Printed in the United States of America

17 18 19 20 21 22 23 24 / LB-SK / 10 9 8 7 6 5 4 3 2 1

For Priscilla Wright

ACKNOWLEDGMENTS

This book is dedicated to Priscilla Wright, who has been a good friend and a constant source of encouragement. She meets me for breakfast, for lunch, even to exercise. What more could a girl ask from a friend?

I'd also like to send a huge thank-you to the Harvest House staff, a truly wonderful group of folks to work with. My agent, Steve Laube, continues to provide insightful, timely, and extremely useful advice and direction. With each book I write, I realize how much I depend on my pre-readers, Kristy Kreymer and Janet Murphy. Thank you, ladies.

My husband, mother, and son continue to support me through this journey as a professional writer. When I doubt myself, you fill me with confidence. When I need a break, you provide it. And when I begin to consume coffee in copious amounts, you never judge. I love you guys.

If my math is correct, this is my nineteenth full-length novel. Some of you have been faithful readers since that first book in 2010, *A Simple Amish Christmas*. Some of you are just finding me. To all of you, I want to offer thanks from the depths of my heart. The fact that you are willing and eager to put aside part of your day to step into my fictional world continues to amaze me. Thank you, and may God be an ever-present hope and comfort in your lives.

And finally, "Always giving thanks to God the Father for everything, in the name of our Lord Jesus Christ" (Ephesians 5:20).

*Those who hope in the L*ORD
will renew their strength.
They will soar on wings like eagles;
they will run and not grow weary,
they will walk and not be faint.

ISAIAH 40:31

In three words I can sum up everything
I've learned about life: It goes on.

ROBERT FROST

One

San Luis Valley, Colorado
September 21

Henry Lapp crouched in a sea of bulrushes and cattails.

A light breeze tickled the hair at the nape of his neck as the distinctive rolling cry of cranes filled the morning. He recognized the call of a marsh wren, a night heron, and an ibis.

As he waited, dawn's light splashed over the Sangre de Cristo Mountains to the east, crossed the San Luis Valley, and settled against the base of the San Juan Mountains in the west. Sunrise turned the marshland into a sea of gold and warmed the brisk fall air. Henry moved behind a clump of bulrushes, the ripened seeds temporarily filling the lens of his Nikon binoculars.

Henry again heard the flat, rattle call of a sandhill crane, a *gar-oo-oo* that never failed to quicken his pulse. He brought his binoculars around to the sound and adjusted his focus. Nearly four feet tall, with a wingspan of at least six feet, the male crane was a beauty to behold. Its gray color provided a perfect camouflage against the fall stalks, rendering the splash of red against its forehead all the more surprising.

The crane took several steps east, and Henry did the same, barely noticing the way his boots sank in the mud.

Lexi stuck close, quivering, eager to chase. He should have left her at home. Throughout most of the preserve, pets were not allowed. He'd chosen this spot so he could bring her. No doubt it was something akin to torture for the beagle to not be able to do what came so naturally, but Henry had been unable to deny her pleading brown eyes when he'd begun stuffing items into his day pack.

With his left hand, he calmed his dog. With his right, he steadied the binoculars. Many people had abandoned binoculars altogether when birdwatching, opting for cameras instead. But Henry had no intention of taking photographs. Being Amish, he didn't own a camera. No, for him the joy was in seeing the majestic creatures, observing them and appreciating the wonder of God's hand in all things.

The male croaked, spread its wings, and jumped, neck stretched long—all for the benefit of its mate. Although he couldn't see her, Henry knew the female was close. She must be among the cattails, searching for breakfast.

He crouched lower, continued to follow the male's direction, and forgot about the arthritis in his knees or how he wished he'd eaten a bigger breakfast.

And then she was there, filling up his lens, slightly smaller and staying close to the juvenile.

"A family unit," he muttered. He could have raised his gaze and seen hundreds, possibly thousands, of the birds, but this chance to observe a family rewarded him more than watching an entire flock of birds ever could.

He crept closer, eager to focus in on the juvenile, which must be nearly six months old. The young bird mimicked the male, jumping and dancing and attempting to imitate the unison call that rang out from the adult male and female. The male had flipped his head upward, the female mirroring him so that her neck was parallel to his. What a beautiful sight.

Henry stepped forward, completely focused on the birds, and his foot struck against something. He lost his balance and began to fall. Lexi jumped out of his way, and Henry tried to focus on saving the binoculars, on not dropping them in the mud.

He was thinking of that, of how precious the binoculars were to him, when he landed on his backside, scaring away the family of three and causing an entire flock of cranes to take flight. He shook his head at his clumsiness and called Lexi closer, but the beagle was now emitting a low, menacing growl.

"Lexi, shush."

The dog paid him no mind. Her growl turned to high-pitched barks, and more cranes rose into the morning sky.

Henry lurched for the dog's collar, and he twisted, turning back in the direction he'd come. That was the moment he saw what made him trip, what Lexi was now backing away from, still alternately growling and yipping.

Hidden among the bulrushes and the cattails lay a woman's body, facedown in the brush.

Stumbling forward, he knelt beside her, swept aside her hair, and placed two fingers to her neck. He couldn't detect a pulse, and she certainly wasn't moving. But then again, his own heartbeat was thundering in his ears, and his hands were shaking. He should get help, run to the visitor center, but first he had to be sure. Gently he rolled the body over, his heart sinking in recognition.

She wouldn't be needing help. That much was for certain. Henry uttered a prayer for her soul even as his gaze froze on the bruise marks around her neck. His tears didn't begin to fall until he looked at her face—unmarred and unlined in death, as if the worries of her life had slipped away and sailed across the vast Colorado sky.

Two

Seven days earlier

Henry directed Oreo to the parking area at the side of Maggie's Diner. "Buggy Parking" was painted on the building above an artistic rendering of a horse and buggy. Henry couldn't help chuckling at the mural every time he saw it. The horse resembled a draft horse, which would never be used to pull a buggy. And the buggy looked like a carriage from the 1800s. But at least the good folks of Monte Vista tried to incorporate Henry's Plain community into their image of the town, which he supposed was a compliment.

Oreo didn't seem to mind the mural's incorrect details. The buggy parking area was unpaved, which was better for standing, and there was grass to crop. Nearby trees provided a fair amount of shade when the sun took a westerly dip.

Only one other buggy was there—Leroy Kauffmann's, by the looks of it. Leroy was a deacon in their church and the wealthiest member in their small community. He was probably meeting someone about selling his fall crops.

Tourists often looked surprised to see an Amish person at a diner, but the truth was Plain folks enjoyed a meal out as much as anyone. Most Amish families had eight to ten children, so for them eating at restaurants was usually reserved for special occasions, such as birthdays or anniversaries. But because Henry was a widower, and a childless one at that, he frequented Maggie's much more often.

"Back in a few, old girl." He tucked his large drawing pad under his arm, patted the mare on her neck, fed her a piece of carrot from his pocket, and turned to enter the diner.

Several people nodded hello as he walked in. Leroy sat at one of the two-seat tables with a man in a cowboy hat. He waved a hand in greeting to Henry, and then he returned to his conversation.

The place was fairly packed with a late-lunch crowd, so Henry was especially pleased his favorite booth was available. It was in the back corner, and he always sat facing away from the front door and toward the window so he could see the mountains to the west. He enjoyed eating there several days a week, and he believed it was one way he could build bridges between the Amish and the *Englisch*.

Though his community strove to remain separate in many of their ways—no electricity, no telephones, and their own parochial school— he also understood it was wise to foster relations when two such different groups lived in close proximity. He could be a good neighbor by supporting local businesses, and certainly that was one reason he came to the diner. But if he were honest, he'd have to admit he also grew tired of eating alone three meals a day. Plus, he liked Maggie's made-from-scratch biscuits and the fact that they served breakfast all day long.

"Coffee with biscuits and gravy, Henry?" The waitress, Sophia Brooks, had started working at Maggie's a little over a month ago, and they'd been on a first-name basis for weeks. It seemed she rarely took a day off. Henry had never seen her at the grocer or the library or the town's park. Work appeared to be her entire life.

She was young and capable, but an almost constant hooded expression on her face spoke of loss and pain—or so it seemed to Henry. As a bishop, he'd dealt with plenty of both in his congregation, as well as in his own life.

"Maggie's biscuits are nearly as *gut* as my *mamm's.*" Henry readily accepted the mug of hot coffee. "But I'm here for the meat loaf special."

"Good choice." Sophia wrote down the details of his order. "I could add biscuits on the side."

"A *wunderbaar* idea."

Sophia nodded and hurried off to check on her other tables.

Business at the diner was brisk, probably because the fall migration of sandhill cranes had begun. Monte Vista was a natural place for folks to stop since it was situated in the middle of the San Luis Valley. Henry sipped his coffee and stared out the window. It was a beautiful area. Four-teen years ago, the Amish here decided to revitalize their dying Plain com-munity by inviting families from Indiana who were ready for a change. Henry didn't realize then how much he would grow to love the place, how right it would feel to be there.

The valley was fifty miles across and one hundred and fifty miles from north to south. The Sangre de Cristo Mountains boasted peaks of ten thousand feet to the east. The San Juan Mountains to the west were a high and rugged portion of the Rockies, some of those peaks topping fourteen thousand feet. Yet the valley itself was flat and filled with farms, which made it a natural resting spot for migratory birds. Since moving to the val-ley, Henry had become quite the birder—a hobby that brought him great joy and cost practically nothing.

Henry enjoyed his meat loaf, mashed potatoes, okra, and coffee, plus two biscuits on the side. When he'd pushed away his empty plate, he stood to go outside.

"Leaving so soon?" Sophia had a coffeepot in one hand and an order pad in the other. She looked rather harried, and in that moment Henry realized she wasn't as young as he'd first assumed. She was probably closer to thirty than twenty.

"Actually, I'd like to stay longer if you don't need the table. But I want to check on my mare."

"Plenty of tables," she assured him. "We're between the lunch rush and the dinner crowd now. I'll refill your mug."

"*Danki.*"

Henry knew Oreo would be fine, but it felt good to stand and stretch a moment. At sixty-five, he'd learned that sitting too long in one position left him stiff. He walked out into the fall air and fed the mare a few sugar cubes from his pocket. The day was beautiful, the sun shining as it usu-ally did in the valley. A slight breeze blew from the north, reminding him winter wasn't far away, and if the weathermen were correct, a significant cold front would move in later in the week.

"Enjoy the sunshine while you can, girl." He patted her nose and then went back inside.

Sophia was helping an old woman to her feet, making sure she had a solid grip on her walker before hurrying around the counter to ring up her check. The woman was accompanied by a nearly bald gentleman who looked as fragile as she did. Whether Amish or *Englisch*, people aged the same. Henry had found the process held agonizing change as well as beautiful moments of grace.

When Sophia glanced up, he nodded once, and then he made his way back to his booth. She'd cleared off the dishes but left the mug, steam rising from freshly poured coffee. He sipped it appreciatively, and then he opened his tablet, pulled out a pencil, and began to sketch.

Henry had spent most of his life actively ignoring his drawing talent, but the situation with the Monte Vista arsonist had changed all of that. He smiled as he drew, thinking of Emma and her admonition that his strange ability was a gift from God. Emma was a good friend—and, he thought, perhaps something more. They were both widowed, and he'd taken to attending social events with her as well as asking her on a buggy ride at least once a week. He wasn't sure where their relationship was headed, if anywhere, but he was enjoying the time they spent together, and for the moment that was enough. Emma seemed to feel the same way.

As often happened, he became lost in the process as he drew. He had no sense of how much time had passed or that his coffee had long grown cold, so he startled when he realized Sophia was standing beside him, again holding a pot of coffee. She raised it, silently asking if he wanted more.

"*Nein*. I've had plenty." Henry glanced around and saw the diner was now mostly empty. "It seems I stayed longer than I intended."

"You were pretty focused on your drawing. May I?" She nodded toward his tablet.

"Sure. Of course." He turned it toward her and motioned for her to sit down.

Sophia's eyes widened in surprise as all color left her face. She pressed trembling fingers to her lips, and when she spoke, there was a note of fear in her words. "How…how did you do that? And why?"

In that moment, Henry couldn't have said what he'd drawn. Sometimes that was the way of things with him. Sometimes his hand rendered what his unconscious mind had seen rather than any particular scene, such as the beautiful mountain vistas outside the window. So he was surprised when he looked at the tablet.

He had produced a nearly photographic rendering of Sophia.

Three

Henry cleared his throat as he tried to determine how much to explain. Sophia's gaze darted around the diner, and then she sank into the booth across from him. "Why did you draw me?"

"I don't always decide what I'm going to draw."

"You don't decide? Did someone tell you to do this?" Now her voice was rising in alarm.

He wasn't sure how a picture could frighten someone so. Well, that wasn't quite true. He remembered how his first drawing, done when he was a young lad of twelve, had spooked his parents. But this was different. Sophia's fear was personal.

"I have this...ability. To draw anything I've seen. I suppose when I came back inside after checking on Oreo, I saw you helping this customer, and the kindness of your gesture caught my attention."

"But this is more like a photograph than a drawing." She glanced up now, her fear replaced by confusion. "You weren't even facing me, Henry. You were facing the wall or maybe the window. How could you remember these details?"

With the drawing angled so they could both see, Sophia's fingers skimmed over it—touching the clock above the register, the sign advertising cinnamon rolls *only $2.99*, the embroidery on the old woman's shirt, and a small scar along the side of her own neck.

She glanced at Henry. Her dark hair was shoulder length and pulled back with a hair band. She quickly put a hand to her neck, covering the mark that appeared in the drawing.

Henry tried to understand her reaction. Many people were surprised when they first saw his drawings. He knew it wasn't just the degree and accuracy of the details. It was that he was somehow able to capture the emotion of the moment. Glancing down at this drawing, he saw that he'd depicted both Sophia's compassion and the elderly woman's look of gratitude and vulnerability as she accepted help.

"How do you do it?" she asked again.

"It's rather difficult to explain."

She stood, walked back behind the counter, and placed the coffeepot on the burner. "I'm taking my break," she hollered toward the passthrough window where the cook set plates of food. Someone answered back, "I'll keep an eye out," and Sophia returned to his table.

She sat down, her arms crossed and her expression grim.

"Try. Try to explain this to me." She reached forward and tapped the drawing. "Because this is sort of freaking me out. It's as if you were watching me, only I know you weren't. And I still don't understand why—"

"I'm sorry I've frightened you. This talent I have is the result of an accident. I was hit with a baseball when I was twelve years old." Henry's hand went to the spot on his head. He couldn't resist touching it whenever he related the story of the accident. "The doctors thought I might die, and my parents...well, they were sore afraid. But I recovered, as you can see."

Henry reached for his mug of now-cold coffee and turned it around in his hands. "Afterward, I found I had this ability to draw things, and not just draw them but accurately render them as in an *Englisch* photograph."

"You have a photographic memory?"

"Not quite. The doctors claim there is no such thing. They say what I have is most similar to eidetic memory."

"And what's that?"

"The ability to view memories like photographs." Henry paused. He'd shared his story with very few people, and he could count on one hand the number of *Englischers* he'd spoken to about it. But he'd frightened her, that much was plain, and because of that he felt he owed her an explanation. "I couldn't have told you the gentleman had a stain on his shirt or the woman wore glasses suspended on a chain. I wouldn't remember those details, but somehow my subconscious recorded them."

"Could you draw before? Before the accident?"

"No better than any other child."

"Henry, are you saying you're a savant?"

He glanced up, surprised at her use of the term. "A label the doctors use, but I'm not quite comfortable with it. Actually, they called me an 'accidental savant.'"

"Like those people who can play Mozart on the piano when they've never had a lesson, or tell you what day of the week your birthday fell on the year you were born?"

"*Ya*, savants come in all types."

Sophia again pulled the drawing toward her and studied it.

"So you didn't come in here today to draw me?"

Henry chuckled. "Indeed I did not."

"You came in for the meat loaf."

"Which was delicious."

"And stayed to draw."

Henry had already shared more than he normally would with a near stranger, and an *Englischer* at that. But something in Sophia's expression pricked at his heart. He remembered the fearful look in her eyes when she'd first seen the drawing. Why? What was she scared of? And what had she asked? *Did someone tell you to do this?*

He didn't understand her concerns, but he wanted to ease them.

"I've hidden my ability for most of my life, but a little over a year ago something happened that changed my mind about that. I'm trying to learn to embrace it as a…well, as a gift from *Gotte*."

She tilted her head but didn't interrupt him.

"My *freind* Emma gave me a few drawing tablets and pencils for a Christmas gift. I sometimes take them to the park or library or—"

"Diner?"

"My first time to do that. Perhaps it wasn't a *gut* idea. I certainly didn't mean to alarm you."

She tapped her fingers against her lips, staring off across the diner. Finally, she raised her eyes to his. "May I keep this?"

"Of course." He tore the sheet from the tablet and passed it across the table to her.

"Thank you." With a weak smile and a nod, she stood and walked away.

Four

Emma Fisher was sixty-two years old, plump but not heavy, with hair that was now completely gray. She lived with her son, daughter-in-law, and grandchildren, and she had quite a schoolgirl crush on her friend and bishop, Henry Lapp.

"Rather an odd reaction," Emma said. Henry had just explained about drawing the young waitress, a woman named Sophia Brooks.

Henry often stopped by her place on his way home from town, and she looked forward to their visits. Now they were strolling through her garden, harvesting the last of the fall vegetables. Her basket held some tomatoes and a few bell peppers. Henry dug around a sprout, pulled out a nice-sized potato, shook off the dirt, and set it beside the rest of her crop.

"It was."

"You know people are often surprised by what you can do."

"It was more than surprise, though. I'm sure she was quite frightened for a moment."

"At what you'd drawn? Because it sounds harmless enough. No doubt your mind was taken with her kindness to the old woman."

"But I don't think she would have reacted the same way if I'd drawn only the old woman. *Nein*, it was more that I'd drawn her. Did I mention her scar?"

Emma shook her head.

"Small one on her neck. As soon as she saw it on the drawing, she brought her hair forward to cover it."

"Many people are self-conscious about scars."

"Perhaps."

"But you think it was something more."

"I'll admit the entire situation makes no sense to me."

He took the basket from her, and they walked to the front porch. Once there, he set the basket near the door, and Emma sank onto one of the rockers. Henry walked to the railing and looked out over the barns and fields. Emma's son, Clyde, had done a good job caring for the place since George died. George had been one of Henry's closest friends and Emma's husband, and at first she had denied her feelings for Henry because it felt like a betrayal.

Time and prayer had assured her it was no such thing. George would be pleased at the turn her friendship with Henry had taken. He would want her to live her life fully. Hadn't those been among his last words? That, and *I love you*.

Henry turned now and studied her. He was older—by two years—but his hair was still brown in places, he'd managed to avoid the extra weight most men put on, and more importantly, his faith and optimism were a balm to her soul. Right now a smile was playing across his face. "This is your fault, Emma."

"Mine?"

"*Ya*, for sure and certain. You bought me the drawing tablets."

"And I'm happy you're using them."

"You also encouraged me to draw more."

"It's a *wunderbaar* gift."

Henry sat down beside her and set his chair to rocking. "At least no murderer is involved this time."

"We can be grateful for that."

Katie Ann burst onto the porch. "*Mammi*— Oh. Hello, Henry."

"Hello, Katie Ann."

"Do you need something, dear?"

Instead of answering, she peered around the porch and asked, "Where's Lexi?"

"I came from town," Henry explained.

"So she's okay?"

"*Ya*. No doubt she's lying on the back porch in a spot of sunshine, dreaming of chasing rabbits. Or maybe she's chasing rabbits."

"You didn't come out here to ask us about Lexi, though." Emma knew how much Katie Ann loved the little dog, but something else was plainly on her mind.

"Doc Berry rang the phone shack early this morning, and Silas just remembered to tell me."

Even as she spoke, Silas drove off in the buggy, waving but not pausing to talk.

Silas was Katie Ann's older brother. At nineteen he was actively courting at least one girl and had fallen into the habit of checking the messages at the phone shack a couple of times every day.

"I'll speak to him when he returns. It's easy enough for him to write you a note and leave it on the table."

"That's what I said!" Katie Ann was seventeen and full of spunk and energy. She had an unbridled love for animals. After trying jobs at a quilt shop, a bakery, and the library, she'd finally found her niche helping Doc Berry on Mondays, Wednesdays, and Fridays. Since today was Thursday, it was safe to assume the message from their local veterinarian was about an emergency call.

"Do you need to be somewhere?"

"She asked me to meet her at the Kline place, but now Silas is gone in one buggy and *Mamm* in the other—"

"Not a problem, Katie Ann." Henry stood. "I'd be happy to drop you off."

Emma watched in surprise as Katie Ann threw herself at Henry, hugged him, murmured her thanks, and then ran off to fetch her workbag.

"She treats you like she used to treat George."

"I'm certainly not trying to step into his shoes."

"I meant that as a compliment, not a critique. It does my heart *gut* to see her excited about something again."

"That mess with the arsonist is behind us."

"Thank *Gotte* you're right. Though some nights I still dream about what happened that day." She glanced toward the woods, to the place where the Monte Vista arsonist had abducted them. "Do you still write to him? In prison?"

"I do."

"And?"

"And you don't need to worry about him, Emma. He's doing well incarcerated, but his sentence was for life with no parole. That won't change even with *gut* behavior."

Emma tsked, slapped her hand over her mouth, and pretended to be overly concerned with the status of a pot of marigolds. She'd noticed herself tsking a lot lately. What did it mean? Why did she do it? When had she fallen into the habit? Tsking sounded old, and while she was fine with the fact that she would soon turn sixty-three, she had no intention of sounding that age.

Katie Ann popped out of the house, her arms wound through a backpack that contained animal medical supplies. "Just let me check on one thing in the barn."

While her granddaughter dashed in the opposite direction, Emma walked with Henry to his buggy.

"I've been thinking about your situation."

"Situation?"

"With Sophia. The waitress."

"Oh, *ya*. That. I'm not entirely sure it's a situation, per se. More a puzzle to be solved."

"I might know a way to solve it. You can take me to dinner there on Saturday."

"Hmm."

"Problem?"

"*Nein.*"

"Did you have other plans?"

"I did, in fact." Henry reached for her hand. "I was going to ask you to the pizza place in town."

"It's a date, only we'll go to the diner instead."

"And what do you think we'll accomplish?"

"Put the girl's mind at ease, maybe? And also, I can tell you if you're imagining things. Women are often a better judge of another person's emotional vibes."

"I won't argue with that."

"You can pick me up Saturday, then." Emma almost laughed at that. Two years ago she would have been terribly embarrassed to admit she was going on a date. Things had changed since then, though. She'd looked death in the face when the arsonist had abducted them. She'd feared for, prayed for, and pleaded for Katie Ann's safety. She'd learned to appreciate each day as well as the small things in life—such as a meal shared at the local diner.

She was no longer embarrassed that the thought of a date made her happy.

One way or another, she and Henry would figure out what was going on with Sophia. It was a small mystery, and a small mystery wasn't a dangerous thing. In fact, it could be quite amusing, something to break up the monotony of fall cleaning.

It wasn't as though they were trying to catch a killer.

Five

We have confirmation.
She's living/working in MV.

> To what end?

No idea at this point.

> Any indication she has information
> re our next harvest?

Negative.

> Could be she's simply following
> the husband's footsteps.

Sentimental journey?

> Something like that.

Safer/simpler to eliminate her.

> MV isn't San Diego. We don't want
> to draw attention.

We do what we need to do.

> Agreed. For now,
> maintain surveillance.

Six

feel somewhat guilty that we're not going to Bread 2 Go."

"They close at four on Saturday, and besides, we're after dinner." Henry wiggled his eyebrows, causing Emma to laugh and let go of any last morsel of guilt.

Her daughter-in-law, Rachel, had made a nice casserole for the family. They'd be enjoying it and then board games afterward. Stephen and Thomas were still young enough to look forward to the time of family fun—though they often laughingly called it *forced family fun*. They were now ten and eleven and delighted in anything that could be remotely considered a game. Silas would be out on a date, but Katie Ann would join in the evening's entertainment. Emma's family was fine without her, and Emma understood she had no reason to feel worried about leaving them for a few hours.

As for Bread 2 Go, Henry was right. The new Amish bakery didn't serve dinner, or even lunch, for that matter. They served bread, pastries, cookies, cakes, cupcakes—basically anything Emma shouldn't eat but loved to. The place had recently been opened by three widows from their community, though they weren't all widows. Ruth Schwartz was and Nancy Kline was, but Franey Graber had been divorced by her husband, which was difficult if a woman was Amish.

Regardless, the women were collectively referred to as the three widows, and the bakeshop they'd opened in town a few weeks ago, named Bread 2 Go, was already a smashing success. They had tables inside, but they also had a drive-through.

Henry parked beside two other buggies and then reached for her hand as they walked to the diner's front door. A brisk north wind was blowing, and Emma was glad she'd chosen to wear her outer bonnet over her *kapp*. Once they were inside, she took off the bonnet and stored it in her coat pocket.

A thin young woman with shoulder-length hair picked up two menus and two sets of silverware.

"Evening, Henry."

"Sophia. I wasn't sure if you'd be working tonight."

"One of the other women called in sick, and I can use the money. Where would you like to sit?"

"Corner booth will be fine," Henry said.

Once they'd sat down, and Sophia had handed them the menus, Emma introduced herself. "I'm Emma—Henry's friend, old friend…"

"Indeed, we go way back."

"That must be nice." Sophia nodded toward a customer who was trying to catch her attention. "I need to take care of that table, and then I'll be back to take your order. Do you both want coffee?"

"Decaf please," Emma said, and Henry nodded in agreement.

Once she'd left, Emma leaned across the table.

"I see what you mean."

"You do?"

"It's as if she's working at being invisible."

"Why would you say that? How can you tell anything after one brief conversation?"

Emma knew he was teasing her. Henry often seemed completely bewildered by women and their ways, but she was pretty sure it was an act. He enjoyed people and studying how they interacted with one another. It was one of several reasons he was a good bishop.

"Her speech is very quiet, her smile timid. She wears no makeup, not even a hint of lipstick."

"You don't wear either of those things."

"I'm Plain. And as you know, it's forbidden."

Henry smiled, and then he moved his hand in a circle, indicating she should continue.

"Most waitresses find some way to brighten their clothes or appearance, some little thing to encourage themselves throughout the day. It might be a ribbon in their hair, or a decorative pin on a shirt pocket. Something to help them through the long hours of their shifts."

"How do you know these things?"

"Work is the same, Henry, whether in a diner or at home, whether *Englisch* or Plain. Remember the proverb our mothers quoted? *Keeping a neat house is like threading beads on a string with no knot.* I'm sure working in a diner is the same."

Henry nodded and removed his hat, setting it on the seat beside him. He was facing the wall and window, looking out at the darkness. Emma had a good view of the busy diner and everything going on there. She saw Nancy Kline's grandson sitting with an Amish girl, though she couldn't make out who it was. His buggy must have been one of the two parked outside. And the other? She craned her neck left and then right, finally spotting Abigail and Daniel Beiler on the far side of the restaurant. Abigail had mentioned it was their anniversary. No doubt they were celebrating.

Henry closed his menu, and Emma realized she'd barely looked at hers. She glanced through the salads, decided she was too hungry for that, looked over and dismissed the sandwiches, and finally set to studying the dinner plates. When Sophia returned, Henry ordered the pot roast. Emma asked Sophia which was better—the chicken and dumplings or the grilled trout.

Sophia shrugged and murmured, "Customers seem to like both."

"I'll take the trout then, as Amish rarely grill their food." She meant it as a joke, but Sophia didn't seem to notice. She filled their coffee mugs, assuring them it was decaf, and hurried off to another table.

"She's busy," Henry explained.

"I can see that, but watch the other two waitresses."

Henry cornered himself in the booth so he could glance over the room. All three waitresses were quite busy. But the other two would laugh at a joke, stop to touch a customer on the shoulder, smile at a baby. Sophia was all business.

"I hadn't noticed it before," Henry admitted, turning back toward her. "At least not consciously."

"But perhaps your subconscious did, or your heart did. Perhaps *Gotte* pricked your spirit. She certainly seems as if she could use a *freind.*"

Emma tried to draw Sophia out when she returned with their meals, but to no avail. It was only when she said, "Henry told me he drew your picture," that the cocoon around the girl seemed to fall away.

"I still don't understand how he's able to do such a thing."

"None of us do, including Henry."

"It's true," he said.

"I've known him for many years, my dear." Emma picked up her knife and fork and cut into the trout, releasing steam and the scent of fish and lemon and garlic. "It's only recently that Henry has embraced his talent and begun sharing what he draws. The picture you have? It's a rare gift to receive."

"Now you're embarrassing me," Henry said.

Emma kept her attention on Sophia. "I hope you took *gut* care of it."

Sophia hesitated, and then she admitted, "I did. It's tucked away safely, where coffee can't get spilled on it."

She smiled then, a genuinely beautiful and vulnerable thing. "Around here? We have the terrible three—grease, ketchup, and coffee. No matter what you wear or what you bring in, you'll end up with one or more of those stains when you leave."

The door to the diner opened, and when Sophia glanced that way, she blanched.

Emma followed her gaze, but only saw Scott Lawson, the newest addition to the Monte Vista Police Department. He was young, Irish, and well mannered. He'd recently given a talk at the library on scams in the area and how to avoid them. Emma had only listened because she'd been waiting on Rachel to check out her new books.

When she turned back toward their waitress, Sophia was gone.

"That was strange," she said.

"What was strange?" Henry finished spreading butter over a biscuit, broke off a good-sized chunk, and popped it into his mouth.

"Sophia. That's what." Emma tried a forkful of fish. "*Gut* food."

"I told you so."

"Now I see why you come here so often."

"Only a few times a week."

"The rice is *gut* too, with fresh carrots and peas in it."

"Almost like Amish cooking."

"Henry Lapp, you are not going to distract me with talk of cooking."

"Why would I attempt such a thing?"

"Sophia was starting to warm up when we were talking about stains. If you want a woman to talk, just ask her about laundry."

"Is that so?"

"And then Scott Lawson came in."

"The new patrolman?"

"The same. Weren't you paying attention at all?"

"I was. To my pot roast. Would you like to try some?"

Emma knew Henry was trying to lighten the conversation, but when she leaned forward and lowered her voice, he suddenly looked serious.

"She's afraid, Henry. That's why she tries to be invisible."

"Afraid of what?"

"I have no idea."

Henry set down his fork, wiped his mouth, and studied Emma for a moment. Finally he said, "What do you think we should do?"

"I'm not sure we should do anything." She tried the corn and nodded in appreciation—fresh not canned. A woman could always tell. "There's one thing, though. Maybe it has to do with her husband."

"Husband?"

"It could. Often it does in these situations."

"These situations?"

"Stop repeating what I say, Henry."

"How do you even know she's married?"

Emma tapped the fourth finger on her left hand. "Indentation. Plain as day if you look. She might not be married now, but she was. Maybe there was some problem, and maybe that's why she's hiding in Monte Vista."

Seven

Sophia once again offered to stay past her shift and close the diner. She preferred waiting until the parking lot was empty before leaving. That way she could tell if anyone was following her.

Caution was a good thing. Paranoia? Not so much.

Keeping those two in balance was a constant struggle.

She gave the tables a final wipe-down, made sure all of the salt and pepper shakers were filled, and was sweeping the floor when Travis Small walked in, whistling. Travis wasn't a tall man, but he definitely wasn't small. She guessed his height at five and a half feet, same as hers, but he had to weigh more than two hundred pounds. His skin was ebony, wrinkled and weathered, giving him a leathery look. His hair was cut close to his scalp and reminded Sophia of white cotton.

He'd told Sophia he was seventy-eight years old, and that he cleaned the diner each night to stay active. Every indication was he was telling the truth. How could she know, though? People often weren't who they appeared to be.

"You keep doing my work, and they're going to fire me."

"Sorry, Travis." Sophia straightened up, stretching her back and glancing outside. "Guess I lost track of time."

"Every night? If you say so."

Sophia handed him the broom, pushed through the double doors to the employees' area, and removed her purse and jacket from her locker. Walking back through the dining area, she paused near the cash register and waited for Travis to look up. "You know that new cop? The one with reddish hair?"

"Guess I've seen him a couple of times."

"You trust him?"

"Now, that's an interesting question." Travis leaned on his broom.

Instead of looking at Sophia, he let his gaze drift over the diner. She tried to see what he must see. Travis had told her he'd grown up in Monte Vista. He often talked about the old days, when everyone knew everyone else. When no tourists traveled through and most folks were farmers.

When the diner was empty and clean, Sophia thought the place took on a tranquil, almost holy atmosphere. Light reflected off the black vinyl of the stools lined up in front of the counter, and the black-and-white checkered floor nearly gleamed. How many people had fallen in love here? Severed relationships? Met new friends? Hidden from their enemies?

It seemed to her that, even more so than town halls or community centers, diners were the heartbeat of a town. Her gut was telling her Monte Vista was a good place, a community filled with hardworking, decent people like Henry and Emma and Travis. More importantly, she needed to be here. Cooper had left her a journal, and those entries had pointed to the San Luis Valley. He wrote cryptically in a shorthand that made her laugh and brought tears to her eyes at the same time. The reason she was there, though—there and alone—never failed to stir an ache in her heart. She didn't know exactly what her husband had uncovered, but it was big enough that he'd paid for it with his life.

She fingered the scar on her neck, resolve flooding her system and wiping away all doubts. She wasn't giving up until she figured out what story Cooper had been chasing.

But she could no longer trust her instincts, and something about the new cop had struck her as off.

"Can't say as I really know him," Travis added.

"He arrived in town a few weeks ago."

"I guess."

Sophia shrugged, acted as if the topic no longer interested her, and pushed open the front door. A cold wind nearly pulled it from her hands, and she was thinking of hanging on to the door so it wouldn't bang when Travis's words pulled her back inside. He appeared to be completely focused on cleaning underneath a table, but his tone had taken on a heaviness that sounded almost like a warning.

"Lots of good officers, and I wouldn't want their job. No, sir. This old man is happy cleaning floors and washing windows. An officer's job requires quick reactions, a knack for reading people, and the ability to make quick decisions. Sometimes life-or-death decisions." He moved over to the next table.

"But then in every group you have the potential to get a bad apple, and that can be a truly terrible thing with someone who is supposed to have our trust." He studied her for a moment and then returned to his sweeping. "As for Officer Lawson, I expect time will tell."

It wasn't only that Lawson stopped by the diner every day. That in itself wasn't so odd. But he often came in on Sophia's shift, and several times she'd caught him watching her. He wasn't the only one. Officer Anderson, who according to the diner's manager, Julie, had been in Monte Vista for years and years, did the same thing. Perhaps they knew something Sophia didn't. Maybe they were protecting her, or they were part of the group that had killed her husband. There was even a chance she was imagining the whole thing.

Sophia turned to look out at the cooling September night. She didn't have time to figure out which side Lawson or Anderson was on, or if they were involved at all. Misreading—and underestimating—either man's intentions could be costly. She'd already made one mistake when it came to the police. She wouldn't again.

She needed to check out of the motel where she'd been staying since coming to Monte Vista. It would be safer to spend the night somewhere else—somewhere they couldn't find her. If people were following her, they wouldn't make a move at the diner, but they might catch her while she was sleeping—if they knew where she was sleeping. The weather wasn't so cold that she couldn't sleep outside, or maybe it would be enough to move to one of the other motels in town. But if the manager there was compromised…

She looked back at the diner, at Travis working on the next section of floor. She felt safe at Maggie's. Maggie herself wasn't around much, having retired. But her niece, Julie, who was the manager, and the other waitresses had taken Sophia under their collective wing, as if she were a young girl who needed protection. They'd managed to help her feel safe during working hours when the booths were full and the bell over the door rang constantly. She could continue to work there a few more days, a week at the most. Her window for finding any evidence was shrinking.

"You okay?" Travis asked.

Sophia realized she'd been standing there, staring at him, her hand on the door.

"Maybe," she answered honestly.

Travis nodded as if that made sense. "Some people you have to watch out for, but never forget every community has good people too."

"How do I know the difference?"

"Listen to your heart. What you see or hear might fool you, but your instincts? If you listen, they will guide you correctly."

"Thank you, Travis."

"For what? Talking to a pretty girl as I clean this floor? That's no hardship at all. Now you be careful, hear?"

As she stepped out into the night, she tried to zone in on her instincts, to discern whatever her subconscious was trying to tell her. Her thoughts and doubts and fears tumbled round, always landing on the same tender spot. The problem was she didn't trust her instincts anymore. Sometime in the middle of everything that had happened, they had gone askew. The scar on her neck was proof of that.

She supposed it didn't matter who was or wasn't watching her.

She knew what she was doing would be dangerous before she stepped onto that Greyhound bus. Nothing had changed in that regard. She also realized the odds of success were slim. But that hadn't stopped her before, and it wasn't going to now.

Eight

She checked out of her motel.

                                   Why?

I didn't ask.

                       Do your job and find out.

I think she's spooked.

                    Any indication she spotted you?

No.

                    Who else has she been talking to?

How would I know?
I can't stay on her 24/7.

                         Where is she now?

Leaving the motel.

                              Follow her.

Intercept?

                               Not yet.

Nine

Their Sunday service was held at the Graber home.

As Henry walked to the house from his buggy, he realized for probably the thousandth time how grateful he was that he had good people to support him in guiding their church. Their leadership consisted of Abe Graber, Clyde Fisher, and Leroy Kauffmann. Each one was selected by lot as the positions became available, which was the Amish way. He'd overseen all three selections.

When a position became open, members—both men and women—nominated a man to fill the position. Henry understood *Englischers* found this to be sexist, but the Plain faith was based on Anabaptist teaching, which, in their opinion, called for a strict interpretation of the Scriptures. He fully understood how much influence women had on the church, and that as a believing body, they could not exist without them. But the official positions of deacon and bishop were always filled by men.

Henry took great pleasure in the process. Bibles were stacked at the back of the church, one for each person nominated. Henry prayerfully slipped a bookmark into one of them. Each man, nominated by at least three other members, was invited into the meeting, where he picked up one of the Bibles. After a prayer and introduction, Henry instructed them to open their Bibles. The one with a bookmark in it was considered chosen by God to serve, and to serve for life.

"Morning, Henry."

"Gudemariye."

Abe was in his midforties, had dark hair and bushy eyebrows, and always wore glasses. "Bit cold today. We'd hoped to have the service outside, but…"

"Perhaps the house is better."

"*Ya*, and we'll have lunch in the barn. Hopefully, the wind will stop blowing by then, and the *youngies* can scatter outside."

Abe hurried off to see if his wife, Susan, needed any last-minute help. The two of them had four children, not a lot by Amish standards. They also provided for Franey, Abe's sister-in-law, who had been divorced by her husband when he left the Amish faith.

Abe was a minister and therefore a preacher. He'd been hesitant to accept the position, but there was no valid reason for denial, except perhaps poor health. Abe was as fit as a workhorse both at the time of his nomination and now. He'd grown into the position of minister, and Henry greatly appreciated having the man in their community.

Clyde and Leroy were already busy putting hymnals on the benches that had been placed in the sitting room and dining area. When services were held inside, which in Colorado was at least half the year, all of the furniture was removed from the main sitting room. Some members would arrive the day before the service to help stack the furniture, most often in a barn, to make room for the benches that had been delivered in a wagon the week before. It was usually crowded, but they always managed to fit.

"*Gudemariye*, Henry." Leroy had recently turned fifty-nine. He was by far the wealthiest member of their group, though you wouldn't know it by his clothing or buggy. His farm was a bit larger than most, and he had slightly younger horses and a bigger barn.

"And to you, Leroy."

"Wind's a blowing, Henry." Clyde Fisher balanced an armful of hymnals with the word *Ausbund* stamped across the front. Clyde was the youngest of the three deacons, only forty-one. He had sandy-blond hair and a physique that showed he was a full-time farmer in the prime of his life. "It's going to blow in all the cranes so you can watch them next week."

"Sure you won't go with me?"

"*Nein.* Watching birds puts me in the mind to hunt, and I know the cranes are protected."

"Deer season will begin in a few weeks."

"Moose has already begun." Clyde combed his fingers through his beard. "*Dat* always said the deer needed to be harvested. The population has grown so that the land can no longer support them, and watching all of them grow thin and hungry is a travesty. The moose, though? They're regal and grand, and for the life of me I cannot imagine shooting one."

Clyde was Emma's son, and he had the same responsibilities Abe did. George Fisher had also been a deacon, and Clyde had been chosen after his father passed. Clyde stepped into his father's shoes, and Henry saw God's hand in that. The two men were very much alike, and the entire family—Emma's family—had become an integral part of their community as well as Henry's personal life.

Abe, Clyde, Leroy, and Henry made up the church's leadership. Leroy didn't preach. Instead, he handled the collection of offerings as well as disbursements to missions and benevolence. This was a good job for Leroy, as he had a head for numbers as well as practical matters. Leroy was a bit severe, but folks soon learned it was nothing personal, just his way. And he provided a good balance to Abe and Clyde, who tended to look at the human and spiritual side of things but sometimes forgot to consider the practical.

In many communities, deacons shared the responsibility of reminding wayward members of their wrongdoings and explaining any confusion about the *Ordnung*, their daily rules for living. But Henry preferred to take that last task upon himself.

Henry was the bishop. He supervised the other three and shared preaching duties with Abe and Clyde. He visited families when they welcomed newborns into their household, guided them when they suffered through times of mourning, researched family lines when marriage intentions were announced, and, of course, he called any necessary meetings. He prayed for and with each of them. He led his flock. He had served as a minister for many years in Goshen, Indiana, and when several of their families decided to move to Monte Vista, he'd stepped into the role of bishop, which he enjoyed more than he would have ever guessed.

He liked people.

He was fond of visiting with elders in the community and finding ways for them to continue to contribute. He liked talking with young people, assisting them through the difficult early years of adulthood. It was among his greatest joys to welcome new members into the faith, baptizing them into a life of Christian servitude and preparing them through classes for what lay ahead.

Soon Abe's home was filled with families. The women sat on one side, the men sat on the other side, and the children clambered back and forth. At the back of the room, Susan and Franey had set up cookies and cups of water. Children sometimes needed a small snack to help them through the three-hour service.

Henry spoke to each family as they came into the home.

He noticed Emma seemed in especially fine spirits. He'd enjoyed their dinner together the night before, and he appreciated her thoughts about Sophia.

Henry gestured toward a back bedroom. Leroy, Clyde, and Abe followed him.

"Abe, would you give the first sermon today?"

"Of course, Henry."

"And Clyde, I'd like you to preach the second."

Clyde nodded in agreement as he thumbed through his Bible, looking for a specific passage.

"Leroy, if you will lead the Scripture reading and the singing, I will offer the opening and closing prayers."

Together they prayed silently, and Henry's mind called up each family in his congregation. They were a relatively small district, for which he was thankful. Once they reached a number too large to fit in a home for a service, they would have to divide into two districts. He wasn't quite ready for that, although he knew God would see them through the process when the time came.

As they prayed, his thoughts drifted to Sophia, and he offered up a prayer of protection and provision for her. The woman seemed troubled, and Emma's reaction had confirmed that he wasn't imagining something was wrong. He couldn't begin to guess what she might be dealing with, but God knew, and God would provide.

From the sitting room, Henry could hear the voices of the men and women and children singing the *Loblied*, their second hymn of praise. It comforted his heart to know this same hymn was being sung in Amish communities everywhere. Though they might differ in other aspects, the tradition of the *Loblied* was permanently a part of their worship.

Henry cleared his throat, and then he prayed aloud for the upcoming service, for the people under their care, and for God's provision and blessing.

Ten

For months now, Emma had allowed Henry to take her home after their church meeting. She enjoyed their buggy rides, times when they could relax and talk about both the important and inconsequential. Or even ride in silence. She was learning that Henry was an extremely relaxing person to be around.

She had another reason for accepting a ride with him. Emma adored being part of a large family, but she had also learned to treasure quiet time. By going home before her son, daughter-in-law, and grandchildren, she had a little time to herself. Henry usually took her home a couple of hours after lunch, always by four. Clyde, Rachel, and their younger boys usually stayed until dark, and Silas and Katie Ann wouldn't come home until much later. They'd enjoy a light dinner and time singing with the other *youngies*. The teenagers would play games, sing, eat, and in general socialize with one another, just like when Emma was a young girl. She had first kissed George at a singing. Six months later, he asked her to be his bride.

"The wind is blowing worse," she said as a cardboard box skittered across the road.

"And from the north." Henry glanced at her and smiled. "Your son says this will blow the cranes down just in time for me to watch them next week."

"They're in our fields. You don't need to go all the way to the national wildlife refuge."

"But I enjoy going to the refuge."

"Apparently."

"And I've already asked Stuart to drive me there."

"Stuart's a real help to our community."

"You should see it, Emma. On your farm, you might see a few cranes—"

"I've counted as many as a dozen."

"At the refuge, there are hundreds, even thousands. It's a thing of astonishing beauty. A real miracle of *Gotte* the way the families stay together, and the way they fly in a group, always taking the same path each spring and fall."

"What day are you going?"

"Thursday. Would you come with me?"

"I'd love to, but I can't."

"Saturday?"

"That's no good either."

"Next week then, on Thursday. I'll confirm it with Stuart."

"It's a date."

She was about to ask him whether she should pack a basket of food for the trip when Henry slowed Oreo. The young waitress Emma had met the night before was trudging down the side of the road, bent into the wind, a backpack bouncing up and down as she walked.

"Why would Sophia be out in this weather?" Henry asked.

"I'm not sure, but we can ask."

Sophia glanced back at them, fear etched across her face.

Emma waved as Henry pulled to a stop.

"Get in the back," she hollered. "It's too cold to be walking."

Sophia looked as if she might argue, but another gust of wind nearly pushed her over. She peered left and then right, as if someone might be watching, and finally nodded in agreement.

"The temperature has certainly dropped," Henry said. "Weather here in the valley can change on a dime."

"Thank you," Sophia murmured as she climbed into the backseat.

Henry called out to his horse, and Emma told her there was a blanket on the floorboard if she'd like to cover up. Henry's buggy had a small heater in the front, but the backseat could be drafty.

"I'm good," Sophia said. "Just getting out of the wind helps."

"Is your car broken, dear?" Emma turned around so she was facing Sophia, who unwound her arms from the backpack and set it on the seat next to her.

"I don't have one," Sophia admitted. "Walking hasn't been a problem until today. You would think winter had arrived early."

"It's only a front pushing through," Henry assured her. "Tomorrow should be sunny and calm, though a tad cooler than last week."

Emma laughed. "Henry Lapp, do you have a weather radio plugged into your buggy dashboard?"

"*Nein.* Leroy told me. He stops in at the library whenever he can to read the *Englisch* weather forecast."

Emma turned her attention back to Sophia. "Where can we take you?"

"Um…the motel?"

"Monte Vista has three. Do you have one in mind?"

It was plain as day that Henry was teasing, but a look of panic again crossed Sophia's face. She glanced left and right and finally said, "The one down the road."

"The Rio Grande. All right."

But when they reached the parking area, Sophia looked even more lost than when they'd picked her up. "Thank you, both, for the ride."

She picked up the backpack and hugged it to her chest. Something in that gesture pierced Emma's heart. What was Sophia struggling with, and how could they help? Why was she walking through the streets of Monte Vista alone? What was she afraid of?

"You're not really staying here, are you?"

"Why would you say that?"

"Because you would have pulled a room key out as we pulled up, and you weren't sure of the name of the motel when Henry mentioned it."

Instead of answering, Sophia said, "I'll be okay. Thank you. Again."

But Emma knew she couldn't leave it at that. She wouldn't sleep a wink thinking of Sophia out on the streets alone.

Sophia was already out of the buggy. Emma turned to Henry and said, "Give us a minute." Then she climbed out of the buggy too and hurried after the young woman. The wind tugged at her dress and nearly pulled the bonnet off her head. It was gusty for sure. She caught up with Sophia in a breezeway between the motel's office and its row of rooms.

"Wait, please," Emma called out, grateful that they were momentarily protected from the wind. "Tell me what's wrong, Sophia. It's obvious you're in some kind of trouble."

"I can't talk about it."

"You need to tell someone. Perhaps we can help."

"No. It wouldn't be…It wouldn't be safe for me to tell you."

Which sounded a bit dramatic to Emma, but she nodded her head as if she understood. "All right. Well, can you tell me where you're spending the night?"

"I don't know."

"You don't know?"

"I don't have a place."

"Do you have any money?"

"Some."

"I'm guessing it's not enough. I'd be happy to loan you what you need for a room."

"I don't need a loan."

"But you can't stay here?"

Sophia shook her head.

"Why, Sophia? Why can't you stay at this motel? I assure you it's clean and the rates are reasonable. Everyone in Monte Vista says so. There's even a drive-in movie theater attached to the back, and you can watch and listen to the movies from your room. Not that I've stayed here, but I've heard people say they enjoyed it."

"No. I can't. It's not safe."

"Not safe?"

"I'll think of something."

Emma suddenly knew what she needed to do. Hadn't Henry reminded them of their Christian duty when he'd led them in prayer at that morning's service? *Whatever you did for one of the least of these brothers and sisters of mine, you did for me.*

"Come back with me."

"What?"

"Come back to the buggy. Henry was taking me to my son's house. We have plenty of room. You can stay with us."

"Why would you do that?"

"Because you need a place to stay, and whoever or whatever you're running from won't think to look for you there."

Sophia hesitated, but eventually she turned back toward the buggy.

Emma tucked her arm in the crook of Sophia's. She wasn't so much worried that Sophia would change her mind, but she looked for all the world like a lost soul. Perhaps offering the hand of friendship, a bed to sleep in, and even a hot cup of coffee would help set right whatever was wrong with her world.

Eleven

Henry couldn't have been more surprised at the turn his day had taken. Their church service had gone well, the whole congregation was there for lunch, and everyone seemed cordial. Afterward, the adults stayed in the barn where the wind couldn't chill them while the *youngies* played baseball and tag. He'd seen a few of the older teens walking in pairs or groups of four. Everyone appeared to be having a peaceful, restful time.

He'd looked forward to the ride home with Emma.

Now their day had careened off on a helter-skelter course. He was reminded of their days looking for Vernon's killer, but he pushed that thought away. Whatever this young woman's troubles were, he couldn't imagine murder being involved.

When they'd first arrived at Emma's house, Sophia had walked slowly up the porch steps, and once inside, stood still in the sitting room. She looked around in surprise. Henry tried to see the room as she did. Two rather worn couches formed an *L* shape and were positioned to face the large potbellied stove. On either side of the stove was a rocking chair. Next to each rocker was a basket holding Emma's and Rachel's sewing projects. In front of the couches was a coffee table, where the family spent many evenings playing board games. Henry had joined them in quite a few hours of Dutch Blitz and checkers. A small bookcase under the front window held board games, books, and copies of the *Budget*.

Only two things adorned the walls. A simple wall clock, approximately two feet tall and made from cherry wood, was positioned to the right of the front door so it could be seen from the sitting room or the kitchen. Emma's father had made the clock and had given it to Emma and George on their wedding day. The other item was a framed, handstitched Bible passage—the twenty-third chapter of Psalms.

Sophia stepped closer to it, close enough to read *The Lord is my shepherd; I shall not want.* She stood there a moment, seemingly lost in thought, and then she turned and followed Emma into the kitchen. She still didn't seem quite at ease, but neither did she look as frightened as when they'd first picked her up.

Emma heated the kettle on the gas-powered stove. As they waited for the water to boil, she told Sophia about her family, hoping to put her at ease. She'd made it through all of the grandchildren when the kettle let out a whistle. She jumped up to pour the hot water over bags of herbal tea. "*Gut* for the nerves," she murmured, setting a mug in front of Sophia.

Sophia continued to glance around, but she didn't speak until they were all settled at the kitchen table.

"You have a beautiful home."

"*Danki.*"

"I'm not familiar with the Amish lifestyle. Until I came to Monte Vista, I'd never met an Amish person. I don't know what I was expecting, but your home...Well, it looks like any other."

"We have no electricity, of course. Which means no television, no electric heat, things like that. It's a simple life—one we're dedicated to."

Sophia nodded as if that made sense. She sipped tentatively from her mug.

"You don't have to talk about your problems with us, Sophia." Henry waited until she raised her eyes to meet his. "But we're here to listen if you'd like to."

"I can't."

"All right."

"You're welcome to stay with us for as long as you want to or need to," Emma assured her. "And there's a community ministerial council that will be happy to find you a place to live when you're ready."

"I won't be staying."

Henry glanced at Emma, who shrugged.

He decided to try a different tack. "You've been working at the diner several weeks now."

"Five. I've been there five weeks."

"Do you like the job?"

"No. What I did—" She glanced down at her hands. "What I did before was on a computer. Easier work by far. The first week at Maggie's, my hands and arms actually cramped at night from carrying heavy trays of food, and my legs...I had no idea standing for eight hours could be so exhausting."

"Why did you take a waitressing job?" Emma asked.

"I needed something. For the time I'm here." She took another deep drink of her tea. A shudder passed over her, and Henry thought she looked as if she might weep. He waited. Eventually, the warm drink and the quiet surroundings calmed her, strengthened her somehow. She drew back her shoulders, sat up straighter, and pulled in a deep breath.

"I appreciate your help. Both of you have been very kind. And obviously, it wouldn't be wise for me to sleep outside tonight. The change in weather took me by surprise."

Henry didn't interrupt. She seemed about to reveal something, but if she had been, she changed her mind abruptly.

"I can't involve you in this, though."

"Perhaps we could help," Emma suggested.

"No. It would be dangerous."

"We have some experience with that." Henry sighed. "My drawing ability has twice now resulted in our being involved with law enforcement. Two murder investigations—"

Sophia jerked her head up so forcefully that she spilled her tea.

"That's not a problem." Emma fetched a dish towel and started wiping up the liquid. "We have four children in this house, and even though two are nearly grown, we still have our fair share of spills."

"Your drawing frightened me." Sophia studied Henry, as if she were still trying to make up her mind about him. "I thought...I became concerned that perhaps you weren't who you appeared to be."

"And now?"

"It seems you're an Amish bishop, just as you've told me."

"That's exactly right!" Henry slid the plate of cookies Emma had set on the table toward Sophia, but she didn't appear to notice.

"They couldn't insert someone into Monte Vista, have him grow a long beard, teach him to drive a horse and buggy, and give him Amish friends in so short a period of time." She seemed to be talking to herself more than to him. She grew silent, but finally she looked at Henry and said, "I believe you are who you say you are."

"Then we're making progress. Now, Sheriff Grayson is a *freind* of mine—"

"No. I can't go to the authorities. I can't trust them."

"Grayson's a *gut* man," Emma said. "He helped us during the last situation."

Sophia stood and began pacing back and forth across the kitchen floor. "I can't go to the authorities. I tried that." Her hand went to the scar on her neck, but she didn't attempt to explain.

"What can we do to help you?" Emma asked.

"I appreciate your letting me stay here. There's no Internet? No cell phones?"

"We have a phone booth half a mile from here if you need to call family or—"

"I don't. It's just that if you have neither of those things, they can't track me." She glanced out the window at the fields stretching toward the far horizon.

They were on the outskirts of Monte Vista here. Not exactly isolated, but the area was private. No one would be sneaking up on them, if that was what she was worried about.

"I'll stay the night, but you needn't concern yourself with my problems. And I promise to be gone in the morning."

Twelve

You won't believe this.

Try me.

She hitched a ride in a buggy.

What are you talking about?

A buggy, like the Amish drive.

And?

Driver took her to a different motel.
She got out and then back in again.

Where did they go after that?

No idea. Once they were out of
town, I couldn't follow without
being seen.

Plate on the buggy?

Nope. Not required in CO.

This is a problem.

Agreed.

Find out who she's made friends
with, who she might have talked to.

And then?

We do what we have to.

Thirteen

Sophia had been surprised many times in the last eight weeks by the twists and turns her life had taken. But still, this might be one of the strangest. She was a houseguest in an Amish home. She was staying with people she barely knew. She was a long way from her loft apartment in San Diego, separated by tragedy and grief and many miles.

Emma's son and daughter-in-law had come home with their two younger boys in time for dinner, which consisted of sandwiches, homemade potato salad, and pie for dessert.

"Your food is better than the diner's," Sophia said. She'd had trouble eating of late, constantly watching over her shoulder and jumping at the slightest noise. But she managed to relax in Emma's home.

How could she not? The only sounds were from farm animals and Emma's family. No television news to hover over. No ringing phones since she had no wireless reception for her cell phone, though she'd popped the battery in for a moment while she was in the bathroom to make sure. Seeing the message *cellular service not available* had filled her with relief rather than worry. She didn't need to talk to anyone, and with no service available, no one could track her current location.

Emma's family was quite welcoming. Clyde and Rachel had taken the notion of an overnight visitor in stride.

"Any *freind* of Henry's is a *freind* of ours." Clyde had smiled warmly and then called the boys outside to help him with the evening's farming chores. They didn't whine or complain when they were called away from their checkers game, though she heard one challenge the other to a race. And then they were gone, sprinting off into the gathering darkness ahead of their father.

She soon learned Rachel was an avid reader. "Mostly Christian fiction and classics. We don't read a lot of contemporary popular fiction, though the occasional title will catch my attention."

They talked books for the next twenty minutes, with Emma smiling and sometimes offering an observation.

"I'm not a big reader myself, but Rachel often shares what she's reading."

"Sometimes I just need to talk about the characters or the plot."

"Perhaps you should join a book club," Sophia suggested.

"An Amish book club. Now there's an interesting idea."

The way Emma and Rachel chuckled at that idea told Sophia it probably wouldn't happen. She knew so little about the Amish way of life. She was rather ashamed of that. In the past she'd been eager to ask questions and learn about new people and different cultures. All of that had stopped on a rainy day in July. Now one thing and one thing only consumed her attention.

"You're looking tired, Sophia." Rachel reached out and patted her hand. "Would you like me to show you to your room?"

She hadn't thought she was tired, not really. Until coming to Emma's, she'd been filled with a desperate, nervous energy. But she knew she'd need to rest if she hoped to accomplish what she'd set out to do. Tomorrow might be her last chance. Certainly, the next few days—

"Katie Ann has an extra bed in her room. And you're welcome to take a shower."

Now, several hours later, she'd been awakened by the sound of a buggy clattering down the lane and the clip-clop of a horse. She assumed the older children, Katie Ann and Silas, had come home. Rather than shattering the night's peacefulness, the sound seemed to fade into it. She had almost fallen back asleep when Katie Ann came into the room, moving quietly, the beam of a flashlight shielded by her hand.

"It's okay. I'm awake."

They talked, but only for a few minutes. Katie Ann was more excited about the work she'd be doing with the local veterinarian the next day than she was about the boy who had asked to give her a ride home.

"For once my *bruder* had no one to take home because his girlfriend left early with a stomach bug, so I thought it would be silly not to ride with him. Besides, Nathan Kline and I are not cut from the same fabric, as *Mammi* would say."

"Why is that? Don't you like him?"

"I like him okay, but with Amish folk, you'll find some are more Plain than others."

"I don't understand."

Katie Ann had changed quickly and slipped beneath her covers. A small nightstand stood between their twin beds, and the room was so dark Sophia couldn't make out much more than the outline of the furniture and the lump in the bed next to hers that was Katie Ann.

"We're all Plain. That is to say, anyone within an Amish community who has joined the church or plans to. We agree to live simply, to follow the *Ordnung*, to commit our lives to our faith and our family."

"What is an *Ordnung*?"

"Rules. Pretty much it's a set of rules. They vary a little from place to place. Some communities allow scooters or solar power or tractors. But overall, the rules are the same. Dress Plain, live humbly, remain separate."

"Separate?"

"*Ya*, well, it's not every day we have an *Englischer* spend the night in our household. But remaining separate speaks more to marrying other Amish, attending parochial school if possible, that sort of thing."

Warming to her subject, she plopped over on her mattress, turning toward Sophia so she could lower her voice. "Working with the local vet? In many communities that wouldn't be allowed, but my family understands how much I love animals. And Henry tells me to pray and listen to *Gotte*'s voice. I'm not sure what that means exactly, but I do think He gave me this love for animals. Do you know what I mean? Is there something you feel like if you don't get to do it, you just might wither and die?"

Katie Ann didn't wait for an answer. "That's how it is with me and working with Doc Berry. Each day I work with her, I can't wait until the next day I work with her. And Nathan doesn't understand that one bit. Tonight he asked me if I wouldn't rather work in the quilt shop or the bakery. *Ack*. He doesn't really know me at all."

Katie Ann sounded young, perhaps ten or fifteen years younger than she was. Sophia tried to remember a time when she hadn't felt old and worried and sad. Had she ever been as carefree as Katie Ann? When had she last been eager for the next day to dawn? Her mind was flooded with memories of how happy she'd been a year ago, how she'd looked forward to each day's assignment, how she'd fallen asleep each night in Cooper's arms. Looking back, those memories seemed to belong to a different person.

This thing that had taken over every aspect of her life had also stolen her hope.

Katie Ann flopped onto her back. "I don't know if I'll ever find a boy, a man, who will love me for who I am, but I don't even care about that right now. Does that make me strange?"

This time she did wait for an answer.

"It doesn't make you strange at all. When you're older—"

"I'm already seventeen."

"When you're twenty or twenty-five or even thirty—"

"Twenty-five is almost an old maid."

Sophia winced in the darkness. At one time she, too, had thought twenty-five was old.

"When you're older, you'll learn to accept who and what you are. You'll be more comfortable with yourself. That's one of the best things about growing older."

And oddly, Sophia searched her heart and found that was still true. If she could go back in time, she would do anything within her power to change what had happened, but she wouldn't change who she was.

As Katie Ann's breathing deepened and evened out, the night sounds crept back into the room.

Sophia had always been able to fix a time in her mind and wake up within a few moments of it—an ability that had helped her tremendously in college. Determined to be up and out of the house before anyone else was stirring, she focused her mind on five o'clock, rolled over, and promptly fell asleep.

She woke to the smell of bacon frying downstairs and Katie Ann's bed empty and made.

Fourteen

Emma had always assumed *Englischers* slept in late, at least until six or seven. So she was surprised when she looked up and saw Sophia standing in the doorway to the kitchen, her backpack slung over her shoulder, dark circles under her eyes. Emma had hoped a night's rest would put their visitor at ease, but if anything she looked more wary than she had the night before.

Emma reached for a mug and asked, "Can I pour you some coffee?"

Sophia hesitated, but apparently she couldn't resist the aroma of freshly brewed coffee.

"Clyde and the boys will be in from the barn in a few minutes. Katie Ann is feeding the chickens, and Rachel is in the laundry room, sorting clothes."

"Thank you." Sophia took a gulp of the coffee, not bothering to doctor it with sugar or cream. Still clutching her drink, she walked to the window and stared out into the receding darkness until she'd drained the mug. She rinsed it, set it in the sink, and finally turned to Emma.

"The food will be ready in a minute. Nothing fancy, but the bacon is crisp and the oatmeal's hot. We have raisins and brown sugar to—"

"I can't stay for breakfast, but thank you for giving me a place to rest. Thank you for your kindness."

"At least let me put some fruit and sweetbread in a bag for you."

"No, Emma. Thank you, but I have to go."

"Where? Certainly no place is open this early. You said last night that you didn't have a shift at the diner today. So where will you go?"

"I can't say."

Emma waited, but Sophia offered no other details. Finally she asked, "Will you be at the diner tomorrow?"

"Maybe. I think so, yes."

"All right. I'm sure Henry will be by to see you there. He seems to enjoy the diner's breakfast better than his own cooking." She moved a pot off the stove burner, wondering what she could possibly say to Sophia to ease the worried look on her face. "Please tell him if there's anything you need. If there's anything we can do."

"You've done enough."

Sophia stepped closer and reached out as if she were going to put her hand on Emma's arm. But Emma saw the ache and exhaustion in her eyes, and without making a conscious decision to do so, she wrapped her arms around the young woman and said, "We will pray for you, that *Gotte* prepares the road before you and makes clear your path."

Nodding her thanks, Sophia turned away. She started for the front door and then stopped in her tracks as if she had suddenly remembered something. Dropping her backpack onto the table, she unzipped it. Emma couldn't see what she pulled out.

"There is one thing you can do for me." Stepping closer to Emma, she pressed a small item into her hand. "Keep this device."

"What is it?" She stared down at the oblong object, smaller than a clothespin but metallic. She'd never seen anything like it and had no idea what it was used for or why it would be so important to Sophia.

"Just keep it." Sophia folded Emma's fingers over the device, held Emma's hands in hers, and seemed to bow her head to pray. Looking up, she added, "Keep it safe, and if…if something happens to me—"

"What could happen to you?"

"If something does, take it to someone you trust."

"Someone I trust?" Emma felt like a parrot, but she couldn't stop herself from repeating what Sophia said.

"You could give it to Henry. I think he would know what to do."

"All right. I can do that for you."

"Thank you, Emma."

Sophia once again wound her arms through the battered backpack's straps. Emma followed her to the front door, and then Sophia stepped out into the early morning. At least the wind had died down. The morning was cold but would warm into a fine fall day.

Sophia paused in their yard for a moment, scanning the horizon from left to right. Cinching the pack higher on her back, it appeared she was carrying a weight far heavier than one person should have to shoulder. Emma watched the young woman walk away. She said a prayer for her safety, and then she dropped the device Sophia had given her into her apron pocket.

Soon the kitchen was filled with her family. Emma loved them so much that at times her heart felt full to overflowing. The boys jostled for seats around the table. Katie Ann came in jabbering about new kittens in the barn. Clyde reminded them to thank the Lord for good food and health and family. Rachel shared a smile with her husband.

As they silently prayed, Emma's mind slipped back to Sophia, to the image of her walking down their dirt lane, the pack once again weighing down her shoulders.

Katie Ann asked about Sophia and seemed disappointed when Emma said she'd already gone. Once the boys had left for school, Clyde and Silas for the barn, and Katie Ann for Doc Berry's, Emma admitted her fears to Rachel.

"She's in some kind of trouble. I only wish we could help her."

"What kind of trouble? And how would we help her?"

"I have no idea."

"She didn't appear to be on drugs or anything like that."

"*Nein.* I don't think so either."

"Man trouble?"

"I suppose it's possible. I think she was married in the past."

"Widowed or divorced?"

Emma shrugged. There was so much she didn't know about Sophia. It was quite odd that their paths had even crossed, but then Henry was one to reach out to a person in need—whether Amish or *Englisch*. Never like this, though. She'd never had an *Englischer*, a total stranger, stay in their home before. They'd given her shelter for one night, but that wasn't much help in the greater scheme of things.

"If she won't tell you…"

"That's the thing, though. Sometimes when you're in trouble so deep you don't see a way out, you feel as if you can't share it with anyone. You feel as if you have to deal with it yourself. And yet those times are when you need help the most."

"We'll pray, then." Rachel pulled a dish out of the rinse water, dried it, and placed it on the shelf. "We might not know what Sophia's troubles are, but *Gotte* does."

Wise words, and ones Emma fully intended to heed.

After she'd spoken with Henry.

As much as she wanted to believe Sophia would be fine, a desperation about the woman bothered her. What could have frightened her so badly that she would roam the streets of Monte Vista, stay with a near stranger, and refuse to talk about what was wrong? Why was she so convinced no one could or would help her?

And what could they possibly do to earn Sophia Brooks's trust?

Fifteen

Henry's duties as bishop didn't pause simply because he had a mystery on his hands. Sophia's problems would have to wait, at least until he visited a few folks in his congregation. Fortunately, everyone on today's list was dog friendly. He whistled for Lexi, who bounded toward the buggy.

She stopped long enough to rub noses with Oreo. Henry had wondered how the old mare would get along with the dog. She'd never been around one before, except maybe in passing. But Oreo had taken to Lexi, even going so far as to lick her clean when she bounded through the mud. In the Monday morning sunshine, the two were a sight to behold, and it occurred to Henry that he wouldn't mind drawing them.

The mare extended her neck forward and down, nuzzling the beagle.

As for Lexi, she sniffed back, and then she rolled over on her belly, which produced more nuzzling from the mare.

"As much as I'm enjoying this, we have people to see."

He hurried to his workshop to retrieve the double-decker birdhouse he'd made from old window shutters. Deborah King had a new baby who was suffering with colic. She also loved gardening and especially the birds that visited her flowers for seed and insects. He thought the birdhouse might be just the thing to lift her spirits.

Twenty minutes later he was standing in her front room, offering it to her.

Deborah's eyes were red—either from allergies or crying. Her prayer *kapp* sat at an awkward angle on her head, her apron was splattered with something from the kitchen, and the room was a bit of a mess, but she managed a halfhearted smile.

"*Danki*, Henry." She ran a hand over the birdhouse. "When Adam comes in from the fields, I go for a walk outside. I always end up in the garden, sitting on the bench he made. It helps to calm my nerves."

Baby Chloe was finally asleep, but Henry had heard her cries from his buggy when he first drove up.

"I can only imagine how difficult this is for you, Deborah, since I've never had a child of my own." Henry ran his fingers through his beard as he gazed out at the fall flowers bordering the vegetable garden. "I suppose the women in our church have given you plenty of advice."

"They have, and we've tried it all—placing a warm towel on her tummy, taking her for rides in the buggy, and of course rocking her more often."

"She's two months now?"

"Just."

"Most colic resolves itself at four months."

"We'll all be crazy by then, or deaf."

"If there's anything I can do, please let me know."

"Of course. And Henry, *danki* for the drawing you did of Chloe and me."

"The drawing was no trouble. In fact, I enjoyed it."

"I don't mind the rule against photographs. I even understand it—our need to remain humble, to not allow pride a toe step into our lives." She pulled out a dust rag from her pocket and swiped at the coffee table. "It's hard when family members live apart, though. We sent your drawing to our families in Pennsylvania, and they passed it from one house to the next. *Mamm* had been terribly upset she couldn't come for a visit when Chloe was first born. She didn't want to miss out on her first month. She especially appreciated being able to see Chloe through your drawing."

"Your mother is coming next month?"

"*Ya.* I can hardly wait."

"Are you sure I can't hang this birdhouse for you?"

"Leave it for me. I'll look forward to spending some time outside this afternoon and finding the perfect spot."

Once back in his buggy, Henry pulled out a scrap of paper. Using the pen he kept in his jacket pocket, he made a note about the King family. Perhaps some of the women in the congregation could come by and spell Deborah a bit—enough time for her to go to town, take a walk, or nap.

Next he visited with Mary Yoder, who had broken her foot when step-ping down off the porch the wrong way.

"I've no one to blame but myself. I was in a hurry and not paying attention."

"These things happen, Mary. I don't think placing blame is necessary. Now tell me about the *grandkinner*."

Mary had twelve *grandkinner* so far, though most of them lived back east. She received circle letters from the family, and she had recently learned that two of her *grandkinner* were now expecting children. She also had two grown children in the area—both girls, one married, one not. Sally was twenty. She was one of those change-of-life babies women joked about. Mary had been forty when she was born. Both Mary and her hus-band, Chester, had shared with Henry their worry that the girl hadn't set-tled down. Henry assured them twenty wasn't so old and that they would all pray for Sally to meet the person she was destined to marry.

Their other daughter, Claudia, had been married for two years and was expecting her first child. Claudia had been diagnosed with uterine tumors when she was only sixteen. She'd had two surgeries to remove them before she married.

"We worried that Claudia wouldn't be able to have children because of the problems she had when she was younger."

"*Gotte* is *gut*."

"All the time," Mary agreed. "The baby's due around Christmas. Since I'm supposed to stay off this foot, I have plenty of time to work on a new project. I'll have a baby quilt, receiving blankets, and even some clothes finished in plenty of time before the birth."

Mary's husband, Chester, was in a less optimistic mood. "We'll starve before she's back on her feet again."

"Aren't Claudia and Sally helping?" Henry asked.

"Of course they are, but those girls never could cook. Not like Mary does."

Henry patted Chester on the shoulder and assured him they would pray for Mary's speedy recovery.

"Pray for my patience. Between my wife, the cranes that keep landing in my fields, and the boys intent on courting Sally, though she continues to find reasons to turn them down..." Chester shook his head, unwilling or unable to finish the thought.

"A kite rises only against the wind," Henry reminded him.

"This kite is worn out, and that proverb never was much help."

Last on his list was a visit with Albert Bontrager. Albert's parents had moved to Kentucky the year before when the Monte Vista arsonist had been frightening families in their community. Albert was supposed to join them after the farm sold. It had surprised everyone when he decided to stay. Because his parents were now living with his uncle, they didn't immediately need the money from the sale of the farm. They'd agreed to give him three years to see if he could make it profitable. At that point he could go to the bank for a loan if he still wanted to remain in the valley. Henry thought Albert's interest in staying had something to do with one of the young ladies in the congregation, but neither had made their intentions public yet.

Albert raised a hand when Henry pulled up next to the barn.

"Morning, Henry. Lexi."

The beagle ran to Albert, sniffed his feet, and then took off for the barn.

"Lots of energy."

"Indeed."

"Come take a look at this, Henry." Albert was bent over a large, shiny panel set on a workbench he'd pulled out into the sun.

"What am I looking at?"

"Solar panel."

"Ah."

"Now, before you tell me it's forbidden, know that I haven't taken it anywhere near the house."

"Can you explain to me how it works?"

"Certainly."

He spent the next ten minutes going on about the contraption, tracing the path from the modules to the inverter.

"So the power is stored here?" Henry pointed to the inverter, both fascinated and concerned about it. Their *Ordnung* expressed in no uncertain terms that there was to be no electrical power to homes, though barns could have generators when a person's business required them.

"*Ya.* This panel simply converts the sun's power. No electrical lines, as you can see. But if you have something like a power tool or small lantern with a battery, you can recharge the battery here. And the best part? It's free. No one can charge us for *Gotte's* sunshine."

"I've heard of other districts allowing solar panels, but I didn't think we'd have to make a decision so soon."

"Some of the communities in New York are allowing it. Seems to me the real issue is not the use of the solar panels, but what we use that power for."

"Explain that to me." Henry crossed his arms and studied the young man in front of him. Albert had always been one to push the limits. Since he'd taken over running the farm, he'd had less time to immerse himself in foolishness. This, though…it seemed Albert had thought it through.

"Well, if we're using it to power a radio that brings the *Englisch* world into our home, then it's not in accordance with our Plain ways—twenty-four-hour news, advertisements, rock and roll." He grinned at this last item, as if he might have an electric guitar hidden somewhere. "But if we use it to charge a weather radio or a flashlight, think how much better it is not to purchase batteries."

"They're expensive."

"And they can't be easily recycled." Albert scratched his clean-shaven jaw. The woman who married Albert Bontrager would have her hands full, but then she'd always be provided for. Albert was a hard worker. "Some batteries can be recharged, though. Have you seen them in the store?"

"*Nein.*"

"Same as any other battery, but *Englischers* plug a doohickey into the wall and recharge them. They can last years that way."

"And you could recharge them with this?"

"*Ya.* Absolutely you could. It's what the panels are designed to do."

"Albert, it occurs to me that you've thought this through, unlike in the past."

"Now you're referring to my battery-powered bicycle."

"And the golf cart."

"It's not as if I were playing golf."

Henry wiggled his hand back and forth. This was the line Albert had danced on for years. Yet it seemed the man before him was maturing.

"Make me a list of acceptable devices that could be powered by this, as well as a chart of basic costs. I'll take it to the elders at our next meeting."

The last stop on Henry's list was the Fishers' house. He'd wanted to give Sophia time to rest and maybe even relax into her surroundings, but it was nearly ten. Surely she'd be up and ready to talk now.

He called out to Lexi, who jumped into the buggy, and then he directed Oreo down the lane and toward Emma's house. Perhaps they could find a way to help the young waitress from Maggie's Diner.

Sixteen

It never occurred to Sophia to worry about how she would get out to the Monte Vista National Wildlife Refuge. She'd stopped giving any thought to such mundane details weeks ago. The refuge was where she needed to be, so she would find a way to get there. Sometimes the manager at work gave her a ride, but today she was on her own.

She walked the first few miles, and then she hitched a ride with a nice elderly couple.

"We're headed to the refuge ourselves," the woman said, raising her binoculars and grinning. She had short white hair that clung to her scalp like a swimming cap, skin wrinkled and pale, and blue eyes that sparkled whenever she spoke. "We go every year, don't we, Burt?"

"That we do, Gloria." Glancing at Sophia in the rearview mirror, he said, "Those are our names—Burt and Gloria Danson."

"Nice to meet you," Sophia said, though she had no intention of sharing any information about herself.

"Been coming here since it first opened in '53."

"We were newlyweds then." Burt cackled, grinned at his wife, and then gripped the wheel of the old sedan all the more tightly. While his wife was tall and thin, Burt was nearly as round as he was tall—or at least that was how they seemed sitting in the front of the vehicle.

"Place has changed more than I would have thought possible." Gloria faced the front again, though she was still talking to Sophia. "When we first came, only normal folks like us were there. Now fancy photographers and people from those nature channels come, and they have food trailers and souvenir stands. Nearly got whacked by one of those drone thingamajigs last year."

"Knocked my hat off my head," Burt confirmed.

"We used to come in the spring, during the crane festival. Now we come in the fall, when there aren't any crowds."

"Or drones."

"Or drones. The trip means a lot to us. It's worth the drive from Colorado Springs to see the cranes." Gloria twisted in her seat to pin Sophia with an inquisitive look. "You're out here alone?"

Sophia nodded.

"When I was your age, women didn't travel alone, but I understand the millennial generation is more independent. We have a granddaughter who went to Europe for three months. Don't we, Burt?"

"Yup. She wanted to see the sights."

"We even had one of those video chats with her. Couldn't figure out how to set it up, but our son came over and showed us. She was standing outside St. Patrick's Cathedral in Dublin. Can you imagine that?"

Sophia closed her eyes, resisting the urge to put her head down and weep. Fortunately, Gloria was again facing the front of the vehicle and didn't notice.

"Is this your first time to see the cranes?"

"Yes. Yes, it is."

"It won't be your last." Gloria patted down her hair, though it was too short to be out of place. She wore dangly purple earrings that matched her purple track suit.

Gloria and Burt parked outside the visitor center. Sophia thanked them for the ride and then slipped away before they could ask about her plans for the day.

She didn't need to look at her husband's notes to know which direction she wanted to go. The San Luis Valley stretched one hundred miles from north to south and half that distance from east to west. The area had three refuge centers in all. Alamosa and Monte Vista were in the south-central end of the valley. Baca Refuge was to the north. She'd visited Baca the week before, and Alamosa the week before that. Neither had the landmarks Cooper described.

She figured out his code easily enough. Why had he used it? Why hadn't he shared any of this information with her? Had he known, even then, that what he was uncovering was dangerous?

She appreciated the way he protected his source as well as his information, but the first hadn't helped him—he was, after all, dead. The second wasn't helping her. She needed to find the location of the next op, and she needed to do it well before Wednesday. It was her only chance to catch the ruthless people responsible for Cooper's murder, and she had no doubt at all that the group operating in Monte Vista was the same group that had killed her husband.

The height of the migration was predicted for the next week, but already the sound of birds filled the air. The parking lot was two-thirds full, and everywhere she looked, Sophia saw folks with backpacks and binoculars. Some, as Gloria had indicated, were also carrying large, expensive cameras. If this was not crowded, she didn't want to be around to see the throngs of people in the spring. The refuge was huge, though, and she imagined that once you moved away from the visitor center, you could find a relatively isolated spot.

The people she was looking for would be a good distance from any witnesses.

Sophia slipped into a group of birders, but when they took the paved trail to the right, she exited left, away from the crowds. The paved road turned east and then branched off to the south in several locations. Sophia did not turn south. Instead she continued another twenty minutes, and then she turned north, hopping over the chain with the sign that read "Authorized Personnel Only." Keeping to the side, she hiked down the gravel road, which soon turned to hard-packed dirt.

She listened for the sound of shots or helicopter blades or off-road vehicles. She heard none of those things, and what she could hear—the cry of birds—didn't pique her curiosity. But the open meadow in front of her did. It exactly matched what Cooper had drawn in his notes.

Seventeen

"Where could she have possibly gone?"

"I don't know, Henry."

A large pot of macaroni and cheese had boiled over on the stove, the washing machine in the mudroom had a busted hose, and Rachel was trying to chase a bird out of the house with a broom. Mornings could be a bit chaotic at the Fisher household, but usually more people were there to help manage things.

"Where's Clyde?" Henry asked, raising his voice to be heard over the sound of Rachel whacking the broom against a cabinet.

"South field."

"Would you like me to get him?"

Emma waved away the idea as she continued to sop up water and macaroni. "Katie Ann has gone to help Doc Berry today. Rachel and I can handle this. Can't we, Rachel?"

For her answer, Rachel again walloped the broom against the cabinet. The bird, a small sparrow, was hopping from place to place, its small head jerking left and right as if to try to figure out where the swoosh of broom bristles was coming from.

Rachel had a legendary fear of birds, but only if they found their way into the house—which seemed to happen more often to her than anyone else.

"I'll take care of this little guy," Henry said, gently removing the broom from her hands.

She glanced around as if surprised to find him there.

"Maybe you could do something about the flood in the mudroom?"

Emma handed Rachel the mop and began to refill the pot with water. Henry picked up the bowl of macaroni and walked out the back door to the pigpen, dumping it into the animals' trough. While he was near the barn, he checked the jars of supplies on the western wall, found some birdseed, and shook out a handful.

It wouldn't do to have the bird fly through the mudroom. Rachel would probably sock the little guy with the wet mop.

Henry walked to the front of the house, scattered the seed from below the front step to the front door, and then propped the door open. Back in the kitchen, he stood across the room from the bird and flapped his arms. The little sparrow took one look at him, hopped from the top of the cabinet to the sink, and then sailed off through the front door, never pausing to peck at the seed.

He found the broom, went outside, and brushed the seed away from the front door, scattering it onto the ground. Closing the screen door behind him, satisfied that he'd done at least one useful thing, he wound his way back into the mudroom and emptied Rachel's bucket. It took another ten minutes for them to mop up the rest of the water, but when they were done the floor was sparkling clean. Together they stood staring at the back of the gas-powered machine.

"I would offer to fix the hose," Henry said, "but I'd probably do more harm than *gut*."

"It was our last load. We can wait until Clyde comes in for lunch. *Danki*, Henry. You saved us." They walked back into the kitchen, where things were calm and clean once more.

"Indeed you did," Emma said, agreeing and handing him a steaming cup of coffee. She'd changed into a dry apron, and Henry thought she looked quite fetching for a woman who'd just had a domestic emergency. "For our thanks I have oatmeal cookies or raisin bread."

"I'll take a slice of the bread."

Rachel excused herself, saying, "I believe I could use a break on the front porch," which they all knew was her code for *I'd like to go read a chapter now*. Henry had never known a Plain woman who liked to read as much as Rachel, but he'd known several men who studied the *Budget* as if it were the Holy Grail.

Emma joined him at the table.

"Now explain to me about Sophia."

"Not much to explain. She seemed to be doing fine. Katie Ann said they had a nice chat last night after she came in late. Nothing specific. Just girl talk, whatever that means."

Henry grunted as if he understood, which he didn't. But because it didn't seem to matter, he opted not to interrupt Emma.

"Sophia came down as I was cooking breakfast. She didn't seem much better than last night. She still had that tired, weary look about her. And then before I knew what was really happening, she was gone."

"Just like that?"

"Just like that."

"Was she going into work?"

"No. She doesn't have a shift today. When I asked her if she'd be there tomorrow, she said she thought she would."

Henry sipped the coffee, savored the bread, and allowed the quiet of the morning to settle his thoughts. After a few moments, he said, "I thought we were supposed to help her."

"Perhaps we did."

"I thought that might entail more than one night's lodging."

"She knows she's welcome to come back, but I don't think she will."

Henry stood, rinsed out his mug, and glanced through the sitting room and out the front door. Lexi was lying on the porch in a ray of sunlight, and he could just make out the hem of Rachel's skirt as she pushed the rocker back and forth. He didn't have to walk out there to know she had a book in her lap. He envied her that—her ability to leave the day's worries behind and enter another world. Perhaps that was what he did when he drew. He wasn't sure. He wasn't familiar enough with his ability yet, even after all these years, to know if it helped or hurt him.

"We can pray," he said as Emma walked him outside.

"I promised her we would."

He said goodbye to Rachel, called Lexi out of her dreams, and finally remembered what he'd meant to tell Emma.

"Chloe still has colic, and Deborah seems to be having a rough time of it."

"Poor thing."

"I was wondering if you could arrange with some of the women to give her a break every other day or so."

"We can, and I should have thought of it myself. None of my children had colic, but I've seen it enough to know how hard it can be on a mother and baby."

"You're a *gut* woman, Emma Fisher." Henry squeezed her hand, and then he climbed into the buggy. Instead of stepping back, Emma stepped closer and lowered her voice.

"I care about Sophia too, Henry. You know I'm in favor of helping anyone who needs it, but the last time we got involved with an *Englischer*, someone ended up in jail."

"The *Englischer* ended up in jail."

"Exactly."

"But we weren't actually involved with—"

"I'm only saying perhaps we should tread carefully here. I don't want you mixed up in something that could cause problems for you."

"I don't believe it's like that. Sophia strikes me as a lost soul, someone who's carrying a heavy burden."

"And we can't help her if she isn't in a place where she's ready to receive help." Emma stepped back from the buggy. "If there's anything I can do…"

"Of course I'd let you know." As Henry drove away, he was surprised he felt energized by the morning's errands. He had a good congregation—all of them, even the cranky ones like Chester Yoder. He also had the abiding friendship of Emma Fisher, and that was enough to brighten even the darkest of days.

Eighteen

Sophia stood staring at the open meadow in front of her.

Definitely big enough to land a helicopter, with no overhead lines to interfere.

And it was far enough from the road that no one would hear, or if they did, they would assume it was coming from the National Guard base in Alamosa.

She had to be sure, though. Fumbling with her pack, she stepped back into the tree line. They could be watching, with drones or satellites or all manner of things she couldn't begin to guess at. She needed to be careful, especially now, when she was so close to discovering the truth.

She glanced up at the sky. Would she even know a drone if one flew past her? Did the people who killed her husband have drones? If they had helicopters, they probably had drones. Even kids had them these days. She'd seen in the paper where a third-grade student had made one out of Legos—a Lego drone kit. What was the world coming to?

She pulled out the small four-inch by three-inch mini composition book Cooper used for notes. She'd teased him about that. *There's a notes app on your phone, dear.* How confident she'd been then, so sure she knew the better way for everything. Cooper had only smiled and said that for some things he preferred old school. Already suspicious of how the police said he died, she'd found the small booklet the day after his funeral, stuffed in the glove compartment of their car, where she'd been searching for a tissue.

That was when she realized something was truly wrong. Cooper kept that notebook on his person at all times. She'd seen him pull it out while

they were at the movies and jot down some note. She remembered running her finger over the red numeral *31* he'd made on the front with a
sharpie marker. Thirty-one notebooks full of sources and notes and drawings and tidbits.

Numbers one through thirty had been filled with what you might find
in any wildlife reporter's notes. Nothing outstanding. Nothing shocking.
But he'd turned the information into good, informative pieces. Rather
than looking for assignments, he'd had to turn some down, insisting that
he wouldn't do it if he couldn't carve out enough time to do a good job.
Cooper had begun to be one of the few reporters who were sought after,
making it possible for them to start putting aside money for a house—
money that she'd blown through the week after his death when she'd hired
an investigative firm that had learned nothing.

His notebooks one through thirty were a testament to that work ethic.
Then came number thirty-one.

She shook off the memories, thumbed through the worn pages, and
found what she was looking for.

He'd sketched a meadow surrounded by fir trees, with a small pond
to the northwest and a large boulder to the east. Sophia glanced up and
ticked off each item in her mind. This was the place. It had to be. Next
to the drawing were the initials BT. She assumed that was his source,
but she couldn't be sure. She hadn't found any other indications of what
the initials might mean. She wasn't sure Cooper had recorded them
anywhere.

But she was sure this was the place. There was no doubt in her mind.

Later, after she'd found book thirty-one, she also found a flash drive
with backups of his notes. Why had he felt a need for both records? Was
there another backup somewhere else—in a safety-deposit box or with
a colleague? She might never know. The files had required a password,
which she'd guessed on her third try. Once inside the files, she'd realized
the depth of his fear—every entry was in code, a code she knew by heart,
the same code she'd used with her sister, Tess, when they were kids. Had
he done that on purpose, knowing only she would be able to understand
what he'd written?

Both the flash drive and the notebook confirmed that Wednesday was
the meet date, or so she'd guessed based on the dates on the next page. The

first three had checks by them. She'd had to look back through her smart-phone calendar app to confirm that he had been out of town on those days. She'd known he'd gone to Colorado, but she had been too busy with her own deadlines to question him about it. He always had his cell phone on him, so she didn't need to know particulars. He called every evening to ask about her day, to tell her he loved her and missed her, and to say he would be back soon.

They had coffee together every morning when he was home. They read the news on their tablets and shared the day's upcoming events.

He'd called her his coffee mate and laughed at his cleverness.

Sophia's throat tightened, her eyes burning with tears. But she'd mourn later. It was a luxury she wouldn't allow herself now. Not when she was so close.

Of the two other dates on the list, one was three days from now, and the other next week. She harbored no illusions about being able to stay around through the next week. She was certain she had been followed. She'd been smart to leave her motel room. Staying with Emma Fisher had been an excellent break. Giving Emma the flash drive? That had been a difficult decision, one she'd had to make quickly as she hurriedly dressed. It was the best solution she could come up with. The information would be safe in Emma's house. No one would look there, and if something did happen to her, she truly believed Emma would get the drive to someone trustworthy.

Which didn't mean she was willing to stay with Emma's family. She could take a chance with her own life trying to catch these people, but it was wrong to risk the lives of others.

The evil people Cooper was closing in on were ruthless. They'd proven that they had no qualms about harming or killing anyone who got in their way. She wasn't paranoid enough to believe all of the authorities were in on it, but she thought some of them might be. Her hand went to her neck, tracing the shape of the small scar there.

What if they had infiltrated the San Diego police? She'd been on her way to the precinct office to turn in what evidence she'd found when someone attacked her. What if they'd warned a corrupt law officer she was heading there, and he'd been waiting for her? Sometimes when she tried to sleep, she could still feel the cold blade against her neck, hear the raspy breathing of her assailant. If it hadn't been for the pepper spray she carried, they might have killed her.

She could be lying in her grave, just like Cooper. If she was going to do this, she'd have to do it alone.

It was Wednesday or never.

Nineteen

On Tuesday morning the diner's parking lot was nearly full. Henry stopped by anyway.

He managed to get seated in Sophia's section, and he placed his regular order. But while she was polite and efficient, she was distracted—either because of all the customers or whatever was wrong in her life.

She smiled at Henry, apologized for having to rush off, and then hurried away to fill someone's coffee mug. To anyone else she would have looked like a harried waitress working through her shift, intent on taking orders, delivering food, and earning tips.

That wasn't what Henry saw, though.

He noticed the way her eyes darted toward the door each time it opened. He saw the scowl that flickered across her face when Scott Lawson walked in. He remembered how she'd been hunched over, carrying her pack, plodding into the cold north wind.

Something was not right with Sophia Brooks, but he had no chance to ask her about it then. He went back late Tuesday afternoon, hoping he'd miss the dinner rush. He was seated in his regular booth, nursing what was left of his coffee after having enjoyed the daily special—a barbecue pulled pork sandwich and sweet potato fries—and waiting to see if he could have a word with Sophia. Finally she walked his way, an order pad sticking out of the front pocket of her apron.

"Henry."

"Sophia."

She waved a pot of coffee toward his mug, eyebrows arched, waiting. He pushed the mug toward her, and she filled it.

"Busy day," he said.

"I guess." Sophia glanced around, as if there must be customers who needed waiting on.

"Place has cleared out. Can you take a break?"

Sophia shrugged, but her eyes rested on him for a moment. Henry thought there was something she wanted to say, some burden she needed to share. Of course, he could have been imagining all that. But he hadn't made up the fact that she was homeless, so something was amiss. Sophia walked behind the counter and said something to the cook on the other side of the pass-through. She poured herself some coffee and returned to Henry's table.

"How have you been?"

She responded with a question of her own. "Why do you care? And I don't mean that as rudely as it sounds. I'm genuinely curious."

Henry didn't answer immediately. He'd learned long ago that pauses in conversations were good. They gave both parties a chance to order their thoughts. After he took another sip of coffee, he said, "You know I'm a bishop."

"I've heard you mention it a time or two."

"As a bishop, it's my calling to lead the people under my care."

"I'm not Amish, Henry."

"*Ya*, that's for sure." He glanced at the tattoo on the inside of her left wrist, which was peeking out from the long-sleeved shirt she wore. "What do the letters CB stand for?"

Sophia closed her eyes for a moment. When she opened them again, Henry saw a young woman who was lost, alone, and for some reason afraid. He thought she wouldn't answer his question, but she ran her right index finger over the tattoo. "Cooper. It stands for Cooper Brooks—my husband."

"And the number?"

"The date we met."

"I didn't realize you were married."

"Widowed." Her bottom lip trembled. She raised the fingers of her right hand to her mouth and pressed them against her lips, as if she could silence the words that needed to be said.

He again gave her a moment, and he wasn't surprised to see her grief change to steely resolve.

"I appreciate your trying to be my friend, even though I can't imagine why you would."

"We all need *freinden*."

"You don't want to be seen with me."

"Why wouldn't I?"

"Because it's not safe."

"How is that?"

"I shouldn't be sitting here at this table with you. You have no idea—" She took a deep breath and lowered her voice. "You have no idea how far their reach is. Any credit card transaction—"

"I always pay cash."

"Any cell phone."

"Never owned one."

"Even the wireless routers in your home can be traced."

"Wireless what?"

She stared out the window for a moment. When she turned her eyes back to him, her emotions seemed to have calmed somewhat. In fact, she almost seemed resigned to whatever was upsetting her.

"Have you ever wondered why life is so unfair?" she asked.

"Often."

Sophia smiled then, a small, tenuous thing. But in it Henry could see the beautiful young woman she once was and might be again.

"You're a bishop."

"*Ya.* I am."

"Then you're supposed to have the answers."

"To everything?"

"That would be helpful."

He finished his coffee, though it was now cold and he didn't really want it. He realized he was stalling. So often he didn't know quite what to say to his parishioners, how to ease their burdens. It would be later, after they'd parted ways, that the right words would come to him, and sometimes he would sit down and write them a note and mail it. But he had the feeling he wouldn't be mailing a note to Sophia Brooks.

"When one becomes bishop in an Amish community, it's not because he knows all the answers or even because he's lived a better life than other people. It's simply that he's chosen. I have been chosen."

"By whom?"

"We have a lottery, and in that way we believe *Gotte* chooses."

"And I thought waitressing was hard. At least I picked this job…" She started to add more, but shook her head.

"It is a burden at times, but it's also a privilege. As to why life is unfair, I've wondered that many times myself. When I see *freinden* suffer. When my own wife passed. When I felt alone and invisible."

"Everyone loves you, Henry. I'm an outsider, and even I can see that."

"I am surrounded by many *gut* people, it's true." His thoughts drifted to the Monte Vista arsonist, and further back than that, to a young girl named Betsy Troyer. "Sometimes—even amid *freinden*—I have felt alone and invisible. On those days, I remembered my parents' voices, schooling me in the ways of Scripture."

"You're talking about the Bible."

Henry nodded. "There are many promises in *Gotte*'s holy Word—promises of His love and care and forgiveness. But none that I know of promise an easy path."

"Then what's the point?" A look of desperation came into Sophia's eyes. "My grandmother kept a Bible near her bed and read it first thing every morning and last thing every night. She died in a tornado. That Bible, those words, didn't protect her from an F4."

"I am sorry for your loss, Sophia. For your many losses." Henry didn't attempt to talk her out of her grief. Instead he said, "Christ promises that when we are weary and burdened, He will give us rest. He will take our yoke, and we can learn from Him, but it's also important to reach out to those around us—to the people He has placed in our path."

"My path is deserted."

"I'm here with you, and so are others like Emma and Katie Ann."

"I barely know any of you."

"We know each other well enough. The holy Scripture says we are to spur one another to love and *gut* deeds, to encourage one another."

"The only person…" Her voice faltered. Sophia bowed her head, whether in prayer or exhaustion, he wasn't sure.

Finally she glanced up, the small, tight smile back in place.

"I probably won't see you again, Henry."

"Why is that?"

"I'm giving my notice this afternoon." She stood, once again taking on the persona of the efficient waitress. "What I mean is, this is my last shift."

Henry stood also and put his hand on her arm. "Sophia, please. Tell me what's wrong. Why are you so afraid? Who are the people you think are after you?"

Shaking her head, she turned away, but then she faced him again, stepped closer, and said, "I think I'm close. I think…maybe this is about to end. But if it goes the other way…"

"Goes what other way?"

"Say a prayer for me, Henry. Okay?"

"Of course."

"And if something happens to me, talk to Emma."

Twenty

Her Amish contact is the bishop.

                              Name?

Henry Lapp.

                              Relation?

None.

                    Maybe it's nothing.

Maybe it's something.

                Continue monitoring SB.

And if the bishop knows?

                    We'll take care of it.

Twenty-One

Sophia resisted the urge to once again place the battery in her cell phone.

She'd charged it a few hours before at work and didn't need to take the unnecessary risk of checking it again. Hitching out to the wildlife preserve had been a bit more difficult than the day before because there was so little traffic. It was already dark when she left Monte Vista, and no bird-watchers were traveling toward the refuge.

She hadn't minded the walk. Even though her feet hurt from standing all day at the diner, she was still filled with a nervous energy. She'd finally been offered a ride in the back of a farmer's pickup, which she'd readily accepted.

When she reached the refuge, a closed, locked gate stretched across the entrance. Waist high, it would stop vehicles but not people. Obviously the rangers weren't worried about tourists making their way into the refuge in the dead of night. She easily climbed over it.

The place was deserted. No cars. No people. No activity of any sort.

She pulled a flashlight covered with red cellophane out of her backpack, shone it at the ground, and retraced her steps to the meadow she'd found the day before.

She didn't have a bedroll, but she did have a jacket and gloves and a scarf. She donned them all before crawling underneath the low-lying boughs of a pine tree. With her back against its trunk, she could see the meadow perfectly. Glancing up through the branches, she could just make out starlight.

She sat there, certain she would lie awake all night, but she drifted asleep in the first hour. Her dreams were filled with disjointed images of Cooper, Henry, Emma, and men wearing ski masks. Cooper stood a few feet away, holding his hand out to her, but she couldn't raise her arm, couldn't move at all. Henry and Emma both held coffee mugs. They spoke softly to one another, and then they turned to watch her, compassion and worry shining in their eyes.

The men leaned close, their breath hitting her face in hot, angry bursts. She couldn't understand a word they were saying. It was as if they spoke another language, or perhaps—in the illogical way of dreams—she was deaf.

Something about the eyes of one man seemed familiar, but each time she looked at him, he glanced away. The other two continued to scream, to push, and finally to hit her.

She woke with a start, her heart racing and palms sweating. She stripped off the gloves and rummaged through her pack for a bottle of water. Only when the cold liquid hit her throat did she calm.

It was simply a dream. She'd faced worse. She would probably face worse again.

She didn't sleep after that. Instead she listened to nature's night sounds and allowed memories of Cooper to come. Their honeymoon in Ireland. How excited he'd been to show her the sights and sounds and food and people. They'd been to Saint Patrick's Cathedral in Dublin, just as Burt and Gloria's granddaughter had. On her bedside table at home sat a picture of them standing near the Cliffs of Moher. She missed their loft in San Diego more than she would have thought possible.

After another hour, Sophia pulled out her phone and stared at the darkened display. She felt torn between a thundering paranoia and the need to speak with her sister. How long had it been? The funeral. Tess had come as soon as Sophia called her, catching the next flight out from JFK. She'd taken care of the arrangements, even though she was younger, even though Sophia had always imagined herself taking care of Tess.

But Tess had always been that way—the practical sister. Their parents had proudly introduced the two girls as *our thinker and our dreamer, not that the two are mutually exclusive.* She could still hear her father's booming voice. Had it really been five years since both her parents had perished in a head-on collision?

It seemed that tragedy had colored her life since that spring day.

She ran a finger over the display, thinking of Tess, wondering if she dared to call her. Henry's words echoed in her mind. *It's important to reach out to those around us—to the people He has placed in our path.* What if this were her last chance to make things right with Tess? Even if she couldn't explain why she'd had to go, she could tell her sister how much she loved her. What would she be willing to give to have received such a message from Cooper?

The sky had begun to lighten and the cries of cranes were becoming more prevalent. Sophia could just make out mineral blocks placed on the far side of the meadow. It must be nearing six, which meant it was nearly eight on the East Coast. If she called now, she might catch Tess on her commute. She pulled the cell phone's battery out of her pocket and turned it over and over in the palm of her hand.

Did she believe as Henry did? Her thoughts were filled with snippets of hymns and Bible verses, memories of sitting between her mother and father in a church pew, sweet recollections of the thing she had lost—family. What was more dear than family? And the only family she had left was Tess.

Breathing the simplest of prayers, Sophia slipped the battery into the phone, pushed the On button, and waited for the icon to indicate she had reception. The screen glowed bright. She glanced across the meadow once more, then thumbed in her sister's number. The phone rang as she pressed the device to her ear, her pulse thudding and sweat prickling her scalp.

Her heart sank as the ringing stopped, and then she heard Tess's recorded voice. Her sister always sounded up, her words seemed to shine with smiley faces, her eyes sparkled as if from some private joke.

Sophia's sadness and regrets fell away. This was the single person who understood her best. Why had she separated herself from someone so important? To protect her? Did she believe Tess would be in danger? Or had she simply wanted, needed, to do this on her own?

She heard a beep and realized she was supposed to be speaking.

She did, the words flowing from her heart. She spoke for a minute and a half, reminded Tess how much she loved her, and finally pushed the End button.

And with that action, she was filled with a cold resolve. She deleted the call log, powered off the disposable phone, and removed the battery. She stored them both in her pack, removed her Canon ESO 760 camera, and placed its strap around her neck. She flexed her hands, neck, and feet. She heard a stirring in the meadow, and then a group of female elk stepped out from the trees, nosing at the blocks and finally pausing to lick them. Cows and bulls—she'd laughed when Cooper first told her what they were called. *Bulls bark, cows mew.* She'd dared him to bark then. He'd chased her around the loft, barking and demanding that she mew as she'd melted into a puddle of laughter and joy and love. That memory filled her heart and drove out the fear and the questions.

She slowly, quietly, gently removed the camera lens cap and began snapping pictures of the cows. She guessed the largest of the three had to be at least four hundred pounds. They were so much larger than the mule deer she'd seen in California that it was almost comical. She clicked away with the Canon, zooming in so the mineral block was in focus and the cows were a blurry foreground. Suddenly the largest of the cows jerked its head up, snorted, and fled from the meadow.

Sophia's pulse raced as she wondered if this was it, if this was the minute when the men who had killed her husband would step out into the open. But no person had spooked the cows. A majestic bull sauntered out of the tree line. He raised his head, sniffing the air, and she snapped a photograph of his antlers that had to be nearly four feet long. If she'd thought the cows were large, she was completely unprepared for the size of this creature. The research she'd done had claimed the average bull weighed seven hundred pounds, and this bull was clearly bigger than average. Suddenly a herd of smaller bulls followed him into the meadow.

She was snapping pictures nearly continuously now.

The bull walked straight to the mineral block and began to nudge and then lick it. Several of the other bulls joined him as the rest grazed the meadow. Sophia realized how beautiful the scene before her was—if only she wasn't trying to catch killers, wasn't risking her life, wasn't determined to avenge Cooper's murder.

She leaned forward, snapping quickly, already thinking about where she would send the files, the notification list she'd created and mailed to herself. She would see that this story made the front page of every paper in the country. Then she'd let the authorities deal with the fallout.

With thoughts of sweet success filling her mind, she realized someone else was in the tree line. Then she became aware of the murmur of voices—possibly a male and female, clipped, and moving closer. She craned her neck to hear, willing the thundering pulse in her ears to quiet and managing to make out the words, "We have a visual…south side…roger."

They were only a few yards away. Clutching the camera to her chest, she cinched the straps of her backpack tighter, took a deep, cleansing breath, and began to run.

Twenty-Two

Threat eliminated.

You did not have authorization.

There wasn't time to call and chat.

You should have made time.

We practically tripped over her.
We need to meet.

Too risky.
Anything linking her to us?

Burner phone. Nothing on it.
Camera.

?

I've already sent it to
the Alamosa drop.

And the harvest?

Done.

Then we proceed with
the agreed-upon schedule.

And the last harvest?

It's a go.

After that?

We clean up and vacate the area.

Easy for you to say.

We'll get you transferred.

Twenty-Three

Henry knelt among the bulrushes and cattails beside Sophia's body, shocked that what she'd feared had come to pass.

Sophia—dead.

It was almost more than he could wrap his mind around, and yet life in the valley continued unaware. Nothing had changed because one woman's life had ended.

The breeze continued to stir the hair at the nape of his neck. The distant cry of cranes still filled the air. Morning light splashed across the San Luis Valley.

Lexi remained close, now quivering and whining deep in her throat.

And Henry understood that everything had changed because the world would never know the woman Sophia might have become. His heart was heavy, grief flowing over him, piercing his heart.

After he turned her over, he might have squatted there beside her body for a few seconds or a few minutes. He wasn't sure. Eventually he became aware that a group of cranes had returned and were scavenging in the vicinity, sunlight was now brightening the day, and Lexi trembled at his feet. There was no doubt in his mind that Sophia was dead. Her arms jutted out from her side at an awkward angle. A light breeze stirred the dark hair draping over her cheek. Her eyes remained closed as if she were sleeping, though it was obvious she had passed from this life to the next.

Henry didn't doubt that she was indeed dead, but something deep inside needed to confirm it again, in case he'd missed something, in case he was wrong. He reached forward again, touched two fingers to her neck and waited. Still no pulse. The skin was cold and stiff to the touch. Henry stood, removed his hat, and murmured a prayer for her soul. Pulling off his jacket, he draped it over her body, hoping it would offer her some measure of dignity. Was there such a thing? Dignity in death? He prayed there was, and that she, even at this moment, was in the loving arms of their heavenly Father.

Sparing her one last glance, he turned and jogged toward the parking area, Lexi at his heels. Flagging down a bird-watcher was easy enough, and of course the *Englischer* had a cell phone. With trembling fingers he placed the 9-1-1 call, and then Henry spoke into the phone.

His voice shook as he gave detailed directions to the dispatcher, the *Englischer* watching him with a growing sense of alarm. But Henry didn't stop to explain. Instead he returned the phone, thanked the man, and hurried back to the body, wanting—needing—to stand guard over her, to protect her from the elements and any curious people passing by. He felt an overwhelming need to afford Sophia that last measure of respect.

He needn't have worried. The bird-watchers had all moved north, following the cranes as they foraged.

Had she been birding and died suddenly? But then why were there bruises around her neck? Had someone strangled her? Why would anyone do such a thing? Who would do such a thing? Who had she been afraid would find her?

And why had he been the one to stumble upon her body here? Why was he, once again, in the middle of a mysterious death?

The questions circled round and round until he raised his eyes to the sky and silently recited Psalm 84. Many of his congregation preferred Psalm 23, but for Henry the eighty-fourth had always been a source of great comfort in most any situation. *How lovely is your dwelling place, Lord Almighty!...Even the sparrow has found a home, and the swallow a nest for herself...Better is one day in your courts than a thousand elsewhere.* The words flowed over his troubled thoughts and distraught soul. He realized his hands were shaking, and he shoved them into his pockets.

Lexi stood close, pressed against his leg, and stared up at him, her eyes wide, worried, even concerned—if a dog could feel such things. Then the police arrived, and Henry stepped back and waited as they set up a perimeter. He understood that the sheriff would want to question him. This wasn't Henry's first murder. He was familiar with the process.

He glanced again at her face, the bruises on her neck, and then the

sun glinted off her necklace. He leaned forward and studied the dog tag.
It held the words of the well-known "Serenity Prayer."

Thirty minutes after they arrived, Roy Grayson hitched up his pants,
readjusted his sheriff's hat to block out the morning sun, and stepped away
from the body. He gave some last instructions to the crime scene techs and
then walked over to where he'd told Henry to wait.

"I messed up your crime scene. I'm sorry."

Grayson didn't dispute that. He did say, "Must have been quite a shock
for you."

The sheriff pulled out a notepad and pen. "Walk me through it. What
you saw, when you saw it, your first impressions, absolutely anything that
comes to mind."

Lexi sank to the ground, head on paws, as Henry began to recount
the events of the last hour. When he was finished, he felt as if he'd lived
through the horrible incident twice.

"Looks to me like she's been dead at least a day," Grayson said. "There's
no identification on her. We'll run her prints. See if any missing persons
reports that match her description have been filed."

"Her name's Sophia Brooks." Henry shrugged when the sheriff leveled
him with a surprised stare. "I was going to tell you earlier, but you were
busy on your phone and radio."

"You know her?"

"She works—worked—at the diner."

"She worked at Maggie's?"

"*Ya*, it's the only diner I know of in Monte Vista."

Grayson ran a hand up and down his jawline and finally admitted,
"Haven't been there in several months myself. Wife has me on a diet. Seems
I've gained twenty pounds in the last year."

Henry had always thought of the sheriff as tall and thin, but now he
noticed the man had put on weight. Grayson pulled off his Stetson, wiped
at the sweat on his balding head, and replaced the hat. His uniform was
neatly pressed, though he did have what appeared to be a coffee stain on
the front of his shirt.

"It's a small town," Henry said. "I'm sure you've seen her around."

"Maybe." Grayson reached for his radio, pushed a button, and told
someone on the other end the victim's name.

"Terrible thing," he said, turning his attention back to Henry.

"Indeed." Henry became aware that the tremor he'd experienced earlier was worse instead of better. The trembling began in his shoulder and worked its way down his arm to his fingers. Just his right hand, though. Strangest thing. He kept his hand in his pocket and closed it into a fist to still the shaking.

"Good place to kill someone or even dump a body," Grayson said. "This place is pretty desolate."

"Kill her?" Henry realized he sounded like a simpleton. Of course she'd been killed. He'd seen the bruises on her neck. It was just all so hard to fathom.

Grayson pierced him with a stare, and then he shook his head. "Ligature marks around the neck. Looks to me like she was strangled. She was facedown when you found her?"

"*Ya.*"

"My guess is they came up behind her. Maybe she was running, or maybe they caught her unaware. Strangled her and left her body here in the reeds. Didn't figure anyone would find her, or even if they did, well, the perp would be long gone by then."

"Unless it was someone local."

"Why would you say that?"

"I don't know." Henry wiped at the sweat running down his face. He suddenly felt inexplicably tired, as if he could barely stand.

"Henry, listen to me. This is quite a shock. I want you to go home and rest."

"But—"

"You can't do anything more here. I appreciate your help so far."

"Help?" Henry's laugh was a distraught thing. "I tromped all over your crime scene, turned over the victim, and probably obliterated any clues."

"There's a good chance we'll come across some evidence yet. You'd be surprised what we can find." Grayson closed the small notebook and stuck it and the pen back into his pocket. "You kept your head, Henry. Can't say as I'm surprised, given our history."

Henry didn't answer that immediately. His mind wanted to slip back to the events of sixteen months prior, but he resisted. Today's troubles were enough. "You said *dumped*. She wasn't killed here?"

"Could have been. Can't imagine what she would have been doing out here, though. Was she a birder as far as you know?"

Henry shook his head.

"We'll know more when we receive the forensics reports."

"And you think it happened yesterday?"

"I'm not a forensic pathologist, but that would be my guess." Grayson blew out a long breath. "Like I said, this is a good spot to hide a body. I'm not a birder myself, but I know this area is large."

"Nearly fifteen thousand acres."

Grayson whistled. "What are the odds?"

"Of me stumbling upon her?"

"Exactly."

"Low, and I can't say as I'm glad I did."

"She's bound to have some family."

"Not that she spoke of."

"We'll find them. It isn't the best part of my job—notifying the next of kin—but at least they will know. It's better than wondering."

Henry nodded in agreement, even while he offered up a prayer for Sophia's loved ones.

"All right. You know the drill. If you think of anything else—"

"Actually, there is something." Henry couldn't think how to phrase what he needed to say. It was going to sound crazy regardless. "She mentioned being afraid."

"Afraid?"

"That someone was following her."

"Why would they do that?"

"She never said."

Grayson sighed and rubbed his brow as if to relieve a headache forming there.

"She told you this?"

"She did."

"All right. I'll see if she mentioned it to anyone at work. Remember, if anything else, anything at all, comes to mind—"

"I'll call you right away."

Grayson glanced back toward the parking area, though it was too far to see it from where they stood. "You have a way home?"

"Stuart was supposed to pick me up about this time."

"Good. If for some reason he doesn't show, tell my deputy to call in and get you a ride."

Henry had turned away when Grayson called out to him. "I might stop by later. Might have some additional questions for you."

Henry raised his right hand, indicating that he understood, and noticed that it trembled still. Calling to Lexi, he tramped off toward the parking lot.

Twenty-Four

You won't believe who found her.

                                    ?

The bishop.

                    How did that happen?

He's a birder.

                    And he just happened
                    to stumble over her?

I know. What are the odds?

            This could work to our advantage.

Exactly.

                    I'll handle it from this end.

Twenty-Five

True to his word, Stuart was waiting in the southwest corner of the parking lot. Henry wasn't too surprised to see he was reading a paperback book and completely ignoring the police activity around him. Like Rachel, Stuart loved to read, which was one reason he'd decided to drive for the Amish. "Lots of down time," he'd once explained.

Henry tapped on the hood of the old pickup.

Stuart jerked his head up and offered a one-handed wave.

Henry opened the passenger door. "In, Lexi."

The little dog jumped up and settled on the floor in front of the passenger seat.

Stuart placed an UNO card in the book to hold his place—a historical book, apparently, with a picture of President Hamilton on the front—and cranked the truck's engine. The vehicle didn't look great with its faded paint, torn seats, and a headliner that tended to droop, but it had always succeeded in taking Henry from point A to point B.

"Cops mess up your birding?" Stuart pulled onto the two-lane road and turned right.

"The birds have scattered, for sure."

"Word is they found a dead body. That the person had been shot two times." Stuart tapped the back of his head, down near the neck. "Double tap, Mafia-style."

"I found it, or rather her. No bullet holes I could see."

Stuart shot him a questioning look. "You found her? Do you know who she was?"

"Her name was Sophia Brooks. Maybe you've seen her at Maggie's?

A little shorter than me, young, brown hair cut near the shoulder." He touched the top of his left shoulder.

"Yeah, sure. Sophia waited on me a couple of times. Nice gal. She seemed a little young and a little lost. You're sure it was her?"

"I am."

Stuart let out a long, low whistle. "Terrible thing."

Henry didn't answer that. It didn't seem as though he needed to. Lexi dropped her head across his foot and fell asleep as they continued to Highway 15 and then turned north toward Monte Vista.

"Awful waste of a life. I know you don't believe that, but…"

"We believe each life is complete."

"You've explained that to me before. You know, back when Vernon…"

Henry had no desire to rehash the death of Vernon Frey, who had been killed in a fire set by the Monte Vista arsonist.

"Still an awful thing for a girl that young to have her life end so abruptly." Stuart set the truck on cruise, though they were only six miles from Monte Vista. "Not a bullet wound, huh? What killed her, then?"

"I couldn't say. There was bruising around her neck. Sheriff Grayson thinks it might have been strangulation, but they'll need to run tests to be certain."

"A terrible thing," he said again.

"She was lying on her stomach, and I felt for a pulse but found none. So I rolled her over, which in hindsight I shouldn't have done. I contaminated his crime scene. Only at the time, I wasn't sure it was a crime scene. Regardless, once I turned her over, it was pretty obvious she was dead. Her body was cold and quite stiff."

"Good grief, Henry. I know you're a bishop and all, and that you're used to death to some degree, but you touched the body? And then I suppose you were questioned by Grayson. Let me take you for a cup of coffee or something. Breakfast? Anything. It's on me."

Henry waved away his concern. "Another time maybe."

"Yeah, okay. I guess after the morning you've had, you'd rather be home."

"I would. I need to clean up anyway. I have dried mud on my hands and knees."

Stuart let him be then, with the only sound that of the tires against pavement. Once they were within two miles of town, Amish homesteads began to dot the countryside. Henry's congregation was spread out around Monte Vista, but the town was only about two square miles, with a population that hovered around 4,500.

Five minutes later, they pulled into Henry's lane. Lexi stirred, yawned, and stretched as if she recognized the sound of the dirt under the truck's tires. Henry had only had the little dog a little more than a year, but she had readily accepted the place as home.

Seeing his house, his workshop, even his garden, which had mostly been harvested, brought a measure of peace to Henry. He hadn't realized how rattled he had been, but then, who wouldn't be? He might be accustomed to matters of life and death, as Stuart had said, but he wasn't used to identifying the dead, especially when it was someone he knew, someone he'd cared about. And he had cared about Sophia, though she'd done her best to keep everyone at a distance.

Stuart pulled the truck to a stop in the circular gravel area in front of Henry's house. "Would you still like to go back out on Saturday?"

Henry reached for his wallet, counted out a little more than Stuart would say he owed, and pressed it into the man's hand. When he opened the door, Lexi bounced out, tearing around to the backyard and back again.

"How about I give you a call tomorrow? I can walk down to the phone shack—" A thought blossomed in his mind, one he quickly pushed away. The last thing he needed to do was get any more involved than he already was. "Would that be all right?"

"Sure thing." Stuart tapped his fingertips against the wheel as Henry exited the truck. "And call if you need anything else. It doesn't, you know, have to be for a ride."

"*Danki*, Stuart."

He shucked off his muddy boots and left them on the porch before walking into his house, Lexi on his heels. He quickly washed and dried his hands, and then almost unconsciously made his way to the kitchen drawer where he kept pens, pencils, and his drawing paper. He pulled out a tablet and looked at it as the thought he'd had in the truck asserted itself, pushing into his consciousness. He could draw what he'd seen, draw it now while the memory was fresh in his mind. Shaking his head, he stuffed the pad back into the drawer and shut it.

The *Englischers* had their cameras. They would record everything the same as Henry's subconscious mind had. And it didn't matter if he drew the scene now or a year from now. His mind and hand would render the same drawing. The memory didn't degrade over time. Or so the doctors had suggested.

No, he didn't need to draw Sophia's death while her body was still being carried to the morgue.

Embracing his unique talent was fine, and he was glad that twice now he'd been able to help put a murderer behind bars. But he wasn't *Englisch*, and he certainly wasn't employed by law enforcement in any way. He didn't need to involve himself with the death of Sophia Brooks. He'd tried to involve himself in her life, and what good had that done? None that he could tell.

No, he didn't think he would spend time drawing what he had seen that morning. He sat at the table, his hands shaking and his heart filled with sadness. Who would murder Sophia? Why? She'd said something about *being close*. What did that mean? Should he have mentioned it to Grayson? At least mentioned that she'd been afraid something might happen to her?

Henry tried to clear his thoughts, to push away the questions that plagued his mind.

Grayson and his team of forensic techs would solve the murder, if indeed it had been one.

His life was Plain and simple, and he'd just as soon keep it that way.

Twenty-Six

It was midafternoon when Emma heard the story from Katie Ann, who heard it from her best friend, Naomi, who was working at the three widows' new bakery in town. The bakery was wildly popular, which explained why they needed extra help. And still everyone was surprised when they'd hired Naomi, who would rather be jotting stories in her notebook than manning a cash register. She tended to be rather absentminded and had been known to show up in town with her *kapp* falling back off her head, two different shoes on her feet, and once with her apron on backward. The girl was a mess but sweet as the apple pie also sold at Bread 2 Go.

"You're sure about this?" Emma dried her hands on a dish towel and sat down at the kitchen table across from Katie Ann, her stomach turning at the news. "You're positive it was Henry who found the woman's body?"

"*Ya.*" Katie Ann pulled in her bottom lip and worried it with her top teeth.

It occurred to Emma that Katie Ann did not need this type of complication in her life. It had taken her months to get over the trauma wrought by the Monte Vista arsonist, and in the end they'd sent her to Florida for a while. She'd come back more mature and calm—not the bright, cheerful schoolgirl she'd once been, but also no longer plagued with nightmares. Now this. Only seventeen years old, and two people had been murdered in her hometown.

Emma reached across the table and covered Katie Ann's hands with her own.

"We will pray for whoever it was, for any family she might have had, and of course for the authorities as they puzzle this out. Perhaps you're

99

mistaken on some of the details. Let's hope so. It could have been an accident of some sort."

"Nancy told Naomi who told me, which makes it nearly straight from Henry's mouth."

"I'm not sure about that."

"Not sure about what?" Rachel walked into the room, holding a book in one hand and a dust rag in the other.

Rachel and Katie Ann looked as much alike as a mother and daughter could. Both had long, thick blond hair, which was properly covered by a *kapp*. They also shared brown eyes, medium height, a small pert nose, and a splash of freckles. The only real difference between them was thirty pounds, but then Katie Ann was young and hadn't birthed four children. Katie Ann also resembled her father, Clyde, but in more subtle ways. Emma's son often teased that he didn't see a bit of himself in the girl, but Emma understood they shared a tendency to stubbornness and a big heart. Plus, Katie Ann preferred working outside, like her father, and was rarely caught looking at a book.

Life was interesting, and families were the best part of it, in Emma's opinion.

"Henry found a dead body," Katie Ann said.

"Are you kidding?" Rachel dropped her book on the kitchen table and reached for her mug of cold coffee. "How? Where?"

"No one is sure how the woman died, but Henry stumbled across her body at the Monte Vista Wildlife Refuge."

"Have they identified her?" Emma asked.

"Naomi wasn't real clear on that. Someone mentioned a movie star, but then someone else said she was just a stranger passing through."

"Not Amish, then." Rachel put the mug back down on the table without drinking from it. "I shouldn't have said that. Any death is a tragedy."

"And yet it's natural to worry about our own." Emma tsked as she walked back to the counter, picked up the shoo-fly pie she'd assembled, and slipped it into the oven.

Rachel and Katie Ann continued wondering aloud about the poor girl found in the marsh, but Emma gradually tuned out the sound of their voices, lost in her own thoughts and worries. She needed to check on Henry. She needed to see for herself that he was all right, that this terrible thing hadn't pushed him over some proverbial edge.

She stood near the kitchen sink, drumming her fingers against the countertop and staring out the window. Deciding to go with her instinct, she turned around and said, "I think I'll take Henry some of that leftover chicken casserole from last night."

Her daughter-in-law and granddaughter exchanged a knowing look.

"It's a cas-se-role," she said slowly, as if by pronouncing her words carefully they'd believe her excuse. "He's probably hungry."

"It's okay to say you want to check on him, *Mamm*."

"*Ya*. We all know you care about Henry in a special way."

Emma shook the dish towel she was holding at Rachel. "You read too many romances."

"They're Christian romances."

"Will you watch my pie?"

"Of course."

"And you…" Emma studied her granddaughter, trying to think of what she could say to the little imp to curb her imagination. But Katie Ann, as usual, was one step ahead of her.

"It's okay, *Mammi*. We all think it's sweet. Now, would you like me to hitch the buggy to Cinnamon, or would you rather walk?"

"I'll walk." She could use the exercise. She'd sworn she wasn't going to eat any of the coffee cake Rachel had served with breakfast, and then she'd promptly consumed two slices—though they were thin slices, which was why she'd needed two. "*Danki* for offering."

She turned and hurried out of the house before she had to answer any more questions about Henry. It wasn't until she was halfway to his place that she realized she'd completely forgotten about the leftover casserole she'd intended to bring.

When Lexi greeted her in the lane, Emma reached into her pocket for the dog biscuit she kept there in case Henry stopped by with his little friend. The beagle accepted it with a yip, carrying it in her mouth as she darted off toward Henry's workshop. She would sometimes carry a biscuit around in her mouth for the entire duration of a visit, as if it was a gift to be treasured rather than a treat to be eaten.

Henry was in the back, working in the shade afforded by the workshop, sanding an old Adirondack chair that looked as if it had seen much better days. He'd taken to fixing old furniture, refinishing it, and then selling it in his shop. Henry once told her giving life to old things reminded him of his work as a bishop, where he hoped to share God's abundant life with his congregation—old and young alike.

Often he whistled or hummed an old hymn as he worked, but today he wasn't whistling. His back was to her, and it seemed that his shoulders were bunched up and tense. As she stood there, watching, he stopped and rubbed his right arm with his left hand before picking up the sandpaper and going back to work.

She called out so as not to startle him.

In the instant he turned and looked at her, the lines between his eyes smoothed and his frown turned into a small smile.

"Emma, what a pleasant surprise."

"I brought you a casserole for dinner."

"That was most thoughtful."

"But I forgot it."

Henry nodded as if that made sense. "I still have plenty of fresh bread and some leftover ham. I'd been planning on sandwiches. Care to stay for dinner? I could take you back in the buggy."

Emma noticed his right hand shook as he set down the piece of sandpaper.

"Dinner sounds tempting. I'd love to, actually. But I promised to finish sewing a new pair of pants for Silas. He's taking Hannah Schwartz out tomorrow night."

"Thought he was dating Sally Yoder."

"I did too."

But they weren't concerned about Emma's grandson. Silas was a good boy. It was only that at nineteen he still hadn't decided he wanted to settle down. Emma had a suspicion he was also dating an *Englisch* girl occasionally, but she didn't bring that up now. No doubt Henry had bigger things on his mind. Bigger than who the *youngies* dated or how the chair he was working on turned out.

Emma had never been one to dance around a subject, and now didn't seem like the time to start. "Tell me if it's true that you found a dead body."

"*Ya.* I did."

"And?"

"You'd better sit down."

Twenty-Seven

It took twenty minutes for Henry to explain everything that happened. By the time he was finished, they'd moved onto the little porch of his workshop, which was just big enough to hold two rockers. The afternoon light stretched across the front half of the porch, so they sat with their bodies in the shade but their legs stuck out in the sun, which was satisfyingly warm. Lexi dozed at their feet.

"I'm sorry, Henry. She seemed like a sweet, if somewhat lost, young woman."

"She did."

"I'm sorry for Sophia and for you."

Henry didn't answer that, and Emma thought she knew why.

"It's normal to be disturbed by it."

"What makes you think I'm disturbed?"

"You're a bishop. You're not a saint."

"True enough."

"These things are upsetting."

"Maybe."

"Maybe? Your right hand is shaking as if you have the palsy."

Henry stared down at the offending hand, turning it over and looking at the back and then again at the palm as if he could find an answer there. "Strangest thing. Started after I made the 9-1-1 phone call, or maybe before that."

"But it started this morning?"

"*Ya.*"

"You're in shock, that's what it is. Watching for birds and literally

103

stumbling upon a corpse would do that to a body. Stumbling upon the corpse of someone you knew… And don't argue with me. We did know her, Henry. It's not as if she were a complete stranger. You're bound to be in shock. Perhaps you should see Doc Wilson."

"You worry too much."

"Do you think so?"

"But I appreciate your concern."

Emma set her chair to rocking. She waited for a minute and then brought up the topic they were both avoiding.

"Do you think you should…" She made the motion of drawing on a page.

"Funny you should mention that. When I came home, the first thing I did was walk to the drawer to pull out a pad of paper."

"That's *gut*. It's *gut* you're embracing your gift."

"I put the paper back. Decided it wasn't my place to become involved in this."

"But you already are."

"Doesn't mean it will do any *gut*."

"You won't know until you try."

Henry stood and repositioned his rocker so he was facing her. "Emma, you've been a *wunderbaar* help to me. At one time, as you know, I thought I should hide this strange ability of mine."

"And I'm glad you're no longer doing so. The drawings you've made in the last year since Vernon's death have been a real blessing to people."

"You suppose?"

"Take the one you drew of the Kings' new baby. They mailed it back east to their family, and Deborah told me her mother was thrilled to be able to see the child. She passed it around to the entire family and then mailed it back so Deborah could put it in her keepsake box."

"She said the same thing to me just the other day."

"And what of the one for Doc Berry?"

"I happened to be at Daniel Beiler's place when Doc Berry arrived to try to save Daniel's workhorse. The horse had caught his hoof in a hole in the field, and he went down hard. If you could have seen Daniel that day, tears streaming down his face as he waited for Doc's verdict. He feared she would recommend putting the horse down. Instead she used her portable

X-ray machine, found out it was only a sprain, and showed Daniel how to wrap it."

"She's a *gut* doc."

"That she is. She went back every day for a week to check on that horse. Daniel shared with me how appreciative he was and how he wished he could have paid her more."

"She takes what we can afford, and somehow it's enough." Emma stared out across Henry's place and saw Oreo chomping grass in the pasture. It was the same with all the Amish. Their horses were an important part of their way of life, and they often lived twenty years or more. They became a part of each family. "I saw the drawing you did, of Doc kneeling next to the horse and Daniel in the background. There was so much emotion in the drawing. It's truly amazing what you are able to do."

"My hope was that the drawing might express our gratitude for Doc Berry's commitment to our community."

"And it did. Katie Ann told me it's now framed and hanging in Doc's office."

Henry sighed and reached down to scratch Lexi between the ears.

"What you're able to draw… They're real works of art."

But they all knew Henry's drawings were more than that. They were a miracle.

Since he'd been hit by a baseball at the young age of twelve, Henry had been able to render anything he saw in photographic detail. No one understood exactly how that worked, but no one in their community doubted it, either. The doctors claimed Henry was an accidental savant, but Emma only knew he was their bishop and a good man.

For years he'd refused to use his gift, certain that it was a curse. But then Vernon Frey had died in a horrible fire, and one of their own had been jailed for the murder. Henry's drawing had led to the arson investigator solving the case.

The last picture he'd drawn, as far as Emma knew, was of Rebecca Yoder just days before her passing. Emma had seen it, and the details Henry included were moving—the woman's hand upon a quilt, her thumb caressing the old stitching, sunlight streaming through the window and landing on a patch of Rebecca's white hair, the expression of complete acceptance and faith on her face. The sketch had seemed more real than any *Englisch* photograph. Emma knew for a fact that Mary and Chester Yoder treasured the drawing.

Then she remembered he'd drawn one other scene since. "You drew Sophia."

Henry nodded.

"But she kept it."

"*Ya.* She told us she put it in a safe place."

"Could you draw it again?"

"I suppose." He tapped his forehead with a finger. "I suppose it's still in here. It would seem that nothing slips away from that portion of my brain."

"Maybe you should." The words were practically a whisper.

"I'll consider it."

She knew he still struggled with how his ability was perceived by others.

"The families in our district appreciate the special talent you have."

"I'm grateful to be surrounded by kind, compassionate people."

"And we are blessed to have you as our bishop."

"Some more conservative Amish districts might have said—"

"What? That your ability is a curse, Henry? Or that it's vain?"

"You know they would have." He smiled now, and Emma suspected it was because her hackles were up. He could always tell.

"There's nothing in our *Ordnung* that speaks against it," she said.

"I happen to agree with you."

"We prayed on it and agreed that, for our district, drawings are fine."

"Some say we'll be carrying smartphones next, snapping photos right and left."

Emma made a *tsk* sound. She pressed her fingers to her lips, certain she could break the habit. "What did you hope to draw when you arrived home this morning?"

"I'm not sure. It was more of a reflex. I can't see how it would help at all."

"Maybe it would help you."

"What do you mean?"

"You saw a terrible thing, Henry. Perhaps your mind needs to express what it captured, to give your heart, and your soul, peace. Perhaps then your trembling will stop."

Henry stood, walked to the edge of the porch, and stared out across his small acreage. Unlike most Amish, Henry didn't have a place big enough for plowing and planting a marketable crop. His farm consisted of a good-sized garden, where he raised vegetables for his own meals, sufficient pasture to allow his mare, Oreo, to exercise, and his home and workshop. His needs were simple, and his woodwork was well liked by the shops in town, well enough to provide what income he needed.

Emma knew all of these things. She understood he was now feeling as though the peaceful life he enjoyed had been torn in two. She appreciated how important it was to him to have a quiet haven where he could recharge. He'd shared those thoughts with her often. They'd become quite close over the last two years.

Now he turned to her, a smile playing across his lips. "You're a wise woman, Emma."

"Is that so?" Heat crept up her neck, causing her to feel like a young girl. "I'll give what you've said some thought."

"Which is all I can ask. Now I'd best get home and start working on those pants for Silas."

"Sure I can't drive you?"

"On an afternoon like this?" The day had warmed so that she no longer needed her sweater. The slightest of breezes rustled the leaves on the surrounding trees, occasionally sending down a shower of red, gold, and orange. "I might decide to go home the long way, just as an excuse to be outside longer."

He walked with her to the end of the lane. When she was about to turn and go, he said, "Sophia was a *gut* girl and only a little lost, as you said. We spoke just the day before yesterday, on Tuesday." He paused. "She wore the 'Serenity Prayer' on a dog tag hanging from a simple chain around her neck. Do you know it?"

"*Ya.* I do."

"A bad person…I don't think a bad person would wear such a thing."

"Sometimes it's not a matter of whether we're *gut* or bad, though. Sometimes the things we suffer through are related more to or possibly even caused by the people we become involved with."

Henry nodded in agreement, stepped closer, and kissed her cheek. Then he turned back toward his workshop. Emma walked home, the kiss a pleasant reminder of their friendship. Or was it more? She'd yet to completely accept her feelings for Henry Lapp. They were taking their time and getting to know one another, which was quite funny because they'd known each other nearly all their lives. But always as friends, never as a potential spouse. Was that what Henry was? If he asked, would she marry him? She'd accepted that she loved Henry, but did she love him in the way that a woman should love a man she hoped to marry?

She honestly didn't know. Her life was fine exactly as it was. Why risk the chance of spoiling what they had, which at this point was a very dear friendship?

Life was messy enough on its own.

Then again, how often did you find someone to love, someone you'd want to grow old with, someone who shared your attitudes toward and beliefs about life? In her experience, only twice, and that wasn't a thing to squander. It was a wonderful gift.

But as she walked home, her thoughts turned away from what she was grateful for, and she barely saw the glorious fall day around her. Instead her mind remained focus on the young waitress who had worn a prayer on a chain around her neck.

Twenty-Eight

Henry finished sanding the Adirondack chair, checked on his mare, fed himself as well as Lexi, and spent an hour in Bible study and prayer. When there was little else to do, he pulled out the pad of paper and pencils and sat down at the kitchen table.

At some point he noticed the room was growing dark, so he lit the lantern on the table and then continued drawing. When he was done, he'd produced four detailed scenes and was so exhausted that he didn't bother to look at them or analyze them in any way. He drank a glass of water, prepared for bed, and turned off the lantern. He fell asleep with Lexi curled up at the foot of his bed. Henry was normally a sound sleeper, but he woke hours later, certain he had missed something.

The little dog didn't move as he reached for his battery lantern. He preferred it to a gas lantern in the middle of the night. It was easier to turn on, and there was less chance of an accident when he was still drowsy. It cast a soft beam of light across the floor. Henry pulled on his trousers and padded into the kitchen. The clock on the wall said it was twelve minutes past three. He'd been asleep for six hours.

He sat down and pulled a fresh sheet of paper toward him. He drew until his fingers had begun to cramp and dawn pushed at the eastern sky. He'd made three more drawings, which he stacked upon the previous four after looking at them all. Then he went to his room, finished dressing, and let Lexi outside. He'd had his first cup of coffee and simple breakfast of an egg and a piece of the widows' sourdough bread when his dog began to bark. He'd at least managed to train her to stay on the porch when someone was approaching. He glanced out the front window to see Grayson's official sheriff's vehicle bumping down his lane.

Henry walked out the front door and stood waiting.

"Easy, girl." One hand, palm open at his side, and Lexi flopped onto the porch. Amazing how smart the little dog was and how much she longed to please him.

The cruiser came to a stop three feet from the porch. Sheriff Grayson and a man Henry didn't know stepped out of the vehicle.

"Morning, Henry." Grayson nodded to the man beside him. "This is Agent Roscoe Delaney. He's with the FBI."

Delaney glanced around as if he'd never seen a farm before, and perhaps he hadn't. Henry knew almost nothing about the FBI, but he did know their agents usually worked out of larger cities. Delaney stepped forward to shake his hand. The man had pale skin, icy blue eyes, and dark-black hair cut close to his scalp. "Pleased to meet you," he said.

"Hate to bother you so early in the morning." The day before Grayson had been clean-shaven, but now he sported the shadow of a beard. He also appeared to be wearing the same uniform, now rumpled, same coffee stain on the front of his shirt. "Could we come inside?"

"Of course." Henry led them into the house, motioning for Lexi to stay where she lay. The little dog threw him a reproving look but sighed and rested her head across her paws. Henry thought of suggesting the kitchen and suddenly remembered the stack of drawings on his table.

Drawings of Sophia.

Something Grayson might understand, given their history, but Delaney most certainly wouldn't.

Henry walked across the sitting room, settled into a rocker, and motioned for the two men to take the couch. They sat on opposite ends, leaving a conspicuous space in the middle. Delaney gave Grayson a pointed look.

"We'd like to ask you a few questions," Grayson said, pulling out the same small pad of paper he'd taken notes on at the wildlife refuge.

"I'm happy to help in any way I can."

Grayson was nodding, but Delaney seemed almost uninterested, glancing around the room and assessing what he saw. Perhaps it was the first time he'd been in an Amish home. Maybe he was looking for the electrical outlets or the television.

"How would you characterize your relationship with Sophia Brooks?"

"I knew her, but casually."

"Explain that to me."

"I eat at Maggie's Diner a few times a week, and Sophia was a waitress there."

Grayson consulted the notes on his pad. "She started at Maggie's six weeks ago."

"That sounds about right."

"Did she mention why she was here?"

"*Nein.*"

"Why she was waitressing?"

"She said she needed a job while she was here."

"Future plans?"

"*Nein.*"

"You're not being particularly helpful, Mr. Lapp." Agent Delaney studied his fingernails. "Perhaps you could tell us what you do know about Ms. Brooks."

"I'd be happy to. She was a personable young woman, worked hard at her job, and people seemed to like her."

"People? Or you?"

"I don't understand."

"I think you do." Delaney sat forward, elbows on his knees, hands clasped together, and a smile tugging at his lips. "For an older man like you, it would be natural for a beautiful young woman like Sophia Brooks to catch your eye."

When Henry didn't answer, Delaney added, "You're Amish, right? I understand dating is limited in your culture, and the women...well, they don't exactly look like Sophia."

"Hey. That's unnecessary." Grayson shifted uncomfortably in his seat.

"Agent Delaney is correct. Sophia was quite beautiful."

"And yet someone killed her."

"So it would seem."

Grayson cleared his throat. "Our preliminary autopsy ruling confirms the cause of death was strangulation."

"She was strangled?"

"Yes."

Henry thought of one drawing on his kitchen table. Some detail wasn't jibing with what Grayson said. He nearly snapped his fingers when he thought of it—her nails had been clean and unbroken.

"Was there any sign that she fought back? Surely she didn't simply lie in the reeds and allow someone to choke the breath out of her."

Grayson stared at his pad a minute, as if he was trying to decide whether to share some piece of information. In the end, he said, "The medical examiner found small leather fibers around the victim's neck, consistent with strangulation by a thin strap. The perpetrator was likely male, strong, and standing over her when the homicide took place."

Henry had pictured hands wrapped around her neck.

Who would use a leather strap?

Why?

"Sophia was killed with a leather strap?"

"Yes, Mr. Lapp." Delaney didn't bother looking his direction. He again scanned the room as if he might find some clue to Sophia's murder there.

"Someone squeezed Sophia's throat so tightly she couldn't breathe. He stood there for at least two minutes, possibly longer, and continued to strangle her until he was certain she wasn't merely unconscious but dead." Delaney stood, walked across the room, and stopped beside the cubbies where Henry placed his hat and coat and, after he'd been birding, binoculars.

He crouched down, studied the binoculars where they hung from their strap, and then turned to pierce Henry with an accusatory glare. "According to Sheriff Grayson, you were wearing these when you found the body."

"I was, as were a couple hundred other bird-watchers at the refuge yesterday."

"And yet you were the one who stumbled on the body. You just happened across Sophia Brooks where she lay hidden in the reeds on a fifteen-thousand-acre preserve."

"*Gotte's wille*, perhaps." This Henry muttered under his breath. If Agent Delaney heard, he gave no indication.

Grayson crossed his right leg over his left knee. "I'm sorry about this, Henry. But I have to ask. Can you tell me where you were Wednesday morning between the hours of five and seven in the morning?"

"Two days ago you mean?"

"Yes."

"I was here, at my home and workshop." He wanted to ask both men if they believed he had anything to do with Sophia's death, but it was plain they did. At least Delaney did, and perhaps he was the one in charge now.

"Can anyone vouch for that?"

Henry's right arm began to tremble. He tucked it closer to his side. "*Nein*. I was alone all day." It was rare indeed that one of his parishioners didn't stop by or that he hadn't been out to see someone, but it did happen. And that early in the morning?

As an afterthought, he asked, "Is that when she died? Wednesday morning?"

"We're not authorized to share information pertinent to the case," Delaney said.

"It's preliminary," Grayson added.

Delaney had examined the rest of the cubbies and their contents. Now he was again studying the binoculars hanging from a peg by a leather strap. "You wouldn't mind if we took these in, would you? I could get a warrant, but it would look better all around if you helped us in our investigation."

Henry stood, anger and disbelief warring with one another in his mind and heart. In the calmest voice he could muster, he said, "I'd like you to leave now."

"Fine." Delaney raised his hands, palms out. "Just don't go anywhere. We'll be back in a few hours, and we'll bring a warrant."

The screen door banged behind Delaney. Henry could see through it, could see the man standing on his front porch and surveying his property.

"He thinks I did it." His voice seemed to come from far away.

He jerked his head around when Grayson didn't answer. Finally, the sheriff lowered his voice and said, "He can think what he wants. Doesn't mean he can prove it. Stay calm. Cooperate. Hopefully we'll get something in on the tip hotline we've set up, or the lab results from the crime scene will point him toward the real killer."

"So you don't believe… You know I didn't do this."

Grayson pulled him back, farther away from the door. "Henry, we both know you didn't do this, but Delaney is like a bloodhound that thinks he's caught a scent. Cooperate. Show him you're on his side. You're innocent, and the forensics will prove it."

Henry nodded, wanting to believe his friend. But he'd been involved with the *Englisch* police before, and he knew what often mattered wasn't the data they found but the way they interpreted it.

He watched Grayson drive away and then walked back into the kitchen in a daze. He glanced at the table and froze when he saw the drawings of Sophia spread across it. His arm began to tremble again as he realized he would probably be in the back of that police car right now if Delaney had seen them. It was bad enough that he didn't have an alibi, but he had little doubt that the agent would view the drawings as an indication that Henry was obsessed with Sophia.

Delaney would be easily convinced that obsession had something to do with a motive for murder.

Twenty-Nine

Emma was crouched in the flower beds, deadheading the faded geranium buds, when she heard a buggy tearing down her lane.

"Is that Henry?" Rachel asked.

"Appears so."

"I've never seen him drive so fast."

"Maybe you should fetch Clyde."

Rachel rushed off in the direction of the barn as Emma hurried toward the buggy.

Oreo looked very pleased with herself, tossing her black head as her white tail slapped back and forth. Henry on the other hand, tumbled out of the buggy looking quite frazzled.

"Is something wrong?" Emma asked.

Instead of answering, he reached into the backseat and pulled out a large paper bag. "Can we go inside?"

"Of course."

By the time they made it to the kitchen, Rachel and Clyde had come through the back door.

"Rachel said there's an emergency?"

"*Ya.* I think so." He set the bag on the table.

They had been through a lot together, but Emma had never seen Henry look as flustered as he did now. His hat was on backward, his shirt had come untucked from his pants, and his suspenders were twisted. His eyes darted around the kitchen as if he expected someone to jump out and shout *boo!*

"Maybe you should sit down and have a glass of water," she said.

"I can't." Henry's hands flapped at his side. "I have to get back before they return."

"Take it easy, Henry." Clyde walked up to his bishop, placed a hand on each shoulder, and looked him directly in the eyes. "Slow down and take a deep breath. Then tell us what's going on."

In a faltering voice, Henry recounted his meeting with Grayson and Delaney. By the time he was finished, they were all sitting at the table, and he'd downed an entire glass of water.

Emma crossed her arms and clutched her elbows. "This Delaney fellow…I wonder why Grayson brought him in."

"I imagine he didn't have a choice." Rachel smiled slightly when they all turned to stare at her. "The Monte Vista National Wildlife Refuge is on federal land, *ya*? Then the murder would be deemed a federal crime."

"How does my sweet, Plain wife know such things?" Clyde reached over and rubbed the back of her neck. "Wait. Don't tell me. It's those books you read."

Rachel blushed prettily, but she didn't deny it.

"They have no reason to even suggest you could be involved in this, Henry." Emma had a flyswatter in her hand, and she whacked it against the floor, whether because of a fly or picturing Delaney, she wasn't completely sure. She just needed to whack something.

"Grayson will be on your side," Clyde said. "He's a *gut* man."

"He is, but I'm not sure he's running the show. Like Rachel suggested, I believe it's a federal matter now."

"You have nothing to hide, Henry. Let them come back to your house with a warrant. Let them take the binoculars. They'll find nothing. You're an innocent man, and the investigation will prove that."

"It could be that I'll need an alibi, though, which I don't have."

Clyde rubbed a hand across his face. "You were home and in your workshop all day? Well, you had to walk from one to the other, probably a couple of times. Your place is close enough to the road that someone could have seen you."

"At seven in the morning?" Henry shook his head. "I usually eat breakfast and then putter around inside the house until eight. No one would have seen that from the road."

"But they need more than just suspicions," Rachel said.

WHEN THE BISHOP NEEDS AN ALIBI

"She's right." Emma waved the flyswatter in the air. "They have to prove your guilt, and we all know they can't do that. In fact, I think we're all panicking over nothing. So a bully came to see you. So what? Let him be a bully. He has no proof, and so he's grasping at straws. So what if no one saw you at home? That could be said of many other people in the early hours of the morning. And how many people own binoculars with a leather strap? Plenty. Nearly every birder in Monte Vista. As Clyde said, you have nothing to hide."

"*Ya*, what you all are saying is true, and I don't know why I'm so...so frazzled." Henry reached again for the glass, which was now empty, and Emma noticed how his hand shook.

"Say, you're really upset about this." She jumped up to refill the glass. "Henry, we won't let anything happen to you."

"The problem is, Henry doesn't entirely trust the *Englisch* legal system." Clyde sat back and drummed his fingers against the table. "Can't say I blame you, either."

"After what happened in Goshen? *Nein.* I don't."

"But you were found innocent," Rachel argued. "Eventually."

"It's the *eventually* that's the problem." Henry clutched the glass Emma gave him in his hand, holding it so tightly Emma feared he might break it. "I was a younger man then. I could withstand the pressure of sitting in an *Englisch* jail cell, but I'll tell you, it's not natural. Now that I'm an older man, I'm not sure how I would handle it."

"You're not going to be jailed, Henry." Emma could see the fear in her friend's eyes, and that upset her more than anything. "This isn't like Goshen."

Henry was their port in a storm. He was always calm, practical, and at peace with whatever was happening. She'd never seen him in a state of panic. Not during the mess in Goshen, not when young Sam Beiler was jailed for a murder he didn't commit, not ever. Her eyes darted left and then right, and then they landed on the large paper bag.

Poking it with the flyswatter, she asked, "What's in there?"

"That's why I'm here. I need you to hide something for me."

Thirty

Emma watched as Henry spread out seven drawings on their table. Four were of Sophia at the diner, one was of her walking down the road in Monte Vista, another was when she'd come to Emma's home, and the final one was at the Monte Vista Natural Wildlife Refuge.

Six of her alive.

One after she'd died.

All of photographic quality. Every inch of each large sheet of paper was covered. As often happened, Emma was surprised at what he had drawn. This thing he could do—this talent that had resulted from a careless boy's accident—never failed to astonish her.

"When did you have time to draw these?" Emma's voice was a whisper.

"Last night and this morning."

"Did Grayson and Delaney see them?" Clyde reached forward to touch one of the drawings. It showed Sophia at the diner, helping the old woman.

It was the same drawing he'd given to Sophia. Emma recognized it immediately from when Henry told her about it. The same drawing that had scared Sophia.

"*Nein.* They didn't."

"You're sure?" Rachel said. "Because we understand your talent, and Grayson should, but this man Delaney? He might view these differently."

"I was thinking the same thing. It's why I brought them here. Delaney is coming back with his warrant, and if he sees these, he might use them as evidence to say I was obsessed with Sophia. He might think I've been drawing her for days or weeks. How could he know I drew all of these last night? And would he believe me if I told him?"

"Of course we'll keep them for you." Emma couldn't deny it. Sometimes Henry's gift frightened her. Not only were these drawings exquisitely detailed, but the faces showed emotions to a degree that made her uncomfortable. It was as if the person's every feeling was visible, maybe even his or her thoughts.

But that was impossible. A picture, a drawing, couldn't do that.

And there was no reason they shouldn't keep the drawings for Henry. They had nothing to hide. No one sitting around this table had a single thing to conceal from Delaney or anyone else, but prudence was a good thing, especially in legal situations.

"Why did you draw these, Henry?" Clyde had picked up the rendering of Sophia at the wildlife refuge. It showed her lying among the reeds, her neck bruised and her eyes shut, the dog tag with the "Serenity Prayer" peeking from beneath the collar of her shirt. It seemed to Emma that even in death she was beautiful, perhaps more so than she had been in life. She'd finally laid down all of her burdens, and her youth seemed to shine despite the lifelessness of her pose.

"Hard to say." Henry began pacing back and forth in front of them. "Emma dropped by yesterday and said it might help with the shock of it all. I prayed on it, let the idea sit with me a while, and then last night before bed I became convinced it was the right thing to do, that it was a way of honoring Sophia's life."

"And you drew all of these last night?" Rachel asked.

"*Nein.* I drew four before I went to bed, after you came to visit, Emma. I decided you were right, that drawing what I'd seen might soothe the ache in my soul. I worked until almost nine o'clock and then went to bed. Didn't think I would sleep, but I did."

"The other three?" Clyde asked.

"I woke in the middle of the night with the feeling that I'd forgotten something, that some details needed to be put down for others to see. That's when I drew the final three."

Emma asked, "And which were those? Which were the ones your dreams or your subconscious—"

"Or the still small voice of the Lord," Clyde said in a murmur.

"*Ya,* or that," Emma continued. "Which were those final three?"

Henry stepped to the table. He pulled out one of the drawings of the diner, the one he'd done of Sophia when she'd arrived at Emma's house, and the drawing from the wildlife refuge. "These are the ones I drew early this morning."

"All right." Clyde slapped the table with his hand and stood, a smile wreathing his face.

It was one of the things Emma loved dearly about her son—his ability to greet life's most challenging times with a positive spirit. He wasn't a perfect man. He lost his temper when things broke in the barn, sometimes he was impatient with the children, and often he left his dirty socks on the floor. But he was a good man with a strong faith, and he was a true friend to Henry. These things she knew for sure and for certain.

"We will pray that this situation is resolved fully and completely. Leave the drawings here. Emma and Rachel and I will study the three you've pulled out when we have an extra moment here and there. It's not as if you're doing something wrong by removing them from your home. They would only bring more and unnecessary scrutiny on you from this Delaney fellow."

"We'll take *gut* care of them, Henry." Rachel scooped up all of the drawings, placing the three he'd done that morning on top, and put them all back in the paper bag.

"There. Don't give them another thought." Emma tried for an optimistic smile, but it felt off, felt forced. She settled for swatting at a fly in midflight. "I'll walk you out to your buggy."

As they stepped outside, she said, "I'm surprised you didn't bring Lexi."

"I guess I wanted her to guard the house."

"Guard it against what?"

"The police? Sophia's killer? I'm not sure, Emma. To be completely honest with you, I have an overwhelming sense of danger, but I don't know which direction it's coming from."

Thirty-One

'm sorry, Emma. The way I arrived, practically in a panic, that wasn't very bishop-like of me."

"Still trying to be perfect?"

He laughed, perhaps his first of the day. "*Nein*, but occasionally my frailty and fears take me by surprise."

"It's the same for all of us. One day I'm on top of the world, sure *Gotte* is on His throne and I've conquered this thing called living." She stopped beside the geranium plant to pinch off one last bloom. "Other days I wonder how I managed to get to the ripe old age of sixty-two and yet still be so clueless."

"Maybe that explains why we're still here. *Gotte* isn't finished with us yet."

"He who began a *gut* work in you will carry it on to completion."

"I should have thought of that."

Emma nudged his shoulder with her own. Together they walked over to Henry's mare, who seemed content to crop at what remained of the summer's grass. Emma looked up, out across the valley and toward the mountains. Soon their peaks would be capped with snow, and they'd be making their way through another Colorado winter. Such were the seasons of life—each one seemed to come too quickly and pass before she'd settled into it.

"I thought life would slow down as I got older," she said.

"The months and years seem to speed by."

"You feel it too?"

"*Ya*." Henry's hand was next to hers, stroking Oreo's neck. "Perhaps because they have become so precious, and we realize they are limited."

"Death is a normal part of life."

Henry nodded in agreement.

"And yet Sophia's death wasn't natural."

"Every life is complete." They were the same words he'd shared with Stuart, the same words he'd uttered through the years over dozens of freshly dug graves. It had been a privilege to help families through their time of suffering, but who would mourn Sophia? Would Grayson be able to locate her family? Did she have friends who would grieve her passing?

Emma scratched the mare between her ears. "Why would anyone want to kill Sophia?"

"I can't think of a reason, but she did seem to think she was in danger."

"She certainly appeared quite troubled the morning she left here. I remember looking out the window and watching her walk down the lane. It seemed to me she carried the burdens of the world on her shoulders."

"I went to see her twice after that," Henry admitted. "Tuesday, early in the morning, but the diner was too crowded to speak with her. She was rushing back and forth between tables. I went back later that afternoon."

"You must have been very concerned."

"I was. I also had a sense that time was running out." His thumb was under his suspender. He looked down, surprised to find it twisted. He wondered how he hadn't noticed that before. He hadn't given a thought to how he looked. He'd been overwhelmed with a need to be with Emma and Clyde and Rachel, to be among friends.

Emma walked behind him, straightened the strap, and gave him a pat on the shoulder.

"*Danki.*"

"*Gem gschehne.*" The old words passed between them, blessings passed on time and again.

Henry unwrapped the reins from the hitching post in front of Emma's house. Funny that he couldn't remember putting them there to begin with. He'd allowed fear to consume him, and he'd run to the Fishers. To Clyde and Rachel and Emma, the people God had given him to stand in the place of family. Henry had family, of course—siblings who lived in Indiana. They wrote letters and spoke on the phone occasionally, but it wasn't the same as having someone you could share a cup of coffee with, share your immediate fears with. Clyde and Rachel and Emma were three people who were incredibly important to him spiritually and physically. He could see that now, that in his time of need, he'd realized he couldn't do life alone.

Bishop or not, he still needed others.

Together they walked to the side of the buggy.

"Were you able to speak with her the second time you went to the diner?"

"For a few moments. We talked of my being a bishop, of our faith, a little of her family. Her grandmother read the Bible each day."

"It's *gut* that she had those memories, that her grandmother was a believer."

"And yet Sophia's life had its share of tragedy."

"True for us all."

"She was widowed."

"Perhaps that explains the sadness about her."

"Maybe." Henry kissed Emma's cheek and then climbed into the buggy. "She told me she was giving notice at the diner, and that she probably wouldn't see me again. She said it wasn't safe to be *freinden* with her, and that she was 'close.'"

"Close to what?"

"I'm not sure."

Emma sighed as she stepped back from the buggy. "Let us know if there's more trouble with the FBI fellow."

"I suspect there will be." Henry pulled on the reins and called out to Oreo. It was only when he was far down the lane that he noticed clouds were building in the west. Rain was rare in the valley, storms few and far between, but it looked as if they were in for a big one.

Which didn't surprise him one bit. The weather had a way of matching the twists and turns of life.

When Henry pulled into his lane, Lexi didn't run out to meet him, which was strange. Perhaps she'd fallen asleep in a patch of sunshine, or maybe she was chasing toads. She'd developed a fascination with them. But he didn't believe either of those things. She'd never failed to meet him before.

He guided Oreo to the barn, unharnessed the horse, and led her to the pasture.

"Where could she be?" he murmured. When he walked into the barn, he noticed the stall door was closed. He always kept it open because he didn't want one of the barn cats getting locked in there without food or water.

Walking toward it, he was overcome by a terrible sense of foreboding, which was ridiculous. This was his barn, and everything was exactly as he'd left it.

Then he opened the door and saw Lexi lying motionless on the ground.

Thirty-Two

Henry sank to the floor next to the little beagle.

He ran his hands up and down her side. She was breathing, though it seemed to be slow and shallow. He couldn't be sure, though. He didn't know how a dog was supposed to breathe. He did know her not waking up was a bad sign.

"Come on, girl. Wake up for me. Show me you're okay. Show me that beagle spirit."

She still didn't open her eyes, but her ear twitched and her tail tapped the ground once.

He continued petting her, talking in a low voice, and praying that his dog wasn't mortally injured. Was it silly to pray for a dog? He didn't think so. He thought if God had His eye on the sparrow, He could watch out for Lexi just as easily.

As he prayed and waited, he tried to think of some scenario where what he was seeing made sense. Had someone drugged her? If so, why would they put her into a horse stall? Or had they chased her? Perhaps she'd run into the horse stall? Or maybe she wasn't drugged at all. Doc Berry would know, but Henry didn't want to leave Lexi long enough to run to the phone shack and place a call. He also didn't want to load her into the buggy. Best to wait and see.

Finally she opened her eyes and locked her gaze on Henry.

"Gave me a scare there. Can you stand up?"

She attempted to do so, her legs wobbly and her eyes closing.

Henry scooped her into his arms and carried her outside into the sunshine, hoping its warmth would bring her around. He sat there on a bench, holding her close until her tail began to tap a steady rhythm and she took an interest in licking his hand.

"That's a *gut* girl. Sure wish you could talk and tell me what's wrong. Maybe you need some water." He set her on the ground with an admonition to "stay."

Lexi, however, had other ideas.

She let out a menacing series of barks, and then she took off across the yard, headed toward the front porch.

"Quickest recovery ever," Henry muttered.

Lexi barreled up the steps, growling and baring her teeth.

Feeling as if his life had spiraled into an Amish nightmare, Henry opened the front door.

His dog tore across the front room, reversed directions, and then moved more slowly with her nose pressed to the floor, ears touching the ground, tail pointed up. She came to a halt in front of the small wooden wall clock. Henry's father had made it from pallet wood that was now at least fifty years old. The four boards were slightly different colors, and the hour numbers were hand painted. Henry could remember being a young child and reading on the sitting room floor, looking up and seeing that it was time to *outen the light* and head to bed.

Lexi sat down, her nose raised high as if she were sniffing the air, and then she began to bay. Henry had heard her do it only once before, when she'd treed a squirrel. The sound reverberated through his bones and instantly raised his anxiety level. But instead of reprimanding her, he walked to the clock, pulled it off the wall, and stared at the front and then the back. Everything looked as it always had. The small battery reminded him of the solar energy he'd spoken to Albert about. Had that been only a few days ago? It seemed another lifetime.

He turned the clock back over and was about to hang it on the nail when he noticed the numeral 3 looked off, as if the paint had run.

Only it wasn't paint. It was some sort of electronic device or mechanism, approximately the size of an acorn. It definitely was man-made, and it had not been there when he'd last changed the battery.

He pulled the device off the clock, held it between his thumb and forefinger, and tried to determine what it was. Why was it there? Who had put it there? The same person who had locked Lexi in the barn stall and possibly drugged her? Or maybe he was becoming paranoid.

At that moment, Lexi jumped up and knocked the object out of his hand, causing it to skitter across the floor.

Henry returned the clock to the wall and then walked over to the device and put it in his pocket. He'd ask Grayson about it later.

Turning toward his dog, he wasn't surprised to see that she'd now stretched out, her head resting on her paws.

"How about some chicken for lunch?"

Which seemed to be all the thanks Lexi wanted or required.

Three hours later, rain had turned to a steady downpour. The storm had raised the temperature, and the day had turned balmy by the time Delaney pulled off the road, slinging mud as he came to an abrupt stop. He'd returned with the warrant and a crime scene crew. Grayson didn't accompany him, and Henry didn't ask why.

He did insist on seeing the warrant that gave Delaney permission to search his property.

"I assure you that I had nothing to do with the death of Sophia Brooks."

"I've heard claims of innocence from dozens of murderers, Mr. Lapp."

"And yet I am innocent."

"So you say. The judge deemed we had enough cause to search your premises." Delaney stepped forward, and if Henry wasn't imagining it, his eyes sparkled. Like Lexi earlier, he was a man on a hunt. He honestly believed he was hot on the trail of the person who had killed Sophia Brooks. "Better to tell us now if you have something you're hiding. Because we will find it."

Henry put his hand in his pocket, fingered the device he'd found on the clock, and thought of showing it to Delaney. Something cautioned him not to. Some instinct told him to keep this between himself and Sheriff Grayson.

Surely they wouldn't ask him to empty his pockets.

He shook his head and said, "Call me if you need anything."

He sat on the porch of his workshop, a small nightstand in front of him that had been painted at least three different shades of blue. He'd purchased it from a yard sale and thought that with a little care and attention he might restore it to its original beauty. The piece was solidly built of good oak wood. It only needed the paint to be sanded off and a few fresh coats of varnish applied.

He held a piece of sandpaper in his hand, but it might as well have been a prop in an *Englisch* movie. His mind was completely focused on what was happening inside his home, and then they moved into his workshop. Several times he saw them carrying clear evidence bags out to their vehicles. He couldn't imagine why they would want his tack hammer or his receipt book. The person logging in the evidence assured him everything would be returned, though she couldn't say when.

When he peeked inside the shop, he saw a trail of fingerprint powder scattered around. He supposed it was in his house too. He'd even seen one of the techs dusting for prints inside his buggy. Henry was familiar with some of the evidence-gathering processes after what had happened in Goshen when young Betsy Troyer was killed. He didn't want to revisit those memories, but they pushed forward, bringing with them a profound sadness.

He noticed, as he sat back down in the rocker with the rain splashing in front of him and the crime scene techs scurrying back and forth, that they carried more computers than they did all those years ago in Indiana. Advances in technology had changed the specifics of their work, though not the general goal—to catch a killer.

Lexi rolled over in the dog bed he'd made for her from an old wooden crate. Feet in the air, she let out a yip-yip-yip and her back legs jerked as if she were running—chasing rabbits in her dreams.

It was two hours before the *Englischers* began packing up. The rain had stopped, though the afternoon remained dark. Lexi stood, stretched, and trotted off toward the barn.

Henry walked over to where the police vehicles were parked, planning to ask Agent Delaney if there was anything else he could do to be helpful. He might not like the man, but supposing that he was trying to do his job and do it well, he could at least offer his assistance. Not because it made him look less guilty, but because it was the right thing to do.

His good intentions lasted all of two minutes.

"While I was waiting on the warrant, I was able to interview a few people." Delaney smoothed down the black tie that matched his pants. He wore a crisp white shirt and a black jacket, though the day was too warm for it.

"Is that so?"

"For someone who only knew Sophia casually, you spent a lot of time talking with her."

"People tend to confide in me. Perhaps because I'm a bishop."

"And is that why you gave her a ride in your buggy? Folks say that's unusual, that single or widowed men don't normally offer rides to single women. That it's considered inappropriate by your kind."

"Our kind?"

Delaney ignored the question. "I would think your deacons would be concerned about your connection with Ms. Brooks."

Henry didn't answer. He was focusing on keeping his temper in check, which wasn't an easy thing to do around Mr. Delaney. The man seemed to have an innate sense for how to offend someone.

"Also you had an argument with her at the diner on the Tuesday before she was killed."

"I did not," Henry replied hotly.

Delaney again flattened his tie against his shirt and stroked it like a child might pet a kitten. He started to walk away, but then he turned and came back, stopping less than a foot from Henry. He lowered his voice, as if he were about to offer some secret advice. "You can deny your association with the deceased all you want, but we are good at what we do. Monte Vista has cameras on the through roads, which confirm that you did give Sophia Brooks a ride. That, in fact, you went to a motel with her. And we have firsthand testimony that you argued with her at Maggie's Diner."

He smiled, waited for Henry to respond, and lowered his voice even more when Henry remained silent. "You had a known association with the deceased. You had means and opportunity to commit her murder. All I need is motive and evidence. And I will find both."

He paused, his smile widening, and then he turned and picked his way across the muddy lane to his vehicle.

Henry couldn't think of a single reason the FBI would single him out as a primary suspect. He did, however, realize the situation was quickly worsening. He went inside, picked up his hat, an umbrella, and his walking stick. Then he called to Lexi and hurried down his lane. A quarter mile down the road was a phone shack.

He placed three calls, leaving messages on each machine.

As he was about to leave, he turned back and again picked up the receiver. When Stuart answered, he informed him he would not be going bird-watching the next day. "And Stuart, I expect you will have a visit from the FBI soon. It would seem I'm the prime suspect, or rather the only suspect, in the murder of Sophia Brooks."

Thirty-Three

Emma had absolutely no intention of stopping at Bread 2 Go. She was a capable baker and didn't need to spend their limited resources on someone else's bread or cookies or cakes. But she and Katie Ann were returning from the library when they noticed a line of cars and buggies parked at the widows' new shop.

"Maybe we should stop." Katie Ann sat forward, peering out the front window of the buggy.

"We don't need a thing."

"True, but haven't you seen all the Shop Local posters? We'd be doing the Monte Vista economy a favor." Her eyes twinkled with mischief. "I know I wouldn't mind one of their cranberry walnut muffins."

"Clyde does love homemade bread, which I haven't had time to make this week."

"Let's do it!"

She had to guide Cinnamon into the adjacent lot because there was nowhere closer to park. But once she approached the bakery, she knew the widows weren't in need of extra customers. Shop Local indeed. The line stretched out the door. It would seem half the San Luis Valley had the same idea, or perhaps they all were craving cranberry walnut muffins.

"This line is going to take forever," Katie Ann muttered.

"A handful of patience is worth more than a bushel of brains."

"I don't know what that means."

"It means you're better off patient than smart." The woman in front of them was dressed in a business suit and wearing high heels. "My grandmother used to tell me that one."

They shared a smile, and then the line moved forward so they were standing inside and Emma could see what all the commotion was about. She'd been there the day Franey, Nancy, and Ruth opened to show a sign of support, but she hadn't been back in the month since. Red-checkered curtains adorned the windows. Tables for two and four were scattered throughout the room, and each one had an old-fashioned glass milk bottle on it, sporting fresh flowers.

"The flowers are part of Naomi's job," Katie Anne said. "She picks them on her way to work. Since she walks, it isn't a problem."

"What will they do in the winter?"

Katie Ann shrugged, and they shuffled forward as a woman clutching her purchase turned away from the register, a smile on her face.

Apparently, people couldn't pass their money over the counter fast enough.

Muffins for two dollars each. A loaf of bread for five. The widows had uncovered a gold mine!

But what struck Emma were the heavenly smells that saturated the place—cinnamon, nutmeg, fresh bread, baked apples. She could close her eyes and pick them out one by one. As they moved closer to the counter, Emma could see two of her friends.

Franey Graber was carrying a large tray of freshly baked pastries to place inside the display counter. She wasn't smiling exactly, but neither was she frowning. It would seem her nickname, Frowning Franey, was in danger of being replaced with something sunnier. Success could do that to a person, or maybe it was having something to look forward to each day. Franey had been abandoned by her husband years before. Technically, he had filed for divorce, which was recognized in the *Englisch* court system but not in Amish communities. It had been a burden for Franey to bear— that was obvious to all who knew her—and yet today she seemed to have a little pep in her step.

Nancy Kline was running the register. She rang up customers' purchases after Naomi Miller pulled whatever item the customer requested and tucked it into a white bakery sack. Nancy had a smile for everyone. She was the natural choice from among the three widows to interact with the public. It occurred to Emma that Nancy could be a model for one of the Amish books Rachel loved to read. A white *kapp* covered her curly gray hair, her cheeks were a healthy pink from the heat of the kitchen, and a fresh white apron covered her dark-blue dress. She looked like everyone's grandma—everyone's Amish grandma.

Ruth Schwartz was the third widow, and Emma couldn't see her, but she could hear her. Ruth was a real talker. She was no doubt manning the drive-through window, which didn't seem too wise to Emma. No wonder the cars were backed up around the building. She heard Ruth ask if the customer thought it would rain more, and then saw Franey roll her eyes as she carried another tray to the front.

Despite their differences, the widows seemed to have hit a real home run. *Englischers* loved freshly baked goods. Who didn't? Emma's stomach growled, and she stepped to the left to get a good look at the pastry case. Maybe it was because she'd moved that she could hear the *Englisch* woman's comment directed to Naomi, the same woman who had spoken to Katie Ann about the proverb.

"Real shame about the girl from Maggie's Diner."

"*Ya.*"

"Read all about it in the paper."

"Can I get you anything else?"

The woman asked for a half dozen oatmeal cookies, and then she leaned forward to whisper in a too-loud voice. "Heard she was a friend of your bishop's."

Naomi finished writing the woman's order on a receipt pad, pulled off the top sheet a little roughly, and placed it on top of the sack with a definitive pat that must have squished the cookies.

"Nancy will check you out."

"Oh, I'm sorry if I offended you, dear. It's natural to feel protective of someone you know, but how well do we ever know anyone? Maybe you think your neighbor is simply an introvert who likes to watch television and complete Sudoku puzzles, and then you find out he's a serial killer. People are unpredictable."

Instead of answering the woman, Naomi turned her attention to the next customers, who happened to be Emma and Katie Ann.

They placed their order, and Emma waited for the woman in the suit to move down to the cash register. Then she leaned forward and asked, "Have you been dealing with that all day?"

"I have without a doubt heard all the questions I care to on the subject. My patience is about gone."

"Is that why it's so crowded?"

"Don't know, but if it is, I'd just as soon they go home."

Emma patted her hand and moved toward Nancy. Katie Ann lingered to say something to Naomi.

"I haven't seen you in here before, Emma. That'll be seven dollars and fifty-two cents."

Emma placed a ten-dollar bill on the counter. "Are they all talking about Henry?"

"About half of them are."

"Did they mention him in the paper?"

"You know I don't read the *Monte Vista Gazette*. The *Budget* is *gut* enough for me."

"I suppose."

But as they walked out of the bakery, Emma spied a newspaper vending machine across the street. She sent Katie Ann across with fifty cents to fetch her a copy, and when she saw what was on the first page, she knew she wouldn't be heading straight home.

Thirty-Four

Katie Ann read the article to Emma as they drove toward Henry's. When she'd finished, they were pulling down his lane. "Perhaps you could take Lexi to the barn so I can talk with Henry."

"*Mammi*, I'm not a child anymore."

"Of course you're not."

"I would love to see Oreo, though. Maybe I could give her a *gut* brushing in case Henry hasn't had time."

"An excellent idea."

"Promise to tell me whatever he says?"

Emma sighed. It wasn't just that Katie Ann was nearly grown. The problem was that she now expected trouble to be lurking around every corner. That was what the Monte Vista arsonist had done to her granddaughter—he had stolen her innocent outlook on life. Unfortunately, her cautious attitude made sense, which was what bothered Emma. She wanted a Plain and simple life for Katie Ann.

"I promise."

Henry was in his workshop, sanding a small table. Katie Ann said hello and then asked for and received his permission to check on the buggy mare.

"Your granddaughter is a *gut* girl," he said as she slipped out the back door.

"*Ya*, she is. But Henry, we didn't stop by so Katie Ann could see the mare. Have you read today's paper?" She pulled the newspaper out of her handbag, unfolded it, and placed it on the workbench, facing him.

"Can't say I have."

"Sophia's murder made the front page."

"No surprise there."

"*Ya*, but they're hinting that you had something to do with it. Read this part." She stabbed the newspaper with her finger. "How can they say such things? Why would they say such things?"

She walked around the table so she was standing beside him and could read as he did. Somehow it was even worse seeing the words in print than it had been when Katie Ann read them aloud to her.

> According to Roscoe Delaney, an agent with the FBI, the bureau has received several credible leads from the tip hotline. When asked if they had a suspect in the murder of Ms. Brooks, Delaney replied, "No comment," but he went on to say they were waiting on lab results, including fingerprint and DNA samples. "Our methods are quite scientific, and that's one thing criminals can't refute—physical evidence. The public can rest assured that we will find the person who did this, and they will be brought to justice."

> Crime scene crews were seen at the home of the local Amish bishop, Henry Lapp. According to anonymous sources, Mr. Lapp had a relationship with Ms. Brooks, though the nature of that relationship remains unclear. "Although Amish are typically viewed as nonviolent, it's not unheard of for an Amish person to be convicted of murder," said a source close to the investigation. "Edward Gingerich was convicted of killing his wife in 1993. Anyone is capable of taking another life."

> When asked if Mr. Lapp was a suspect in the murder investigation, Sheriff Grayson said he could not comment on an ongoing investigation and referred us back to the FBI agent in charge, Delaney.

> Agent Delaney had no comment.

"No comment! He might as well have said you're guilty."

Henry glanced at her, eyebrows raised. But instead of answering, he folded the paper and placed it back in her hands.

"That part about Edward Gingerich makes me so mad. That man was ill—mentally and emotionally—"

"And spiritually."

"*Ya*. He wasn't in his right mind. Even the courts said so. The way they make it sound, Plain folks are lining up right and left to kill one another. Henry, they cannot do this to you. It's not right. They're slandering your name with absolutely no proof."

"The gem cannot be polished without friction, nor the man perfected without trials."

"Do not quote proverbs to me."

Henry ducked his head, smiled, and said, "I know the plans I have for you…plans to prosper you and not to harm you—"

"Plans for a hope and a future. *Ya*, I know the Scriptures, but I'm scared." Tears stung her eyes, and Emma turned toward the open doorway to brush them away.

Henry gave her a minute, and then he said, "Let's walk to the barn and see how Katie Ann is getting on with Oreo."

Katie Ann stood in the middle of the pasture, brushing the mare down with sure, strong strokes. The sun shone down on them both and on Lexi, who sat studying them with her head on her paws. The sight calmed Emma's heart and helped to dispel the panic that threatened to overtake her.

"You're a *gut freind*, Emma."

"I care about you. We all care about you."

"*Ya. Gotte* has blessed me with a *gut* community—people who will stand by me and believe in me."

"You're telling me dark days are ahead."

"I fear it's true."

"Why, Henry? Why did you have to be the one to find her? Why did someone kill her? And why are we again involved with the *Englisch* police?"

Henry waited a moment and then crossed his arms on the wooden fence and cast a sideways gaze at her. "I hope you're not expecting an answer."

"Not really—*nein*."

"*Gut*, because I'm fresh out of answers."

"You're calmer, though. Calmer than you were yesterday."

"I've had time to pray on it and study the Scriptures."

"Including Jeremiah."

"*Ya*, always a favorite book of mine. Jeremiah lived through the siege and destruction of Jerusalem, and yet he remained convinced of *Gotte's* goodness."

"I know the plans I have for you…"

"Jeremiah didn't doubt *Gotte* even when the world around him descended into chaos."

"As has ours."

"Indeed."

Katie Ann led Oreo in a half circle so she could stand on her bucket and brush the other side. The horse seemed perfectly content to stay there, wait patiently, and allow Katie Ann to care for her. As for Katie Ann, she'd momentarily forgotten their worries—Emma could tell as much from her posture and the way her laugh rang out across the pasture. Emma believed God had a plan for her granddaughter, a good plan. But she didn't understand why Henry was once again going through a terrible time. He was a decent man and had been faithful to God, to his calling.

Yet if she believed God didn't make mistakes…

"You're deep in thought over there," Henry said.

"I just don't understand."

"But we don't have to understand. We're not even called to understand. We only have to remain faithful."

"What will you do?"

"Finish the nightstand I was working on, take Lexi for a walk, minister to our congregation—"

"You know what I mean. What will you do about the investigation?"

"I can't do anything as far as the *Englischers* are concerned. I have a meeting later this afternoon with the church leadership, including Clyde, in case I'm unable to perform my duties."

"You mean in case you're arrested."

"*Ya.* That's what I mean." Henry turned and clasped her hands. "You'll keep the faith, right, Emma? You'll promise me that you will remain optimistic, that you won't allow what's happening to damage your trust in God's goodness, that you'll pray for me and for the officers involved as well?"

"Of course."

Henry paused, searched her eyes, and then smiled. "*Gut.* Together we will see what *Gotte* has in store."

As they waited for Katie Ann to finish with the horse, they talked of church and crops and the weather. It should have settled Emma's nerves to speak of everyday things. Instead she felt an overwhelming sadness building in her soul, like storm clouds on the horizon.

She didn't want Henry to go through more hardship.

She didn't want to be separated from him, and she certainly wanted him to be able to continue as their bishop.

As she drove away, Emma's thoughts shifted to how to keep Henry out of jail. He didn't kill Sophia Brooks. Someone else did. They didn't have to find the person responsible. They only had to cast enough doubt to turn the investigator's attention somewhere else.

Thirty-Five

Leroy Kauffmann pushed away from the table, crossed his arms, and frowned at no one in particular. "It makes no sense—financially— for the investigators to pursue this course. In the end, they'll have to backtrack. It's a terrible waste of time and resources."

"I happen to agree with you." Henry reached down to pet Lexi, who was sleeping at his feet. "Unfortunately, I appear to be their best suspect."

"From what I heard in town, you're their only suspect." Abe pushed up his glasses. "Incompetent. That's what they are."

"And yet they must have found something." Clyde rubbed a hand across his jaw. "I'm not saying they're right. We all know Henry didn't do this, but they must have found some evidence that pointed to you."

"Like what?" Leroy asked. "What could they possibly have found?"

"You admit that you gave Sophia a ride in your buggy, so they will have found her prints there." Abe leaned toward Henry. "So what? Why would it matter?"

"It's not as if you were alone with her." Clyde sat up straighter. "There's something you're not telling us. Out with it, Henry. I know that look, which seems to say you're trying to protect us from something."

"I didn't tell Delaney that Emma was with me when I picked up Sophia."

"What?" Clyde's voice rose in alarm. "Why not?"

"First of all, because he didn't ask me if anyone else was with me. Second, I don't want her pulled into this if it can be helped."

"But Henry, Emma proves you weren't alone with Sophia."

"Which only speaks to my reputation, something I trust you all have faith in. No, the alibi I need is for Wednesday morning. Unfortunately, I was completely alone then."

"And you think they will arrest you?"

"Probably at our social tomorrow for maximum effect." Because they had a church meeting only every other week, on the off weeks they often met together for a time of fellowship. Usually this occurred at several different homes, but Henry thought it might be best if this once they all met together. Leroy, Abe, and Clyde quickly agreed.

"We stand as a united body," Abe said. "Best to show that in an obvious way."

"We'll have the women spread the word, and I'll talk to Lewis." Leroy sat back, a smile playing on his lips. "Let him know to expect a crowd."

"I still don't understand why the investigators are wasting their time on you." Clyde looked completely miserable.

Henry felt sorry that his friends, his deacons, were having to deal with this. He felt bad that the entire congregation would once again be thrust into the middle of a murder investigation, but he believed—with all his heart—that God had a purpose even in this.

"They'll want to make a big splash for the newspapers, which will probably sell more copies than arresting me while I'm sanding in my workshop." He sat back, certain he was on the right track, though he wished it wasn't so. "There's another reason. By arresting me publicly, they'll be trying to shake your confidence in me."

"Proving they don't understand Plain folk."

"The reason I called you here was to prepare you for what might happen. There's always a chance I could be wrong, that the investigation has spiraled in another direction."

"Don't worry about the community." Leroy stood, pushed in his chair, and straightened his shoulders. "If this happens, and I pray it doesn't, we will take up the slack as far as responsibilities go."

"I know Katie Ann will be happy to take care of Oreo and Lexi," Clyde said.

"We'll make up a schedule for visiting these folks." Abe folded the paper Henry had given him. "We'll take care of it, Henry."

"Services will continue as normal," Clyde assured him.

"I appreciate your willingness to jump in to help. I hope you know

I consider each of you more than a deacon. I consider each of you a *gut freind.*"

"A friend loves at all times."

"And a brother is born for a time of adversity."

"Proverbs, I believe. Seventeenth chapter and seventeenth verse."

Henry wanted to laugh then. The three men standing in front of him had managed to calm any anxiety he felt and bring joy to his heart.

As they walked outside, Henry glanced up and marveled at the night sky. So much natural beauty, so much of God's grace, despite the evilness of man. Perhaps there was a sermon in that.

✛

Henry received a warm welcome at their fellowship the next day. Time and again he was patted on the back, advised not to worry, and promised that prayers were being uttered on his behalf. The day was bright and sunny, as most days in the valley were, but the air had a hint of fall. Temperatures were expected to drop overnight.

The time of fellowship was held at Lewis Glick's farm. Lewis was unmarried, though Henry was aware that he was writing to an Amish woman in Maine. Lewis had come to him for advice on that. They'd become close over the last two years. Lewis struggled with drug addiction, and Henry acted as his accountability partner—an *Englisch* term if there ever was one. What had started as a back injury had quickly led to dependence on hydrocodone and OxyContin. He'd been clean for more than a year, and Henry could tell from the look of things on his farm that he was working hard each day and being successful. What Lewis needed was a woman, a family to stay clean for. *A plump wife and a big barn never did any man harm.* Lewis had laughed when Henry shared his mother's frequently quoted proverb.

The house was too small for their entire congregation, so the noon meal was set up in the barn—giant platters of baked chicken, sliced ham, and various types of sandwiches. And every vegetable dish Henry could imagine, including a seven-bean salad that was one of his favorites. The dessert table was a beauty to behold with the freshly baked cakes, pies, and cookies. It occurred to him that those were the things he'd like to draw—images of everyday life.

They'd finished praying for the meal, and Henry had proceeded to share a bit of Scripture from the book of Isaiah, the fourteenth chapter.

"Surely, as I have planned, so it will be, and as I have purposed, so it will happen."

Someone glanced toward the open barn doors, and then another person turned, and another.

He heard the sound of *Englisch* cars approaching.

Though his heart sank, Henry cleared his throat and continued. "I will crush the Assyrian in my land; on my mountains I will trample him down. His yoke will be taken from my people, and his burden removed from their shoulders."

Agent Delaney walked into the room, followed by two other agents. He paused at the back of the room and cocked his head, and so Henry continued.

"This is the plan determined for the whole world; this is the hand stretched out over all nations. For the Lord Almighty has purposed, and who can thwart him? His hand is stretched out, and who can turn it back?"

Henry heard several *amens* as he closed his Bible and handed it to Clyde.

Delaney walked down the middle of the barn, between tables fashioned from sawhorses on both sides. Both men and women turned to watch his approach.

A child asked, "Who is that, *Mammi*?"

A baby began to cry.

Delaney was once again dressed in a starched white shirt and black pants, but this time he had a paisley tie. Henry tried not to react to the smirk on his face. The FBI agent stopped a few feet from Henry and said loudly enough for someone outside the barn to hear, "Henry Lapp, you are under arrest for the murder of Sophia Brooks."

There were no gasps of surprise. Instead, his congregation stood, silent but focused on their bishop. He noticed a few had their heads bowed in prayer. That was good. Prayer was the one thing that could rescue him from this situation.

"Hands behind your back, please." Leaning closer, Delaney added, "Wouldn't want to make a scene in front of all these good church folk."

Henry nodded once and placed his hands behind his back.

Delaney snapped the handcuffs onto his wrists, checking to make sure they were good and tight, as if Henry might be some kind of escape artist.

"You have the right to remain silent. Anything you say can and will be used against you in a court of law." Delaney grasped the handcuffs and placed his other hand on Henry's back, propelling him back down the aisle, past his congregation and friends. "You have the right to an attorney. If you cannot afford an attorney, one will be provided for you."

Emma's head was raised, her expression steady and calm.

Katie Ann looked as if she was about to cry, but she pulled in her bottom lip and reached for her grandmother's hand.

They were outside next to the cruiser when Delaney turned toward him and said in a lower voice, "Do you understand the rights I have just read to you?"

"I do."

Satisfied, Delaney put a hand on top of his head and guided him into the backseat of the cruiser. He started the vehicle and drove leisurely down the lane. When they turned onto the blacktop, Henry noticed the news photographers lined up, snapping pictures.

Thirty-Six

He's being booked
and processed now.

                Is there enough evidence
                        to make it stick?

We planted everything we had.

                And the surveillance device?

Stopped working.

                        He found it?

Doubtful. It was well hidden and
one of the smallest on the market.

                Then what happened?

Technical glitch. It doesn't matter.
He's not at his home. He's at the jail.
And we have eyes there.

                        Keep me apprised.

Framing an innocent man
 doesn't sit well with me.

But killing the girl does?

We had no choice.

We still have no choice.

Thirty-Seven

Henry remained silent on the ride to the station and through the process of being photographed, fingerprinted, and escorted to his cell. Once there, he sat on the cot, braced his elbows on his knees, interlaced his fingers, and prayed.

He started off praying for himself—that God would protect him, would guide his steps and his words, would strengthen his faith. But then he thought of the faces he'd seen as he left Lewis's barn. He started praying for Emma and her family, for Katie Ann that she might grow in faith, for his deacons. He prayed for Deborah and Adam King and for their infant daughter, Chloe. He petitioned God to bless the three widows—Ruth and Nancy and Franey—and help their new business to be a success, that they might be a blessing to both *Englisch* and Amish.

He prayed for Sophia Brooks's family, whoever they might be.

And he surprised himself when he began praying for Sheriff Grayson and the other officers, even Agent Delaney. But was it so odd? They needed guidance if they were going to find the guilty person. A little divine intervention wouldn't hurt.

A young woman who must have been a rookie officer brought him lunch. He wasn't hungry, but he thanked her and drained the cup of water.

He wondered what was taking so long. Why weren't they questioning him? Perhaps they thought by leaving him alone he would begin to squirm, appreciate the desperation of the situation he was in, and confess everything.

But Henry had nothing to confess.

He prayed some more, and then he sat back on the cot, his back braced against the wall, and closed his eyes. He never intended to fall asleep.

The sound of heavy footsteps approaching woke him.

Delaney did not come to fetch him. Instead, a younger man stopped outside his cell. The nameplate on his uniform pocket said *Lawson*. Henry suddenly remembered what Emma had said about Sophia being worried or frightened when Lawson walked into the diner. Why would she have been afraid of a police officer?

Lawson had copper-colored hair, eyes that hovered between green and gray, and a youthful manner. If Henry didn't know better, he would have thought he saw sympathy in the young officer's eyes.

"I need to put the cuffs back on."

Henry turned and placed his arms behind his back.

"I appreciate that." Lawson turned him around and motioned for him to walk out of the cell and down the hall. "And for the record, I wasn't for arresting you in front of your congregation."

"You're new here, aren't you?"

"I am, and so no one asks my opinion." Lawson shrugged as if it made no difference to him.

He walked beside Henry as they cleared the jail cells, turned the corner, and passed two offices. Henry glanced into the main room where the officers worked. He noticed that most of the men and women who made up the police department seemed to be there, along with the mayor and a National Wildlife Refuge employee in uniform. They were all watching him as he walked by, and they seemed to be waiting for something. Perhaps they were simply curious. It wasn't that common for a murderer to be caught in their small town—twice as far as Henry knew, and he had been involved both times. What were the odds? Slim. The odds were astronomically slim, and Henry felt again that God must have a purpose in placing him here at this time.

They stopped beside the interrogation room—a place Henry was quite familiar with. He pushed the memories from Indiana away. The door to the room had a window in it, which Lawson tapped on before inserting a key into the lock and opening the door. The walls were painted a drab gray, the only furnishings four chairs and a rectangular metal table. A long, reflective window made up most of the west wall. It was the same room where Sheriff Grayson had questioned Sam Beiler. That time, Henry had been present as a sign of support for Sam and because the young man didn't have a lawyer.

Sheriff Grayson wasn't present today.

Agent Delaney sat on the far side of the table. Beside him was Jared Anderson. Henry had only spoken to the man a few times, though he'd been with the Monte Vista police force for as long as Henry had been there. He was a jolly sort with a quick smile, or at least he seemed to be. Sometimes Henry had the distinct impression that the smile and chuckle were part of a mask he wore, though he couldn't have said why he thought that. Perhaps because then, like now, his expression didn't seem to reach his eyes.

Regardless, he had always been amenable to Amish folk moving into the area. Henry guessed his race to be Caucasian and his age in the late fifties or early sixties. His build was medium and soft around the middle. His hair was graying. It was rumored that he'd been passed over for a promotion but didn't care, that he was happy being the number two man in the police department. Not that Henry listened to rumors, but people in small towns had little to discuss over their lunch. Any news was fodder for the *Englisch* or Amish grapevines.

Neither the presence of Delaney nor that of Anderson surprised him, though Henry had been hoping Grayson would sit in on the questioning. In fact, his absence throughout the entire arrest had been rather odd, a thought Henry filed in the back of his mind for later.

But the third person in the room did puzzle him. A young, slender black woman stood, looked directly at Henry, and said, "My name is Kiana Sitton, and I'm your lawyer."

She wore black slacks, a white blouse, and a gray blazer. Her hair was stylishly cut and softly framed her oblong face. Her eyes caught Henry's attention—they were calm and patient and intelligent.

"I didn't ask for a lawyer."

"We can talk about that later. For now, I need you to tell these gentlemen you authorize me to represent you."

Henry didn't see as he had any choice. No other lawyers were lining up outside the door to defend him, and he probably wouldn't do well representing himself in an *Englisch* courtroom. So he said simply, "*Ya.* I do."

Kiana turned to Officer Lawson and said, "Remove the handcuffs, please."

Lawson glanced at Delaney, who nodded.

"*Danki*," Henry said.

He took a seat beside the lawyer, who had taken out her cell phone, pushed a button, and placed the device in the middle of the table.

"The date is Sunday, September 24. Location—Monte Vista police station. Matter—Questioning of Henry Lapp regarding the murder of Sophia Brooks."

"Actually, Mr. Lapp has been charged with the murder of Sophia Brooks. This is his chance to save the people of Monte Vista a considerable amount of money by confessing."

Kiana cocked her head, as if Delaney had said something amusing. Then she resumed speaking to the recorder. "For the record, my name is Kiana Sitton, and I am the lawyer for Mr. Lapp. Now I'd like everyone in the room to identify themselves."

Delaney narrowed his eyes at the lawyer, ran a hand down the length of his tie, and said, "Agent Roscoe Delaney, special agent in charge, FBI."

"Jared Anderson, police officer, Monte Vista Police Department."

They all looked at Henry, and he realized it was his turn. "Henry Lapp, bishop."

Kiana had whipped out a pad of paper and a pen from her leather bag. A gold-and-silver bracelet caught the fluorescent light and sparkled and winked, or so it seemed to Henry.

"Enough of the formalities." Delaney slapped a hand against the table. "You were read your rights upon your arrest. With those rights in mind, would you like to offer a statement in regard to the death of Sophia Brooks?"

Henry shook his head.

"You'll need to answer verbally." Kiana nodded toward the phone. "So it will be recorded."

"*Nein*. I don't."

Delaney smiled as if that answer amused him. "All right. Perhaps you can tell us what Sophia was doing at your home."

"She wasn't. She's never been in my home."

Delaney pulled a sheet of paper from a small stack next to him and pushed it across to Kiana. "Forensic results say otherwise. We found her prints in virtually every room of your house."

"I don't understand," Henry said, confusion literally clouding his vision. Sophia had never been to his house. How could what Delaney was saying be true?

"So her fingerprints were found at his house." Kiana pushed the sheet back across the table. "The murder wasn't committed at the home. This means nothing."

"It establishes that he had more than a casual relationship with the deceased."

"How do you know she didn't enter his house and have a look around? It's common knowledge that the Amish don't lock their homes."

Henry jerked his head in her direction. Who was this woman? She wasn't from Monte Vista. At least he'd never seen her before. How did she know anything about being Plain? Though she was right on that point. He'd never locked the door to his home or his workshop.

"We also have testimony that he was seen arguing with Sophia at the diner." Delaney pushed another sheet toward the lawyer.

Kiana studied the sheet for a moment, jotted down a few notes, and then slid it smoothly back across the table. Henry noticed that in addition to the bracelet, she wore what looked like a diamond watch and several expensive rings.

"As far as I know, it's not against the law to have an argument."

"If that's your defense, this case is going to be easier than I thought." Delaney leaned back in his chair and studied Henry. Then he sat up straight, smoothed his tie, and tapped the sheets of paper on the table. "You were known to visit her often, to insist on being seated in her area of the diner. You were seen arguing with her—"

"We never shared cross words."

"You gave her a ride in your buggy, took her to a motel, and then took her home. What happened then, Henry? Were you pursuing a romantic relationship with Sophia? Did she have second thoughts? Did she try to get away? Is that why you killed her? Is that why you strangled her and dumped her body at the wildlife refuge? Did she reject you? A lovers' spat, perhaps?"

Henry felt his face flush and his pulse accelerate. It was bad enough that they were saying these things about him, but they were also disrespecting Sophia's memory.

"Or maybe you loaned her money. She was practically homeless, staying at the cheapest motel in town. Maybe she asked you for money, and in your...generosity, you gave it to her. It would be understandable if you became angry when she couldn't or wouldn't pay it back." Delaney crossed his arms on the table, a small smile playing on his lips though his gaze remained cold and piercing. "Maybe you tried to convert her, and she wasn't willing to become Amish. Which is it, Henry? Tell us. Why did you kill Sophia Brooks?"

Thirty-Eight

Emma, Clyde, Rachel, Katie Ann, and Silas sat at the kitchen table, Henry's drawings spread around them.

"I've heard about Henry's ability, but I didn't realize—" Silas leaned closer to the drawing of Sophia helping the old woman. Emma's grandson's two interests were farming and courting. Emma had been surprised when he'd insisted on coming home with them after the fellowship luncheon.

Katie Ann wrapped a *kapp* string around her index finger. "Reminds me of those books we had when we were young. Remember them, *Mammi? I Spy?*"

"You'd sit for hours staring at those books, trying to find the objects listed on the right-hand side of the page."

"Only this time we don't know what we're looking for." Rachel sipped her cup of coffee and glanced out the window when she heard Stephen and Thomas run past. She glanced up at Emma and nodded slightly. It was good that they were working on this together and that the younger boys weren't involved. They should be outside playing on a beautiful fall afternoon.

"We're not even sure there's anything to find," Emma said. "I hope there is, but it could be there aren't any clues here to be had."

"Giving up already, are you?" Clyde winked at her and then went back to studying his drawing. He'd taken the one of Sophia lying in the field. It seemed most likely to contain a clue. Perhaps the killer had left something behind, some mark or telltale sign.

"I keep thinking about the last time I saw her at the diner." Emma picked up her picture, held it at arm's length, and then pulled it in closer. "She seemed so on edge, as if she thought someone in the diner meant to harm her."

"Maybe she was paranoid," Rachel said. "People with mental instability can seem fine one moment and exhibit radical paranoia the next. I read a book about that once. Only medication can help the situation. Perhaps Sophia was mentally ill."

"I'd agree if it wasn't for the fact that she's dead." Emma cocked her head, trying to view the drawing from a different angle. "But even in this scene, she seems...worried. Look at how her brow is creased. And her eyes? They're not on what she's writing on the pad. They're scanning the room."

Silas stood up and came behind her. "Any idea who all these people are? It's amazing that Henry could remember who was there that day."

"He doesn't remember, not in a way he could articulate. It's only that a part of his mind records it."

Katie Ann stood and joined her brother. "That's the new officer in the corner. What's his name?"

"Lawson." Emma snapped her fingers. "When he first walked in, Sophia jumped as though someone had pinched her. This shows her expression, which looks fearful to me."

"Or at least, as you said, worried," Silas offered.

"I think what Henry has drawn here is from the same day I joined him for dinner, but I can't be sure. Notice he doesn't draw himself."

"He doesn't see himself. He draws what he sees." Rachel leaned forward, warming to the subject. "Think of an *Englisch* camera. Henry's eye, his mind, is like that."

"And his hand is like a printer." Katie Ann grinned for a moment, and then she went back to studying the drawing.

"I wonder how he chooses what he's going to draw." Clyde pushed his drawing aside and leaned forward to study Emma's, though he was looking at it upside down.

But it was Rachel who started asking questions—important questions that caused them all to think critically about the people in the drawing rather than just stare at them.

"Why is this woman wearing earmuffs? It hasn't been cold enough for that. And this person typing on their...what is that?"

"A laptop," Silas said. "You know, a portable computer."

"Who does that in public?"

"Lots of people do. Maggie's has free Wi-Fi."

"Free what?" Clyde gave his son a what-do-you-know-about-this look.

Silas held up both of his hands, palms out. "I don't have a phone or a computer. If I spent money on that, I'd have less to take Hannah out."

"I thought you were courting Sally." Katie Ann nudged her brother's shoulder. "You're not cheating on her, are you?"

"*Nein*. Sally dropped me. Said we weren't compatible."

"What does that mean?"

"It means she'd rather step out with Nathan Kline."

Katie Ann scrunched up her face as though she'd taken a good bite from a lemon, but Emma appreciated that she didn't answer him. She'd once told Emma she thought Nathan wanted a traditional Amish wife, that he spoke poorly of her working with Doc Berry. But she didn't mention that now. Perhaps she'd learned *if you can't say something nice...*

Silas cleared his throat. "Anyway, it's one of the reasons the diner stays so busy. Lots of people stop in to do some work on their devices while they're eating lunch."

Clyde harrumphed and Emma *tsked* at the same time. She immediately snapped her mouth shut. She was going to break that habit if she had to wire her jaws together.

"All right, but look at this guy. It looks as though he's asleep." Rachel tapped the sheet. "No one goes to a diner to sleep."

"And this man is sort of watching Sophia, or at least he's looking in that direction." Emma sat back and crossed her arms. "Of course, Sophia was a pretty woman, and younger than most of the waitresses there."

"This person is in several of the drawings, wearing a national park uniform and has a large scuff across the right shoe."

"Can't tell if it's a woman or man."

"Yeah, the person is either bent down or turned the wrong way. We never have a good view."

"If Henry doesn't see him—"

"Or her."

"Then it's not in the drawing."

"Let's make a list." Clyde stood and strode across the room to a kitchen drawer. He pulled out a pad of paper and pen, which he then dropped on the table. "We have four pictures of Sophia at the diner. Let's list who's in each picture and see if we have any repeats."

"But we don't even know their names."

"That's okay. Make up a name. Earmuff girl."

"Computer man."

"Sleeper guy."

Suddenly the weight pressing on Emma's heart lightened. The task before them seemed something they could accomplish. While it was true that Henry was in jail, she couldn't do anything about that. She'd have to trust that God had a plan and do the best she could from where she was. At the moment, that meant creating a list.

And just maybe that list would point them to a killer.

Thirty-Nine

Henry's hearing was held first thing Monday morning.

Officer Anderson had ushered him over to the courthouse, along with another officer whose name he didn't catch. They'd led him to a conference room where Kiana Sitton was waiting. Today she wore a tailored black suit, an ivory-colored blouse, and patent leather heels.

"Aren't things moving awfully fast?" he asked her.

"They are."

"How did you become my lawyer? How did you even know I needed one?"

Kiana waited until the officer closed the door, affording them some privacy. It went without saying that he would be waiting on the other side. Kiana scooted her chair closer and lowered her voice.

"Roy Grayson sent me."

"Sheriff Grayson?"

"The same."

"Because..."

"Because I have some experience defending both Amish and Mennonite." She went on to cite a few cases in other areas of Colorado. "And there's another, more important reason. Grayson thinks you're being railroaded, and he wanted someone to help you, to keep an eye on you."

"Where is he?"

Kiana shook her head as if that didn't matter, or maybe she couldn't say. "He wanted me to pass on a message. He'll be in touch as soon as he can."

"You certainly seem competent enough, and I thank you for your help. We haven't talked about your fee—"

"A conversation for another day. What matters today is that Special Agent in Charge Delaney is trying to push this case through on a fast track because his evidence is circumstantial at best."

"Why is he hurrying with it?" Henry honestly wanted to know. He'd puzzled over it before falling into a fitful slumber the night before. Something about this entire situation didn't make sense to him. "What is his motivation?"

Kiana studied him a moment and then sat down in the chair next to him, waiting until he'd met her gaze before she spoke. "My best guess is that he's ambitious. He's trying to move up the command chain, and a quick conviction will help him do that."

"But I'm innocent."

"Something we do not have to prove."

"He must prove my guilt."

"Exactly. The burden of proof is on the government, something you're probably familiar with from the situation in Goshen."

Henry gave one brief, definitive nod. He wasn't surprised that she knew about his past. She looked like the kind of person who would do her homework.

"I've read the transcripts, Henry. Sheriff Grayson had a copy from when you were involved with the Monte Vista arsonist. He emailed copies to me before you were even arrested, which shows how worried he was. I'd like you to tell me what happened with Betsy Troyer. We have a few minutes before the hearing, and the more I know, the better I'm able to represent you."

Henry stared out the window for a moment, resisting the memories of those dark days. But if he trusted this woman, if she was going to help him, then he needed to tell her what he could. "It was nearly seventeen years ago. A young girl from our church district, Betsy Troyer, was killed. I was charged for that murder when I took a drawing to the police. They thought I had to be guilty to have been able to re-create such a thing and because of my knowledge of certain texts."

"I've read about your ability. Tell me why you were at her house to begin with."

"Her parents were worried about her behavior, and they asked me to stop by and speak with her. I took one of my church elders with me, as is proper. When we arrived at the house, she wouldn't come downstairs, so we went up to her room."

"And later, after she went missing, you drew the scene of her room."

"I did. I thought it might help."

"So what happened?"

"I was arrested for her murder and held for trial."

"That must have been very hard for you."

"It was, though I'm sure those days were even harder for Betsy's parents. Before the trial commenced, one of the investigators decided to take a closer look at what I had drawn. My vision—or whatever you want to call it—caught an image of a text that came in on Betsy's phone while we were there. Her parents claimed she had no phone. It was later determined that they had thrown it into a pond when they found it."

"And they didn't admit that when you were arrested?"

"They didn't think it was relevant." Henry pulled in a deep breath. "They didn't understand how it could lead to catching Betsy's killer."

Kiana pulled out a sheet of paper. "According to the records from the trial, the cell service provider was able to provide transcripts of all her recent texts. One text was from a drifter Betsy had been seeing."

"The same text I had drawn."

"So you're telling me your drawing is what caused the police to start looking for a phone, one her parents claimed didn't exist."

"*Ya.* Eventually I was released, and the drifter, a man named Gene Wooten, was convicted of Betsy's murder. He's currently serving a life sentence."

"But you were held for more than three months because they wouldn't listen."

"That's not the worst of it. Gene Wooten nearly killed another girl in the meantime." Henry wondered if he would be forced to once again serve time in an *Englisch* jail. "For a long time after that, I didn't draw, didn't use my gift or ability or whatever you call it. It's something that can be misunderstood."

Kiana stuffed the papers back into her briefcase. "All right. Thank you for sharing that with me. I've petitioned the judge to not allow any reference to your situation in Goshen."

"*Danki.*"

"Or the situation here where you were involved with the Monte Vista arsonist."

Henry studied a spot on the opposite wall. "Is it possible that either of those situations, that my involvement in them, might help my case? That it might show I was willing to assist the government?"

"This isn't a television show, Mr. Lapp."

When Henry looked at her quizzically, she added, "The police don't seek or appreciate help from citizens other than what might be called in to their tip line. That's a far different thing from your drawings, which Delaney would twist into something sinister and foreboding."

When she shook her head, small pearl earrings swayed back and forth. "I want you to follow my lead in there. Answer only questions directed to you by Judge Trentini, and keep your answers succinct."

He again nodded that he understood.

"Do not be affected by anything Delaney says or does—or, for that matter, by anything anyone says or does in the courtroom."

"Who else would be there?"

"I don't guess you've seen today's newspapers."

"No one brought me a paper in my cell, if that's what you're asking. At home, we rarely read them."

She pulled copies of *USA Today*, the *New York Times*, and the *Washington Post* from her leather bag. They all had pictures of him being ushered into the Monte Vista police vehicle.

BISHOP CHARGED WITH MURDER

A PLAIN AND SIMPLE DEATH

MURDER IN THE SAN LUIS VALLEY

"Over the last twenty years, people have become somewhat fascinated with our way of life. When someone who is Plain runs afoul of the law, it often makes the front page."

"And Delaney is going to take full advantage of the spotlight. He wants this one." She paused a moment, maybe to be certain he understood the gravity of the situation. "Because this is a federal case, you won't recognize most of the people in the room. This won't be like the trial for the Monte Vista arsonist or the one for Betsy Troyer's murder."

"How does it differ?"

"Charges are brought by the U.S. attorney, so his representative will be here. Also Judge Trentini will preside."

"I'm not familiar with that name."

"He's from the federal district court in Colorado Springs. Another indication that Delaney is trying to fast-track this. He must have called in some favors for the judge to show up less than twenty-four hours after your arrest."

"Are you worried?"

"It's my job to be worried, Henry. It's your job to do what I say. I don't need you flipping out when we're in the courtroom."

"Flipping out?"

"Becoming emotional or angry. Looking smug. Looking bored. Any of those things can sway a judge away from leniency."

"And that's what we want?"

"What we want is you out of jail. Then our real work will begin. We don't have to prove your innocence, but at the same time we want to be untangling what's happened and clearing your name."

Officer Anderson knocked on the door, entered, and escorted them into the courtroom. Henry was wearing the same clothes he'd arrived in. He supposed if the judge ruled he was to stay in jail, then he would be issued a jumpsuit.

It was rare that Henry looked at a room or person or situation and had a desire to draw it. His gift didn't work that way, but maybe he was becoming more aware of what he could do, of the ability God had blessed him with. When he stepped into the courtroom, he was nearly overwhelmed with the desire to find a pencil and paper and draw the scene before him.

The courtroom was full. Several officers sat on the side of the room where Delaney had taken up camp. Henry assumed it was the prosecutor's side. He also recognized a few of the people from the crime scene crew. At the back of the room were news reporters. The judge must have given them orders already, because no cameras were in evidence. However, they all had pads of paper in front of them and were scribbling madly, as if there was already something to report.

But it was the left side of the room that twisted Henry's heart. He hadn't realized he had so many friends in Monte Vista. The life of an Amish bishop, especially a widowed one, was by definition somewhat solitary. Yes, he was a part of the entire community, but they weren't his family, not in the physical sense of the word. Today he realized they were his family in the important sense of the word. As far as he could tell, every single person from his congregation was there. The rows were packed with Plain folk—young and old, male and female, and mixed among them were *Englischers*.

People they had helped after a storm.

People they purchased things from and sold things to.

People who had embraced their presence in this small community.

He had to search the crowd to find Emma, and he wasn't a bit surprised to see the entire Fisher family had managed to take up the row directly behind where Anderson was leading them.

Henry barely had time to process all of these things when the bailiff walked to the front of the room and said, "All rise. The Monte Vista court for the district of central southern Colorado is in session, Federal Judge Connor Trentini presiding."

Forty

When Emma first entered the courtroom, she caught herself glancing around, looking to see if any of the individuals they had identified in Henry's drawing were present. She spotted two right off, but then the room grew quite crowded, and it became difficult to see much of anything other than the press of people.

When the side door opened and Henry walked in with someone she assumed to be his lawyer, Emma felt such a surge of affection and protectiveness for their bishop that she had to glance down at the floor. She closed her eyes, prayed for composure and a clear mind, and looked up in time to see Henry smile at her as he shuffled into the front row. Emma wanted to lean forward and speak to him, say a word of encouragement, and assure him everyone was praying.

But then a man in uniform stepped forward and announced the judge, and everyone was standing, so they stood too, and then the judge was telling them to sit.

Emma studied Judge Trentini as he spoke, giving directions to the reporters and visitors, to the prosecutor, and to Henry and his lawyer. She barely listened to what he was saying, thinking it didn't pertain to her much, but she longed to know whether Henry's future was in good hands. Who was this man? Was he a good judge or merely a man who had risen in the judicial system?

She didn't know if she could tell such things from looking at a person, but if she could, then Judge Trentini was measuring up just fine. He was older than she expected, with only little wisps of white hair. He wore large, owlish glasses, and his skin was weathered and dark. Though he was small in stature, it was plain that he stood for no foolishness in his court.

"This will serve as both a pretrial hearing and an arraignment," he explained, though Emma reckoned everyone but her community already understood this. "I have reviewed the arrest of Henry W. Lapp as well as the postarrest investigation report. The defendant will rise."

Henry stood, and Emma was relieved to see that his right arm was no longer shaking. In fact, he looked calm and serene. She wondered at that. He'd been frightened as a rabbit being chased by a coyote when he'd first come to her home with the drawings. Sometime in the last three days, between Friday morning and today, he'd found a peace that passed understanding. She was glad for that and said a quick prayer of thanksgiving.

Standing beside him was his lawyer, who looked every bit up to the challenge of defending Henry. Emma had heard that the woman's name was Kiana Sitton. She couldn't imagine where Henry had found her or how he'd managed to procure her services so quickly.

"Mr. Lapp, do you understand the crime you have been charged with?"

"I do."

"And how do you plead to the charge of murder in the case of Mrs. Sophia Brooks, sir?"

"Not guilty."

The judge blinked several times. He didn't look surprised exactly, but more as if he was preparing himself for what lay ahead, gathering his thoughts and how he should voice them. Emma liked that. She liked that he was taking his time and actually looking at Henry. Finally the judge shuffled some papers and said, "You may take a seat."

He turned his attention to Agent Delaney's side of the bench. "As we have the body of the deceased, and we have a preliminary forensic report establishing that she died of unnatural causes, the charge of murder is appropriate. However, I find your evidence against Mr. Lapp to be a bit weak. What does the prosecution say?"

The man beside Agent Delaney stood. He was middle-aged and bald, and Emma disliked him instantly.

"We believe Mr. Lapp had opportunity and motive, and in addition we have forensic evidence—"

"Yes, I have that report here, but I fail to see how it establishes a direct connection to Ms. Brooks's murder."

Delaney jumped up and whispered something to the man who must have been his lawyer. That man nodded once and said, "The federal government believes we can prove that, in the early morning hours of September 20, Mr. Lapp took Mrs. Brooks to the Monte Vista National Wildlife Refuge, murdered her, and left her body among the reeds."

Kiana popped out of her chair. "And then returned to the scene the next morning, the twenty-first, and called 9-1-1, saying he'd found the body? Why would he do that?"

There was a murmur among the crowd, but one look from the judge silenced everyone. Kiana sat back down, though she perched on the edge of her seat, ready to intervene again.

"We believe Mr. Lapp experienced instant and extreme remorse given his position of leadership in the community."

"Instant and extreme remorse, huh?" Trentini raised a single eyebrow, indicating his skepticism.

"In addition, the federal government believes it to be of utmost importance that we assure the public the killer has been removed from the area, that the public lands in the San Luis Valley are in fact safe for every man, woman, and child to enjoy. We ask the judge to deny bail."

"Objection, Your Honor." Henry's lawyer had again popped out of her seat. She stood ramrod straight, her voice calm and her demeanor relaxed. Emma couldn't imagine having such a job, but she was glad that somehow Henry had found someone competent to represent him. "My client has no past criminal history and gives no indication that he is a flight risk, especially given that his mode of transportation is a horse and buggy."

A ripple of laughter cascaded through the crowd, and Emma felt her mood swing to optimism.

Judge Trentini nodded as he wrote something down. "I am releasing Mr. Lapp on his own recognizance, though he will be required to wear an electronic monitoring device. Mr. Lapp, you are not to tamper with this device in any way."

He went on to explain that if Henry stepped outside of a predesignated area, the device would send a signal to the police department, who would arrest him and bring him back to the jail.

Emma felt a little dizzy at the thought of Henry wearing something that could track him, but then it wasn't as if he had anything to hide.

"This trial is slated to begin on November 1. I expect to be made aware of any changes in either the prosecution's case or the defendant's status."

And then Judge Trentini banged his gavel, and they were all dismissed.

Forty-One

He's being released.

You're certain?

I was in the courtroom.

This could be a problem.

How?

He could start nosing around.

He's wearing a monitor.

The first good news today.

And Delaney's lawyer argued to
keep him off the wildlife refuge.

Even better.

That might not stop him, though.
He strikes me as the nosy sort.

If we have to, we take him out.

That would bring too much
scrutiny on us.

You're afraid of that now?

You should be.

Talk to me about tomorrow
night's pickup.

Everything's ready.

Then stop worrying.

Forty-Two

Henry was processed out of the jail faster than he imagined. He walked into the lobby and found Clyde waiting for him.

"Thought you might need a ride home."

"*Danki.*" They stepped out into a warm September day, one bright with fall leaves and busy with folks driving and walking up and down Main Street. Henry hadn't realized how much he'd missed everything in just twenty-four hours. He hadn't allowed himself to focus on life outside the jail's walls. But now that he saw it, he was nearly overwhelmed with gratitude that he was for the moment free.

"With weather like this, I might have enjoyed the walk."

"*Ya*, but little Lexi here was eager to see you."

Clyde laughed when Henry opened the door to the buggy. The small dog had been sitting on the seat, looking out the window. She threw herself at Henry and began licking his face.

"Katie Ann enjoyed watching after her. So much so that she's started pestering me about getting one."

"It's not a bad idea. She's a *gut* guard dog and a pleasant companion to have around."

Clyde grunted at that, and Henry let the subject drop. He understood his deacon wasn't short on companions. He had his mother, his wife, their four children—and soon the children would marry and bring spouses and then have children of their own. It was the Amish way of life to be

169

surrounded by family, and companionship wasn't usually an issue. Henry's life had been different, but then it had blessings of its own.

"How does that contraption work?" Clyde asked, nodding toward the ankle bracelet.

It was bigger and chunkier than Henry had imagined, though how could he have known what to expect? He didn't remember ever seeing such a thing or even hearing about one.

"The way Lawson explained it to me—he's a very nice young man, by the way—is that there's a homing device—"

"I've heard of homing pigeons," Clyde muttered.

"This device inside the monitor sends out a radio frequency at timed intervals."

"Can you feel it when the signal is sent?"

"*Nein.*"

"And the signal tells them what?"

"My location."

"So you're limited in where you can and can't go?"

"Exactly."

"Does it shock you or something if you step out of the area?"

"*Nein.* The light is green now." He pointed to a small light on the side of the monitor. "Which means I'm within my allowed area. My understanding is that it will turn red and send an alert to the police department if I go somewhere I shouldn't."

"Can you leave your property once I take you home?"

"I can. I just have to stay in the Monte Vista region. No trips to Alamosa, which I hadn't planned on anyway. I'll be able to visit the folks in our church, which is a real blessing."

"Better than sitting in a jail cell, I suppose."

"Indeed." Henry glanced out the window. The fall migration of the sandhill cranes was nearing its peak, and now he would miss that. "No birding for me this year. Not allowed to go out to the wildlife refuge. Delaney cast enough doubt on my character that the judge wants to make sure I'm not a menace to any unsuspecting bird-watchers."

"That's a shame. I know you're disappointed, but the cranes will be through here again in the spring, and this will be behind us then."

"I hope you're right."

"I know I'm right." Clyde thrust his chin forward as he spoke, which made Henry want to laugh. His friends were bound and determined to assert his innocence. It was a balm to his soul.

"How'd you get the lawyer?"

"Sheriff Grayson contacted her. She has some experience with others like us who have run afoul of the law."

"Plain? She has experience defending Plain folk?"

"She didn't have time to explain before this morning's hearing, but as we waited for them to process my release, I asked her about her experience. She mentioned a Mennonite gentleman she helped with a drug charge. She convinced the judge to consider his lack of criminal history as well as his limited role in the enterprise. Worked well for all involved. The man is out now and staying clean. Another man was imprisoned for failing to follow his municipality's fire code. She worked out a compromise."

"When will you see her again? To plan your defense?"

"Later this week. She's going out of town for another trial, but she assured me she'd be working on my case."

"It's *gut*, Henry. *Gut* that you have someone on your side who is knowledgeable about *Englisch* laws and their court system."

They passed the rest of the drive in silence. Henry allowed Lexi to sit on his lap. She was content now that he was with her. He'd once read that dogs lived in the present moment, and that was the reason for their joyful personality. Judging by the expression on Lexi's face, Henry would have to agree with that. As they neared his place, Clyde slowed his mare before pulling slightly on the right rein so she would turn down the lane.

"Other than her experience, why would Grayson contact her?" he asked, returning to the subject of Henry's lawyer.

"I'm not sure."

"Have you asked him?"

"That's the strange thing—or one of the strange things. He's not around, but he sent a message through Miss Sitton. He wanted her to tell me he would be in touch soon."

They were quiet as Clyde drove the buggy up to the house. When Henry opened the door, Lexi bounded out. Clyde started to get out of the buggy, but Henry stayed him with a hand on his arm. "You've given up enough of your day to my concerns. I know there's work waiting for you at home."

Clyde nodded once.

"I appreciate it, though. You don't realize how dear home is until you spend a night away."

"We're glad to have you back, and you're right. I do have work at home, so I'll get on for now." Clyde ran a hand over his beard before turning to meet Henry's gaze. "But I'll be back tonight. We all will."

"All?"

"Emma, Rachel, Silas, Katie Ann. We've all been studying your drawings. We think we've found something."

Henry nodded as if that made sense, though he couldn't imagine what they'd found. He barely remembered the drawings, though he could vividly recall the panic he'd felt when he'd hurried to Emma's, when he'd asked her to keep them safe. That panic seemed so distant now as to have belonged to someone else.

"All right. Tonight, then?"

"After dinner. Get some rest beforehand. I imagine you need it after the twenty-four hours you've had." Clyde smiled. "And the women left you some food in the house. They were certain you starved with the *Englisch* cooking at the jail."

Henry climbed the steps of his front porch, and then he turned and watched Clyde drive back down his lane.

He didn't know what was going to happen next. He couldn't predict how the trial would go or how he would prove his innocence. He still lacked an alibi.

But he knew he had friends, good friends. And together they would find a way to weather this storm.

Forty-Three

Henry ate too much for lunch—ham salad spread on fresh bread, a large helping of potato salad, and oatmeal cookies with a cup of hot tea. He hadn't been in jail long, but he'd still missed Plain food—the freshness and richness of the ingredients, knowing that his friends' hands had kneaded the dough and sliced the bread. In all likelihood someone had butchered a pig and seasoned and smoked the ham. The cookies were filled with raisins and nuts.

"We have a *gut* life, Lexi."

The beagle rolled over on her back, and Henry couldn't resist reaching down to scratch her speckled stomach.

Determined to stay awake, he moved to the rocker in the sitting room. It was good to relax in a patch of sun and read from the Scriptures, a family Bible in the old language and handed down from his grandfather. Henry read the German text, comforted by verses he had been raised hearing from his bishop and his parents and his grandparents. Verses he had shared with others throughout the years. Promises of comfort and hope and an eternal reward.

Perhaps it was that familiarity that allowed him to relax, finally, and then fall into a restful sleep. When he woke, the sun indicated it was late afternoon. "We should see to Oreo."

Lexi stretched and trotted to the door, her tail wagging so hard it caused her entire body to shift from side to side. "I should have named you Wiggles."

An hour in the barn and another in the workshop helped to reinforce the routine he'd known all his life. He was almost able to forget the ankle monitor.

He'd eaten so much for lunch that he wasn't hungry at all for dinner. Instead, he drank a glass of milk while standing at the sink, looking out at the sunset. As he was admiring the view—the beauty and simplicity of it— three cranes landed in what was left of his garden. He'd planted bulrush and berry bushes on the south side of his field where the water tended to stand if they had any rain at all. His fingers itched for his binoculars, but then he remembered Delaney had taken them.

He leaned closer to the window and confirmed that he was seeing a family—a male, female, and juvenile. They pecked at the seeds and meandered through what was left of his garden. Some of the farmers in the area had entered into an agreement to sell parts of their harvest to the Crops for Cranes. Henry thought that was an excellent plan. It reminded him of the verses in Leviticus where God's people were instructed to leave a small portion of their harvest for the poor and foreigner. It was good and right that they should do so—a sort of natural tithe.

The female stretched her neck, and even from where Henry stood inside the house, he could hear her soft purr echoing across his garden.

"She's saying get ready to fly, little guy."

The juvenile mimicked its parent, and then they were rising into the sky, a group of three against the darkening blue of the sky.

"Perhaps *Gotte* brought the cranes to us since we can't go to them."

Lexi whined and dropped her head on her paws, apparently skeptical as to Henry's observation. He laughed, surprised that he could do so given his circumstances, and proceeded to make fresh coffee and set out mugs, cream, and sugar.

Twenty minutes later, Lexi's ears perked up, and she jumped to her feet and scampered to the door.

"Your hearing is much better than mine." Henry stood on the porch, the dog at his side as Clyde's buggy trundled down his lane for the second time that day. As his friend had promised, he'd brought his family.

They all moved inside, apparently eager to share whatever they had found.

"*Gut* to have you back, Henry." Rachel was carrying what Henry was sure had to be a fresh-baked pie. It smelled like apple. "I'll just go into the kitchen and slice this up."

Katie Ann paused to scoop up the dog. "Lexi missed you, Henry."

"Silas stayed home with the younger boys." Clyde clapped him on the shoulder. "Usually he's stepping out with one girl or another, but he said this is important, and he'd be happy to stay home and help. Already *gut* things are coming from your trouble."

And then it was only Henry and Emma standing in the doorway to his home.

"You wouldn't believe how I've prayed that you would be right here, right here where you are, and soon, by this evening—if at all possible." When she looked up at him, he saw the depth of her fear and her compassion. It was humbling to think that someone could care for him so much.

"*Gotte* is *gut*, Emma."

"All the time. But Henry, I don't ever want to see you in a courtroom again." Her eyes were wide, intense—and beautiful. "We'll figure this out. We'll figure it out together, and we'll put this behind us. Agreed?"

"*Ya*. I can agree to that." He squeezed her hand, and then on second thought followed his instincts and leaned in to kiss her on the cheek.

She colored a pretty shade of pink and said, "There will be time for courting when we've solved this, Henry Lapp. Until then, we need to stay focused."

To which he had to laugh, because in that moment she reminded him of Lexi, intent on protecting the one she loved. Did Emma love him the way he was beginning to love her? Henry hoped so. He wanted to talk to her about his feelings, about their future and what it should look like, but Emma was right. There would be time for that later.

When he walked into the kitchen, he saw that Rachel had placed five small plates on the counter, each with a slice of pie and a dollop of whipped cream. She'd also poured four mugs of coffee and one glass of milk. Both the lantern over the table and the one by the stove had been lit, casting a warm glow around the room, though it was only just beginning to grow dark outside.

"Looks like a social," he said, and suddenly the single glass of milk he'd had for dinner didn't seem like enough. He gladly accepted the slice of pie Rachel handed him.

"No reason we can't eat while we solve this mystery." Katie Ann had spread the drawings he'd done out on the table.

"We spent a few hours studying these," Clyde explained. "And we've made a list of people who appear in more than one picture—people who might have been watching or following Sophia."

"All right. Let's hear it." But Henry had no sooner sat down with his pie and coffee than Lexi began to bark again, followed by the sound of an *Englisch* car driving down his lane. Bright lights swept across the front windows.

"Let's hope they haven't come to arrest me again," he mumbled as he hurried from the kitchen.

Emma followed him to the front door. Henry had the absurd notion that if the police were there to arrest him again, she would throw herself in front of him. Surely one determined Amish woman could stop injustice.

But the police weren't waiting on Henry's front porch. A young *Englisch* woman of medium height, with shoulder-length light-brown hair and dark-brown eyes, stood there. The skin around her nose and eyes looked red, swollen, chafed. He thought she looked completely exhausted, as if even standing there took all of the energy she possessed.

"Can I help you?" Henry asked.

"I'm here to see…that is, I'd like to speak to Henry Lapp."

"I'm Henry."

The woman glanced at something on her phone, then back up at Henry. She hesitated, then swayed, and Henry worried that she might take a tumble. But she drew herself up to her full height, which couldn't have been even five and a half feet, and asked, "Are you the Henry who knew Sophia? Did you try to help my sister?"

Forty-Four

Emma pulled the young woman into the house before she collapsed on the porch. "*Ya*, we knew Sophia. We're so sorry for your loss. It's a real tragedy."

Lexi sniffed the woman's shoes, determined she wasn't a threat, and trotted back into the kitchen.

Sophia's sister halted just inside the room, staring in wide-eyed wonder. "You don't have electricity. Just like it says in the book." She dropped her phone into her handbag and pulled out a slim paperback book with the photograph of two Amish girls on the front. At least it was tastefully done. The girls were facing away from the camera.

"*Ya*. Just like in the book," Emma agreed. "Why don't you come into the kitchen?"

Henry raised his eyebrows, so Emma held back as Rachel walked out to greet their guest.

"You're sure this is a *gut* idea?" Henry asked.

"How can it hurt?"

"Things have a way of twisting and turning in unexpected directions, as you and I know all too well."

"But Henry, she's grieving. It's plain to see she's devastated by what's happened. Surely our first responsibility is to minister to her."

"You have a terrible habit of sounding more bishop-y than I do."

She sighed, relieved that he could joke about their situation. "Let's go see why she's here."

Katie Ann and Rachel were guiding Sophia's sister to a chair. She accepted a mug of coffee, but her hands were shaking so badly that she had to place it on the table, which was when she noticed the drawings.

"What…what are these?"

"I can explain," Henry said evenly.

"They're all of Sophia. Every one of them." Tears began to fall down her cheeks.

Emma expected an accusation then, that Henry had been infatuated with her, that Henry had been stalking her, that Henry had killed her. Instead, the young woman picked up one of the drawings, the one with Sophia helping the old woman. She hesitantly ran her fingertips across the page, touching the inside of Sophia's wrist that was marked by the tattoo. "It's like Sophia said. It's more than a drawing. It's more like a photograph."

She set it down and took a big gulp of coffee before she realized they were all watching her. "I haven't even introduced myself. I'm Tess Savalas. I'm Sophia's younger sister."

"You look very much alike," Rachel said. "Same cheekbones, same nose."

"I suppose we do, or rather we did." She swiped at the tears running down her cheeks. "I always thought her hair was shinier and her face was prettier."

Emma sat down next to her. "It's natural enough to envy your older *schweschder*—sister."

"Yes. I guess that's what it was." She drank more of her coffee and then stared down into it. "I still can't believe she's dead."

"Your sister was a very kind woman," Henry said. "Everyone in this room knew her, and we will miss her, though of course our grief can't compare to yours."

"I was so surprised when she mentioned you." Tess raised her eyes to Henry's as he sank into the chair across from her. "She doesn't usually talk about strangers. Sophia was something of an introvert. Her circle of friends—well, they were good friends, but few in number. When the police…when they called, I knew I had to come. They offered to ship the… the body, but I needed to see where she'd spent the final weeks of her life. How she'd spent them. I didn't expect this." She waved her hands toward the drawings. "It's like a chronicle of her last days."

"Perhaps I should explain—"

"How you can do this? I read all about that." When they looked at her in surprise, she again reached for her book on Amish people. "That's right. You don't read the paper much. I guess you don't know, but the newspapers wrote all about you and what you can do."

"How did you know where to find Henry?" Clyde asked. "And why? I don't mean to be rude, but he's been falsely accused, and it's been a terrible forty-eight hours. Why did you come here this evening? What is it you hope to accomplish?"

She squared her shoulders and turned her attention to Clyde. "It was easy enough to find him."

Emma could tell Tess Savalas was made of strong stuff. Just one more way she resembled her sister.

"Just ask in town, and they'll point you in the right direction. I stopped by the police station first, of course. I met with Officer Anderson, who assured me you would be tried and convicted. That you wouldn't get away with this." She let her gaze travel around the room until she reached Henry, and then she spoke directly to him. "But I know you didn't do it."

"And how do you know that?" Henry's response was so softly spoken, so tenuous, that Emma leaned forward in her chair.

"Because Sophia told me. She told me I could trust you. And she said if anything happened to her, I should come and find you."

"You spoke with her?"

"No. She left me a voice mail message, I think a few hours before she died. Though I didn't tell that officer as much. I'd be more than willing to speak to the judge, but honestly, I'm not sure who else I should trust." She picked up the picture of Sophia walking down the road in the wind. "I hate that she was so alone. That she was frightened."

"She was frightened," Emma agreed. "But she wasn't alone. Henry could tell something was wrong, and so he…well, he tried to minister to her."

"And that's why she spent the night at your house? You're Emma, right?"

Emma nodded, and then she realized Tess didn't know everyone in the room. She quickly introduced her family before continuing with her questions. "What did she tell you, Tess? When she called and left you a message, what did she say?"

Tess blinked rapidly. Instead of answering, she turned to Rachel and held up her mug. "Could I possibly…"

"Of course."

Katie Ann jumped up as well. "And pie. We have homemade pie. It's *gut*, and you look as if you haven't eaten."

Lexi's ears perked up at the word *pie*, but she didn't bother climbing out of her bed.

Tess shrugged, which Katie Ann took as a yes. Rachel had cut the pie into eight pieces and three were left in the pan. Katie Ann plopped two of them onto a saucer and put it in front of Tess, gently pushing the drawings out of the way. Emma noticed that she covered up the one of Sophia's body in the reeds. She smiled at her granddaughter, grateful for her quick thinking and her compassionate spirit.

"This is very good. I can't believe I'm eating pie, though, while my sister is lying on a slab in your county morgue."

"I'm sure she would want you to take care of yourself." Rachel had refilled her coffee mug and sat down next to Clyde.

No one spoke as Tess ate three heaping bites of pie. Her attention turned again to the drawings, and she pulled the stack toward herself, thumbing through each one until she came to the final picture, the picture of Sophia lying among the reeds of the refuge wetland.

"You want to know why I'm here." She stared at the drawing another moment before looking up.

"I'm here to find the person responsible for killing Sophia, and I will do that. One way or another. For some reason, I think you all can be more help than the police, who seem to have already decided Henry is the guilty person. But Henry didn't do this." She leveled her gaze at him. "I barely know you, but I know you didn't do this because Sophia liked you. She trusted you, and she told me to find you, to talk to you if something happened."

"But do you realize what you're insinuating?" Clyde sat forward now, his shoulders bunched, a deep furrow between his eyes, and his hands clasped together. "If Henry didn't kill Sophia—and we agree with you that he didn't—then someone else did. Someone in these drawings, is what we suspect. We don't know why or whether they're still in the area or even if they will kill again."

And then Henry voiced what Emma had been thinking. "Perhaps it's not wise for you to be here, Tess. Someone killed your *schweschder*, and whoever it was probably wouldn't hesitate to kill you too."

Forty-Five

Tess's expression took on an even more determined look. "I appreciate what you're saying, but that doesn't change my mind. I'm determined to find who did this, with or without your help."

Henry combed his fingers through his beard. Because he'd been married, he had a full beard, now mostly gray. But Henry had been a widower for many years, and he understood the pain of loss—how it could color a person's world. He didn't want that for this young woman, and he wanted justice for Sophia. Against his best intentions, he felt himself being drawn into her crusade.

His friends had come over with one goal in mind—to establish doubt as far as Henry's guilt. At best, they would find a way to present an alibi for his whereabouts on the morning of Wednesday, September 20. It was a defensive strategy, and as such was a vastly different thing than trying to find a killer. Henry knew that well enough. He also knew Emma and Rachel and Clyde understood what they were about to undertake. Perhaps young Katie Ann did as well. She'd been integrally involved in catching the Monte Vista arsonist. Henry wished it wasn't so. She was much too young to be exposed to such things. But then God's ways were not his ways.

"We will help in any way we can." The rest of the group visibly relaxed at Henry's words. They had felt the draw to help her as well. That was good. The Spirit was speaking to them in the same way, encouraging them to help this lost soul. "Perhaps you should start with the message Sophia left you. Could you tell us, word for word, what she said?"

"I can do better than that. I still have the message." She pulled her phone out of her purse, and then hesitated when her eyes landed on the slim paperback book. "But you don't allow phones in your home. Should I go outside?"

"These are extenuating circumstances," Henry said.

When Tess glanced at Clyde, he laughed. "Henry's our bishop. It's his job to decide what exceptions can be made to our *Ordnung*, but in this case—as his deacon—I happen to agree with him."

"All right. I didn't want to get anyone in trouble."

She placed the phone on the table, tapped a couple of buttons, and then Sophia's voice was coming over the speaker.

Tess, it's me. Sophia. I wanted…I needed to call you. I should have done it sooner, and I'm sorry. I'm sorry for so many things, but mostly that I didn't call you when I needed you. I did it for a good reason—to protect you—but I see now that there was no reason good enough to shut you out.

I think I know who killed Cooper. Not the person's name, but what they're involved in. Actually, I don't know exactly what they're doing. I hope to find that out tonight. It all has to do with something Cooper found out. He was about to expose someone, and they killed him so he couldn't. I know the police said it was a street mugging, but that doesn't make any sense. Cooper would have never been in that part of town that late at night. I know him, and I knew—even when you came down to help with the funeral, but I didn't tell you—I knew something wasn't right about it all. And then I found his notes…

Tess, I have to turn off my phone now. If I survive the night, then I'll call you back in a day or so. Once I've turned the evidence in. Once I've figured out who to turn it in to. But if I don't make it, if you hear that something's happened to me, then I want you to know how much I care about you. The truth is, you've been the best sister a girl could hope for, even if you did borrow my makeup and get a stain on my favorite dress when you went out with Danny Vento.

There was a pause, and Henry thought that was the end of the recording, but then Sophia cleared her throat and continued.

My friend Henry says we can trust God's words, His promises. Do you still believe that? I think I do, and maybe that's why I'm brave enough to go through with this. Henry also says we're supposed to encourage one another, to spur each other to love and good deeds. If something happens to me, finish this, Tess. Don't put yourself in danger, but take what I've put together and hand it over to the authorities. Emma Fisher has my files. Find Henry, Henry Lapp in Monte Vista, Colorado. He's an Amish bishop, and he will take you to Emma.

I love you, sis.

The recording ended. Tears were once again running down Tess's cheeks. Katie Ann stood, walked around the table, and wrapped her arms around her. When she finally pulled away from Tess, who was sniffling and dabbing at her nose with her shirtsleeve, Katie Ann said, "Henry has a fine horse. Would you like to see it? A walk outside might…well, it might help."

Tess nodded. Lexi jumped up to join them, and the three fled into the warm night.

The door had barely shut behind them when Henry, Clyde, and Rachel all turned on Emma at once.

"Files?" Clyde frowned in confusion. "You said nothing about files."

Emma was already shaking her head. "I don't know anything about any files."

"She said you have them, though, so she must have given them to you." Rachel leaned back in her chair. "You were only with her twice—"

"Three times," Henry said. "At the diner, in my buggy when we brought her here, and at your home the morning she left. One of those times, Sophia gave you something. And if I'm right, it contains the information we need to find whoever killed her."

Forty-Six

Emma continued to shake her head as they all stared at her. "I can't think of a thing she gave me. Certainly not any files."

"All right. Let's leave that for a minute," Henry said. "Sometimes when you think of something else, you can remember the thing you forgot."

"Or maybe Sophia meant to give me something but didn't, though why would she give it to me and not you? I barely knew the girl."

"*Gut* point," Clyde said. "If it happened while you were in the diner or the buggy, she probably would have given it to Henry. So it had to have been while she was at the house after Henry left that evening or the next morning."

"She left in a hurry," Rachel said. "I came out of the laundry room, and she was gone."

Emma's hand flew to her mouth.

"You've remembered." Henry sat up straighter. "You've remembered what it was."

"*Ya*. Well, I don't know what it was, but I do know where it is—in my apron pocket."

"Files fit into your pocket?" Clyde shook his head. "That can't be right."

"Which is probably why I forgot. It was a little thing." She held up her thumb and forefinger, a gap as big as a clothespin between them. "It was some little object. She gave it to me and said—"

Now she stopped and dropped her head, staring at her lap. Embarrassment and grief washed over her. How could she have forgotten? "She told me to give it to you, Henry. She said if anything happened, to make sure that I gave it to you. But I slipped it into my pocket, and I haven't worn that apron again because the hem was starting to unravel. I don't think I've even washed it."

"And you think this thing could be what Sophia told Tess about?"

"Maybe. I don't know."

She felt miserable. How could she have forgotten something so important? But so much had happened in the last week. It was then she realized that it had been exactly seven days since she'd spoken to Sophia. And in that time the poor girl had been murdered, and Henry had been charged with the crime.

"You've had a lot on your mind, *Mamm*." Clyde reached across and clumsily patted her hand. "Don't blame yourself."

"And you couldn't have saved her even if you'd given it to me the same day. I'm sure I would have had no idea what it was, let alone what to do with it."

"It might be something to put into their computers," Rachel said. "Phones and computers. *Englischers* save all sorts of records on them, and they call them files."

Henry tapped his fingers against the table. "Emma can find it, and then we'll ask Tess. For now, tell me what you saw in the drawings."

By the time they'd laid it all out, Emma was feeling better. What had happened was terrible, but it wasn't her fault. And while Sophia's files might hold clues, Henry's drawings did as well. She was sure of that.

Katie Ann and Tess walked back into the room as they were finishing the list. Lexi trotted over to her water bowl, drank noisily from it, and then curled up at Henry's feet, her head across his shoes.

Tess's color was better, though her eyes were still puffy, and she kept wiping at her nose with tissues Katie Ann gave her. Crying was probably a healthy sign. Emma could only imagine how much pain the girl was in, but keeping those emotions bottled up couldn't be healthy. No, it would be far better to cry it out and face the feelings.

There was something else. Emma's thoughts slipped back to her childhood. A terrible storm had passed through their town in Indiana, damaging many homes and barns and obliterating the crops. She'd walked in one evening to find her father on his knees, pouring his heart out to God. Her mother had pulled her aside. "Sometimes *Gotte* calms the storm, but sometimes He lets the storm rage and calms His child." At the time, she hadn't understood that at all, but maybe now she did. Tess was calming before their eyes. She was sharing her burden with them, though the storm around her continued to rage.

"What is this list?" Tess asked, staring down at the sheet of paper they'd written on.

"I believe Sophia thought someone was following her." Henry studied the picture of Sophia helping the older woman, the one that showed the scar on her neck. "When I drew this picture, she was quite frightened, and I think it was because of this detail. This scar on her neck."

"She didn't have that when I saw her last."

"You're sure?"

"Positive."

"And how long ago was that?"

"After Cooper died." She sank into a chair. "I flew into San Diego to help with the funeral."

"Is now a *gut* time to do this?" Emma asked. "Perhaps you need to get some rest, and we could go back at it again tomorrow."

"I couldn't sleep. I'm too keyed up."

"All right, but tell us if you want to stop." Rachel nudged the drawing toward Tess. "Do you notice anything else? Anything that could be important that we wouldn't see?"

"Her hair. It's a little longer. When I saw her—"

"When was this?" Clyde asked.

"Middle of July. Cooper was killed on July 15. I remember because that was our mother's birthday."

Katie Ann glanced at her own mother, and then reached over and snagged her hand.

"Anything else different?" Katie Ann asked.

"Her hair was lighter than the shading appears here, like mine."

"The Sophia we knew had dark-brown hair," Emma said.

"So she dyed her hair and let it grow longer." Katie Ann picked up another of the drawings from the diner. In it, Sophia was carrying a tray of food to a table. "Maybe she was trying to make herself look different."

Tess nodded in agreement and pulled Henry's tablet toward her, the same tablet they'd been making their list on. She drew a line across the page, left to right. On the far left, she tagged the line and wrote *Cooper's death*. Under this she put the date 7-15. On the far right she put *Sophia's death*, with the date 9-20.

"I didn't know she'd left San Diego. She didn't answer my calls, but she would text occasionally. I thought she needed her space and time to grieve. I didn't know she was keeping all this from me."

"Sophia knew how much you cared for her," Henry said. He waited a few seconds and then pointed to the left of her line. "She'd been working at Maggie's Diner for six weeks."

"All right. That would put the date at around August 1."

"And she must have come here for a reason," Katie Ann said. "No one just picks Monte Vista off a map. We're too small."

When her parents looked at her quizzically, she added, "Which is what I like—nice and small."

Clyde drummed his fingers against the table. "Sometime between when you saw Sophia in San Diego and when Henry drew this first picture of her at the diner, she got that scar on her neck."

Tess notched a spot halfway between 7-15 and 8-1. She drew a question mark below it and above it the word *scar*.

"It was a week ago Sunday that she spent the night with me," Emma said. "That would have been…"

"The seventeenth! I remember because I came home from the singing, and she was in my room. We had a nice long talk, which seemed odd since I didn't know her, but Sophia—she was easy to talk to." Katie Ann had been smiling as she remembered, but her expression quickly grew somber. "If only we knew what files she was talking about."

"We might have figured that out," Henry said. "Emma remembered that Sophia gave her something."

"This big." Emma again demonstrated with her thumb and forefinger. "Plastic or maybe some kind of metal. Very light."

Tess dug around in her handbag and pulled out a small green device. "Did it look like this?"

"*Ya.* Same size, only not green."

"It's a flash drive. It's what we put computer files on. Do you know where it is?"

"I put it in the pocket of my apron, which is either in the dirty laundry basket or my sewing basket. I can't remember."

"Please tell me you didn't wash it."

"*Nein.* I don't think so. Why? Would water and soap ruin it?"

"Possibly." Tess was up out of her chair and drawing the strap of her purse over her shoulder. "Can we go and get it?"

"We can." Henry didn't stand. "But perhaps we should talk about the list first."

Slowly, Tess sat back down and nodded in agreement.

Clyde crossed his arms on the table and leaned forward. "Henry drew four scenes from the diner. One when she was helping the older woman, one carrying a tray of food, another as she stood at the window to the kitchen, and this final one where she's checking someone out at the register. We noticed that in each of them, we see some of the same people."

"Which doesn't mean anything necessarily," Katie Ann was quick to point out. "Small town and all. You're bound to run across the same people again and again."

"That's true, so for instance, we see Jared Anderson, the Monte Vista police officer you met, Tess, in three of the four pictures. But only one where he's looking directly at your *schweschder.*"

Tess shook her head in amazement. "I know I read about accidental savants, but seeing these…are you sure they're accurate? That what you drew is exactly as it happened?"

"*Ya,*" Henry said simply. "We're sure."

When she still looked doubtful, Emma explained, "His mind is like a camera since the accident."

"With the baseball. I read about that."

Emma wondered how the *Englisch* newspapers had so much information on Henry, but what difference did it make? They had nothing to hide, and his ability was nothing to be ashamed of. "He doesn't remember things consciously. In fact, he misplaces his reading glasses at least three times a week."

"It's possible I should buy another pair for backup."

"It would save you a lot of aggravation." Emma turned back to Tess. "His memory isn't perfect. But what he draws? That comes from the subconscious part of his brain—"

"The camera," Tess said.

"Exactly," everyone said in unison.

"All right. So we have this officer in three of the pictures."

"Right, but in two of them he's looking elsewhere—at his phone once, and out the window once." Katie Ann pulled out the four drawings from the diner and laid them side by side.

"Only one time he's looking at your *schweschder*," Emma said.

"He's frowning."

"True, but he could be frowning about any number of things—a call that just came in, something that happened earlier that day, even his bill." Rachel turned her coffee mug around in her hands, though it was empty.

"Who else did you find?"

"That's where it gets interesting," Henry said. "A wildlife employee is in every picture. We can tell by the uniform."

Emma leaned closer to the drawing. "Can't tell if it's a man or woman, but there's a long scuff mark across the toe of his or her right shoe."

"There's a rancher in three of them, and a member of our community in two."

"A member of your community? An Amish person?"

Emma noticed Henry and Clyde share a quick glance. Now probably wasn't the time to bring up the fact that Leroy was one of their deacons. Surely he had nothing to do with Sophia's death, but it only seemed fair to list him while they were listing *Englischers*.

"We think one of these people might have been watching Sophia," Henry explained. "Maybe not harmed her, but knew something about what she was doing here and could possibly lead us to the killer."

Forty-Seven

They decided Tess would take Emma, Katie Ann, and the bag of drawings in her car to retrieve the flash drive, while Clyde and Rachel rode home in the buggy. Henry would harness Oreo and meet Tess at the diner, where, as they now knew from Silas, there was free Wi-Fi.

"I could read the files anywhere, but I think we might want to check a few things online as well."

"The diner's open until eleven," Henry said. "And the dinner crowd will be gone."

"Are you sure you don't want me to come to the diner too?" Clyde asked.

"Or me?" Rachel said. "I could catch a ride with Tess and Emma."

"*Nein.* You've all done enough for one day, and I know the morning starts at four in your home."

"Don't hesitate to wake us up if you need us." Rachel squeezed Henry's hand and then walked outside.

Tess was already in her car, making a phone call.

Emma was the last to leave. She only said, "Be careful," and then kissed his cheek—as he had kissed hers. It was such a simple thing. Something a grandmother might do to a grandchild, and yet it filled Henry's heart with no small measure of joy. When you were a widower as long as he'd been, you could sometimes go days or weeks with no physical contact. But it wasn't the kiss. It was that Emma felt comfortable enough to kiss him and that she cared so much.

He was thinking on those things as he walked back inside, retrieved his jacket and hat, and then—as was his custom—picked up the pocket change on his dresser. There among the nickels and quarters, he saw the device he'd found on his clock. After some thought he'd taken a hammer to it, smashing it once. What was left was flatter and hopefully no longer working. He was certainly glad he hadn't had it in his pocket when he was arrested. He wasn't ready to hand it over to the Monte Vista police. Perhaps Tess could tell him what it was. He gathered it up with the change, dropped it all into his pocket, and walked outside toward the barn.

Lexi danced at his feet.

"Too late for you to go with me this time, girl. Stay here and guard the place, and I'll be back as soon as I can."

It was just past eight, and he was carrying a battery lantern, so when Lexi stopped suddenly, stood on point, and began to growl, Henry knew in what direction she was looking. Was Sophia's killer here? Had he been foolish to feel safe on his own property?

"Tell that beast not to bite me, Henry." Sheriff Grayson remained in the shadows, but when Henry raised the lantern he could see him well enough. Grayson wore jeans, a long-sleeved flannel shirt, and a baseball cap.

Henry blew out a sigh of relief. "Give an old man a heart attack."

"My apologies, but I didn't feel like I could walk up to your door and knock."

"And why is that?"

"Because they could be watching."

"They?"

"The people who killed Sophia Brooks." Grayson motioned toward his lantern. "Maybe you could douse the light."

Henry did as he asked. "Should we go inside?"

"Out would be better. I want to see anyone who's coming."

Henry thought Grayson was being a bit paranoid. Lexi would let them know if anyone was approaching.

As if reading his mind, Grayson said, "They don't have to get that close if they have a high-powered rifle and a nightscope."

"You're scared."

"I'm cautious, and you need to be too."

Grayson nodded toward the other side of the barn, where they could sit on a bench situated against the barn's south wall and watch out over the field. The large water trough might provide some protection from spying eyes—or bullets.

"I see Kiana got you out of jail."

"She did. *Danki* for sending her. I was surprised she didn't ask for a retainer."

"I vouched for you." Grayson crossed his arms, deep in thought. "She's good, she doesn't have any direct ties around here, and she's had some experience defending Amish before. She was the obvious choice."

"But how did you know I would need a lawyer? She said you think I'm being railroaded?"

"This was a setup from the word go."

"Explain that to me."

Henry's eyesight was adjusting to the darkness. He could see that his friend looked tired, that he had three days of stubble on his face when he normally shaved every day, and that he'd walked through high weeds to reach him. The hems of his jeans were covered with bits of brush.

"I'm not even sure I can explain it to myself. Look, you placed the emergency call to 9-1-1 at 7:25 on the morning of September 21."

"Sounds right."

"I was on scene by 8:10. We talked, and you left."

"Stuart brought me home. I got here a little before ten."

"Right, but Agent Delaney called before I had even left the crime scene."

"Is that unusual?"

"You bet it is. Usually we assess a scene, and if we decide it falls under another jurisdiction, we make the appropriate calls. I was planning to contact him as soon as I got back to the office."

"But he called you first."

"How did he even know about the case? When I asked him, he changed the subject, started asking me questions about who I had interviewed so far."

"Which was me."

"I hadn't even been to the diner yet."

"All right. So Delaney gets tipped off about the case somehow, and he takes it over before you've had a chance to make a call or file a report."

"He stayed on scene until late that night, Thursday, and we came to see you early Friday morning."

"The day I found the device."

"What device?"

Instead of answering, Henry pulled out the small electronic object he'd discovered in the wall clock. He put it in Grayson's hand and explained how he'd found Lexi unconscious in the horse stall and how when she came to, she'd led him to the device.

"What happened to it?"

"I smashed it with a hammer."

"Obviously."

"Wasn't sure what it was, but I didn't like the idea of it doing whatever it was supposed to do inside my house."

"Next time take it to the barn."

"I hope there won't be a next time."

Grayson grunted in agreement. "I don't like this at all."

"What is it?"

"A surveillance device, and a fairly sophisticated one, by the looks of it. Can I keep this?"

"Of course."

"Tell me about how you found Lexi."

"She was in the stall with the door shut, something I take care not to do. She looked as if she was sleeping, only I couldn't wake her."

"Any sign that she'd been kicked or hit?"

"*Nein.* No bumps at all. She was simply out, and then she wasn't."

"It sounds as if she was drugged."

"Why would someone drug my dog?"

"The better question is why they didn't just kill her, though you might have reported such a thing to the police."

"Why put her in the stall? Wasn't it enough to drug her?"

"Maybe they were sending you a message, Henry. What we know for certain is that someone was here, at your place, and left this surveillance device. Someone's watching you, Henry."

"Who?"

"The same person trying to frame you for Sophia's murder."

That sat between them for a moment. Henry braced his elbows on his knees and stared at his dog. Finally he said, "You were telling me about Delaney. About the day he came back to collect evidence."

"I was not happy with how the previous interview had gone. Delaney was jumping to conclusions, which isn't like him."

"He's an aggressive sort of fellow."

"True, and he always has been. I've worked with him on a couple of other cases. He's blunt and forceful, but he's also always been methodical. With you it was as if he had information he wasn't sharing, some reason to believe you were involved."

"But I wasn't."

"Of course you weren't."

"How can you be so sure?" Henry asked softly.

"Because I know you, Henry. I have enough instinct to know who is and who isn't a killer, and yes, I understand that people can fool you sometimes. But I know you, plus killers rarely call police to the murder scene. Nothing about what Delaney was assuming made sense. After we left here, I called him on it."

"I can imagine how that went."

"Not well." Grayson pulled off the ball cap and ran a hand over the top of his head. "There's more. An hour after we left here, I received a call from my supervisor telling me I'm required to take a vacation every year, and I haven't done so in the last twelve months."

"Is that true?"

"Yes, but no one has ever called me on it before. I eventually get around to using my time. I was basically relieved of duty. I was told, in no uncertain terms, that I was to let Delaney handle the case, and that I should not report into the station for fourteen days."

"Does that mean your supervisor is in on this, whatever this is?"

"Not necessarily, but it does mean someone has the ability to remove me from the case."

Henry tried to wrap his mind around everything Grayson was saying. Lexi had hopped up on the bench between them and was leaning against him. He placed his arm around her and scratched under her chin.

"Delaney somehow found out about the investigation from another source."

"Someone who wanted him on it. That's what I'm thinking."

"And for some reason he zeroed in on me."

"From what I heard—"

"Heard from whom?"

"A few guys at the station I'm in touch with. From what I heard, Delaney got your name from the tip hotline."

"I guess that's possible. I did know Sophia, and I did give her a ride in my buggy."

Grayson was shaking his head vehemently. "No way. Those tip hotlines receive all sorts of calls, and it takes days at the very least to comb through them. They help the most with cold cases highlighted on a news program or in local papers. None of that had happened with your case. The chances of Delaney receiving a tip, an actionable piece of information in that time frame, is almost nil."

Henry didn't answer right away. He knew Grayson was his friend, and he trusted him to have his best interests at heart, but he didn't want to misinterpret. Finally he stood, faced Grayson, and asked, "Are you saying Agent Delaney is involved in this?"

"I'm saying he could be. Until we find out for certain who the murderer is, who had cause to want Sophia dead, I want you to stay out of it. Lie low."

"Lie low?"

"Stay here on the farm."

"I'm a bishop. I can't hide out here. People in my church need me. I have visits to make and church business to attend to."

Grayson wasn't listening, though. "I'd rather you didn't live alone, but since you do... Any chance you'd consider keeping a cell phone on you?"

"I will not."

"Figured as much."

"Don't worry about me. *Gotte* is my protector, and I have Lexi." Henry's dog scratched at her collar, lost her balance, and fell off the bench. She wasn't exactly giving the impression of a guard dog.

"Henry, this isn't a lone person who has a screw knocked loose."

"Like last time."

"This person is nothing like the Monte Vista arsonist. Whoever did this is someone with resources and friends within the law enforcement community. This is big, and I'm going to figure it out. But I need a little more time, which means I need you to stay out of it."

"I'm afraid that's impossible." And then Henry told the sheriff about Sophia's sister, the drawings he'd done, and the computer device Emma had gone to fetch.

Forty-Eight

When Emma, Tess, and Katie Ann arrived at the farm, they hurried up the porch steps and into the house. Emma introduced Tess to the boys, and then she rushed to the mudroom to search through the dirty laundry.

Years earlier, Clyde had hammered together a string of bins—one for heavily soiled clothes, another for whites, and a third for towels and sheets.

"I remember now. I hadn't washed the apron yet because I was still trying to decide whether to try to mend the hem or use the fabric for a quilt, not that it would matter. Either way it needed to be washed."

Stephen and Thomas hadn't been remotely interested in their *Englisch* visitor. They remained on the sitting room floor, engrossed in a game of checkers. Silas met them at the door, one question tumbling over another. Katie Ann briefly filled him in on what had happened, and then they followed Emma into the mudroom where the washer was. Tess stood clasping her hands in front of her. Silas crossed his arms and looked ready to take on anyone who threatened his family. Katie Ann hovered in the background, a look of concern on her face.

Emma was tossing everything from the white clothes bin onto the floor.

"I have no idea how we can have so much laundry when we just did laundry earlier today. We do laundry every Monday. Where does it all come from? Why wasn't it here this morning when we were tackling it after Henry's hearing? Some days I think the boys purposely hide their dirty things and then fill up the basket after we're done. Must be some strange form of entertainment to watch my eyes grow wider with each piece of soiled—"

Emma stopped rambling and leaned forward to fetch the last item out of the bin.

"Is that it?" Tess asked.

"*Ya.*"

"Is the flash drive there?"

Emma's hands were shaking as she searched first the right pocket and then the left.

"*Nein.* It's not."

"But you said—"

"I know. It should be here. I remember slipping it into my pocket when Sophia gave it to me."

Katie Ann had moved into the room and was watching her grandmother and Tess. "Then it has to be there."

"But it's not." Emma wanted to sink to the floor and bury her head in her hands. She'd been so sure the device was in her apron pocket. Had she remembered wrong? Had she remembered what she wished had happened instead of what had actually happened? Had Sophia given her the small device, or had she dreamed up the entire thing?

Katie Ann brushed past her and practically crawled into the bin. She leaned so far into it, nothing was visible but the back of her dress and the soles of her shoes. When she emerged, she was holding up a piece of plastic no larger than a clothespin. "Is this it?"

"Yes," Tess said, her voice softer, disbelieving, but wanting to believe. "That's it."

"Must have fallen out of your pocket, *Mammi.* It was in the far corner of the bin."

"Would you like to look at it here?" Emma asked. "With your computer? I think Henry would say it's okay this once."

"No. Once I open whatever is on there, I'm going to want to sit and read it all the way through. And as I said, we might need the Internet too."

Katie Ann placed the device in Tess's hand. "I hope it has the information you need."

Tess nodded solemnly, and then she began walking toward the front door. She turned back to Emma suddenly, nearly bumping into her. Emma had her purse slung over her arm.

"You should stay here," she said. "Stay with your family."

"Katie Ann will do that."

"*Ya*, of course I will."

"I'm going with you. It's better if you're not alone for such a thing, and you don't even know where the diner is."

"It's a small town, Emma. I'm sure I can find it."

"We'll go together. Unless you'd rather be alone?"

Tess glanced up at her, and she had such an expression of vulnerability on her face that Emma's heart went out to the young woman. She'd been through so much in the last couple of months, and then to learn of her sister's murder, to realize her brother-in-law's death wasn't the result of a mugging, to now feel responsible for finding the killer who'd probably ended both their lives? That was a lot for one person to shoulder.

"I would like for you to go with me, but I was trying to be polite."

Emma nodded, and then she turned to Katie Ann and Silas. "Tell your parents I might be late, and they shouldn't wait up."

"Are you sure that's a *gut* idea?" Silas asked.

"We'll be fine. We'll be in the diner. No one would hurt us there."

"Okay," he said, though his tone lacked conviction.

Emma was at the door when Katie Ann called out, "Promise to be careful."

"Of course."

As they stepped outside, Clyde pulled up in the buggy.

"Did you find it?" he asked.

"*Ya*. We're going to the diner now. Don't wait up for me. Tess or Henry will bring me home when we're done. You need your sleep."

"Be careful, *Mamm*." Rachel hopped out of the buggy and embraced Emma.

It was nice to have her family worry about her, but it wasn't as if she planned on going to search for the killer in the middle of the night.

She slid into the front seat of Tess's car, and they made their way back down the dirt lane, turned onto the county road, and then sped through the darkness.

Forty-Nine

Henry pulled his buggy onto the blacktop, his thoughts swirling with everything Grayson had said. What did it mean? Who had the means and the ability and the motive to misdirect a federal investigation? Why would they do so? That one was obvious—so their own actions wouldn't be scrutinized. Which meant the killer had to be in a position of authority, or he had a close relationship with someone in authority. Either way, that significantly increased the danger and difficulty they were up against.

He was less than a quarter mile down the road when he became aware of flashing red lights behind him. He pulled on Oreo's rein, guiding her onto the shoulder, and waited.

The night was quiet except for the heavy breathing of the mare and footsteps walking toward him in the darkness.

Agent Delaney flipped on his flashlight, momentarily blinding Henry. "Was I speeding, Officer?"

Delaney didn't so much as smile. "I'm the special agent in charge of this investigation, not an officer." He redirected the light and craned his neck to see better into the buggy, not that there was much to see.

An old towel lay across the passenger side of the front seat. He'd placed it there for when Lexi rode with him, but despite his concern for her, he'd decided it was more prudent to leave her at home. He had no idea how long he'd be gone, and he didn't want her waiting in the buggy for hours on end.

Agent Delaney turned his cold blue eyes to study Henry. "Rather late to be out, especially for an Amish person."

"But not against the law."

"I didn't say it was." He smoothed down his black tie.

No other vehicles were on the road, and they were still a few miles from town. Henry thought of Grayson's assertion that Delaney might be involved. Henry had personally come face-to-face with two murderers before. They hadn't shared any common characteristics. He wouldn't have known they were capable of taking another life just from their physical appearance. What about this man standing before him now? How could he possibly know if the person in charge of the investigation was working with them or against them?

"I'd be careful, Mr. Lapp. We can trace you with the monitor you're wearing. We can follow anywhere you go."

"I'm aware."

"We're building a case here."

"And it's my hope you'll be successful doing so. You'll have to change the focus of your investigation, though, if you hope to find Sophia's murderer, because I most certainly did not harm that girl."

Delaney stared at him silently. The look on his face said that he did not believe Henry was hoping they'd find the killer. The look—practically disdain—said he was convinced Henry was the guilty person.

"Why do you think I would do such a thing?"

"I've learned not to doubt what people are guilty of."

"And yet you must have some evidence pointing you to me. I'd like to know what it is."

"Your lawyer will be made aware of it during the disclosure portion of the trial."

"But what if we could solve the murder before then, before this person hurts someone else?"

"Oh, I'll make sure that doesn't happen, because we're going to be watching you night and day."

"A waste of your resources since I'm innocent."

"The trial will determine your innocence or guilt. The only reason I'm still here is to collect more evidence and oversee your transfer into federal custody." He leaned in, as if sharing a secret. "It's possible the judge may have believed your lawyer's spiel about you not being a flight risk. Or maybe, like me, he wanted to give you a little rope to better hang yourself."

"Hang myself? I assure you I have no intention of incriminating myself in any way."

"And yet you're on this road, late at night, rushing off to something rather urgent by the way you were hurrying down the road."

"Again, not against the law unless I was speeding. Was I speeding, Agent Delaney?"

"I've worked more than two hundred cases, Mr. Lapp. When a guilty party—"

"Which I'm not."

"When a guilty party feels the pressure, we typically see three responses—fight, flight, or freeze. We're simply waiting and watching to see which you choose."

Delaney stepped away from the buggy and flicked his hand as if to indicate he was done with the conversation.

Argue with a fool, and someone watching might not be able to tell the difference.

As far as Henry could tell, no one was watching, but he was beginning to think Delaney was a fool. He followed his mother's advice, the old proverb ringing in his ears, and chose not to further engage the man. Instead he called out to Oreo.

The horse trotted down the road, and Delaney followed, making no attempt to hide his surveillance. Which was fine. All he would see was a meeting at a diner, and it wasn't as if he'd be able to listen in on the conversation.

Fifty

The bright lights of Maggie's Diner spilled out into the night.

Henry guided his buggy to the side of the building and then hurried into the diner. He paused to nod once in the direction of Agent Delaney, who had pulled to a stop in front of the building. From the angle of his vehicle, he seemed to have parked so he could see what went on inside. For some reason it was important to Henry that Delaney understand he knew he was being watched and that he wasn't intimidated by that. He had nothing to hide. He was tempted to invite the agent in to join them.

Emma and Tess were already sitting at a table on the far side of the room. Henry took the seat opposite Emma, beside Tess. On the chair opposite Tess was the bag with his drawings. He was glad someone had thought to bring them. They still might contain a clue, though he couldn't imagine what—other than what the Fisher family had already pointed out. Some people appeared in more than one picture. The waitress had brought coffee for each of them, and she said to wave her down if they decided they wanted anything to eat.

Henry gave them a detailed account of his encounter with Delaney.

"He might be listening," Tess admitted. "I haven't made it a topic of research, but crime shows on television show they can with parabolic microphones and that sort of thing."

When Emma and Henry only stared at her, she shook her head. "Don't worry about it. We can't allow ourselves to be concerned with him right now. We need to focus on finding Sophia's killer."

"Except there's a small chance Delaney is involved," Henry said, his voice low.

Emma choked on her coffee, and Tess stopped typing on her computer.

"Say that again." Tess closed the top of the laptop and waited, her hands folded on top of it as if in prayer.

Though he had no idea what a parabolic microphone could or couldn't pick up, he told the two women about finding Grayson near his barn and shared a concise version of what the sheriff said.

Quiet descended over the table as the three took a moment to assess what they were up against. Finally, Tess shrugged and opened the computer. "Whether he's in this or not, I still think the answers are on the flash drive. Why else would Sophia have left it with Emma?"

"I don't understand why she would leave anything with me. She barely knew me."

"But she trusted you. She trusted you both. That much is obvious."

Tess pulled the flash drive from her pocket and slipped it into a slot on the side of the computer. Henry locked eyes with Emma. He wasn't sure what Tess hoped to find on the device, and he held little hope that Sophia had known the person who murdered her. If she had, she could have avoided being anywhere near him or her. But she was caught by surprise, so how could what was on the device be of any help?

Emma reached across the table, touched his arm, and pointed toward the front door.

Jared Anderson had walked into the diner, stopped, and was staring in their direction. But he didn't approach their table. Instead, he said something to their waitress, and she led him to a booth on the other side of the room.

"Maybe he's here for the pie," Emma said.

"Or Delaney sent him in here to watch us."

Tess glanced up at Anderson, momentarily distracted from whatever was happening on her laptop. "He seemed kind and sympathetic when I met him earlier, but he was so convinced of your guilt. I'm sorry you've been caught up in this. I know you didn't kill Sophia, and I regret that this has disrupted your life."

"You have no need to apologize," Henry assured her.

Officer Anderson didn't try to hide the fact that he was staring their way. He did place an order with the waitress without even looking at the menu.

"He was in three of your pictures." Emma turned her coffee mug around in her hands. "Do you think that's significant?"

"Could be. Or it could be a coincidence."

"But what would his motive be? Why would he want to kill Sophia? She was a quiet girl. She didn't cause any trouble. I just can't imagine why anyone would want to harm her."

"It has to all go back to Cooper," Tess said. "He discovered something, maybe by accident. And whoever was involved was afraid he'd expose them."

"Maybe Cooper confronted whoever it was." Henry was speaking to Tess and Emma, but he continued to watch Officer Anderson. "Maybe he threatened to turn the evidence over to the authorities."

"It's possible," Tess said, agreeing. "Cooper wrote for nature magazines. He'd been doing it for years, making a modest living, and then recently he hit it big. He had feature pieces in *National Geographic*, *National Parks*, *National Wildlife*, and one in *Scientific American*. Sophia told me he had more work than he could handle. He was turning down assignments."

"He must have been very *gut* at what he did," Emma said.

"He loved nature, and he loved sharing it with the people who read his articles." Tess blinked rapidly.

It hurt Henry to see the woman so distraught, so desperate to find the person guilty of her sister's murder. None of them were detectives, and the only thing that connected them was an affection for Sophia.

"He thought we were on this too much." Tess tapped the laptop. "He would tease both me and Sophia about it. She was a blogger, and so all of her writing was done on the computer. It was never actually printed."

"And what do you do?" Emma asked.

"Analyze funds—stocks, things like that. Mainly my work is for large groups of investors, like teacher unions. It's why I live in New York City, though I suppose I could do it anywhere. Being in the city puts me close to the action." She shook her head. "It's as far from what Cooper and Sophia did as night is from day."

She returned her attention to her laptop and tapped away for a few minutes. Henry had been trying to remember what was in the drawings he'd done. Anderson had been in three—he was sure Emma was right about that. But what had his expression been? Was he staring at Sophia or past her? He was just about to ask Emma to pull out the drawings when Tess sighed in frustration.

"Problem?" he asked.

"Yes. Look for yourself."

Emma brought her chair around so Tess was sitting between her and Henry. She was staring at the monitor. A cursor blinked inside a small box in the middle of the screen. Above the box, in red letters, were the words *Invalid Password.*

"What does that mean?" Emma asked.

"Sophia locked the files with a password, and I can't access them unless I can guess what that password is."

"Do you have a limited number of guesses?"

"I don't think so. If I did, then it would say something like 'three tries remaining.'"

"All right. So we only need to think of the password. Would it be something obvious like her birthdate or name?"

"I tried those. Even tried her address and the address of our family home. None of those worked. It could be anything."

"Let's make a list," Emma said. "Otherwise you'll forget what you've tried."

She pulled a receipt and a pen out of her purse, and they began making a list on the back.

That's what they were doing when the waitress who had brought them coffee returned, only this time she wasn't there to ask for their order.

"Are you Sophia's family?" The woman's name tag said *Julie.* She was nearly as round as she was tall, with gray hair cut just below her ears. Lines spidered out from her eyes and mouth. Henry couldn't guess whether they were laugh lines or worry lines. At the moment, though, she definitely looked worried—or if not worried, then concerned.

"I'm Sophia's sister," Tess said.

"My name's Julie. Julie Hobbs. I wanted to say how sorry I am. Sophia was a good worker. I'm the manager here. I'm the person who hired her. She kept to herself, but she never caused any trouble. What happened to her was terrible."

"Thank you," Tess said, her voice a mere whisper.

"I'm about to go off shift," Julie said. "I don't want to intrude, but if you have a moment, I'd like to talk to you about Sophia."

"Do you know who might have wished to harm her?" Henry asked.

"No. I don't. But I knew something was wrong, and then it seemed like people were too interested in her. Do you know what I mean?"

Henry and Emma and Tess all nodded their heads simultaneously.

Julie glanced up and across the room. "I have to take care of my tables, and then I'll clock out. I think you need to know—you deserve to know—about the people who were following Sophia."

Fifty-One

Ten minutes later, Emma had moved her chair back to its original place and placed the bag with the drawings on her lap to make room for Julie. The manager quickly and succinctly told them about Sophia's time at the diner and how, over the last six weeks, she had come to view Sophia as a younger sister. She and the other waitresses had also gone out of their way to protect her.

"You're sure about this?" Emma glanced around the diner. Officer Anderson had apparently received a call, because he'd left after eating only half his meal. He'd pierced them with one final glare before hurrying out to his squad car. No other officers were currently in the dining room.

"Am I sure about Anderson? Yes, I'm sure. We rarely saw him here until Sophia started working, and then we saw him nearly every day she was scheduled. I don't know how he knew when she was working. It's not as if she had a car she parked out back or anything."

"You don't think it was a coincidence?" Henry asked.

"Could have been, I guess. Except if he came in and she wasn't working, he always acted as though he was just stopping by to get a cup of coffee to go. I teased her about it once. Said maybe he had a crush on her or something, but Sophia looked scared at first and then angry."

"Did she speak to him about it?"

"No. Not that I know of. In fact, we kind of ran interference for her."

"What does that mean?" Emma asked.

"If Anderson sat in her section, we'd tell her to go on break, or we'd pretend she was very busy and one of the other waitresses would take his order. It wasn't something we talked about or decided—we just did it. Waitresses…well, we kind of stick together."

Emma understood that. It was the same in Amish circles. If a man seemed interested in a woman, but that woman didn't return his feelings, then other women would try to make the situation less awkward. She supposed everyone had been the recipient of unwanted attention at one time or another. It was an embarrassing, uncomfortable feeling.

"All of us knew Sophia didn't belong here," Julie said.

"What do you mean?" Tess asked.

"Too smart. Too young. Too pretty." Julie rubbed her left hand with her right. Emma noticed that the knuckles of her left hand were swollen, probably from arthritis. Waitressing would be difficult at any age, but at Julie's age it must be particularly hard.

"We think she was investigating something," Tess admitted.

"Like what?" Julie continued to rub her knuckles. Emma had a jar of lotion at home that might help. She'd have to remember to drop some by.

"Her husband's death. He wrote for nature magazines, and we think he was killed because of something he stumbled across, maybe something he was going to write an article on."

"That's terrible." Julie thought a minute, and then she shook her head. "She never said anything about that. Sophia kept to herself. She wasn't rude or anything, but she didn't have a lot to say. Didn't talk about boyfriends or a husband. She never mentioned she'd been married."

Emma remembered the tattoo Henry had drawn. When he'd asked Sophia about it, she'd said it was her husband's initials and the date they met. But she hadn't volunteered the information that she was a widow until that conversation. She must have been a very private person.

Julie was staring across the room now, as if she was trying to remember something. Finally she said, "I guess I just thought she was some kind of nature buff."

"Why would you think that?" Henry asked.

"Because she moved here. Why move to Monte Vista unless you either have family here, know someone here, or you're interested in the mountains or the sand dunes or something to do specifically with this area? The times I gave her a ride, it was always out to one of the nature parks."

"You gave her rides?" Emma leaned forward as she picked up the pen—poised over the receipt where they'd been making their list of possible passwords.

"Yeah, a few times."

"Do you remember where, exactly?"

"Sure. The Alamosa, Monte Vista, and Baca Refuges, and one time to the Sand Dunes National Park."

Emma jotted down all of the names.

"Why would she go out there?" Tess asked.

"I don't know. When I'd ask, she'd shrug and change the subject."

"Did you tell all of this to Officer Anderson?" Henry asked. "Or Agent Delaney?"

"No. I didn't." A stubborn look settled over Julie's face. "I answered their questions. We all did. But offer information? Uh-uh. It seemed to me they'd already made up their minds who had done it, no offense intended."

"None taken," Henry said.

"We knew you couldn't have done it, Mr. Lapp. You have a good reputation in this town. Maybe you don't remember, but a couple of years ago a storm came through, and your people—your church people—came over and helped my parents put a roof back on their barn. Truth is, they shouldn't be on that farm at their age, but they refuse to move. The insurance was stalling and winter was coming, and we didn't know what to do. Some of your people showed up without anyone asking. And they didn't help only my parents, either. They provided assistance to quite a few of the families around here."

"We try to help folks when and where we can."

"People who help their neighbors that way are not killers. I don't mean to say you're perfect. We see the kids smoking behind the diner or driving jalopies that shouldn't even be on the road."

"*Rumspringa* is a difficult time for our *youngies*."

"My point is that most of us are glad you moved to the valley, and we don't believe you had anything to do with Sophia's death. If you ask me, find out what she was doing here, and you'll find out who would have wanted to kill her. And maybe if you could figure out why Anderson was so interested, that would help too."

"When you first came over, you said people were following Sophia, as in more than one."

"Anderson wasn't the only one. That new officer—Lawson—seemed to be watching her closely too. Of course, with Lawson it could have just been the normal interest a man shows a woman. He's new here and doesn't know that many people yet. I can't say why, but he didn't strike me as nearly as threatening as Anderson. Maybe that's just my own prejudices showing, though."

Julie peered out across the diner, which was emptying out. Emma was surprised to glance at the clock and see it was nearly ten. When had she last been out this late? But she wasn't a bit tired. She felt as if they were getting close to solving the mystery of why Sophia had come to Monte Vista. Finding her murderer wouldn't be quite so easy, and Emma understood that you couldn't solve a murder in one night. More often, you stumbled upon the answer—at least, that was how it had been with the Monte Vista arsonist.

She didn't even know if that was the reason she was here—to solve a murder. It seemed like a lofty goal. But she did care about Sophia and about Tess. She'd like to find the person responsible, to see justice served.

She was involved for another reason too. She was worried about Henry. What she wanted more than anything else was to prove his innocence. She wanted to provide him with an alibi, but short of that, they would just have to find who else could have been responsible. That was her goal, and she didn't care if it took all night to do it.

Julie leaned in and lowered her voice. "Twice, when I was giving her a ride, I noticed a dark-colored truck following us."

"What kind of truck?" Tess asked.

"Couldn't tell exactly. It looked as if it could be state park or national park or something else with a symbol on the side. I never had the right angle where I could make out the insignia or the make or license number."

"You're sure the vehicle was following you?"

"Yeah. It stayed back, but I could tell. The second time I took the long route and pretended I needed to pick up some dry cleaning, and that truck followed me into Alamosa and then back out again."

"And after you dropped her off?"

"Well, that was the strange thing. Both times, once I dropped her off, they turned down a side road and sped away."

"So they took a risk following you to know where she was going, but once they'd determined that, they didn't stay around to find out why."

"Or they already knew the why and didn't stay because it would have been too obvious."

"Did you mention it to Sophia?"

"I did…once. She shrugged as if she expected as much."

They all fell silent for a moment, digesting what they'd learned. Henry stared out the window, and then he turned back to Julie, a smile playing on his face. "A less serious question, but why is this place called Maggie's Diner?"

Julie laughed, and the lines around her eyes seemed to melt away. "My aunt's name. The crane festival started in the 1950s. She came with my uncle to see the birds, and a year later they'd sold their home and property in the Texas panhandle and moved here. She opened this place in 1957."

"Is she still around?" Tess asked.

"Turned ninety-four earlier this year, and she still comes to the diner now and then just to make sure we're doing things right."

There wasn't much to say after that. Tess thanked Julie for talking with them. Emma mentioned the hand lotion and said she'd bring some by the next time she was in town. Once the manager had left the table, they stared down at the paper where Emma had added *Alamosa, Monte Vista, Baca,* and *Sand Dunes* to the list of possible passwords.

"Do you have a place to stay tonight?" Henry asked.

"Yes. I have a room at the motel."

"All right. I think I should go home and wait on Grayson to show back up. He needs to know Anderson might be involved."

"And tell him about the truck," Tess said. "Her killer could have been someone working at the refuge. If so, then it might make sense that she was killed there."

Henry nodded, stood, and pushed in his chair. "Would you like me to give you a ride home, Emma?"

She looked over at Tess, who was now typing each of the possible passwords into the box on her computer. She'd stop after each attempt and scratch off the word on the list.

"I'll stay here with Tess."

"Thank you, Emma." Tess glanced up from the computer. "Thank you both, and I'll give her a ride home. We only have another hour until they close."

"All right. Be careful, and let's all remember to pray that *Gotte* will guide our steps and make safe our way."

As Tess resumed her process of trying passwords, Emma watched Henry walk out to his buggy. She couldn't be certain, but she thought she saw a brown pickup with some sort of emblem on the door pull out of the parking area across the street and follow Henry's buggy down the road.

Fifty-Two

The hands on the clock crept past ten.

Emma felt as though she wasn't being helpful at all. So she pushed their coffee mugs away and pulled out Henry's drawings. There was a clue in one of them. She was sure of it. Why did Henry have this ability if not to help others? Okay, perhaps it was sometimes simply to comfort their hearts, as in the drawing of the Kings' baby. But it could also be that God had given him this talent to help rid the world of evil.

That sounded a bit preposterous even to Emma.

But he had been drawn to Sophia. He'd felt a real calling to befriend her. Perhaps God had put him in the right place at the right time to make a difference.

"This isn't working," Tess said. "None of these are the password. It could be anything."

"What would you use?" Emma was staring at the drawing of Sophia in the diner, the one where she was helping the old woman.

"Usually some combination of numbers and letters."

"An important date or name. Something of significance to you."

"Exactly. Sometimes a combination of lowercase and uppercase, but always something easy for me to remember."

Emma's heart rate kicked up a beat. She could be wrong. She didn't want to get Tess's hopes up, but what did they have to lose?

She turned the drawing around so it was facing Tess, and she pointed at the tattoo on Sophia's wrist. "How about something like this?"

Tess reached out and touched the drawing the way she had when she'd first seen it on the kitchen table at Henry's house.

"It's amazing that he can draw with such detail. And you're sure it's accurate? The articles I read about him were right?"

"*Ya.*" She got up to sit beside Tess. "But what the articles probably didn't say, what the writers couldn't possibly have known, was that Henry struggled with his gift for many years. He felt it was a curse—not that we believe in such things."

"Why would he think something so amazing was bad?"

Emma considered her words carefully. She'd thought about this many times. She had prayed for Henry's acceptance of what to her was certainly a blessing. Through those prayers, she'd learned to also appreciate why and how he struggled.

"When Henry draws, he's not actually aware of what he's drawing. He's sort of on…"

"Autopilot?"

"*Ya.* That sounds right. His mind, his hand, simply reproduces what it has recorded."

"Every detail."

"And you can see how that might be a problem. He doesn't pick and choose what should or shouldn't be drawn. He doesn't…I guess he can't stop and consider how it might affect someone who looks at his drawing. Think about it. If you could freeze a scene and catch everyone's reaction, not what they wanted you to see when they know a picture is being taken, but their inner heart reaction."

"He reveals their emotions."

"Both *gut* and bad."

"I love this drawing of Sophia. It shows how much she cares about the old woman, and the look the old man and woman are giving her? It's almost heartbreaking. They're so grateful for her help, for her kindness."

"And yet this drawing is the same one that frightened Sophia. Henry thinks it's because he caught the scar on her neck, something she wasn't comfortable showing."

"Like I said before, I don't even know how she got that scar. It's recent. Certainly since Cooper died."

"Maybe she was trying to grow her hair out to cover it. Maybe she didn't want to have any defining marks someone could identify her by."

"Like a tattoo."

"Exactly." Emma studied the drawing, her mind sliding back to the night she'd met Sophia in the diner. "The few times I saw Sophia, she wore long sleeves, which isn't that unusual here in the valley in September, but I never would have guessed that she had a tattoo."

Tess touched the place in the drawing where her sister's sleeve had pulled up, revealing her wrist and therefore the tattoo. "Henry knew, though, and he drew it."

"His mind knew, which I guess is the same thing."

With trembling fingers, Tess entered the letters and numbers from the tattoo into the box on her computer screen—CB021412. The box disappeared, and in its place popped up a list of what Emma assumed were files. Both Emma and Tess stared at the screen, speechless, surprised that they'd finally found a way past the password screen.

Emma peered closely at the titles. "Looks like journal entries."

Tess clicked on the most recent entry—one dated two days before Sophia's death—and the screen filled with Sophia's final note.

> I'm lying here in Emma's house, listening to the sounds of this Plain family begin another day. Katie Ann already crept out of the room, no doubt trying not to wake me.
>
> When I first arrived in Monte Vista I was frightened and angry and determined. I'm no longer frightened. What else could they do to me? They took the person I loved the most in all this world. However, I am still angry. Why did something so unfair, so cruel, so unnecessary happen to Cooper? I'm angry that whoever did kill him no doubt continues to walk the earth. If so, why doesn't God strike them down? I suspect Henry would say God's ways are not our ways.
>
> My anger has made me even more determined than before. I now know Cooper was contacted by an informant who witnessed illegal activity in Glacier National Park. Cooper flew out to investigate. (All he told me was that he was on an important story—that this one could bring in big money and make a difference at the same time.) While at Glacier, Cooper caught someone who was on a low level within this "organization." He convinced the man to remain involved and feed

him information. He assured him that doing so would miti-
gate any future charges he might face.

I don't know why he didn't go to the police at that point.

I've read through his journal countless times. The code wasn't
hard to crack once I remembered the stories I'd told him
about Tess and me writing notes with our own secret language. Cooper used that code to ensure no one else could read
his entries. Because he took those precautions, I think he must
have realized what he was doing was dangerous. I also believe
he had reason to doubt the authorities. His level of caution
indicates this was/is a high-dollar operation with involvement
across law enforcement, corporate, and possibly judicial levels.

Once I'd broken his code, it was only a matter of rewriting the
entries to make sense of them. However, he was cryptic in his
notes, which has left some guesswork on my part as to where
the next meet is supposed to be. Only two more are scheduled,
so I have only two chances to get this right. The next pickup
is supposed to be at the Monte Vista refuge tomorrow night,
or before dawn Wednesday morning. I've gone back and read
his last entry. He left good directions. I'll find the spot today
and go back tomorrow night. I'll get the evidence Cooper was
after, and then I'll take it to Henry. He'll know who to trust.

If I'm even reading Cooper's journal entries correctly.

And if I've underestimated these people, and someone else
is now reading this journal entry, please finish what I started,
what Cooper started. Don't let his death be for nothing.

I'm going to save my journal to a flash drive and give it to
Emma. If it's safe anywhere, it will be here—on an Amish
farm.

Fifty-Three

Emma and Tess stared at each other, and then they both read the journal entry again. It wasn't long, taking up less than two pages of the document.

"That's where they killed her—at the Monte Vista refuge."

Emma nodded her head. Her throat was suddenly dry. She reached for her glass of water and took a long drink, and then she glanced up at the clock on the wall.

"Only fifteen minutes until they close. We could take this back to your motel room."

"We could."

"Or we could go to the authorities."

Tess shook her head, and Emma knew why. Could they trust the Monte Vista police? What if one or both of the officers showing an interest in Sophia had been involved in her murder? Emma didn't know how to contact Grayson.

Her hand trembling, Tess pushed a few buttons on the computer, and then they were looking at Cooper's last entry. To Emma it looked like gibberish. Tess switched over to Sophia's document and highlighted *I remembered the stories I'd told him about Tess and me writing notes with our own secret language.*

"Do you know what that means?"

"Yes." She closed her eyes for a moment, the barest hint of a smile playing on her lips.

"Is it difficult to translate?"

"No. It's surprisingly simple."

"It is?"

"Yeah. We used it when we were kids. Probably we'd read too many Nancy Drew mysteries." Tess pulled the receipt, which was now half full of failed passwords, toward her. Emma handed her the pen.

Glancing from Cooper's entry to the receipt, she quickly replaced the code with the corresponding letters.

Vjg hkpcn rkemwr…

The final pickup…

"See? You replace each letter with one two spaces before it. All the *v*'s are *t*'s. All the *j*'s are *h*'s. And so on and so forth."

There was no need to read the entire thing. The final paragraph of his entry told them what they needed to know, and once they'd read it, Emma understood there was no time to read more than that last portion. Cooper's last words said it all.

The final pickup will be at the Sand Dunes, three a.m. on September 26.

That line was followed by a lengthier description. By the time Tess finished translating it, a waitress had changed the sign to "Closed" and was beginning to lift chairs off the floor so someone could sweep and mop it.

"Just one more minute," Emma said.

"I'm here another hour, honey. Take your time." This waitress was thin, with dark skin, tired eyes, and a ready smile. Was she one of the women who had run interference for Sophia? Emma felt a sudden tenderness toward this woman she didn't know. She smiled her gratitude and turned her attention back to Tess.

"The final pickup is tonight."

"At least the final one he knew about."

"Right. Cooper included the directions, which he must have been given by the informant."

"But who was the informant?"

"I don't know. We might be able to work it out if we looked back through every entry. We should save that for later, though." Tess glanced at the clock. "We need to go. We need to go now."

"We don't even know what they're picking up. What could that phrase even mean?"

"It doesn't matter. Whatever it was, they were willing to kill for it. Which is why we need to go there. We need to find out." Tess shut down the computer and started to stuff it into her large shoulder bag. She froze suddenly, the laptop still gripped between her fingers. "What am I saying? I can't ask you to go with me."

She pulled the computer back out of the bag and pushed it into Emma's hands. "Keep this. If something happens—"

"Uh-uh."

"Listen to me, Emma—"

"*Nein.* You're not going alone."

"But Emma—"

"I can't let you do that, Tess."

"It could be dangerous."

Emma thought about that. She remembered Sophia walking away from their home, down the lane, headed to find the exact location of the pickup at the Monte Vista Refuge. She couldn't have realized it would also be the place of her death, though she must have feared that what had happened to Cooper would happen to her. She didn't let her fear stop her, though. The result was that the people behind this operation had committed murder yet again.

What were they protecting? Why would they be willing to go to such lengths? How could they justify murdering perfectly innocent people?

Emma shook the questions from her mind. "Promise me we won't confront them."

"Of course not."

"You'll use—" She waved her hand at Tess's phone. "Use your phone. Do something with that."

"I can take pictures or even stream a video."

"Whatever. We go in, go to the last place Cooper described—"

"His description combined with Sophia's code makes it so simple. I'm sure we can find it."

"We'll find the spot, gather some evidence, and then we'll skedaddle."

In response to that, Tess dropped the computer into her bag and held up her hand, palm out. Emma slapped it as she'd seen *Englischers* do. It felt rather silly but also good. It felt right to be involved in something that could rectify one of the wrongs in the world. They couldn't bring Sophia or Cooper back, but they could do whatever was within their power to stop anyone involved in their deaths.

Tess tossed enough money on the table to cover their three coffees plus a generous tip.

They hurried out the door, its bell chiming as they stepped into the night.

Emma glanced left. Tess glanced right. The parking lot seemed to be empty. No police cars or mysterious dark trucks. No one watching their next move. In fact, the main street of Monte Vista was empty. The town was tucked in for the night, everyone snug and warm at home. Everyone except Sophia's killer.

And Emma and Tess—two women on a mission for justice.

Fifty-Four

Henry had unhitched Oreo and set her to graze in the pasture. Lexi greeted him as if they'd been separated for weeks instead of hours. It was late, but Henry found himself wide awake, his mind spinning with everything he'd learned in the last twelve hours.

Sheriff Grayson was certain there was a conspiracy. Special Agent Roscoe Delaney might or might not be involved. The files on Sophia's small computer device were password protected. Tess was certain the person who killed Sophia had also killed Sophia's husband, Cooper.

Henry wasn't sure how to contact Grayson, but he wanted to talk things over with the man and see if he had any additional insight.

He'd walked back out to the barn and was now sitting on the bench, the same place he'd sat with Grayson a few hours earlier. Lexi waited patiently at his feet. She stared at him for a moment, as if she were questioning why they were outside instead of in bed. When Henry didn't explain, she turned in a circle three times and collapsed to the ground with a sigh. Five minutes later she was making doggie snore sounds.

As a bishop, Henry saw his fair share of the dark side of people, but rarely did that darkness lead to murder. It was the final step in a path away from God, or so it seemed to him. The taking of a life was a sin against nature, against man, and against the Almighty. It wasn't an unforgivable sin, but it separated man from his fellow man in a fundamental way.

And what could drive a person to such a thing?

Passion, instability, envy, revenge, jealousy, greed.

The person who killed Sophia had felt one of those things and had been willing to kill not just once but twice because of it. Moreover, there was a good chance the person was in the pictures Henry had drawn. He wasn't sure of that, but it felt right. Why else had God put him and Sophia on the same path? If, as Emma insisted, his ability was truly a gift from God, then perhaps God was again using him.

To solve a murder mystery.

An Amish bishop.

Henry shook his head at the absurdity of it all, but he didn't go to bed. He waited, somehow certain Grayson would return. The minutes ticked by, and Henry started to drift off himself when Lexi gave a low, menacing growl. Suddenly the little dog leaped to her feet, snarling and barking and darting back and forth from the corner of the barn to Henry.

"I thought you were training her," Grayson said.

"It's only been a few hours since we saw you last."

"Which means you haven't even tried."

"Not really."

Grayson sat down beside him with a groan. "Tell me why you're out here."

"We figured out a few things—Tess and Emma and I."

He detailed what the waitress had said about Officers Anderson and Lawson.

"I have a hard time believing either of those two could be involved."

"Because…"

"Lawson is new. I hired him myself." He sat forward, elbows braced on his knees, and rubbed his eyes.

"How long has it been since you slept?"

Instead of answering that question, Grayson said, "Though his application came to me in an unusual way. Lawson was requesting a transfer from another division in a different state. Everything was in order, and he interviewed well. Someone had written a note and stuck it on the top of the file. I can't remember who, but it must have been someone with authority. I interviewed him over the phone and offered him the job. We checked his references, and they were glowing."

"Could it be a coincidence that he transferred to your department so soon after Sophia moved here?"

"I don't believe in coincidences, but the spot was open because one of my officers retired. That had been planned for six months. Whoever is behind all of this couldn't have had anything to do with that."

"But they could have seen the opening—"

"And figured it would be a prime opportunity to put someone in my crew."

"Is that what you think happened?"

"No. I don't. I'm not discounting what the waitress told you, but maybe Lawson just had an infatuation with Sophia. She was a pretty woman."

"What about Anderson?"

"That one is a little more difficult."

"Why?"

"I don't like him. Never have, and that feeling has only grown stronger over the years. It's not that he's done anything wrong. He's something of a whiner. He'll do what I ask, but he makes sure everyone knows he's going out of his way to do it."

"He wants to be recognized."

"Maybe. He was never going to get a promotion. He knew that. He just doesn't have what it takes to lead other men, and he certainly isn't an investigator. His work is a little sloppy. I guess I'm saying he does the minimum amount of work required. He knows how not to get fired, but that's about it."

"Not a rousing recommendation."

"No, it isn't, but it doesn't make him complicit in a murder case either."

Henry stood and stretched, and then he told Grayson about his most recent encounter with Delaney. "Based on what you said earlier, either Agent Delaney is involved or he's being deliberately misled."

He studied Grayson, who had suddenly sat up straighter, squared his shoulders, and pushed his right fist into his left hand.

"You just remembered something."

"I did."

"Care to share it?"

"When the murder was called in, I didn't want Anderson working it. I didn't trust him to do things right. So instead I put him on the telephones. He would have been the person working the tip hotline."

Grayson didn't speak for a moment. Then he stood and said, "I have some people to call, a few details to chase down."

"And then?"

"I'm going to skip my immediate supervisor and hand this over to his boss, a man I've known since college and someone I trust."

"Do you have enough evidence to do that?"

"Not yet, but I will. Together he and I will decide how best to proceed."

"Is there anything I can do?"

"You've done enough. I want you to stay here, Henry. Stay on your farm, and nothing can happen to you."

"How can you say that with any certainty? They drugged my dog and left some sort of electronic device in my house."

"So they're watching you. That doesn't mean they're willing to trot over here and kill you. It would be too obvious. They wouldn't take that risk." He paced back and forth for a moment, as if he were testing a theory and deciding if it was sound. Finally, he turned to Henry and said, "They don't know you've figured anything out or that you found the device. No doubt they're hoping it simply malfunctioned. Stay here. Attend to your regular business, and hopefully we'll have that ankle bracelet off in the next twenty-four hours."

Which sounded pretty good to Henry.

Reaching into his back pocket, Grayson removed his wallet and pulled out a business card. "This has my personal phone number on it. Call me if there's anything I need to know."

He adjusted the ball cap on his head and turned to go, but then he turned back to Henry. "If you talk to Emma or Tess, tell them to stand down."

"Stand down?"

"Stay out of it. Tell them to stay out of it. I'll take care of this, but I don't want them running around playing sleuth. The people who killed Sophia and her husband are dangerous."

Henry knew Grayson was right.

Emma was a commonsense person. He imagined she was already home, tucked into bed and surrounded by her family.

He didn't know what Tess would do, but the woman had looked utterly exhausted at the diner. He hoped they'd called it a night. Tess had promised to give Emma a ride home, and he suspected she'd gone to her motel room after that. She'd be safe there.

Henry watched Grayson jog across his pasture, and then, a few moments later, he heard the engine of a truck turn over. In a short time, a dark-colored Ford passed down the road, illuminated by the lone streetlight.

What was it the waitress had said? The times she'd given Sophia a ride, they'd been followed by a dark-colored truck.

He momentarily wondered if Grayson could be somehow involved in this, but he knew that couldn't be true. Grayson was a good man. He was determined to help Henry despite his superiors ordering him off the job. It wasn't the first time, either. Grayson had helped Henry before. No, he couldn't be involved in what had happened to Sophia, though it was possible that the killer drove a truck similar to Grayson's.

"I'm jumping at shadows, Lexi." The little dog rolled onto her back, all four feet in the air. Henry gave her a thorough tummy rub and then motioned toward the house. "We should head inside. Old bishops and young dogs need their sleep same as anyone else."

Lexi looked disinclined to move. She lay there in the dirt, content and staring at Henry as if he should take a spot beside her.

"Come on, girl. Maybe there's a treat for you inside."

Lexi's ears perked up first, and then her tail began thumping. Finally, she bounded to her feet.

"There's no telling what tomorrow will bring, but hopefully it'll bring Sophia's murderer into police custody."

And with that happy thought, he hustled across the yard and into his house.

Fifty-Five

Tess had driven less than a mile when Emma said, "Pull over. There. In that parking area."

She turned the automobile into the lot and parked it next to the horse and buggy waiting there. The words across the front of the building, Bread 2 Go, were clearly visible by the parking lot lights, though the inside of the shop was dark and the sign hanging in the window had been turned to "Closed." Three ladies stood beside the buggy—Ruth Schwartz, Franey Graber, and Nancy Kline.

"Wait here. I need to speak to them."

"All right, but hurry, Emma."

Emma jumped out of the vehicle and jogged over to where her three friends were waiting.

"Emma. What are you doing out so late? And with an *Englischer* to boot?" Franey frowned at Tess's car. When Tess waved at her, she shrugged and turned back toward Emma. "Are you all right?"

"*Ya.* We were at the diner, and they closed."

"Of course they closed. It's past eleven." Nancy stepped forward and put her hand on Emma's arm. "I can tell something's wrong. What is it?"

Ruth clasped her hands in front of her. "We heard Henry was released. How is he doing? I can't imagine having to wear one of those awful devices. It's terrible that they would think him capable of such a thing, and after all Henry has done to help this community—"

"The *Englischer* is Sophia's *schweschder*." Emma didn't like interrupting Ruth, but then the woman could prattle on. "We're in a bit of a hurry."

"Hurry?" Franey squinted toward the car again, as if she could intimidate

Tess into jumping out of it and confessing whatever foolish errand they might be on. "Why? Where could you possibly be going at this hour?"

"Do you need help?" Nancy looked ready to climb into the back of Tess's car.

Ruth stood swiveling her gaze between the car and Emma. Her mouth gaped open, either surprised that she'd been interrupted or shocked that Emma was once again involved in a murder investigation.

"I don't have time to explain, but I need you to do me a favor. If I'm not back by daybreak, tell Henry and Clyde we've gone to the sand dunes."

"Henry?"

"Clyde?"

"Sand dunes?"

Emma almost laughed at the looks on her friends' faces. "We're chasing down a few clues."

"At this hour?"

"I don't have time to explain. Just say you'll do this one thing for me. Please don't worry them tonight. I think…that is, I hope to be home well before daybreak. Just stop by to check on your way into town in the morning."

"Not tonight?" Nancy asked.

"*Nein.* Tomorrow is fine."

"But Emma—"

"If I'm not back by morning, tell them we're going to the sand dunes where Highway 150 crosses Mosca Creek—one mile east and to the north of the creek. A trail there leads north through the woods to a clearing. Can you remember that?"

"*Ya.* Of course we can," Franey said.

The three women nodded their heads as one.

Emma was back at the car when she thought to ask, "Why are you three out so late?"

"Sold everything in the shop. Our shelves were bare, so we had to get a leg up on tomorrow's baking." Nancy's tone conveyed everything there was to say about how pleased she was about that. "Who knew *Englischers* liked fresh bread so much?"

"Who indeed?" Emma murmured, sliding back into the front seat and fastening her seat belt.

"You know those people?" Tess asked.

"*Ya.* They're *freinden.*"

"Friends?"

"*Ya. Gut* ones." Emma stared into the side-view mirror. Her friends hadn't moved. They were watching the car drive away, and Nancy raised her hand and waved. It was as if Emma were watching her life fade into the distance as she raced off into the unknown.

Tess accelerated as they headed east on Highway 150, the lights of Monte Vista fading in Emma's side-view mirror. No cars were following them, that was for certain. The evening was moonless, with only the light of a million stars and the beam from Tess's headlights to guide their way.

"Tell me about Sophia. That is, if you feel like talking about her."

Tess glanced at her and then stared out at the road, as if she needed to keep all of her attention on what was ahead of them. But Emma knew from experience that grief was easier to bear when it was shared. She'd needed to talk about her husband, George, after he'd died. Sharing precious memories with her son, daughter-in-law, grandchildren, and even Henry had helped to heal the aching places in her heart.

"Sophia was always the unconventional one," Tess said. "She didn't much care what other people thought."

"Give me an example."

"In high school, she would sometimes wear her hair in pigtails. No one did that. It was a hairstyle for third graders. Sophia would comb her hair into two pigtails, one on each side of her head, and tie ribbons into her hair—little slips of ribbon our mom had lying around her craft room. If anyone else had tried it, they would have been laughed out of the lunchroom. When Sophia tried it, you'd think she'd started a trend."

"She was popular?"

"In a way, though not like a cheerleader or anything. It's more that she was just fun to be around. She didn't complain a lot, and she wasn't as moody as most of us were. Being around her was encouraging. Even as we grew older, I'd call her when I was down, and by the time we'd finished talking..." Tess's voice grew soft. She cleared her throat once and then again. "By the time we finished talking, I would feel better."

"She sounds like a very *gut* person."

"She was." Tess smiled and darted a look at Emma. "Not that she was

perfect, mind you. One time she snuck out of the house to meet a friend—
they were going to walk across town to spy on a boy."

"Oh my."

"She wasn't even dating yet. It was like a middle school crush. When
my parents found out, Mom gave her a lecture, and Dad planted a rosebush outside her window."

"I might have to remember that one when my grandsons get older. I
suspect they're going to be a handful."

"She liked to read too much. And blogging?" Tess shook her head. "She
made an okay living, I guess, but Sophia was smart. She could have been
anything—a doctor or teacher or camp director. She was very good with
children. I always thought…I always thought she and Cooper would have
a houseful of kids."

And in that instant, Emma was reminded that Tess had lost more than
her sister. She'd also lost her brother-in-law and the chance to have nieces
and nephews. She silently vowed to pray for this woman long after their
paths parted.

"Your parents have passed?" Emma asked.

"A few years ago."

"I'm sorry, Tess. It sounds like you're alone, and I know it must feel that
way too. But you're not. I'm your *freind*. Henry is your *freind*, and I imagine many people care about you back in New York City."

Tess nodded, but she didn't agree or disagree.

The Sangre de Cristo Mountains loomed in front of them.

"How tall are they?" Tess asked.

"Thirteen thousand feet? Something like that. When we first moved
here, I loved looking at them on the horizon. I suppose, over the years, I've
stopped noticing them, but they are beautiful."

"We're going to find whoever did this, Emma. We're going to find the
people responsible for Sophia's death, and then we're going to make sure
justice is served."

Emma prayed it was true, but over the years she'd learned that justice
often took a different form than what she imagined.

Fifty-Six

Sophia's directions had been clear. Once they'd deciphered the code, it made perfect sense, and Emma felt confident they would find the right spot. They simply had to drive toward the entrance to the Great Sand Dunes National Park, slow where Highway 150 crossed Mosca Creek, and then pull over and park one mile east and to the north of the creek. They'd walk the rest of the way.

The dunes were the tallest in North America. Emma had been there once when the children were younger, when they'd first moved to Monte Vista. Since then, it seemed that the years slipped by, and there had been less time for sightseeing. Or maybe they'd taken the natural beauty around them for granted. Well, she had. Silas and Katie Ann managed to visit the dunes several times a year. Sometimes the teens would hire a driver and go on a day hike there when work on the farm allowed.

Being part of a high-altitude desert, the temperatures could be quite extreme. It was fortunate they were attempting to catch a killer in September. In the summer, the sand surface could reach 150 degrees, and in the winter, minus 20. Emma said a silent prayer of thanksgiving that they were chasing criminals in the moderate weather of fall.

A bobcat darted across the road, but Tess barely slowed down. She was focused on one thing—reaching the pickup point before Sophia's killers. And who could blame her? It was the last pickup noted in Cooper's journal. If they didn't catch whoever it was tonight, chances were they never would.

"I wonder if we should have alerted the police," Emma said.

"How could we? From the sound of it, only Grayson can definitely be trusted. And we don't know where he is or how to reach him."

"Surely there's someone else there we can trust."

"But who?" Tess glanced at her.

In the glow of the dashboard lights, Emma could make out the strain on the woman's face. When was the last time she'd slept? It had been less than a week since Sophia was killed, but Tess looked as if she'd been ravaged by worry and grief in that time.

"I don't know," Emma admitted. "Normally I would say Sheriff Grayson, but Henry had no way to contact him. Grayson told him he would be in touch, but that could be tonight or even tomorrow."

"And we couldn't wait." Tess ran her left hand up and down her right arm, as if she were cold, though the temperature was pleasant inside the car. "Thank you for coming with me, Emma. You didn't have to."

Emma let that observation fade into the night. There was no use in second-guessing what they were doing. The mountains now towered against the horizon. She couldn't so much see them in the darkness as she could sense that they were there. Looking out her window, she saw no stars, but if she craned her head and looked up, she could make out the band of light from the millions or even billions of stars that made up the Milky Way.

People thought the Amish didn't appreciate science, but that wasn't so. Rachel was such a reader, and the grandchildren had such inquisitive minds that books from the library were always lying around. Often they were scientific in nature. Just the week before, Emma had caught Clyde reading about snow and rainfall in the mountains and how the valley acted as a watershed for that precipitation. Amish didn't reject logic, but neither did they feel a need to question everything they saw. For them, it was a matter of balance.

"How big is this place?" Tess asked.

"Huge. More than forty thousand acres."

"And tall. The dunes are so tall."

"Seven hundred and fifty feet above the valley floor."

"How do you remember those things? Are you like Henry? Are you a savant?" There was a teasing note in Tess's question. Or perhaps it was nerves.

"*Nein*. It's easy enough to remember what my *grandkinner* tell me. Silas is interested in the resources of the area. He's a farmer—at least I think he will be. But he loves to go with his *freinden* to the different areas in the valley. He loves to be outside in nature."

"And he's visited this area?"

"Several times, and Katie Ann is always coming home talking about the elk, mountain lions, turkeys, and grouse."

"Anything dangerous?"

"Elk can be, and of course a mountain lion is a fierce but beautiful creature. Black bears have even been spotted in this area."

"Did you say black bears?" Tess jerked the wheel to pull her vehicle back squarely in their lane. "Black bears are dangerous, aren't they? Or is that brown bears? I can never remember."

"I suppose black bears can be. The thing to remember is that they're not sitting around waiting for people to pass by. Katie Ann says this area belonged to the animals first, and we're just visiting."

"She sounds like a special girl."

"That she is."

"Still, I wish I had one of those bells you wear around your neck to warn away the bears."

"It would be hard to sneak up on a murderer if you're wearing a bell."

"Good point."

"Plus, some people call those a dinner bell."

"How about bear spray?"

Instead of answering, Emma remembered something Silas told her the winter before. "Do you know how to tell the difference between black bear poop and grizzly bear poop?"

"Um...no."

"Black bear poop is smaller and contains lots of berries and squirrel fur."

"Ew."

"Grizzly bear poop has bells in it and smells like pepper."

"Not funny, Emma." Tess shook her head in mock despair, or maybe it was real despair. "I've never met an Amish person before, but if you'd asked me a week ago, I wouldn't have guessed that you'd be willing to chase a murderer or that you had a sense of humor. I might have given both of those things fifty-fifty odds."

Emma shrugged. Too many people watched television shows about the Amish, in her opinion. Watched them and believed what they saw there was true.

They were nearly to the spot where the directions indicated they were to turn off the road. Tess slowed and peered through the windshield.

"Despite the size of this place, Cooper had the spot exactly marked. The person he had on the inside, whoever it was, must have been well trusted in the organization to know these sorts of details."

"Someone who didn't approve of what they were doing," Emma said.

"But didn't know how to get out."

"So instead he, or she, shared the story with a journalist."

"Hoping to stop whatever is happening."

"But that story didn't stop them. It didn't even see the light of day as far as we can tell. It only resulted in Cooper being killed."

"Which would have been enough to send the informant scrambling for cover." Tess rubbed the tips of her fingers across her forehead.

They parked off the road on the shoulder. The clock on the dashboard read 12:22. If the pickup was at 3:00, then they had two and a half hours to get in place.

"Do you think it's okay to leave the car here?" Emma asked.

"Shouldn't be anyone else out. And I don't see that we have any option."

Emma knew she was right. And besides, if something happened to them, at least the police would find the car. She pushed that thought away. Nothing was going to happen. They were going to hide near the pickup point, take some pictures or video on Tess's camera, and then scamper back to safety. They got out of the car and searched the surrounding woods for a trail of some sort, but saw nothing. Tess started back at the far side of the road and walked more slowly, Emma inches behind her.

"There," Emma whispered.

Tess played the beam of her flashlight on the ground where there was indeed the faintest outline of a trail. "This is the spot. It has to be."

They set off at a slow but steady pace, down the trail and into the woods. Emma was grateful for her tennis shoes. The path was damp in places and rocky in others. She pulled her sweater more tightly around her. The temperature felt as if it had dropped at least ten degrees in the last hour. The trail widened, and she moved up to walk beside Tess.

"I'm not sure what we're expecting to see," she admitted, her voice a hushed whisper.

"Whatever they're picking up, that's what we're going to see. We're going to find out what this is about, what is worth killing people for."

"Sophia's husband included directions, dates, even times in his journal, but he never said specifically what is happening. Why do you think that is?"

"Three possibilities. Maybe he knew and wrote about it in a different journal entry—we only read a few. Or possibly he knew and didn't want to put it in writing yet. In case someone found his notes and could decipher them."

"And the last possibility?"

"He didn't know, at least not for certain."

"What about Sophia?"

"She figured it out, probably even had proof. That's why they killed her."

A shiver raced down Emma's spine, and it wasn't from the cold. She'd agreed to tag along because Tess was coming whether she did or not. Emma didn't think she could live with knowing that she might have somehow protected the young girl but didn't. She wished, though, that they had made the time to call one of the phone shacks and leave a message with someone other than the widows.

She'd told Clyde and Rachel not to wait up, but if either of them checked to see if she was home and found she wasn't, they'd be worried. And Henry would have no idea Tess hadn't taken her home.

"And we're only taking pictures? With your…" She waved toward Tess's phone.

"Or a video. That's all we need to do. Once we have the proof, I plan to send it directly to the news media. Then the investigators can come in and figure out the details, but they won't be able to deny it. I'll post it on YouTube if I have to."

"You who?"

"YouTube."

"I don't understand what that is."

"It's a video sharing site on the Internet."

"Ah." Emma had an overwhelming longing to be back home, where no one worried about phones or videos or tubes that shared videos.

They continued down the path for another ten minutes before Tess reached out and tugged on Emma's arm, bringing her to an abrupt stop. To their right was a small meadow. They crept through twenty feet of forest. Pine trees rose high above them, and the sound of a creek gurgled in the distance.

"This is it," Tess whispered as they reached the edge of the clearing. They stood there for a moment, staring and wondering what could possibly take place here. The area wasn't that large. It was bigger than the *Englisch* football field behind the high school, but not by much.

Emma and Tess pulled back, leaves crunching beneath their feet. They worked their way around the meadow to the opposite side and huddled in a grove of nearby trees. An owl hooted in the distance. Some small animal skittered across the ground. A light breeze stirred the trees.

Now it was a matter of waiting. According to the journal, the drop-off or pickup or whatever it was should occur at three in the morning. Emma hoped so, as she had to be home by four thirty to help prepare breakfast. Life on a farm paused for no man or murder mystery. Cows needed milking, regardless.

"I'm sorry," Emma said. "I'm very sorry about Sophia. She was a nice girl, a *gut* person."

When Tess didn't answer, Emma pushed on. "Catching the people responsible won't bring her back."

"I know that. I know it won't."

They were sitting side by side, shoulder to shoulder, under the cover of the pine trees. Emma felt the young woman reach up and brush at her cheeks.

"But it's the right thing to do." Tess's voice dropped to a low whisper. "These people…whatever they're doing, they're willing to kill for it."

"True."

"Which means they won't stop. They're likely to kill again."

"It's a definite possibility."

"And that's why we're here. To stop them."

Emma didn't answer that right away. How could she? Tess was right, but she also wasn't speaking to the heart of the matter. Whether or not they caught the people responsible for Sophia's murder, Tess would have to deal with the ache in her heart. She would have to decide if she wanted to focus on the bitterness she felt or on the love she had shared with her sister.

But Emma didn't say those things. She didn't think Tess was ready to hear them. So instead, she reached over and clasped Tess's hand in hers.

Fifty-Seven

When Henry reached the house, he didn't go straight to bed. He rinsed out a cup and placed it in the drainer, walked into the sitting room, and picked up the copy of the *Budget* he'd left on the coffee table. He folded it and placed it on the table next to his chair. The clock was ticking toward twelve, and he couldn't have said why he was still awake, why he was stalling, why he didn't want to give in to the draw of sleep.

He walked into his bedroom and Lexi followed, jumping up on the end of his bed and turning in a circle three times before settling down. "My *mamm* would have a fit if she could see you lying there, though now that I think about it, maybe she can. Who knows what those who have gone on before can or can't see?"

Lexi rested her head on her paws, but she kept her eyes locked on Henry.

"If she can see you lying on the end of my bed—something she would have never permitted—perhaps she also saw you help us catch the Monte Vista arsonist."

Lexi stared at Henry and whimpered softly.

"And then again, you found the surveillance device."

She shut one eye and continued to study him with the other.

"Given those two cases, I suspect her rules would have softened."

For her answer, Lexi closed her eyes and rolled onto her side.

Henry knew he should sleep. Most likely the next day would be even more trying than the last. It was clear they were closer to catching Sophia's murderer than Agent Delaney, probably because Delaney had stopped looking. In the agent's mind, he'd already caught Sophia's murderer.

Instead of dwelling on that, Henry's mind turned to Tess and the grief she must be feeling. Without making a conscious decision to do so, Henry did what was so often his habit when troubled. He slipped to his knees, bowed his head, and petitioned his heavenly Father on behalf of Tess. He prayed for her, for Emma, and even for Agent Delaney. He prayed for himself, that he might know how to comfort Tess and point her toward the truth of the gospel, and then he began to name each of the church members in their community, along with their needs and their blessings. He couldn't have said how long he talked to God, but his spirit calmed, and the anxiousness of his thoughts settled into an easy peace—a peace that passed all understanding.

Lexi's soft snores reminded him that morning would come as it always did—right on time regardless of his habits. He stood, knees popping, and reached for his nightclothes. After he changed, he climbed into bed and immediately sank into a deep sleep.

He dreamed of his mother, and she seemed to be trying to tell him something. Lexi was in the dream, too, rising up on her back legs, her front paws reaching for Henry, trying to catch his attention. Henry glanced back at his mother, who didn't appear to notice the dog at all. He thought that was rather odd. She'd always been a stickler about animals in the house. Surely she would say something one way or the other, but in the way of dreams, he couldn't open his mouth to ask her about it.

Her left hand was clasped around her waist and her right hand was urging him up, urging him on. He was momentarily frightened. But then he leaned closer, really studied her, and realized there was a solid assurance in her eyes, though she continued to urge him to get moving. He was trying to figure that out, trying to decide exactly what she wanted, when he was yanked from the dream.

Lexi bounded to her feet and began to bark as if the house were on fire. Henry sat up, disoriented at first, and then he heard the clatter of buggy wheels.

In the middle of the night?

Henry hushed Lexi as he pulled on clothes and shoes, grabbed his battery-operated lantern, and rushed to the front door. The time on the clock near the door said thirty-seven minutes past one in the morning. He stepped out onto the porch as the buggy pulled to a stop. He raised his lantern, and Nancy Kline tumbled out of the buggy.

"What's wrong?" Henry asked.

Of the three widows, Henry thought, Nancy had adjusted best to the changes life had thrown her way. Her disposition remained sunny, her words were never bitter, and she rarely complained. She was a good woman, and probably she was the glue that held together the group of three who had opened Bread 2 Go.

What was she doing here?

Lexi trotted over, smelled the horse, the buggy wheel, and Nancy's shoes before ambling toward a bush near the front porch.

"I didn't mean to alarm you, Henry."

"It's past midnight."

"*Ya*, I know."

"Come up onto the porch. Have a seat. You look—upset."

Nancy followed him up the steps and perched on the edge of a rocker. She glanced around and then reached up and patted her *kapp* into place, tucked in a few stray hairs, and clasped her hands. "She told us not to tell you. We were to wait until morning."

"She?"

"Emma."

"Is she all right?"

"She was. At least she seemed to be, but something feels wrong."

Henry set the lantern on the porch floor, turned the other rocker so he was facing Nancy, and sat down. He prayed it wasn't so, that Emma wasn't in danger. Perhaps Nancy was overreacting, though she was normally quite levelheaded about things. "When did you see her?"

"Several hours ago. The three of us were leaving the shop."

"I had no idea you work so late."

"Normally we don't, but we had to bake tonight. Business has been better than expected."

"I guess so."

"I took Franey and Ruth to their place—we ride in together, you know. It helps our families to use one buggy instead of three. I went home myself, but I couldn't settle down. I even tried some of that herbal tea Doc recommends. Finally I decided to come and see you, but the strange thing? Once I had the mare hitched up, she seemed to come here on her own." Nancy frowned. "Anyway, I'm here because of Emma."

"What about her?"

"I'm afraid she's in danger."

"Tell me exactly what happened."

"She was with an *Englisch* woman."

"Tess?"

"I suppose so. Emma said the woman is Sophia's *schweschder*, but I didn't see her myself. She stayed in the car."

"I left Emma at the diner earlier this evening. She was with Tess." Henry tried to understand what Nancy was telling him. "They were going to work on Tess's computer, and then she was going to take Emma home."

"I suppose something must have happened between when you left and when I saw them."

"They weren't going home?"

"*Nein.* They were headed to the sand dunes."

"*What?*" Henry shot to his feet.

"'Chasing down a few clues,' Emma said. She told us if she wasn't back by daylight to tell you and Clyde where they'd gone."

Henry paced back and forth. "They must have figured out the password."

"What password?"

"And whatever files were on the device must have pointed them to the sand dunes."

"Files?"

"Did she say anything else, Nancy? Anything more specific?"

"*Ya.* She did. She said they were going to the dunes, where Highway 150 crosses Mosca Creek—one mile east and to the north of the creek. And there's a trail to the north through the woods that leads to a clearing. But why would they go there? And is this about Sophia's murder?"

Instead of answering, Henry said, "Can you wait for a moment?"

"*Ya.* But Henry, do you think we should call the police?"

"Not yet."

Henry called to Lexi. The dog normally came to him immediately, except for the time she'd taken off after the arsonist. Now she hopped down the steps and stood facing in the opposite direction, her entire body on alert, tail wagging and nose in the air.

"Not this time, Lexi. In the house."

She gave him a reproachful look, but she obeyed.

"That is some little dog." Nancy shook her head in amazement.

Henry hurried inside. He wasn't waiting around for Grayson, and he didn't know who else he could trust in the police department.

No, this time he was on his own. He was going after Emma.

He scribbled a note for Sheriff Grayson and then folded it and stuck it in his pocket. He got the change from his dresser, snagged his hat from one of his cubbies and his jacket from a hook above the bins, and checked his pocket to be sure he had Grayson's card. "I'll be back as soon as I can," he said to Lexi. "And if I can't get back, I'll send someone else."

He closed the door behind him, careful not to lock it.

As their bishop, Henry felt he needed to talk to the widows about not working so late, but that conversation would have to wait for another time. It would seem all three women had a bad case of the entrepreneurial bug, not that being a business owner was bad. But Amish women did not work until all hours of the night.

"Let's go," he said.

"Sure, *ya*." They were in the buggy before Nancy thought to ask, "Where are we going?"

"You're going home for the night."

"And you?"

"Drop me off at the phone shack."

Fifty-Eight

The phone shack was close, easily within walking distance, but Henry was suddenly convinced a clock was ticking and there was no time to spare, no room for error.

"I'm happy to wait," Nancy said as she pulled in front of the small building.

"*Nein.* You go on home." Henry climbed out of the buggy, but at the last minute he turned back to Nancy and said, "You did the right thing telling me tonight."

"Will you call Clyde?"

Henry almost said yes, but then he shook his head. "Perhaps Emma was right. There's no point in worrying her family if they're simply running out there to check on a few clues."

"But why in the middle of the night?" Nancy's brow creased in concern. "And they're going to be worried anyway when she's not home."

"They know she was with me and Tess. Perhaps they'll think the two of them are working on the computer files at Tess's motel. Let's not cause a panic until we're sure there's cause for alarm."

Nancy nodded and waited until Henry had walked into the phone shack before calling out to her mare and setting her into a trot down the road.

Henry pulled in a deep breath, closed his eyes, and allowed the restored quietness of the night to calm his soul. What he'd told Nancy was true. She had done the right thing. But he hadn't mentioned that he felt a strong foreboding that Emma was in danger. There was no need to frighten the woman when there was nothing she could or should do about it.

He reached into his pocket, pulled out a quarter, and placed it inside the coffee can beside the phone. Then he picked up the receiver and punched in Stuart's phone number. Henry knew it by heart, and if he hadn't, then it was listed on the sheet of paper taped to the counter— all the *Englisch* drivers were listed there. Henry didn't need only a driver, though. He needed a friend.

Stuart answered the phone on the third ring, his voice gravelly from sleep.

"I'm sorry to bother you."

"Henry? What's wrong?"

"I need a ride, and I realize it's late. I'd be willing to pay more—"

"Obviously this is an emergency. Should I pick you up at your place?"

"*Nein.* The phone shack to the north of my home is fine."

Stuart hung up without asking another question, which said something about the man, in Henry's opinion. He realized relationships were not always smooth between Amish and *Englisch* drivers. Sometimes the *Englischers* mocked the Amish for being willing to ride in a car but not wanting to own one. Sometimes Amish didn't realize how rude they were being by speaking in Pennsylvania Dutch rather than *Englisch* while riding in the car. These things and more had caused some hurt feelings over the years, but they'd worked very hard in Monte Vista to cultivate a smooth relationship with those around them.

As Plain people, they felt called to remain separate, to live their lives differently, to put God and family first above all else. But they also needed to be an example of Christ to their community. Henry had felt passionate about this from the time he first became a bishop all those years ago. He'd impressed the same attitude on his church members regularly throughout his years of leading them.

The result was that the relationship between Amish and *Englisch* in Monte Vista was an amiable one. Often their *youngies* worked in *Englisch* businesses, and likewise the *Englischers* were happy to carry Amish-made items in their shops, such as the small pieces of woodwork Henry made. It was beneficial for everyone, and Henry prayed it would remain so.

As he sat on the doorstep of the phone shack, waiting for Stuart, he mulled over these things. The fact that Stuart had agreed to pick him up in the middle of the night, without knowing where they were going or why, said a lot about the man. His instinct had served him well. Stuart was more than a driver. He was a friend.

By the time Stuart pulled off the road, Henry was standing, waiting for the vehicle to come to a stop.

"*Danki*, Stuart," he said as he climbed into the truck and fastened his seat belt. The clock on the dashboard said two o'clock. He couldn't have said why, but he had a sense of sand slipping through an hourglass. He thought of the dream, of his mother urging him to move quickly.

"We're going to need to hurry."

"Where are we headed?"

"Sand Dunes National Park."

Stuart pulled back out onto the road and turned in the direction of the park.

"I appreciate your coming at such an inconvenient hour."

Stuart tucked his chin and stared at Henry over the top of his glasses.

"What? I can't thank a *freind*?"

"You can, and you're welcome."

He thought Stuart would say no more, but then he asked, "How long have I been driving you, Henry?"

"Years."

"Five years. I retired five years ago, and I had a crazy idea that I could drive Amish folk, have time to read while I was waiting, and adjust my hours to those of my wife."

"It's worked well for both of us."

"Your community has been very supportive." Stuart drummed his fingers against the steering wheel. "In all that time, you've always paid me fairly, or more than fairly, and you've never called me in the middle of the night."

"*Ya.* This is something of an unusual circumstance."

"Obviously. Which is why I came without question. I want to help if I can."

"But you don't know what you're helping with, Stuart."

To that Stuart grinned. "You know I love a good mystery."

"*Ya*, but it just occurs to me, if I tell you what's going on, then you could be aiding and abetting a fugitive." Henry pointed toward his ankle monitor. "Maybe I should have called a taxi."

"We both know there are no taxis in Monte Vista, and to call one from Alamosa? That would be terribly expensive."

"Indeed."

"You're always quoting proverbs to me, Henry. Want to hear one of my mom's favorites?"

"Sure, though I didn't realize *Englischers* have proverbs."

"We read the Bible same as you do, or some of us read it. Can't say I understand everything in there, especially not in the book of Proverbs. But this isn't from the Bible. It's just a saying my mom was fond of."

"Must be the way of mothers."

"This was it: In for a penny, in for a pound."

Henry was silent for a minute, and then a smile spread across his face. "And does that describe you? Are you in for a pound?"

"I am."

"Perhaps I should tell you what we're doing, then."

Fifty-Nine

When Henry finished recounting his visit from Grayson, Agent Delaney pulling him over, the impromptu meeting with Emma and Tess at the diner, the second visit from Grayson, and then Nancy's visit to his house, Stuart let out a long, low whistle.

"I thought you lived a Plain and simple life."

"*Ya*. I did. Until this."

"Uh-huh, and the other thing."

"*Ya*, that too. But in between the Monte Vista arsonist and Sophia's murder, things have been relatively quiet."

Stuart shifted in his seat as he peered into his rearview mirror. "No one's following us now. We have the road to ourselves."

"A *gut* thing, in this case."

"So what's your plan? You want me to just drop you off on the side of the road?"

"*Ya*, where Highway 150 crosses Mosca Creek—one mile east and to the north of the creek."

"And I just drive away and leave you there, where you might be in the crosshairs of a killer?"

Henry waved that thought away. "*Gotte* will protect me."

"Uh-huh. What about how God helps those who help themselves?"

"That one actually isn't in the Bible. Some scholars attribute it to Ben Franklin. Others say it originated from Algernon Sydney. Regardless, it's definitely not in the Bible."

"Never argue with a bishop."

"Indeed."

Stuart slowed a little as they neared the sand dunes.

"I'm not just leaving you here, Henry. Do you even have a weapon?"

"*Nein.* We're pacifists. We don't believe in carrying weapons."

"Do you mind if I ask why you're doing this?"

"Because Tess and Emma could be in danger."

"And why couldn't you call the police?" Stuart held up a hand to stop his protests. "Right. You don't trust them."

"I trust Grayson." Henry pulled the card out of his pocket and the message he had scribbled for the sheriff. The message was only two lines. *I've left to find Emma and Tess, who have gone to the sand dunes to gather evidence. They may be in trouble.*

He wondered, not for the first time, why he hadn't called Grayson from the phone shack. Why hadn't he called Grayson instead of Stuart? Because Grayson would tell him to stay home. As an officer of the law, he'd be obligated to insist that Henry respect the terms of his release from the Monte Vista jail. Henry understood the importance of that, but he needed to be with Emma. He needed to make sure she wasn't in any killer's "crosshairs," as Stuart had so eloquently put it.

But he didn't say any of that to Stuart. Instead, he handed him the card and the note.

"That's a message for Sheriff Grayson, explaining what I think has happened and what I plan to do, and on the card is his private number. Give him a call once you're back in Monte Vista."

"Why wait?"

"Because I need to do this, and I have no doubt Grayson will try to stop me."

"All right, but just to be clear, we're sure he's one of the good guys?"

"*Ya,* we're sure."

Stuart blew out a long breath as he pulled off the road, slowed, and came to a stop behind Tess's car.

"I don't feel good about this, Henry."

"Go home and call Grayson once you get there. He might not answer right away, but he'll call you back. You have a cell phone, right?"

"Of course."

"Tell him..." Henry stared out the window. He wouldn't ask Stuart to lie, but neither did he want Grayson immediately on their trail. Perhaps what Emma and Tess were after wasn't even in the woods near the sand dunes. Maybe they'd read the information on the small flash drive wrong. Perhaps they'd made assumptions that would prove, ultimately, to be unfounded.

There was another reason he didn't want Grayson hot on their trail. Grayson would be required to report to the authorities that Henry had fled outside his allowed zone. Perhaps the federal agents or the Monte Vista police already knew that because of a signal. Regardless, Grayson wouldn't be able to keep this between them. He had a job to do, and he wouldn't hesitate because of their friendship.

Grayson wasn't the one Henry didn't trust. He didn't trust who Grayson might be required to work with. At the very least, Grayson would have to alert Agent Delaney, and possibly Officers Anderson and Lawson as well. Henry didn't know which side of the equation those men were on.

He needed an hour's head start, maybe two, to figure things out. He needed time to back up Tess and Emma and to decide their next step before the official authorities became involved.

"If you don't mind—"

"Of course I don't. I'm here. Aren't I?"

"Indeed you are, and I thank you for that. Go back to my house. Once you arrive there, wait one hour before you call Grayson."

"But Henry—"

"I need you to do this for me, Stuart, and I need you to do it my way. Give me time to find Tess and Emma and convince them to come back to Monte Vista. I think...I'm sure I can persuade them to hand whatever information they've found over to Grayson."

"All right. One hour."

"Wait at my house. It will be easier for him to find you there. Also, if anyone else comes by with information for me..." He couldn't think who that might be, but the night had progressed well beyond his imagination already. "Tell them I said to give you the information. You decide what you should pass on to Grayson."

"Only Grayson?"

"*Ya.* He's the only one you can trust. Don't tell anyone else. Grayson said he'd be back as soon as he could, and it could be that he'll answer his phone before then. Wait for him and bring him here."

"Here—where? Henry, this place is huge."

"There's a trail there in the woods. I'm supposed to follow it to a clearing."

"I don't think you should—"

"I'm not going to let her die, Stuart. I'm not going to let either one of them die."

In the end Stuart had agreed, with a frown pulling at his face and the cryptic words, "Just be careful."

Henry had opened the door and was stepping out into the night when Stuart called him back.

"Take this." Stuart pulled a flashlight from the glove compartment and pushed it into his hands. "And Godspeed."

"May He be with you as well."

Henry stood for a moment, watching as Stuart turned the old truck around and then floored the gas pedal. As if getting back to Henry's place faster would hurry the time until he could call Grayson.

Henry didn't feel his age as he walked past Tess's car and made a right at the creek, following its bank until a trail diverted to the right. The time must be close to three in the morning, he was following a barely recognizable trail into the woods, and he might be approaching a killer. But none of those things bothered him at the moment.

His joints didn't hurt, he wasn't tired, and he felt sure that following Emma and Tess was the right thing to do.

Three things to be thankful for, and he was sure there were more.

If he lived to see the dawn, he'd commit himself to being more grateful.

Sixty

It felt as if they'd been sitting beneath the boughs on the pine trees for days, but Emma's watch assured her it had been only a few hours. The pickup was supposed to take place at three, and they both agreed this was the place described in Cooper's notes—or was it Sophia's notes? The events and discoveries of the night were all blurring together in Emma's mind. Nothing about this meadow looked special. It did not look like a place for illegal activity, a place to harbor criminals, or a place where a pickup of any sort would take place.

On the far side of the grassy area, Emma could just make out a few elk licking on a block of some sort. She supposed the rangers put them out to supplement their diet, though she couldn't imagine why they would need any source of food the area couldn't provide. Hadn't the wildlife been here for hundreds of years, long before man set up a visitor center and camping areas?

It could be a mineral block or a salt block, but she couldn't think of a good reason for either of those.

She was about to mention it to Tess when her thoughts were interrupted by the whir of helicopter blades.

They both instinctively ducked down, but whoever was in the helicopter wasn't paying any attention to the surrounding area. A large spotlight flashed on. It seemed to come from the underbelly of the helicopter and was focused on the elk at the far end of the meadow. As for the animals, Emma suddenly fully understood the term *frozen like a deer in headlights*. The elk, giant and majestic, looked incapable of moving. Before they could adjust to the light or respond in any way, someone leaned out of the helicopter and fired rapidly with a rifle. The smaller of the three elk stag-gered in a circle before collapsing. Another attempted to run, ramming headfirst into a tree and then falling to its knees. The largest of the three caused Emma to emit a strangled cry.

Every detail of what was happening stood out in marked contrast to the darkness around them. She had once visited Doc Berry when Katie Ann was assisting her as she performed minor surgery on a tabby cat. A bright spotlight had flooded the operating table with illumination, reveal-ing every detail of the cat's fur, the incision the doctor had made, even the drops of blood on the scalpel. Emma considered herself made of tough stuff, but she'd almost fainted at the sight of bright red blood on the stainless-steel blade.

Watching the elk stagger about, she was reminded of that small cat. Both animals seemed utterly helpless. The beast was huge, with impressive antlers and a reddish hue to its hair. It had also been shot, though Emma saw no blood. Perhaps they hadn't used bullets. The bull high-stepped in a circle, obviously disoriented, but he remained upright. In the circle of bright light coming from the helicopter, someone stepped out of the woods, raised a rifle, and shot again. Emma couldn't hear much because of the helicopter's rotating blades. It hovered there, waiting. The pilot made no attempt to land.

Emma thought maybe she'd fallen asleep and was imagining things. This couldn't be happening. It was like a bizarre dream that made no sense. But the evidence was right in front of her.

The helicopter was real. The armed men were real. They still waited, rifles raised, as if they might need to shoot the animal again.

The bull elk was certainly real. It stood and barked, reminding Emma of Henry's little dog. Then, as if in slow motion, the magnificent beast collapsed.

Emma clutched Tess's arm, but she seemed unaware that they might be in any danger. In fact, she had stepped out of the protection of the tree line, holding the phone up and catching the entire thing on, Emma assumed, a video.

Two additional men ran from the woods opposite them. Both dropped to their knees beside the largest elk, but Emma couldn't see what they were doing. Then the helicopter moved, and a kind of sling was lowered.

The four men on the ground raised the elk with some difficulty, and a fifth person—a smaller person Emma hadn't noticed before—pulled the sling under the beast. Once the bull was secured, the smaller person, who Emma realized must be a woman, signaled the helicopter pilot.

The sling was raised, and the bull disappeared into the helicopter.

The process was repeated two more times. They'd obviously done this before, as they worked with sure, efficient movements. Once the last animal was loaded, one of the men on the ground signaled the pilot in the helicopter. It rose and sped away into the night, its spotlight now doused. Several of the men ran back into the woods, and Emma heard an engine growl to life as a vehicle sped away. The man and woman left behind turned on flashlights and began cleaning up the meadow, picking up the mineral blocks, scouring the ground—probably for any evidence they had been there—and finally heading back into the woods, back in the direction they had come.

In the sudden silence, Emma could hear her pulse thundering through her veins.

"What just happened?" she hissed.

Tess was checking the video on her phone. "We got them. We got the evidence."

Tess stopped talking to Emma, turned the camera to face herself and said, "We're two miles southeast of the entrance to the Great Sand Dunes National Park."

"What are you doing, Tess?"

"What you just saw was someone stealing elk from the park. Please share this post."

"We should go."

Tess continued to ignore Emma, focusing instead on the phone, which was apparently still recording. "This video must go out to as many people as possible. These people killed my sister and my brother-in-law. You can help me stop them."

She seemed oblivious to the fact that they were now standing alone on the edge of the tree line. It was a miracle that no one had seen them, but then they'd been hovering in the darkness rather than the bright light of the helicopter.

"Why would anyone steal an elk?" Emma wondered aloud.

Tess wasn't the one who answered.

"Because they bring good money."

The voice was clipped, cold, and feminine. Emma knew without turning that it was the woman she'd seen pull the sling under the elk. Who else could it have been? What woman other than her and Tess would be in this meadow in the middle of the night? Emma suddenly understood that they'd miscalculated rather badly. They hadn't been as invisible as she'd thought.

Tess's hand froze, holding the phone still, not daring to make a move.

"Drop the phone and take two steps back."

"And if I don't?" Tess's voice was practically a snarl, a cry of anguish and anger. "Are you going to kill me like you did my sister?"

"I will. I'll shoot you right where you stand."

Sixty-One

Henry had started running as soon as he heard the sound of the helicopter.

He'd nearly stumbled into the clearing, coming to a halt when the spotlight from the helicopter lit up the meadow like broad daylight. He'd pulled back into the shadows and waited.

He could just make out Tess, standing on the far side of the grassy area and holding up her cell phone. It was amazing that no one else noticed her, but then their attention was on the elk. He thought he saw Emma standing beside her, but he couldn't be sure.

He'd watched as several men and one woman rushed forward and harvested the animals. They were lifted in giant slings, one at a time, and then one of the men gave a signal and the helicopter rose and darted away. Most of the men left, rushing back through the woods, but the woman and one man had stayed, apparently to clean up the site and make sure no evidence was left. Henry had known that was his chance, so he'd begun to make his way around the meadow, hoping to get to Tess and Emma and convince them to leave now that they had whatever proof they'd come for.

But by the time he'd worked his way back into the woods and around the meadow, the woman was holding a rifle on Tess and Emma, saying, "I'll shoot you right where you stand."

He realized with a start that he'd seen the ranger before, in the diner. Had she been following Sophia? Had she killed Sophia?

Tess was still clutching her phone, and the woman was saying something Henry couldn't hear, her voice lower and more menacing. The man with her glanced Henry's way. Henry dropped to the ground, hoping he hadn't been spotted. His heart hammered in his chest, and he lay there with his face pressed into newly fallen leaves. Finally he dared to glance up, praying they wouldn't see him. No one was looking his direction. Why would they be? He was lying in the middle of the woods in the dark.

His mind combed through his alternatives as he slowly rose to his feet.

He could go back to the road and try to wave down help, but it might be hours before anyone passed by. He could walk over to the entrance of the park, but no one would be there for hours.

What other option did he have?

He could rush into the meadow and defend Tess and Emma. If it came to that, he would, but his presence might tip the scales the other way. It was two against two at this point, and the woman had a rifle. If he made his presence known, she would feel outnumbered, threatened, and even more desperate.

Henry also felt a rising sense of desperation, but another part of his heart, of his mind, told him there was no reason to panic. God had surely directed their path. How else could they explain being here? The woman in front of him, the woman now threatening Tess and Emma, had most likely killed Sophia and probably Sophia's husband too. Why else would she be holding a gun on the two women? Who would have thought an Amish bishop, a grandmother, and a financial adviser could accomplish what the police hadn't?

Surely God had given them the victory.

His spirits rose as he remembered the dream about his mother. She'd been urging him on. Something more came to him as he hid in the darkness of the woods. His mother's left hand, clutched around her middle, had come out in a familiar gesture—palm down, urging him to move slower, more carefully. She'd done that often when he was a young lad, prone to rush about without thinking. "Slower, Henry." Her voice had held an abundance of affection mixed with caution. In the dream, it had been the same. While she had urged him to action, she'd also cautioned him.

Henry couldn't have said whether his dream was a vision from God. It seemed a bit bold, even absurd, to believe that God would intervene in such a way. And yet, wasn't that the truth of the gospel, that their heavenly Father was willing to intercede on their behalf?

So instead of allowing fear to slow his steps and thoughts, he chose to focus on what could be done. He crouched where he was waiting and prayed for an opportunity, a chance to make this right, a way to protect the woman he loved and a young lady he barely knew.

Sixty-Two

Emma glanced down in time to catch a tiny glimpse of the screen on Tess's phone. All she could make out before the screen went dark were the words "live stream complete." Then Tess pushed a button on the side of the phone and dropped it on the ground.

Emma was a little surprised Tess had so readily done as asked.

"Step back. Both of you."

A man joined the woman. He was tall and thin, wearing jeans that were marginally too long and a camouflage jacket over his T-shirt. The jacket was too short and didn't quite reach to his wrists. He seemed to be all arms and legs. Emma guessed his age to be somewhere between seventeen and twenty, but probably closer to the first. He carried a flashlight covered with some type of red cellophane and pointed at the ground.

"Jimmy, pick up that phone."

He glanced nervously at the woman, and then he did as he was told.

"You want me to destroy it?"

"No. We need to see who they called. Put it in your pocket for now."

Emma still felt panic threatening to push through her veins, but her heart rate was calming. They hadn't been shot yet, and she was beginning to take in the details of what she was seeing. The woman was wearing a National Park service uniform. In fact, something looked vaguely familiar about her. Emma glanced down and, though she could barely see by the light of the flashlight, spotted a deep scuff across the toe of the ranger's right shoe—just like in Henry's drawing.

Jimmy shifted from one foot to the other. Emma was certain she'd never seen him before. How had someone so young managed to get caught up in such a terrible thing?

"Did you kill those elk?" Tess asked.

"That's none of your business." The woman motioned for Jimmy to shine his flashlight on Tess and Emma. "Put the light on their feet."

She peered through the darkness at them and then said, "You, in the dress, step back. Now over. Not that far. Just…" She stepped forward and pulled Emma to the left a few steps and then forward again. Apparently satisfied that they were lined up perfectly, she nodded once.

"Is this one of those illegal hunts?" Tess asked. "It must be."

"Did we look like we were hunting?"

"This is why you killed Cooper? To protect some business deal? Somehow he found out, and he was about to expose you."

"Cooper didn't take the hint when we told him to drop the story." The woman's tone was contemptuous.

Emma guessed the woman couldn't imagine anyone arguing with her, daring to oppose her. She wasn't passionately upset, but her calm and cool demeanor sent a chill through Emma's soul. She would take a life as easily as she'd nabbed the elk. Nothing would stand in her way because she was right and justified in what she was doing, or so her attitude seemed to suggest.

"And no, we didn't kill the elk. Do I look like a rich person who gets her jollies spotlighting animals?"

"What then? Why did you just take them?"

"You're selling them to a managed wildlife facility," Emma said.

Katie Ann had gone with Doc Berry to one of the managed properties. She'd come back describing the giant racks on the elk, how the wild animals came running as soon as the feeders went off, and the controversy regarding high fences. "You're increasing the gene pool of their herd."

"The Amish chick is pretty smart," the woman said.

Chick? Emma almost rolled her eyes.

"How could this be worth killing people?" Tess asked.

"You have no idea what people will pay for an elk of that size." The woman took a step closer to Tess, who didn't back down at all.

"And so you steal them? From here and Glacier and who knows where else?"

Jimmy's light splayed over the two women, and Emma could see the ranger's name embroidered on a tag and affixed to the pocket of her uniform. Paddock. Emma had never heard the name before, but she suspected it was her real name. Paddock acted like a woman who wouldn't try to hide who she was. As if she were above the law. As if no one would dare to question her right to be here. And if she was a ranger, as it seemed she was, then probably no one would question her. It was the perfect setup. She had access to the entire park.

Tess took another step forward. There were now less than five feet between them. Just as it seemed Tess was about to confront the ranger, Paddock raised the rifle. Her hand didn't shake on it, and Emma understood that she wouldn't hesitate to shoot. She certainly wouldn't miss at less than five feet.

Tess froze, her hands raised in the air, as if she could protect herself that way.

"Enough tranquilizer is in one of these darts to incapacitate a seven-hundred-pound bull. If I shoot you, it'll be as fatal as a bullet."

Emma pulled Tess back and kept her hand on the woman's arm. They needed to stay calm, to think of a way out of this.

Paddock didn't glance away from them, but she said, "Jimmy, bring the truck around."

"Where are we going to take them?"

"Just do what I said."

Jimmy practically jumped, and he didn't ask any more questions.

"Leave the light," Paddock added.

He nodded twice, gulped, and set the flashlight down, its beam slicing across the ground. Then he darted off into the darkness.

"Where are you taking us?" Tess asked.

"Back of beyond, where they won't find your bodies." Paddock didn't seem at all remorseful about what she had done or was about to do.

If anything, Emma would have said her manner was businesslike. It was all in an evening's work.

"Will the animals be all right?" Emma asked. It wasn't her primary concern at this point, but she wanted to keep the woman talking. "It's obvious you care about them."

When Paddock cocked her head, as if puzzled by the question, Emma pushed on. "The way you checked on them. I could tell."

"Perhaps I was just protecting my investment."

"Maybe, but you seemed to care. About the bull, I mean."

"He was a beauty." Paddock glanced across the meadow to where the elk had been. Nothing remained to prove what they had done. Who would miss three elk from a national park? The only proof, the only evidence they had, was Emma's and Tess's word against this park ranger—that and the video Tess had taken on her phone.

"Actually, I'm a wildlife expert," Paddock admitted. "Trust me when I say those three will be well taken care of. They'll have a better life than they do here."

"I doubt the elk would agree with you." Tess's voice quavered with anger.

"This isn't Disney, you know. Elk want what every animal wants—food, water, safety, and other animals like them. That bull will have all those things, and the fact that my bank account will be fatter because of it? Well, I don't consider that a sin."

"You killed my sister." The words came out like a screech owl, pain dripping from every syllable.

"Shut your mouth," Paddock growled, her tone low and threatening.

Fortunately, at that point they all heard a truck engine, and then Jimmy was pulling into the clearing in a large, dual cab pickup that looked to Emma as if it were several feet off the ground. Why would anyone drive such a thing? And how did you get into it?

Then she realized it was dark colored with an emblem on the side of the door. Was this the truck that followed Sophia? Before she could ask any questions, Paddock directed them toward the truck's open door with her rifle.

Emma thought Paddock would insist on slipping into the driver's seat. She seemed the kind of person who liked to be in charge. But she motioned for the two of them to get in the backseat and told Jimmy, "You're driving."

"Where are we going?"

"Don't worry about that. Keep an eye on them while I make a call." She pulled a service revolver out of her utility belt and handed it to Jimmy with a final order.

"Shoot them if they try to get away."

Sixty-Three

We have a problem.

What now?

Two witnesses.

?

A lady who claims to be Sophia's
sister and an Amish chick.

What did they see?

Everything.

Buy their silence.

Sophia's sister isn't going
to settle for money.

You're probably right.

Paddock typed furiously, frustrated that she couldn't pick up the phone and simply call the man. But he was insistent that any communication be done via texts, as if they couldn't be intercepted like anything else.

There's more. They seem to know
we're connected to the other
pickups.

All right. Do what needs to be done.

Here?

No. Pick another place
farther from the pickup point.

I was thinking the sand dunes.
Easier to hide the bodies there.

I told you before,
I don't want to know the details.

Of course you don't.

You have a problem with
the way I'm running things?

After this I want out.

Was the pickup successful?

Yes.

Then stop complaining. Your money
will be wired within the hour.

Sixty-Four

Henry waited until the truck began to pull away, and then he ran and hopped into the bed, banging his shin badly against the lowered tailgate. Why the tailgate was lowered, he couldn't have said, but he managed to pull himself farther in, among various types of equipment.

It was something of a miracle that he'd made it into the truck bed because the vehicle had a high suspension. It must have been used by the park service for off-road trips—rescues maybe. It also had a loud diesel engine. Henry knew that sound because he'd heard the trucks often enough at the diner. Now he lay in the back of one, straining to hear what was being said inside, but the mechanical whine of the engine blocked out the voices. The woman was definitely a park ranger, not merely impersonating one. Or at least that was his sense of things.

Why would she be involved in this? What exactly was her role?

He'd only caught random words from the conversation between her and Tess and Emma.

The ranger's body language said it all, though. She was comfortable holding the rifle, slightly impatient with this unexpected delay, and clearly in charge of the young man.

He'd wanted to insert himself into the situation, but something had convinced him to hang back, and it was probably a good thing he had. Otherwise, he'd be riding inside the cab, the gun pointed at him as well. And that would do his friends absolutely no good.

He tried to assess exactly how much trouble they were in.

Stuart had been eager to help. He had even wanted to go with Henry. There was no doubt Stuart would do as he'd asked—go back to his house, call Grayson, and wait there for help to arrive. He'd impressed upon Stuart that Grayson was the only one they could trust. Henry hoped the sheriff had answered right away. But if not, Stuart would wait.

It wasn't a great plan, but it was the only one Henry had been able to come up with.

He wished he'd told Stuart to let Lexi out of the house and feed her. Honestly, though, he shouldn't be worrying about the dog at a time like this. But he did worry about her. Suddenly he remembered that Stuart had two dogs of his own—Labradoodles his wife had insisted on bringing home. He had eventually fallen in love with them, and he'd even shown Henry pictures of the two beasts sitting on his living room couch.

If he allowed the dogs on his couch, if he was that sort of dog person, then Henry didn't have to worry about Lexi. Stuart would hear the dog barking or whining and let her out, even find the food in the mudroom. He would take care of Lexi and alert Grayson, so all Henry needed to worry about was keeping the women alive until help arrived.

As the truck bumped and swerved, Henry prayed, asking God to fill his mind with wisdom, his heart with assurance, and his soul with strength.

And then he didn't have time to even think.

The truck slowed down and abruptly came to a stop beneath a streetlight. If only a park camera were hung there, but as Henry continued to crane his neck to check, he didn't see one.

The ranger grumbled some sort of order, which Henry assumed was to the young man. The driver's side door of the truck opened, Henry heard the squeak of a gate being rolled back, the door closed again, and they drove through before the truck stopped again.

The man was walking back to close the gate, now behind them.

Henry lay down flat, but then he elevated his head just enough to see what was happening. And at that exact moment, the man turned around. And stopped.

Henry didn't speak or move.

And then the young man shook his head once, just a short jerk Henry might have imagined, and walked past him to get back in the truck.

The truck proceeded down a two-lane blacktop road.

Had the man seen him? Henry's heart rate once again accelerated. His mind darted back and forth, wondering if he should jump out of the truck, but he would never be able to keep up on foot. And he wouldn't consider abandoning Tess and Emma now. No, if the man had seen him, then he would deal with the outcome of that later. The critical thing was to stay as close to the group as possible.

Henry quickly lifted his head to take in as much as he could before they went too far. They weren't at the main entrance to the national park. There was no visitor center, and he saw no signs other than one across the gate. Henry couldn't read it because it was facing back toward the road. He could see a lock on the gate, though. This must be a service road for park employees, which meant the ranger was taking them to the back of beyond, to a place remote enough that there was little chance of anyone seeing them.

No more witnesses.

She already had two she needed to get rid of. Maybe when she'd been on the phone, typing something into it but not speaking, maybe she'd received orders to take them here. Henry couldn't know. He didn't fully understand how cellular phones worked. He'd only used a cell phone once, when he'd called 9-1-1 after finding Sophia's body. From the look of consternation on the woman's face, he could guess she was reporting what had happened and that she didn't like the response.

And what of the man? Had Henry imagined the fellow had looked straight at him and shaken his head? He didn't think so, but what did it mean? Why didn't he holler, *We have a stowaway. Come look!*

He was involved with this woman in some way, but perhaps he had fallen in too deep. Maybe he was rethinking his associations and actions. It was possible he wanted a way out, or he was willing to steal animals but not to murder innocent people. It was conceivable, and Henry prayed it was true, that the young man was having second thoughts.

If so, it was possible he would be willing to help them.

It was also possible Henry had imagined the entire thing.

Sixty-Five

Emma couldn't quite fathom what was happening. Something had changed back in the clearing. What, though? She needed to put the pieces of this puzzle together, and do it quickly.

There'd been a moment, when the woman had stepped away to use her cell phone, that the young man had looked as if he wanted to say something. But then Paddock had stomped back to the truck, climbed into the passenger's seat, and told him, "You drive while I keep an eye on those two."

As they'd pulled away, Emma had heard a thump in the back of the truck. It sounded too big to be an animal, but she couldn't think of any other possibility in the middle of the night and in such a remote location.

More than anything, Emma wanted to talk to Tess. They needed to come up with a plan, and she wanted to know what exactly Tess had succeeded in doing on her phone.

But she didn't have a chance for a private conversation.

First, Jimmy was driving, practically jumping to do whatever Paddock ordered. When they'd stopped at the gate, Paddock had turned around and held the pistol on them, daring them to make a move. Now they were winding their way down a back road. Twice Jimmy had looked in the rearview mirror and locked eyes with Emma. Was he trying to tell her something? Did he want to help them escape? That seemed like too much to hope for.

They passed a sign that said "High-Clearance Vehicles Only" followed by another that said "Point of No Return" with an arrow pointed in the direction they were going. And then the sound of the road changed, and Emma realized they were driving on hard-packed dirt rather than asphalt.

Point of No Return sounded ominous to Emma, but she didn't believe it. She wouldn't allow her mind or her heart to go to such a dark place.

God hadn't allowed her to live this long, and He hadn't helped her escape the Monte Vista arsonist, only to let her die in the middle of the sand dunes. Besides, He wasn't done with her yet. She was far from perfect. She cared too much about the extra twenty pounds she carried, fussed over the gray hairs that wouldn't stay in place, and had been known to covet the newer clothes or nicer homes of her neighbors. No, she was not perfect, but God had promised to complete a good work within her. There was still plenty of work to be done.

This, along with a burning desire to see her family again—to see Henry again—pushed away the fear that had earlier thumped at the door to her heart. Tess no longer had the phone, but maybe she'd successfully sent the evidence on to someone else. Emma nudged her foot against Tess's and mimed holding a cell phone in her hands. Tess shook her head. Not a good sign.

The road twisted and turned, and then they pulled into what might have been a parking area. It was deserted. Emma guessed the time was close to four in the morning. Clyde and Rachel would be worried. She hoped the grandchildren would be asleep and blissfully ignorant of the jam their grandmother was in.

"Get out." Paddock was once again pointing the pistol at them.

Emma and Tess climbed out of the truck. Emma moved slowly, carefully, not wanting to startle the woman.

Jimmy stood there, once again holding the flashlight and waiting for instructions. Paddock had left the rifle in the truck, the one with the tranquilizer darts. Now she held a pistol with her right hand, and with her left she tapped each of her fingers against her thumb—once, twice, and then a third time.

"Don't try anything stupid."

"What would we try? Do you think we're going to run away?" Emma twitched her head to the right and then to the left. "Where would we go?"

"That was going to be my next point. I'd just as soon kill you here, but Clayton—"

She didn't exactly slap her hand over her mouth, but Emma could tell she wished she could take that last word back. Clayton. Emma didn't know anyone named Clayton, but maybe Sheriff Grayson would, which was another reason she had to stay alive. She wanted to pass on the names of all those responsible for the murders of Sophia and Cooper Brooks.

Tess was being suspiciously quiet. Emma wondered if all they'd been through had been too much, pushing the young woman over some abyss. But then she caught her eyeing the back of Jimmy's jeans, where he'd pocketed her cell phone. If she could get hold of that phone, perhaps they could call for help.

"Jimmy, lead the way."

"To where?"

"Top of the trail. Same place as before."

What did that mean? Had they killed someone else in addition to Sophia and Cooper? Emma shared a worried look with Tess.

Jimmy pushed the button on his flashlight and tapped it against his hand. Shrugging, he said, "Fine, but I need another flashlight." He walked toward the back of the truck and disappeared into the darkness.

Emma could hear him, though. He was pushing stuff around and grumbling. After a couple of minutes, he emerged carrying a different flashlight, this one also wrapped in red cellophane, and wearing a backpack.

Paddock threw him a questioning glance. "I didn't tell you to get a pack."

"Always hike prepared. You know as well as I do how dangerous these trails can be, especially at night."

Paddock rolled her eyes and then pointed her flashlight toward the ground. Before she had a chance to bark any more orders, Tess slipped into line behind Jimmy. He didn't seem to have any problem picking out the trail in the darkness, his light bouncing on the ground in front of him. Around them the trees seemed to press in, and overhead they shut out the starlight.

How could he be sure he was going the right direction? Even with the flashlight, he couldn't see more than a couple of feet. Perhaps his eyes had adjusted faster than Emma's. She felt as though she were trying to walk through the root cellar with no light on. She quickly caught up with them, determined to put herself between Tess and Paddock. If Tess could get close enough to Jimmy, maybe she could grab the phone.

Emma thought she heard something behind them. It was probably a moose or an elk, but for a fleeting moment, she had a vision of help arriving en masse—sheriffs and agents and park rangers who hadn't joined up with the dark side.

It didn't happen.

They were still alone, hiking into the wilderness with an unstable ranger and her sidekick.

Jimmy led the way down a barely discernible trail through the forest and past a grove of ponderosa pines. Emma became aware of the sound of water and wondered what creek they were passing. She wasn't familiar enough with the area to know. But she recognized the Sangre de Cristo Mountains rising up in the darkness to their right, and she occasionally caught a glimpse through the trees of the sand dunes to their left. They were headed north.

The trees fell away and the wind picked up as the trail gained elevation. Emma shut her mind to that and focused instead on pulling her sweater more tightly around her shoulders and putting one foot in front of the other. The wind pushed against her, nearly toppling her off balance and whipping her dress around her legs. She glanced up and saw Tess attempting to hold down her hair that swirled around her head, no doubt obscuring her vision. Emma was grateful for the bonnet she wore over her prayer *kapp*. Who said Plain clothing wasn't practical? Though she wouldn't recommend climbing a steep trail in a dress.

They walked for what Emma guessed to be about twenty minutes, her shoes filling with sand. She could taste it in her mouth, feel its grit against her skin, and the wind whipped it around, causing her eyes to burn and water. The way became steeper with each turn of the trail, and then Jimmy slowed and turned left.

Emma didn't want to take that left turn, but Paddock nudged her in the back with the barrel of the gun.

"Keep going and stay in a straight line," she hissed.

Emma stepped off the trail, careful to stay directly behind Tess. She kept her eyes on the ground and attempted to focus on the feel of the wind against her skin. Her pulse was thundering and her palms were sweating. She felt somewhat light headed, and then realized she was taking quick, shallow breaths. The ground tilted, and she stumbled, forging on when

Paddock snarled something incomprehensible. Her legs were beginning to tremble, and suddenly she couldn't think clearly, couldn't fathom why they were here or what she should do.

She needed to get somewhere safe. She needed to lie down.

But, of course, those things weren't possible. She pulled in a full, deep breath and hugged her arms around her torso.

Breathe deeply. Wasn't that what the doctor had told her when she'd asked him about this? "It's probably part postmenopause and part acrophobia."

And what had he suggested as the best cure for a fear of heights? Stay away from high precipices. Stay on the ground. Avoid stressful situations.

No wonder she was hyperventilating. She couldn't imagine a more stressful situation than the one they were in.

But she could control this. She could and would remain calm. All she had to do was keep going, keep putting one foot in front of the other, and never ever look down.

But then Jimmy stopped, and Tess bumped into him, and Emma couldn't avoid looking out any longer. She chose to look up, and the world began to tilt as she attempted to take in the millions of stars above their heads.

"Faint on me, and we'll throw your body off this dune."

Emma glanced at Paddock and noticed that she was again touching each of her fingers to her thumb in some type of nervous twitch.

"What's the difference?" Tess asked. "You're going to kill us anyway."

"Good point, but I thought you might like a moment to pray, or whatever it is you do."

Finally there was nowhere for Emma to look except in front of them, at the miles and miles of sand dunes that dropped off into darkness, to the floor of the San Luis Valley.

Her heart was now beating so hard that she raised a hand to rub her chest.

A sudden and intense nausea forced bile up and into her throat. The muscles in her legs began to shake. There was a heaviness on her chest as she struggled for a deep breath.

Now was not the time for a panic attack.

She'd been held at gunpoint for more than an hour, and she'd remained reasonably calm. But her body was rebelling against this—a fear of falling off the sand dune.

Paddock had said she was giving them time to pray, but the only prayer that came to Emma's lips was *The Lord is my shepherd*. She closed her eyes again, relieved not to have to look at the edge of the sand cliff they stood on, and she began to silently recite the twenty-third psalm.

She was vaguely aware of Paddock saying, "Watch them," to Jimmy, and then she stepped away. Emma opened her eyes, wondering what could be more important than the murder this woman was intent on committing. She watched in amazement as Paddock pulled out her cell phone and pointed it toward them. She held it up at arm's length and eye level. There was a bright flash, and she stared down at the small screen for a moment. Apparently satisfied with what she saw there, she turned away from them and walked a few paces in the opposite direction.

Sixty-Six

We're here.

Then do it.

It'll cost you.

Meaning what?

Paddock's rage nearly blinded her. This idiot sat in his million-dollar home and expected her to take all the risks. Well, it was time that he pay her what she was clearly worth.

I want one million dollars.

She stopped typing and sent the photo she'd just taken.

One million, or I share this picture
with the authorities.

And land in jail? I don't think so.

You know I'm smarter than that.

Meaning what?

The phone can't be traced to me.
Also, I'll be three countries away
before I hit Send.

You don't want to double-cross me.

And you don't want to doubt
that I would do it.

Fine. I'll take care of your money
when the banks open.

Now. And I want proof of the
transfer.

Ten minutes, but do
all three of them.

Sixty-Seven

The young man's name was Jimmy. Henry had heard the woman say, "Jimmy, lead the way," when they stopped in the parking area.

Jimmy was with the woman, and Henry had seen him hold the gun on Emma and Tess. But Jimmy didn't seem to be on the woman's side. Over the years Henry had learned things were often not as they seemed. When you walked up on a situation, you were witnessing only five minutes of a very long story. There was no way to know what had happened before, and you often didn't know what happened after, either.

It was best to keep an open mind.

For the moment, it appeared that Jimmy was somehow, inexplicably, on their side.

The woman's name was Paddock, or so Jimmy had said. She was dressed in a national park employee uniform. Henry might have thought she'd stolen it, but he'd caught the light from Jimmy's flashlight reflecting off her uniform. What were the odds she would have stolen a uniform with someone's name on it? She was a park employee all right—a ranger by the looks of things, which made this entire situation all the more puzzling.

Henry squatted at a point just below the top of the ridge, like Jimmy had told him to do, but he could still peer over the top.

Paddock stood off to the side. She was once again typing on her phone.

Emma and Tess waited at the highest point of the dune. The wind was whipping Emma's dress and Tess's hair. Jimmy stood close to Tess and handed her something, but Henry couldn't see what it was. His eyes had adjusted to the dark as much as they were going to. He felt lucky to be able to see at all, given the moonless night, but then they were standing on the edge of a cliff beneath the stars. The three of them—Emma and Tess and Jimmy—were silhouetted against the heavenly light that had guided men and women since Adam and Eve had left the garden.

The hike up from the parking area had been difficult, but all the walks with Lexi had helped keep Henry in fair shape. The problem had been the two sand boards he carried, the ones Jimmy had shoved toward him in the darkness while he was still crouched in the bed of the truck.

"Take the sleds, just in case," he had murmured. "Get the women away from Paddock when I give you the signal."

"Take them where?"

"Bottom of the dunes. Hide until help arrives."

Henry didn't have much faith that any sort of help was on the way—at least not yet. Not unless Stuart had connected immediately with Grayson. Even then, Grayson would have to alert others, find the trail and the meadow, somehow figure out that they'd been carted off in a national park truck...it was all more than Henry could imagine. But he had no other plan to rescue Emma and Tess, so he did as Jimmy said and carried a sand board under each arm. They were fiberglass and lighter than he would have thought, though climbing the trail carrying them had proved a bit arduous.

Paddock put her phone in her pocket, turned back toward Jimmy and Tess and Emma, and raised her gun. Only Jimmy was no longer there. Somehow he'd managed to circle around behind her while she was staring at the phone. He shouted "Now!" as he ran toward her.

Paddock pivoted toward Jimmy's voice, and a gun went off, but Henry didn't wait to see who had been shot.

He was running toward Emma and Tess.

"Slide down the dune! Quickly!" He tossed one of the boards at Tess, who jumped on and launched herself off the precipice.

Emma's eyes widened and her voice came out in a strangled whisper. "I can't—"

But Henry didn't wait to hear the rest. He dropped the other board, pushed Emma onto it in a sitting position, and then plopped down behind her, his arms around her waist. He pushed off with all of his might, praying Emma had instinctively grabbed the board's handles.

They sailed out and over the top of the sand dune. For a moment, Henry understood what it must feel like to fly, what the cranes experienced each time they soared up and away.

And then they hit the sand hard, jarring his teeth.

Another shot rang out, and Henry felt a burning pain in his left arm, but he didn't have time to consider why. He had to concentrate. Paddock was using a handgun, and they were certainly out of range of any additional shots. The sound of her firing again and again echoed across the dunes. He heard another gunshot from above, but this one landed in the sand to the right. It didn't seem likely that Jimmy would help them escape and then try to kill them, so Paddock must still be shooting. He had to get Emma away from Paddock. He prayed that Jimmy was okay but feared he wasn't.

Emma didn't scream. She didn't try to pull them off the board. Henry still had his arms wrapped around her, and he felt as if they were one.

They plunged into the night, bouncing against the dune again and again.

Their sled slowed on one of the plateaus, Emma shouted something, and then she pointed to the left. He could just make out Tess plunging over another hill, so he adjusted their sled, pushed with both his feet and his hands, though his left hand refused to cooperate, and then they were flying again. Sand smacked them in the face. Paddock shouted something into the night.

Starlight fell softly on their path.

When they finally stopped and Henry was sure they had reached the bottom, he stood on shaky legs and reached down a hand to help Emma up. There was enough starlight to make out the silhouette of her, and Henry breathed a prayer of gratitude that she was alive.

Emma swayed back and forth, her head swiveled left and right, and then she walked into his arms. "That was terrifying, Henry."

"It was quite the ride."

"I thought I was going to fall off the top of that cliff."

"It was only a sand dune, and actually I pushed you."

"But how…why…when did you—"

Before he could think which question to answer first, Tess trudged toward them. "What do you think is happening up there?"

"I heard shots," Emma said.

"So did I. Probably that woman, Paddock, though clearly we were out of range. She's desperate. I don't think it could have been Jimmy shooting." When both women turned to stare at him, Henry added, "We should hide. He said to hide until help comes."

He picked up the board with his right arm, led them around a smaller dune, and then let go of the board so it dropped into the sand. "If we can't see the top, they can't see us."

Tess stepped closer as she dropped her board next to his. She reached out, touched his left arm, and then rubbed her thumb against her fingers. "Henry, you're bleeding. I think you've been shot."

"What?" Emma's voice rose in panic.

Henry put one finger to his lips. "Sound carries out here. I don't think Paddock will follow, but we should keep our voices down."

He twisted his head to get a better look at his left shoulder. "That's why it was burning."

Blood had poured down his sleeve. Funny how he hadn't noticed that before, but then adrenaline was still pumping through his veins. "I knew it was hurting, but I didn't realize…"

And then he was light headed, the rush of blood buzzing in his ears, and his legs no longer steady.

"Over here, Henry. Sit down and let me…" Emma clasped her hands in front of her. "Oh my…"

"We need to stop the bleeding." Tess looked around, as if there might be medical supplies hidden somewhere, and then she said, "Your apron. Tear off a strip."

Emma snatched up the bottom of her apron and yanked hard on the hem, trying to tear away a two-inch-wide section, but the cotton was thick and wouldn't rip.

"Use this," Henry said, fishing out his pocketknife.

She opened the small blade, poked the tip through the fabric, and yanked on it, causing a nice-sized tear. The section tore away easily.

"I've never…"

"I have." Tess took the fabric from her. "Hold out your arm, Henry."

She wound the fabric over, around, down and back again, then repeated the process until she had used the entire section. When she reached the end of the fabric she reached for the knife, split the material in two, pulled the ends in opposite directions, and then tied a knot. "I don't think it will bleed through. How do you feel?"

"Light headed for a minute. But better now, I think."

Emma and Tess plopped to the ground next to him. They sat in a tight circle, sheltered from the wind—and hidden from Paddock—by the dune.

"Jimmy's on our side?" Emma asked.

But it was Tess who answered. "I suspected as much. Remember when Paddock first forced us into the truck? While she was on her phone, he almost talked to us..."

"She came back too soon."

"Right."

"He saw me in the back of the truck when he went to close the gate," Henry said. "I thought...I guess I thought maybe he'd looked right through me. He just gave one shake of his head, and I convinced myself I'd imagined it."

"But then he went around to speak to you," Emma said. "When we parked at the Point of No Return."

"*Ya.* He was throwing stuff around, making a lot of noise."

"He told Paddock he needed another flashlight." Tess hugged her knees in the circle of her arms. "I wondered what he was doing back there."

"I have no idea what was in the backpack he took, but maybe there was a phone. He pushed the sleds into my arms and told me to wait for his signal and then get you two away from Paddock."

"And he gave me my phone back." Tess pulled the device out of her back pocket. "I couldn't figure that out, why he would give it back to me."

"Does it still work?" Emma asked. "Can you call someone?"

Tess pushed some buttons, but the screen didn't light up. "Battery's dead. I guess I used it all up when I was taking the video."

"Did you—what did you call it? Load up the video?" Emma looked as if she wanted to grab the phone out of Tess's hands.

"No. I streamed it live. I was going to load it once we made it back to the car."

"What does that mean?" Henry asked.

"It means anyone who was on that site at that moment, at the exact moment I was recording, would have seen it."

"Do you think anyone did?" Emma reached for Henry's right hand, as if she needed emotional strength to hear Tess's reply.

But Henry knew what she was going to say, because he could read her body language, the way her shoulders slumped. Her head dropped, and her voice flattened out. "Not many. Middle of the night? On a weeknight? Most people would be asleep because they have work tomorrow."

"What do we do now?" Emma asked Henry.

"We do what that young man who risked his life said to do. We wait."

Sixty-Eight

Tess sat on Emma's right, her head back against the wall of sand, clearly asleep. Henry sat on Emma's left, his legs resting on top of the sand boards. Emma would never have believed she could fall asleep in such a situation, but her body had different plans. As they waited in the darkness, her hand clasped in Henry's and her head resting on his uninjured shoulder, her eyes grew heavier, until she could no longer fight the need to close them.

She woke to the sound of cranes.

Stretching, she realized her legs were sore from the hike through the woods and up the dune, and when she tried to swallow, she felt as if she'd suffered a long bout of tonsillitis. How long had it been since she'd had a sip of water? Her stomach gurgled, reminding her it was time to eat. She ran her tongue over her teeth and grimaced at the taste and feel of sand in her mouth. Her skin, too, seemed covered with the stuff.

But none of that mattered. What mattered was that they were still alive.

She glanced at Henry and could make out only the silhouette of him in the waning darkness. Then her eye caught on the ankle device he'd been forced to wear. A small light on it flashed red every few seconds, which she supposed meant he was out of the allowed area. Well, at least it still worked, even if Tess's phone didn't. Too bad they couldn't call someone with it. Technology seemed like a complete waste of time and money to Emma. You couldn't depend on things like phones and monitoring devices.

You could depend on your friends and your faith. You could depend on your heart to lead you in the right direction. You could depend on God, even when you didn't understand His ways.

The sun peeked over the horizon, splashing the dunes with a dazzling display of pink, blue, violet, and orange.

"A beautiful sight, *ya*?"

"It is." Emma glanced at the man who had become her best friend in the last year. "Are you all right, Henry? How is your arm? And don't try to spare me the truth."

"It's quite stiff," he admitted, trying to raise it and grimacing. "Sore, but the bleeding seems to have stopped. You and Tess made a *gut* bandage."

"I was so afraid." Emma blinked rapidly, not wanting to cry, not wanting to give in to the terror and fear of the night before. "What about Jimmy? Do you think he…"

"There's no way for us to know. There hasn't been any sound at all from the top of the dunes. Pretty quiet all night."

"You stayed awake?"

Henry nodded.

Emma felt that she needed to be strong for Tess and Henry, but she couldn't stop herself from asking the next question. "*Gotte*'s still in control, right? Despite the fact that we're hiding behind a sand dune, we have no supplies, we're in the middle of a forty-four-thousand-acre national park, no one knows where we are, and there's a madwoman still on the loose."

"Sounds dire when you put it that way, but *ya*. I'm sure *Gotte* is still in control. Can you imagine a woman like Paddock outmaneuvering Him? *Nein*."

"When you put it that way, I have no choice but to agree with you."

"Remember Joseph and everything he went through when his *bruders* threw him into a cistern and sold him into slavery? Bible scholars say those holes in the ground used to collect water were usually fifteen to twenty feet deep. Think about that."

"I'd rather not."

"The situation must have seemed pretty bleak to Joseph, sitting in the bottom of that cistern. But *Gotte* still had His eye on him and His hand on Joseph's life. Remember, Joseph said to his *bruders*, 'You intended to harm me, but God intended it for good.'"

Emma thought about that. Paddock certainly did intend to harm them. How could God use that for good? But they were together. Henry's injury didn't seem to be life-threatening. They were basically safe for the moment, and they could all bear witness to Paddock's deeds if they could only make it back home. With their testimony, the authorities could put Paddock away, and she wouldn't be able to hurt anyone else.

You intended to harm me, but God intended it for good.

"Henry Lapp, you're a *gut* bishop. *Nein*, don't stop me. You have a *gut* heart, and you use your knowledge of the Bible to encourage, to bolster our spirits when we…" She blinked rapidly, determined to finish what she needed to say. "When we doubt and when we're afraid."

"We all doubt sometimes, Emma, and we've all known fear."

"I suppose that's true." She thought of when he'd arrived at their farm, carrying the bag of drawings, terrified that Delaney would find them. Henry Lapp wasn't perfect, but he was a good and godly man. "You know just what to say and what Scripture to share to help us in our faith. Those words about Joseph? They were exactly what I needed to hear to calm my heart."

"We're going to survive this, Emma."

Something whizzed by them too quickly for Emma to see. She supposed it was a bird of some sort, which caused her mind to recall the list of animals she'd shared with Tess. She suspected many more animals than she knew of lived in these dunes—snakes and spiders and who knew what else. Surely nothing that could fly could harm them, but what of the other creatures? Were they in danger? Given enough time, they could die of thirst or starvation, but she had a feeling this situation would be resolved well before then. She believed help would arrive—eventually.

But who had survived the battle at the top of the dunes?

In every direction she looked were giant mounds of sand. They seemed to stretch to the horizon, and she knew from personal experience that they also loomed above them. She didn't have to turn around. Didn't need to see the direction they'd come. Didn't want to see the height Henry had pushed her from. That push had saved her life, though.

Paddock might have managed to get away, but at least she hadn't won. The police would put out a warrant for her arrest. Eventually she would be caught.

You intended to harm me, but God intended it for good.

Emma didn't want to contradict her bishop. She was encouraged by the words he quoted from Genesis, but she was also a pragmatist. "It's not like we can walk out of here."

"We will if we have to."

"We might run right into Paddock, or whoever she's working for."

"Which is why we should stay here and wait."

Emma wanted to laugh.

"You insist on being an optimist even after all we've been through." She gestured toward the monitor around his ankle. "Even after they accused you of killing Sophia and made you wear that thing."

Instead of answering her, Henry nodded toward a group of cranes flying across the morning sky. "This area contains the habitat cranes need to survive. In particular, the cattail and bulrush. Is it a plant you know?"

Emma shook her head.

"You have read about it before, though. It's the same plant used to make a bed for baby Moses before he was placed in the Nile River."

"No kidding?"

"No kidding. It lightens my heart every time I think of it. The plant was there and provided the materials to safely move Moses down the river and into the sight of Pharaoh's daughter, who took him and provided a home for him. As you know, Moses's *schweschder* Miriam offered to find a Hebrew woman to nurse the baby, and so Moses's mother was able to care for the infant. A miracle indeed. *Gotte's* ways are not our ways, Emma, but we can trust Him nonetheless."

Sixty-Nine

They'd been speaking in hushed tones, but the rising sun succeeded in waking Tess. She startled into an upright position, looked around at Emma and Henry, and then stared out at the natural beauty in front of her. Emma saw the moment when she remembered her sister's death. Her posture stiffened, she gripped her hands into fists, and her breathing grew more ragged.

Emma rubbed her back in small circles. "It's all right, Tess. We're here with you. Help is on its way."

"I just…I suddenly remembered Sophia and Cooper and last night and Paddock."

"Probably you're in shock."

"And you're not?"

"*Ya*, I think we all are. Henry was just telling me Bible stories."

Henry had moved in front of them. He squatted there, smiling. "Emma has a fear of heights. She needs distracting sometimes, and Scripture is *gut* for calming the heart."

Rubbing her eyes with her fists, something that reminded Emma of a small child, Tess asked, "Do you think I'll see Sophia again one day, Henry? Do you believe that?"

"I do. The Bible says that in heaven there will be no more death or mourning or crying or pain. That's a promise, Tess. Give your life into our Father's hands, and you can rest assured in those promises."

"I *want* to believe."

"Then you can. It's a decision, Tess, and you can decide to trust *Gotte's* Word."

Emma thought the young woman was going to answer him, but they were interrupted by shouts from above.

"Stay here," Henry whispered. "I'll make sure it's the good guys."

He stood and hurried around the dune they were sheltering behind.

Emma had an overwhelming urge to rush after him, but Tess put a hand on her arm and drew her back. "We should wait."

They peeked around the edge of the dune and saw Henry waving his good arm over his head, and then they heard the whine of motors approaching.

"Over there," Tess said.

Coming around the bend was not one or two, but half a dozen golf carts. Emma supposed they were emergency vehicles of some sort, but they looked so incongruent with the peaceful, natural scene in front of her that laughter bubbled up and past her lips. Realizing she sounded slightly hysterical, she clamped a hand over her mouth, but she needn't have worried.

Tess was paying no attention to her. She'd sunk into the sand, sitting cross-legged with her head in her hands, muttering over and over, "They found us."

"It's going to be all right, Tess. We're rescued."

"And Paddock?"

"I don't know, but they've either caught her or she's on the run."

"If she's running—"

"Then the police will cast a wide net and catch her. It's their job now. Maybe it always was."

"I couldn't just let whoever killed Sophia get away. You understand, don't you, Emma? Why I had to come out here last night?"

"I do."

"I never meant to put you—to put all of us in danger."

"You didn't. Paddock did, and she will be answering for that as well."

"Thank you for caring so much for a stranger."

"We are strangers no more, Tess Savalas. After last night? I'd say we're *freinden*."

Seventy

Henry didn't recognize most of the men and women in the golf carts, but he did know Sheriff Grayson and Agent Delaney. He also recognized the new officer, Scott Lawson. From the way the three men were talking, Henry figured Grayson had decided both Lawson and Delaney were on the right side of things.

"I told you to stay home," Grayson said by way of greeting, and then he took in the bandage on Henry's arm. "How'd you manage to get yourself hurt?"

"Guess when Paddock started shooting, I should have zigged, not zagged. But I'm alive." In truth his left arm felt stiff and tender, but he didn't think it was their most immediate need. "Emma and Tess need water and—"

"We'll take care of them, Henry. You too."

"What about Jimmy? I'm afraid Paddock shot him."

"Jimmy's the one who called us. He's being transferred to the hospital as we speak. Now sit down and let the paramedic take a look at your arm." Grayson's tone was tough, but he made no attempt to stop the smile on his face. "We've had a very busy morning."

"Did you catch them?"

"Paddock's on the run, but we have a BOLO out. Her vehicle was spotted heading toward Colorado Springs. She was smart enough to get off the main highways, where we have license plate readers, but we'll catch her. Don't worry about that."

"Do you have the evidence you need?"

"We have some, and we'll find more." He slapped Henry on the back and hurried over to one of the crime scene techs.

Agent Delaney was giving orders right and left. When Henry saw him pull out a walkie-talkie and look toward the top of the dune, he realized they had officers and agents up there as well.

"Where did all of these people come from?" he asked the paramedic. "I see more officers here than we have on the Monte Vista police force."

"Some are local. Some are feds." The paramedic was an older black man with a bald head. He pushed a bottle of water into Henry's hands, and then he shone a light in his eyes and waved something over his forehead, stared at it, and said, "No fever. That's a positive sign."

"Why would I have a fever?" Henry took a long drink from the bottle. He hadn't realized until that moment exactly how thirsty he was. He hadn't realized that water was such a blessing.

"You would have a fever if infection had already set in."

"It's only been a few hours."

"You'd be surprised."

"I didn't realize I'd been shot. It was Tess who noticed, and then she and Emma insisted on...on taking care of it."

"You were smart to wrap it up and leave it. That reduced your risk of infection from outside bacteria. I'd rather not change that bandage here with all the sand blowing about. If it's okay with you, we'll send you back to the visitor center, and one of the paramedics there will take care of you."

"Fine by me."

The old guy picked up his medical supplies, which were in something resembling a toolbox. "Great. I'll go check on the ladies, then."

Henry didn't want to be in the way. Emma or Tess might be uncomfortable with him there as the paramedic shone his light and took their vitals. He gave Emma a slight wave and walked over to the only person who didn't look occupied at the time—Officer Lawson.

"I suppose this means you're not a part of it."

"It?" The young man turned toward him, his eyes crinkling at the corners and sunlight bouncing off his copper-colored hair. "I guess I was and I wasn't."

Henry waited, and Lawson laughed. "It's plain as the beard on your face that you have a few questions. I'll answer them if I can."

"You didn't come here simply to fill the vacancy in Sheriff Grayson's department?"

"I did not."

"Do you work for the feds?"

"I work on a joint task force that was established between the Federal Bureau of Investigation and the National Park Service."

"You knew what Paddock was doing."

"We knew someone was poaching animals—large animals—and we knew it was a sizable operation involving millions of dollars."

"Millions?"

The young man nodded. "They would bait the animals, tranquilize them, and then transport them to the buyer."

"The story Cooper Brooks was following."

"We suspected his death wasn't random, but we couldn't prove it, and we couldn't investigate—at least not openly—without tipping our hand to Paddock and the others involved. It was important they not suspect how much we knew."

"Sophia?"

"She arrived here shortly after I did."

Henry thought of Grayson's suspicions and the waitress's concern that Lawson was infatuated with her. "You were protecting her."

"I tried." A look of regret passed over his face. "I'm just sorry I wasn't able to prevent her murder."

"You aren't guilty of that. You didn't strangle her."

"No, I didn't." Lawson's jaw clenched, and Henry realized he wasn't as young as he'd first thought. "But I will see that the people responsible are prosecuted to the full extent of the law. You can count on that."

"Grayson seems confident Paddock will be caught."

"We know a lot about her—how she operates and where she'll run." Delaney shouted something in their direction, and Lawson said, "Looks like I'm needed."

He shook hands with Henry and then hurried off.

Henry walked over to where the paramedic was finishing up with Tess and Emma. They were both holding bottles of water. The paramedic noted the empty water bottle in Henry's hands, pulled another out of the cooler next to him, and said, "Keep drinking."

"He says we're in *gut* shape, Henry. We just needed some water."

Emma smiled, and Henry had the sudden desire—the need—to put his arms around her. Instead of doing so, he said, "That's *gut*, Emma."

It seemed insufficient, barely touching the depth of gratitude he felt that she wasn't harmed.

Before he could put those thoughts into words, Tess walked up to them. "I don't know how to thank you."

"No need."

"But there is, Henry. You got involved in something you could have ignored. You were a friend to Sophia, and you were kind to me. You both showed amazing courage."

"Courage is simply fear that has said its prayers." Henry nearly laughed when Emma rolled her eyes, but weren't the proverbs of their parents and grandparents always spot-on? It seemed to Henry that they were, that he was only beginning to understand the wisdom there.

"Maybe," Tess conceded. "Maybe there's something to that."

She squeezed Henry's good arm and pulled Emma into a hug. The women stood there, arms around each other as sunlight caused the sand to sparkle, the sound of cranes filling the air.

Seventy-One

They were all loaded into the golf carts and driven to the visitor center. Henry supposed the place was closed temporarily, as he didn't see any other tourists—no bird-watchers at all. They had the place to themselves.

"It's a crime scene," Grayson explained. "Can't let anyone in until we collect all of the evidence. First order of business is getting your arm looked at."

Two additional paramedics had been waiting for their arrival.

"Looks like it grazed your deltoid. You're lucky it didn't go any deeper, or you could be looking at surgery and rehab." The young Hispanic woman cleaned and rebandaged Henry's arm, reminding him to "see your physician within the next twenty-four hours."

After he had put his shirt back on, Henry glanced up and looked out the window in time to see Anderson being loaded into a police cruiser.

"What's he doing here?" Emma asked as she came up beside him.

"I don't know, but he was involved in this somehow." He walked over to the window and thought he saw Anderson glare his way, but he could have been imagining it. The officer driving blipped the siren once, but left his lights off as he proceeded out of the parking area.

Sheriff Grayson walked in, but he didn't ask them any questions. Though Henry had seen him at the bottom of the dune, Grayson now pumped his hand as though they were dear old friends, which he supposed they were. Grayson made sure they had additional bottles of water to drink, and some snacks were spread out across one of the counters. Henry chose a glazed donut. "Not as *gut* as the widows' baking, but it's not bad."

He would have preferred coffee, but the paramedics had insisted they needed to hydrate.

"My family's going to be very worried," Emma said.

"I sent an officer out to let them know you're fine." Grayson took off his hat and ran a hand over the top of his head. "Henry mentioned that you ladies are in possession of a flash drive? I'm going to need that."

Tess dug it out of her pocket and handed it to him. He thanked her, and then he asked, "Password protected, right?"

Emma and Tess shared a smile.

"Capital C, capital B, 021412," Tess said, her eyes shining with unshed tears.

"We're going to need you to wait here until we can get your statement. I know you're tired, and I apologize." Grayson hurried out of the building.

Henry and Emma were patient. After all, they were used to the unhurried tempo of farm life. They weren't surprised or terribly put out when things moved slowly. Tess, however, paced the room, threw questions out at no one in particular, and mumbled to herself.

Finally, Grayson came back, but he wasn't alone. Agent Delaney was with him.

Like the other times Henry had been in the agent's presence, the man wore a crisp white shirt, black jacket, and a tie—this one again black so it matched his pants. He was still pale, still had short black hair and blue eyes. But now those eyes struck Henry as shrewd rather than frosty—the only difference being that he was no longer looking at Henry in an accusatory way.

They pulled their chairs into a circle and got down to business.

"Mr. Lapp—"

"Henry."

"Henry, I owe you an apology. Grayson vouched for you, but I wouldn't listen."

"To be fair, you were being misled."

"I was. The tip hotline lit up within an hour of my being on scene, and a good portion of those tips incriminated you."

"Then it's understandable that you would question my innocence."

"Actually, it's not understandable. I was too eager to close this one. I'm sorry."

"Apology accepted," Henry said.

Delaney looked surprised to be forgiven so easily, but he nodded once, pulled out his phone, and pushed some buttons as he muttered, "I need to record this."

He proceeded to pepper them with questions.

Forty-five minutes later, he clicked off the recording.

"Now can you tell us what's going on?" Tess asked. "I'm not leaving here until I have answers. Why was Sophia killed? She had evidence, didn't she? Evidence about what they were doing?"

Delaney sank back into his chair. "Officially, I'm not allowed to share details of an ongoing investigation."

The special agent stared out the window, and then he allowed his gaze to travel across the three of them. "You three have been through a lot, and we believe your actions will lead directly to the arrest of someone the bureau's been chasing a long time."

He blew out a long breath. "I don't bend the rules often, but this time I'd say you've earned some answers."

"Why was Sophia killed?"

"Your sister had evidence of the crime taking place. We found a burner phone and a camera in a Dumpster near Paddock's truck. She abandoned it in a gas station parking lot in Walsenburg, where she stole a different vehicle. We have the plate number, and the vehicle had onboard navigation. We're tracking her now."

"Will you catch her?" Emma asked.

"There's every reason to believe we will, Mrs. Fisher."

"The phone was my sister's?"

"Apparently, Sophia bought it when she first moved to Monte Vista. I'm sure when we search phone records for that number, we'll find the voice mail recording your sister made to you. More pertinent to this investigation, Sophia took photographs of a pickup at the Monte Vista Refuge, one similar to what you three described. The camera Paddock left behind was Sophia's too."

"So they were stealing animals?" Emma asked.

"Technically, it's called poaching—the illegal hunting or capture of animals on land that is not your own. In this case, on national park land, which makes it a federal crime."

"And they would kill for that?"

"A large bull elk like the one you saw airlifted out? The antlers alone would be worth thousands of dollars, but they weren't hunting these animals. We believe, based on evidence we've recovered, they were selling them to managed land places. You know, private hunts, that sort of thing."

"So someone stole them to sell them to someone else, and the person who purchased them planned to kill them or allow them to be hunted." Tess's voice rose. "And then they killed Cooper and my sister to cover it up?"

"We suspect we'll learn the people who were purchasing the animals planned to use them as breeding stock. And the reason your sister and her husband were killed? Greed, one of the most common motives for murder."

Seventy-Two

'll agree with you about greed being a common motive for murder."
Henry struggled to order his thoughts. "But fifty thousand, even a hundred thousand, isn't that much money, not to an *Englischer*."

"Multiply that many times over. I suspect we'll find this has been going on for some time."

"Who was Clayton?" Emma asked. "I heard that name when Paddock was on the phone."

Grayson looked as if he wanted to answer, but Delaney stopped him. "We can't share that information, not at this point."

"Officer Anderson is under arrest?"

"Yes. We caught him trying to destroy some of the call logs at headquarters. He'd been contacted and told to turn the investigation toward you, Henry. He's the one who fabricated anonymous tips about your having an argument with Sophia, your taking her to a hotel—"

"Which I did."

"The tip said you were there for more than an hour. We now know from the CCTV footage that isn't true. I'm not sure how Anderson thought he could get away with it, but I know why. He confessed to receiving a large payment, which he claims he needed for his retirement."

"Was he also responsible for your getting removed from the case?"

"Yes. He fabricated some complaints and sent them up the chain. It was enough to convince someone I needed time off."

Tess ran a thumb across her bottom lip, back and forth, back and forth. Plainly she was struggling between relief that the killers had been found and grief over the loss of her sister. "I want them all in jail."

"And I believe that will happen. It was very clever of you to take the video."

"But it didn't load."

"You live streamed it. When you did, our tip hotline as well as the local police switchboard lit up with people calling in what they'd seen. It's amazing how many people are online in the middle of the night." Delaney shrugged as if he couldn't fathom the ways of today's generation.

"How did you find us?" Emma asked. "I thought we would sit behind that sand dune for days. We were in the back of the park amid the hills. How did you find our exact location? How did you get there so quickly?"

"James Brownfield."

"Who?" Henry asked.

"You know him as Jimmy," Delaney said. "I don't have all of the information, but he is a federal investigator who had gone undercover to catch the poachers and their operation."

"So he wasn't actually helping Paddock."

"No, Ms. Savalas. Agent Brownfield wanted to stay and apologize to you for that. He wasn't with Paddock the night she killed your sister. They'd sent him to the other end of the supply chain to oversee the arrival of the animals. He thinks if he had been here, he could have saved her."

"It's not his fault," Henry said.

"No, it's not. And when I first arrived to investigate the murder of a young woman on national park land, I wasn't immediately made aware of the other investigation." Delaney rested his elbows on his knees and stared down at the floor. When he glanced up, he looked almost like a normal man rather than a hardened agent. "If we had coordinated better, we might have been able to capture Paddock before you three were in danger."

"Sophia would still be dead," Tess whispered.

"True, but it's unfortunate that we had no way to link the murder of Sophia Brooks to the unlawful capture of wildlife in the national parks. In retrospect, we should have made that connection earlier."

"I heard gunshots." Henry's hand went up and unconsciously touched his bandaged shoulder. "Several shots as I was rushing to push Tess and Emma out of the way."

"Agent Brownfield had circled back around behind Paddock. She managed to get a shot off, and he was hit in the leg." Delaney glanced at his watch. "He should be in surgery right now. CareFlight transported him to the hospital in Alamosa."

"Is he going to be all right?" Emma asked.

"He is. He lost quite a bit of blood, but the bullet passed through cleanly. Agent Brownfield managed to crawl off into the woods, where he called for backup. In the meantime, he told us, she continued shooting at you."

Emma leaned forward, rubbing her forehead. Henry worried that she was getting sick, possibly even with one of her migraines. It would be no surprise if the night had taken its toll on her health, but then she snapped her fingers and sat up straighter.

"I remember now. I remember what was bothering me. When Jimmy asked where Paddock was taking us, she said *same place as last time*. What did that mean? Did they kill someone else?"

"No. They did not, but I can't tell you any more than that."

Delaney stood and smoothed down his tie. "If you have no more questions, I'm sure they need me in the field. Again, I want to offer my condolences to you, Ms. Savalas, and I'd like to thank all three of you for your help. I'm sure the federal prosecutor tasked with trying this case will be in contact regarding your testimony."

He'd made it to the door, and Grayson was standing to indicate the meeting was over, when Emma said, "How did you find us? I know Jimmy, or rather Agent Brownfield, told you where we jumped off the dune, but how did you find us so quickly?"

"Easy," Grayson said. "Henry's monitor led us right to you."

"Speaking of that, you'll be able to remove it now…right?" Emma's voice held such hope that Henry nearly laughed.

"I'll contact the judge."

"So the monitor helped you find me?"

"Once Stuart told me where you'd gone, I called the local office, and they used one of our drones to locate the signal."

"A drone?" Emma shook her head, as if she had trouble trying to picture what he was saying.

"About this big." Grayson cupped his hands as if he were holding a small animal. "Doesn't make much sound, moves quickly—"

"Like a bird."

"Yes." Grayson smiled. "Exactly like a bird."

Emma glanced at Henry, and he knew her well enough to understand she was remembering the words from Genesis.

You intended to harm me, but God intended it for good.

Delaney had opened the door, letting in a breeze that carried the scent of falling leaves and the call of distant cranes. He reached into his pocket and pulled out the flash drive that had held Cooper's notes and Sophia's journal. He fingered the device and turned back to Emma and Tess. "How did you figure out the password?"

The two women shared a smile, and Henry had to repress a chuckle. It didn't seem right to laugh in this situation, but then life took such strange twists and turns that he did find amusing, even amid tragedy.

He'd often considered that day when a baseball slugged him in the head and left him unconscious as the worst day of his life. It had marked him forever as different. It had changed the path of his days, but God had used even such a thing as an accident with a baseball.

"Henry's drawing," Tess said. "He'd drawn my sister, down to the last detail, including her tattoo."

"CB—her husband, Cooper Brooks," Emma said.

"And 021412, the day they met," Tess added.

Delaney nodded, as if what she was saying made sense. He'd never seen Henry's drawings, and he didn't ask to now. He thanked them again, walked out the door, and climbed into his black SUV.

Seventy-Three

Emma's family practically smothered her in hugs, and she didn't mind one bit. Over and over she assured Stephen and Thomas that she was all right. They'd hurried home from school on their lunch break to "check on *Mammi*." Finally convinced that she was fine, they'd each grabbed an apple out of the fruit bowl and assured Rachel it was all they needed, and then they took off running down the lane.

"Does my heart *gut* to see those two living a normal, calm, and simple life."

Clyde had grunted at that. "Perhaps now we all can, if you and Henry will stop getting involved with murders."

Silas stood with his back to the kitchen counter, arms crossed, grinning at Emma as if he was inexplicably proud of her.

She sank onto a kitchen chair and gave them the quick version of what had happened, hitting only the highlights. Clyde, Rachel, Silas, and Katie Ann stared at her, mouths open, eyes wide, and then they all started asking questions at once.

Rachel was the one who came to her senses and said, "The details can wait. You're home, you're safe, and you're probably starving."

Emma admitted that she hadn't managed to eat anything at the park office.

She promised to share all of the details later. Silas gave her a hug and said, "Glad you're home, *Mammi*. Maybe you should be like other grandmothers and take up a hobby. You know, other than solving murders."

Clyde patted her clumsily on the shoulder and headed back out to the fields.

Rachel and Katie Ann insisted on making her a lunch of warm soup, cheese, and fresh bread.

"This bread is *wunderbaar*. Did you make it?" she asked Rachel.

"You know better. My bread-baking abilities are marginal at best."

"We were so worried when you weren't here this morning." Katie Ann perched on the edge of a chair across from her. "The widows came by, wanting to know if you were home yet. When their whole story came out, I thought *Dat* was going to drive the buggy all the way to the sand dunes."

"But then an officer arrived to tell us you were fine." Rachel blew on her coffee and smiled over the rim of the mug.

"I went into town to let the widows know." Katie Ann smiled mischievously. "Figured while I was there I should buy a few things—bread, cookies, and even a pie for later this evening. So we can celebrate. The widows seem quite proud they could pass on your message. To hear them tell it, they're responsible for solving Sophia's murder and returning the valley to safety."

Emma laughed. "There will be no stopping them now. They were already selling out of everything they could make."

"And now the newspeople are there." Katie Ann squirreled up her nose. "They're like flies on a summer day. I won't be going back until they grow tired of the story. I'm proud of you, *Mammi*, but I'd rather my photograph not be on the front page of the *Monte Vista Gazette*."

"Why are they hanging out at the bakery?"

"Are you kidding?" Rachel ran a hand up and down her neck. "Bread 2 Go is becoming quite the meeting place. Think about it. They're positioned at the crossroads. They see everyone who comes and goes. And you know how Ruth loves to talk."

"Why didn't you tell the widows to come and see us last night?" Katie Ann rubbed her fingertips over the table her grandfather had made before she was born.

"I didn't want to worry you."

Rachel's eyebrows shot up.

"I thought you might be asleep."

"While you were still out?"

"I am a grown woman."

"And a member of this family. Even though you told us not to wait up, of course we did. We were worried. But then Clyde said you were with Henry and Tess, and that maybe you'd decided to stay the night at Tess's motel rather than come home so late. So we went to bed. We just didn't sleep very well."

"And how did Henry know to follow us to the dunes? I never thought to ask him."

"Nancy went by herself to tell him you'd gone out there."

"Why would she do that when I told her to wait until morning?"

Rachel shrugged, but Katie Ann grinned and said, "She told me the Holy Spirit prompted her to do it, that the mare practically took off toward Henry's house on her own."

"If she hadn't…" A tremor passed through Emma's body, and she suddenly wished she hadn't eaten lunch after all. If Nancy hadn't told Henry, he wouldn't have arrived in time to jump into the back of the truck. He wouldn't have followed them up the trail. Unless Jimmy had somehow saved them on his own, they'd have been shot by a murderous park ranger while they perched at the top of a sand dune.

"Are you okay?" Rachel scooted to the edge of her chair.

"Fine. Only a little tired." Emma shook her head, still amazed at how things had turned out. "I am sorry I worried you, but you shouldn't—"

"I know." Rachel held up a hand to stop her protest. "You're a grown woman and can take care of yourself, but after what happened with the Monte Vista arsonist, you can't blame a daughter-in-law for being concerned."

Her nausea passed, and Emma reached for another slice of warm bread to butter it. "Oh, I won't blame you for it. I'll thank you. Having a family worry means someone cares about you. I'm sorry, though, to have put you through it."

"Why did you go with Sophia's *schweschder, Mammi*?" Katie Ann leaned forward in her chair, arms crossed and a puzzled look on her face. "You had to know it would be dangerous."

"I suppose I thought it might be, but mostly I didn't want Tess to have to go through anything else alone. It seemed that she'd been through so much already."

"But you barely knew her," Rachel pointed out.

"True." Emma took a bite of the bread, savored the freshness of it, the richness of the butter. Life was good. Far better than she deserved. She'd be on her knees before bed, thanking the Lord for all of the blessings in her life.

"She's not going to explain it any better than that," Rachel teased.

"Only because I don't know how. I'm learning that sometimes you know a person far better than would seem possible. You're right. I had known Tess less than twenty-four hours, and in truth I didn't know Sophia so well either."

"*Gotte* bless her soul," Rachel murmured.

"I know what you mean, though." Katie Ann sat back, twirling one *kapp* string between her forefinger and thumb. "Sometimes when I go with Doc Berry to help with an animal, especially with a horse, it seems I've known that animal all my life. We have an instant connection, even though I've never set eyes on it before. It's like something I read in one of *Mamm*'s books. We're kindred spirits."

Rachel reached over and patted her daughter's hand. "*Gut* to know you're reading a little."

"How could I not? You have books everywhere in this house. It's as if we have an Amish library." Katie Ann turned her attention back to her grandmother. "Is that what you mean? That you felt as though Sophia was a kindred spirit, and you shared a special bond? Maybe that bond was Henry."

"It could be you're right. I saw how much he was worried about her, and so I wanted to help. As for Tess, I kept thinking of the golden rule, of how I would want to be treated if I were lost and alone."

Katie Ann jumped out of her chair and wrapped her arms around Emma. "But you're not lost or alone. You have us."

She stepped back and grinned impishly. "And you have Henry too."

Then she bounded out of the house, toward the barn and the animals she loved so much.

"It's *gut* to see the children, to see them running across the fields and toward the barns, to know they're safe and happy."

"It's just as *gut* to know the same about you." Rachel slipped a book out of her apron pocket and slid it onto the table. "We love you, *Mamm*. You mean the world to us."

Emma wanted to answer that, but she didn't trust herself to do so without breaking into tears. She certainly didn't want to alarm Rachel more than she already had, so she ducked her head and scooped the last bit of soup out of her bowl.

The spoon felt inexplicably heavy, and she became aware of the fact that her eyes were burning.

"You're exhausted. How about a nap since you couldn't have slept much last night?"

It had been a joke between them for years, that Amish women didn't nap, unlike the heroines in the books Rachel read.

"I suppose this once…"

"*Ya*, just this once." Rachel whisked the dishes off the table, helped Emma to stand, though she was perfectly capable of standing by herself, and walked her to her bedroom.

The last thing Emma was aware of was her daughter-in-law pulling back the covers and closing the blinds. And then she fell into a deep, untroubled sleep.

Seventy-Four

Henry spent the afternoon at home. Lunch was followed by a short nap in his rocker, and then he paid attention to his dog and attended to a few small projects in his workshop. He needed the normalcy of routine. It was hard to fathom what they'd been through in such a short time. It had been less than a week since Sophia died, two days since he'd been arrested for her murder, twelve hours since Paddock had tried to kill them.

His arm was still stiff from where the bullet had grazed him, but he had absolutely no intention of going to the doctor. It was barely more than a scratch. If he ran to the doctor every time he cut a finger on a piece of wood or scratched his arms in the barn, he'd accomplish nothing in a day, not to mention the money he'd waste. So instead of heading over to see Doc Wilson, he took some of the Advil he found in the back of a kitchen cabinet. Then he sat out on the front porch and watched the sun make its westward trek, Lexi content to lie at his feet.

No one interrupted the silence.

His congregation would understand that he needed a little time alone—time to pray and to rest and to come to terms with all that had happened. As he did those things, Henry was aware of how much his friends cared about him.

The widows had left blueberry oatmeal muffins in a basket on the porch. Stuart had penciled a note and left it under his saltshaker on the table, telling him to call if he needed a ride anywhere. Someone had brought by fresh milk and eggs. Emma's grandson Silas had cared for Oreo. A child's drawing of Henry with a giant head, a body heart shaped like a valentine, and extra-long arms had been stuffed into his mailbox.

He could have spent the entire afternoon counting his blessings, and he did some of that. But he also petitioned God for the well-being of Tess Savalas. He prayed for Emma, that she would suffer no ill effects from their breakneck plunge down the dunes. He prayed that her spirit would be calm and her heart at peace. He lifted up the young man he knew as Jimmy to the Lord and prayed for his injury. He thanked God for the widows and for Stuart and for Sheriff Grayson. He even managed to utter a word of gratitude for Agent Delaney, whom perhaps he had misjudged.

He thanked God for His protection, for the loving community he'd been placed in the middle of, and for the strange and unusual gift he'd been given. As darkness descended, he had an early dinner and went to bed soon after.

The next day he heard the sound of an approaching horse before he'd finished his morning coffee. Abe hopped out of the buggy with a grin on his face and a package in his hand. "Chocolate zucchini bread from Susan."

"She'll fatten me up yet."

"She thought you might say that and wants you to know you've earned the extra calories this week."

Henry accepted the package and invited Abe in for a cup of coffee.

"I'd love to, but I've a list of errands longer than my arm."

"You didn't have to stop by."

"Are you kidding? Susan wouldn't let me rest until I'd seen you were fine with my own eyes. Of course, we all knew you were. You know how it is." He pushed his glasses up with his index finger. "Word gets around."

"Indeed it does."

"Also, she wanted you to know that she went by and saw Deborah King yesterday. The baby's still a bit colicky, but Deborah seems to be faring better. According to Susan, she didn't burst into tears even once."

"A real improvement."

Abe climbed back into his buggy. Then he leaned out and said, "I checked in on Chester because I knew you were worried about him getting in his winter crop. He only had a little left, and we knocked it out yesterday afternoon."

"You're a *gut* man, Abe Graber."

"My bishop taught me well."

Abe resettled his hat on his head, raised a hand in farewell, and turned the buggy back up Henry's lane.

Henry had checked on Oreo and was working in his garden when Grayson showed up.

"I wanted you to hear it from me. We arrested Carla Paddock last night."

"No one was hurt?"

"Caught her outside the Colorado Springs airport. She'd booked a private charter, hoping to stay under the radar."

"But you were tracking the car she stole."

"Exactly."

"How did she not guess that?"

Grayson shrugged. "Arrogance? I've learned you can never fully understand some people's thinking. It's a waste of energy to try. She gave up once she understood she was surrounded."

Henry blew out a sigh of relief. He hadn't realized how worried he'd been. "That's *gut*. We can put this behind us now."

"I'd say you've earned a rest."

"And maybe you can take some of that vacation you were supposed to be on."

Grayson reached into his car and pulled out a device that looked like a pair of pliers. "How about we get that bracelet off you?"

Henry nearly laughed then. "You're sure it's okay with the judge?"

"I received a call from him an hour ago. He said you could come into the office or—"

"Here's fine."

Five minutes later, Henry stood in the garden, watching the sheriff drive back down his lane and turn onto the blacktop. They'd made a good team, but he was content to return to the life of a bishop and craftsman.

By the time he made it over to his workshop and began sanding a garden bench, he heard the sound of another buggy, and then Leroy Kauffmann walked into the room.

"*Gudemariye*," Leroy said.

"And to you."

"Wanted to check to see if you need anything."

"I don't, but it's *gut* to see you."

Henry thought of the drawings Tess still had, of the one showing Leroy shrewdly watching Sophia. He'd never actually doubted the man standing in front of him. He was a good man and an excellent deacon, though given to bouts of somberness.

He would always wonder, though, if he didn't ask. "You know I did some drawings of Sophia."

"*Ya*, I heard." Leroy picked up a birdhouse from the worktable, ran his fingertips back and forth across the smoothly sanded wood.

"I was trying to find some clue as to what had happened and why. In the process, I inadvertently captured other people who were in the diner at the time."

Leroy glanced up sharply.

"You were in two of the pictures, looking none too happy."

"And?"

"Well, Leroy, I was wondering if perhaps you wanted to share what was bothering you."

The momentary look of defiance slipped from Leroy's expression. He sank onto a stool and admitted, "I've been worried about Jesse."

Henry waited.

"He seems more rebellious than ever."

"I wasn't aware your son was struggling."

"Most people aren't aware. I don't think he even realizes it." Leroy pulled off his hat and rubbed one side of his head roughly as if he could bat around his thoughts hard enough to make sense of them. "I know one of the days you're speaking of. I saw you in the diner as well. I should have come over and said hello."

"Figured you were busy."

"I was meeting with some men who wanted to purchase a part of my crop for the cranes."

"And?"

"We're still in negotiation, but as we were eating, I saw Jesse walking by the diner. He was using one of those *Englisch* cell phones. The lad wastes his money on the most foolish things."

Henry waited, knowing there was more by the look on Leroy's face.

"He's dating not one, but two girls—one Plain and the other *Englisch*."

Henry had no children, but he could imagine what Leroy was going through—how he must pick up his burden of concern when he opened his eyes each morning, carry it all day, and finally set it down when he drifted off to sleep. "It's hard not to worry over those we love. However, Jesse is…what? Twenty years old?"

"Twenty-one."

"The time of *rumspringa* often extends into the early twenties."

"I thought we'd avoided it altogether, that Jesse was confident and sure of our way of life."

"Yet you understand it is our custom to allow the *youngies* to try *Englisch* things, to let them experience that way of life before choosing whether to live *Englisch* or join the church and live under the *Ordnung*."

"*Ya*. Of course I know that. But it's difficult when it's your own child."

"Except he's not a child anymore."

"I know that too."

Henry stood, walked over, and picked up the birdhouse Leroy had been examining. "I imagine Bethany is worried as well."

"She is."

"Give her this for me. I want you both to remember that *Gotte* is watching over Jesse, same as He watches over the sparrow."

Leroy closed his eyes for a moment, nodded, and then accepted the gift.

They walked out to Leroy's buggy, Lexi running circles at their feet, the sun rising into the vast, blue Colorado sky.

This was his life. Being a bishop to his congregation, being a friend to his neighbors, trying to carry God's light into his small corner of the world. It was a good life, and as he watched Leroy drive away, he realized he was only occasionally lonely.

But there was a remedy for that.

The question was whether he had the courage to pursue it.

Seventy-Five

Emma slept for a solid two hours the day she was rescued, another ten hours that night, and still she took a nap after lunch the next day. Perhaps her body was recovering from what she'd been through. Perhaps stress and fear took a higher toll than a day of domestic chores.

She woke from her nap feeling more like her old self, eager to bake a batch of cookies for the boys' after-school snack and help Rachel with dinner. The afternoon passed quickly, and they were setting the dishes on the table when she heard a knock at the front door.

"I'll get that." She hurried through the sitting room, surprised to see Henry standing there, his hat in his hands.

"We were just sitting down to eat."

"I've come at a bad time."

"Not at all. You know there's always room for you at our table."

By the time they'd walked into the kitchen, the children were already moving down the bench to make room for Henry. Everyone bowed their head for the usual silent blessing of the food, but Henry cleared his throat, looked at Clyde, and said, "May I?"

"Of course."

"We want to thank You, heavenly Father, for Your gifts. For the gift of life and of friendship, for Your hand of protection over our lives, for allowing this beautiful family to share another meal again, for placing me in the position to be their bishop. For all of these things, and of course for the food before us, we give You thanks in the name of Christ."

Amens rolled around the table like the wind playing gently across the crops.

And then dishes were passed—ham and carrots and mashed potato rolls and gravy and salad and a large pitcher of water. Emma was content to enjoy the meal and listen to the conversations around her. Clyde and Silas discussing the crops. Katie Ann telling her mother about an injured bird she'd found in the barn loft—she'd managed to wrap its wing and was going to take it with her to Doc Berry's on Friday. The boys describing to Henry a fish they'd caught the weekend before with their father.

"And we're going back on Saturday," Stephen said.

"You should come with us, Henry." Thomas pulled another potato roll off the serving plate.

"Oh, I don't know."

"Don't you like to fish?" Stephen asked. "I thought everyone liked to fish."

"Well, *ya*. I do, actually."

"Then you'll come." Clyde pointed his fork at his bishop. "It would do you *gut* to rest once in a while, and there's nothing quite as calming as a few hours spent with a fishing pole in your hand."

Henry's smile caused something in Emma's heart to ache. For a moment he looked so grateful, so pleased to be included in their plans, and then he covered it up by scratching at his beard and saying, "I suppose I could clear out a few hours in the afternoon."

Once dinner was over and the dishes were cleared from the table, the children took off to do their evening chores. Rachel poured coffee into four mugs and passed three to Clyde, Emma, and Henry.

Emma thought the older children would stay to hear the story of what had happened on the sand dunes. But Katie Ann was worried about the bird and said she'd "get the scoop from *Mamm* tomorrow."

Silas apparently had a girl to meet. "As long as you're okay, that's what matters. Not the how of it."

Which was pretty much the same way Emma felt, but Rachel and Clyde wanted details.

So they spent the next hour going over the events that led to Carla Paddock's arrest.

"I can't imagine you climbing to the top of a sand dune, *Mamm*," Clyde said. "Remember the time *Dat* hired a driver to take us up into the mountains? You had to sit with your head between your knees because the height made you so dizzy."

"*Gut* thing Henry pushed me over the ridge, or I would have stood there, frozen, until that woman shot me."

"*Gotte* wouldn't have allowed that to happen, Emma." Henry reached over and squeezed her hand. "It wasn't your day to trade this life for the next."

"So in the end, your drawings led Emma and Tess to the killer." When everyone turned to stare at Rachel, she said, "The password for the computer storage device. Emma and Tess saw it on the drawing, on the tattoo on Sophia's arm. Without that, they never would have accessed the files. If they hadn't read Sophia's online journal and Cooper's notes, they'd never have gone out to the sand dunes. They wouldn't have known the location for the pickup."

No one spoke for a moment, and then Henry said, "Perhaps you're right. If so, then I put your life at risk, Emma, and I'm sorry."

"*Tsk.*" Emma grinned at the sound coming out of her mouth. It seemed so normal. Who really cared if it was the same sound her mother used to make? Age afforded one certain privileges, and perhaps tsking was one of them. "It wasn't my day. Remember? And besides, all's well that—"

"Ends well. Yeah, yeah." Clyde nodded in agreement. "The important thing is that the guilty person has been arrested and is no longer a threat to anyone."

Henry stood and walked to the sink to rinse out his coffee mug.

Rachel leaned over to stare at his feet, and then she said, "You seem to have lost your ankle monitor."

"Grayson removed it when he came by earlier today."

"And Tess?" Emma asked. "Where is she now?"

"Staying in town for a few days in case Grayson or Delaney need her. She left me a message at the phone shack. Her plane leaves tomorrow, but she'd like to meet at the diner in the morning. Would you like to join us?"

"I'd love to."

Rachel sipped her coffee. "If Tess hadn't come to Monte Vista, if she hadn't sought us out, *Mamm* never would have remembered the flash drive Sophia gave her."

"You probably would have washed it." Clyde smiled.

Clyde had a habit of leaving bits of paper in his pockets, small scraps he'd write notes on. It had taken Rachel the first ten years of their marriage to remember to check garments for notes before washing them. Emma knew her son had learned the habit from his father. She still had a few of George's notes—precious memories of a man who had brought joy and happiness to her life for many years.

Make appointment with the farrier.

Bring down more hay from the loft.

Pick up a rosebush for Emma.

Emma treasured each piece of paper, each memory. Even as she looked across the table and admitted to herself how much she cared for Henry, she understood that George had helped her become the woman she was. Henry's friendship and George's love had been highlights of her life.

"If either of us had washed it..." Rachel stared down into her mug.

Paddock would still be free, planning the next pickup and willing to kill anyone who got in her way. It was a sobering thought.

"Tess came here because Sophia called her." Emma tapped her fingers against the table. "After talking to Henry, she called her *schweschder*. Remember? We all heard the message. Sophia wanted to tell Tess how much she cared about her. Sophia was going to find her husband's killer, regardless how much it put her own life in danger. But after meeting you"—she reached out and touched Henry's shoulder—"she took the time to contact her *schweschder*. She made things right with what was left of her family."

"Tess is the reason we were able to lead the police to Paddock," Henry agreed. "At great personal risk, she sought us out and insisted on solving the mystery. She's a very stubborn, very brave woman."

After that there wasn't much to say on the subject.

Henry claimed to be done solving murders.

Emma vowed she was going to begin knitting again. "Silas had a great idea. He suggested I be like other grandmothers and take up a hobby. Preferably something I can do at home, on the porch, at ground level."

Which caused everyone to laugh. When Rachel stood to take care of the dinner dishes, Emma insisted on helping her, and Henry said something to Clyde she couldn't hear.

Clyde glanced at Emma, nodded his head once, and they trooped out the back door toward the barn.

"I wonder what that was about," Emma said.

"I don't know, but did you see the way Henry was looking at you?"

"Looking at me?"

"During dinner."

"He looked at me during dinner?"

"Like he couldn't get enough of the sight of you. I think it frightened him, your life being in danger."

Emma almost tsked, but she decided once a night was probably enough of that. No need to completely indulge being old and cranky. Besides, she didn't feel old. After all they'd been through the last week, and after two days of sleeping as much as she could, she felt surprisingly alive and energetic. There might be something to taking an afternoon nap after all.

"How do you feel about him?"

"About who?"

"Henry. Who else?" Rachel rinsed a plate and passed it to Emma.

"Of course I care for him. He's been a *gut freind* nearly all of my life and a *gut* bishop too." But deep in her heart she knew that wasn't what Rachel was asking. Emma dried three more plates and added, "I loved Clyde's *dat*. I suppose a part of me always will, but I love Henry too. Is that silly? Someone in their sixties thinking about such things?"

"It's not silly at all. They say sixty is the new forty."

"Who says that?"

"People."

"What does it mean?"

Rachel washed the last plate and set it in the rinse water. She dried her hands before turning to place one on each of Emma's shoulders. "It means you're as young as you feel."

"I'm not, though. My knees pop and crackle, I have white eyelashes that poke out in funny directions, and my hands look like an old person's."

"Your heart, *Mamm*. I suppose I was referring to your heart."

Seventy-Six

Henry and Emma sat across from Tess in the corner booth of Maggie's Diner.

It was at the height of the breakfast rush, and the place was bustling. Most of the bar stools along the counter were full, their chrome and leather sparkling in the light beginning to shine through the large plate glass windows.

Folks chatted and ate and discussed the weather as the sun rose over the San Luis Valley, and Emma noticed how the waitresses moved back and forth across the checkered floor, waiting on customers, feeding the masses, spreading good cheer in their own special way.

The bell over the door jingled, and Sheriff Grayson stepped inside, looked around, and then walked to their table to join them. They spoke of inconsequential things until they'd placed their order. Then Grayson folded his arms on the table and proceeded to catch them up on the investigation.

"The feds have put a lot of people on this, and information is still coming in, so I don't know everything. But Delaney briefed me last night, and I do know more than the twenty-four-hour news outlets."

As one they turned their heads to look out the window. The news media people had been camped both at Bread 2 Go and the diner. What had been a dozen television vans had been reduced to two. Henry suspected they'd be gone in another day or so, chasing another story. What had happened in the San Luis Valley was quickly becoming yesterday's news, and he rather preferred it that way.

"Everything points to this being a multimillion-dollar operation."

Grayson sipped the coffee brought to him by their waitress, grimaced, and grabbed a package of sugar. "Feds are still attempting to trace all of the purchases, which they're able to do because Paddock kept detailed records. Apparently, she's a bit OCD."

"OCD?" Emma glanced at Henry and then back at Grayson. "What is OCD?"

"Obsessive-compulsive disorder. It's a type of anxiety that causes people to do things in a repetitive or meticulous way."

"Like this?" Emma touched each of her fingers to her thumb.

"I noticed that too," Tess said. "I thought it might be a signal or something, but then why bother with signals when you're the one holding the gun?"

"I guess it could be a symptom of OCD," Grayson said. "Maybe she was counting in her head. No doubt it was a compulsion of some sort. People with this disorder can be as smart or smarter than anyone else, but they have an overwhelming need to address an irrational fear. In this case, Paddock needed things to be in order even though she was part of a dangerous poaching scheme."

"She told us to get in line." Tess turned to Emma. "Remember? When she first confronted us with the rifle. She kept moving you around, like she needed to line us up exactly so."

"And when we turned toward the dunes, she warned me to stay in a straight line. I couldn't figure out what difference it made."

"Sounds like a deeply disturbed person," Henry said.

"And yet it worked to our benefit," the sheriff said.

"How so?" Emma asked.

"She kept things she should have destroyed, like Sophia's camera. Her photos are more proof we can use in the upcoming trials."

"Her compulsion wouldn't allow her to throw it away?" Henry shook his head in disbelief.

"Correct. Paddock had to know, on one level, that she shouldn't be keeping records, but we think she couldn't help herself. We found them handwritten on an accounting tablet back at her place—names, dates, amounts, animals sold. It's a treasure trove of information."

"And that's *gut*?" Emma asked.

"Yes. Those records will help the feds specifically locate and charge all persons involved. Her records, those precise dates and amounts, will help us trace the funds. In the end, it will go a long way to ensuring all parties involved are held accountable in federal court for their actions."

"Millions of dollars…for elk." Emma shook her head. "It's still hard to imagine."

"Oh, they didn't poach only elk. They took bighorn sheep, cougars, deer, and even a bear. It was quite the operation, and it had been going on for almost three years."

"Do you know the name of Cooper's source? BT?" Tess asked.

"I do not. I suspect Delaney does, but he hasn't shared it with me." Grayson raised his eyes and waited for Tess to meet his gaze. "There's something else. The final autopsy reports are in. Your sister was hit with a tranquilizer before she was strangled."

"Like they used on the animals." Emma reached out and clasped Tess's hand. "Paddock told us it could be a lethal dose."

"It wasn't, but the thing is, she was unconscious when she was killed. She didn't feel anything. It's one of the reasons she didn't fight back."

"They shot her with a tranquilizer gun?"

"Yes, like the one Paddock was carrying the night she abducted you two."

"And then one of her men strangled her?"

Grayson nodded, Emma continued to hold Tess's hand, and Henry closed his eyes as if in prayer. No one said anything for the space of a few moments. Emma guessed Tess would eventually be relieved to know her sister didn't suffer, but right now the poor woman was probably in shock. Too much had happened in too short a period of time.

The waitress brought their food—plates piled high with pancakes and eggs and bacon and pan-fried potatoes. Once she'd refilled their coffee mugs and told them to holler if they needed anything, Grayson continued.

"Paddock was second in charge. The real mastermind was a man named Clayton Clarke."

"The name she mentioned by mistake," Tess said.

"And the person she was texting." Grayson picked up the saltshaker, thought better of it, and settled for pepper instead.

"I wondered what she was doing on her phone."

"At first she was confirming instructions, but in the end she was threatening Mr. Clarke."

"Who is he?" Emma asked.

"He runs a nonprofit called Wildlife Protection Society. We think that's where he made his contacts, people he approached about buying genetically superior animals. Delaney suspects he'll find Clarke was able to funnel the money through that charity."

"So he wasn't setting up hunts?" Emma stabbed at a pancake with her fork.

"No. His real business was providing breeding stock to game management places."

"Have you arrested him?" Tess asked.

"Last night," Grayson said. "Paddock gave up his name within the first hour of her questioning, angling for a plea bargain."

"Will she get it?" Henry asked.

Grayson shrugged and scooped up a forkful of potatoes. "Possibly. Not a reduction in sentence, but Delaney said they would consider petitioning the judge for a better facility, one for white-collar crime, if she continued to work with the investigators."

"But her crime was violent," Tess said.

"It was, and yet not as violent as many of the offenders in federal prison. She doesn't deserve to be on the street, not for a very long time, if ever. But the death penalty? I don't know. It seems to me that life in prison might be punishment enough in this case."

"These people killed my sister and my brother-in-law. Maybe others."

"And they will pay for those crimes."

No one said anything as that sobering thought sank in. Emma felt a profound sadness. What a terrible waste of the gift of life. But perhaps in prison each person involved would have time to consider their deeds and repent for them, to accept the forgiveness of Christ.

Emma thought her appetite should be affected by the topic, but she looked down at her plate dismayed to see that she'd eaten nearly all of her pancakes. She set down her fork and glanced around the table. "So Clayton Clarke ordered the killings, but Paddock carried them out?"

"She did. At least we know she killed Sophia. We have proof of that. Probably Clarke is responsible for the murder of your brother-in-law, though we are still investigating that aspect of the case."

"Why would she do such a thing?" Emma asked. "How could she justify doing such a thing?"

"I can't answer that." Grayson sat back and crossed his arms. "I'm not sure anyone can."

"I should have known better than to put us in that kind of danger," Tess said. "These people had committed murder, yet I thought I could record whatever they were doing and reveal their deeds to the world. If it hadn't been for Jimmy…"

"I try to avoid going down the road of what-ifs," Grayson said.

But Tess wasn't listening. "What if Jimmy hadn't been able to call for help? What if you hadn't answered Stuart's call right away? Or Henry's monitor had malfunctioned? What if no one had called into the police department alerting you to my live streamed video?"

Emma put a hand on Tess's arm to calm her rising panic. "Too bad we don't still have it to add to the boatload of proof you're compiling."

"Actually, we do." Grayson smiled at the look of surprise on Tess's face. "The social media site you used maintains copies of everything live streamed for thirty days in case something like this happens. After that it's erased. I've already seen the footage myself. It will be enough to put Paddock away for the rest of her life for poaching alone. Add in the murder charges, and you can be sure she won't be out on the street again."

They finished their meal in silence. The waitress came to take away their plates, and then Julie Hobbs stopped by their table to say she was glad to see they were okay.

"You helped a lot, and we're grateful," Tess said.

"I don't know how much I helped. Your sister's still gone, but I like to think catching those responsible has eased your pain some."

Emma grabbed her purse off the seat and pawed around in it. "I brought something for you."

She pulled out a small jar of salve. "For your arthritis. If it helps, I can bring more."

Julie seemed embarrassed, but she pocketed the jar of salve and promised she'd give it a try.

Emma's thoughts were pulled back to the investigation when Tess suddenly crossed her arms on the table and leaned forward.

"Tell us about Jimmy."

Grayson glanced around, as if considering whether he should share the information. Finally he shrugged and said, "Agent Brownfield was undercover in Clarke's organization, and that team had just tied what was happening with Clarke to this area—to Monte Vista. Jimmy had been here in Monte Vista for the last month."

"That explains why he was keeping an eye on Sophia."

"Paddock didn't realize he was doing that, but Jimmy had figured out Sophia was here to discover who killed her husband. He didn't want her to get hurt and hoped she'd give up on her search and go home."

"Obviously, he didn't know my sister," Tess said. "She could be quite stubborn."

"What did Jimmy know at that point?" Emma asked.

"Only that someone was taking animals off national park land, but they needed more proof to build a solid case. Jimmy went undercover, pretending to be a teen hooked on video games who wanted to take the hunting and killing of wildlife to the next level. At that point, he had no idea Clarke's and Paddock's crimes involved murder. When he checked into Cooper Brooks's death, it looked like a mugging to him, just as the San Diego police had determined. He didn't understand why Sophia was here or what she hoped to find until later."

Emma snapped her fingers. "When Jimmy asked where Paddock was taking us, she said *same place as last time*. What did that mean? Delaney said it didn't mean they killed someone else."

"On the previous pickup, the one where Sophia was killed, one of the bull elks had a reaction to the tranquilizer. He was dead before they could unload him. The helicopter dropped the animal at the top of the dune, the same place where you were taken, and left it there. Paddock and Agent Brownfield made sure it slid down the back of the dune, where scavengers would take care of the remains."

"Surely there would still be bones," Henry said. "Something to indicate what had been done."

"More than likely, but the dunes are constantly shifting. Any carcass would have been covered with sand within a few days, and we've found no evidence of that particular crime. We're still looking."

"What about the scar on Sophia's neck?" Emma asked. "I remember seeing it in the drawings, and Tess said Sophia didn't have it at her husband's funeral."

"She didn't," Tess confirmed.

Grayson sat back, crossed his arms, and studied the other folks in the diner. "Sophia had tried to go to the police before when she was in San Diego. Clayton Clarke's people were already on to her at that point. As she was walking toward the police station, someone attacked her and held a knife to her throat. She only managed to get away because she was carrying pepper spray. However, the incident left a scar where the knife scraped against her skin."

And then there was nothing else to ask.

Grayson thanked them again for their help, told Henry he'd check on him later in the week, and wished Tess safe travels. He stood to leave, and then he reached into his pocket and pulled out the device Henry had found in his clock. Only now it was in an evidence bag. "I was right. This was an extremely expensive surveillance device."

"Why would they be watching me?"

"That's a question we haven't answered yet, but we will. It had Paddock's fingerprints on it. She admitted to planting Sophia's fingerprints in your home."

"If it weren't for Lexi, she would have listened in on everything we said." Henry shook his head in disbelief.

"If you ever want to get rid of the beagle, she might make a good police dog."

"Not a chance," Emma and Henry said at once.

When he was gone, it was just the three of them, and Emma realized she was going to miss the young woman she'd known such a short time.

"We're sorry, Tess." Henry waited until she raised her gaze to his. "We are deeply sorry for the tragedy you have suffered through and for your losses. We will both pray for you, that *Gotte* will be close and present and a real help in your time of need."

Tess sucked in her bottom lip, but no tears spilled from her eyes.

She squeezed Emma's hand, pulled her purse strap over her shoulder, and stood. When Henry stood too, she stepped closer and put her arms around him before embracing Emma. Wiping the tears from her cheeks, she turned and walked out of the diner.

Seventy-Seven

Monte Vista National Wildlife Refuge
One week later

Henry led Emma to his favorite viewing spot and motioned for her to crouch down in a sea of bulrushes and cattails. Emma raised one eyebrow, but she hiked up her dress so as not to trip over it and squatted beside him. Lexi sat quietly, her nose raised high, smelling, sensing, and abundantly pleased with the outing.

A soft breeze tickled the hair at the nape of Emma's neck.

There was just enough light for Henry to see and recognize how beautiful she was. He was thinking on that, on how to say such a thing and not sound foolish, when the distinctive, rolling cry of cranes filled the morning.

Emma placed her hand on his arm, glanced at him, and smiled. "So many of them."

"*Ya.*"

"And is that"—she cocked her head—"a marsh wren calling?"

"It is."

Emma was a fast learner, which didn't surprise him.

As they waited, dawn's light splashed over the Sangre de Cristo Mountains to the east, crossed the San Luis Valley, and settled on the foothills of the Rockies, bringing the sand dunes into sharp contrast against the mountains. Sunrise turned the marshland into a sea of gold. It reminded him of the enduring nature of God, of their rich harvest of blessings, and of the joy that was theirs to claim.

The heavens declare the glory of God.

"Indeed they do," he mumbled.

"What did you say?"

"Look. There." He passed her the binoculars and pointed to a spot ten yards away and northeast.

He heard the flat rattle call again. The air filled with one *gar-oo-oo* and then another and another.

"I've seen the cranes before," Emma whispered, "but I never stopped to look at them, to watch them."

The adult male nearest them took several steps east. Henry, Emma, and Lexi followed.

They watched the regal creatures for the next hour, moving whenever another group caught their fancy.

As the sun's light rose against the face of the Rockies, Henry glanced around and recognized the section of marsh they had come to. He remembered finding Sophia among the bulrushes and cattails. He would never have wished to become involved in such a thing, but he had been, and there was no changing the past. God's ways were not man's, were certainly not Henry's.

He reminded himself of the good that had come from even such a tragedy as this. Sophia had now been laid to rest. Her sister had found a measure of peace, although Tess would be grieving for some time. She had sent him a short note saying she'd contacted her local pastor and attended church on Sunday. She was young in the faith but intent on seeking God's answers.

As for Sophia, Henry continued to feel a deep loss for the young woman. It was a great solace to him to know that before he'd even stumbled across her body, Sophia's soul had been reunited with their heavenly Father.

Lexi flattened her belly against the mud, stretching her legs in front of and behind her, and then she glanced up at him with a pleading look.

Henry reached for Emma's hand.

"Can I interest you in some breakfast?"

"Maybe one of those slices of spinach and bacon quiche from the diner would be *gut*."

"And hot coffee."

"Perhaps a sticky bun to round it all out."

They walked for a few minutes before Henry found the courage to say, "I spoke to Clyde last week about us."

"Us?"

"I care for you, Emma. Surely you know that I do."

"You do?" She shook her head as if she couldn't fathom why she was repeating his last word each time he spoke. He gave her a moment, and she finally said, "I care for you as well, Henry. But what does that have to do with my son?"

When they reached the edge of the marsh, Henry pulled her over to a bench positioned near the walkway and they both sat down.

"I thought it best to ask his permission. I'd like you to marry me, Emma."

"Marry you?"

"Indeed."

"Oh."

"Oh?"

Emma tugged at both of the strings on her prayer *kapp*, reminding him of a much younger girl. Then she smiled, and his anxiety over asking her melted. "That is... *Ya,* I'd like that very much."

He looked down at their hands, or rather at her hands resting in his. He'd been unaware that he'd reached for them, just as he'd been unaware that he was falling in love with this marvelous woman, someone who had been his friend practically all of his life.

"You don't think we're too old?"

"Rachel says sixty is the new forty."

"What does that mean?"

"I'm not sure. She tried to explain it..." Emma smiled so that the skin around her eyes crinkled. "Perhaps it means we have plenty of years ahead of us, *Gotte* willing."

"*Ya, Gotte* willing."

Lexi put her paws up on the bench and sniffed at Emma and then Henry.

"She seems to approve," Emma said.

"Indeed."

They stood and started for the parking area, where Stuart was waiting to give them a lift back to Monte Vista.

"Where will we live, Henry? When will we marry? When should we tell the congregation?"

"All *gut* questions."

"I suppose it's something we can think on. It's not as if we're in a rush like two *youngies*."

"I am in a rush, though. I want to spend my days and nights with you, share coffee with you on the front porch, and help to raise your great-grandchildren."

"No great-grandchildren expected, though I believe Silas will marry soon."

"And then Katie Ann."

"It all happens so fast."

"Children are a blessing of the Lord, as are grandchildren."

"And great-grandchildren." Emma smiled and touched his arm. "Before the new year, then."

"*Ya*, before then."

Lexi trotted at their heels as they left the marsh, the cranes rising and settling behind them like waves of majestic grain.

Discussion Questions

1. Our main character, Henry Lapp, feels drawn to Sophia Brooks. He believes he is supposed to help her in some way. Is this realistic? Are we ever "called" to help someone outside our circle of friends? What biblical examples can you think of that might relate to this? (Hint: Read Luke 10:25-37.)

2. Henry just happens to stumble across Sophia's body. Is this believable? Could God have directed his steps in this way so that her body could be found and Tess could have at least that small measure of comfort? Proverbs 20:24 says, "A person's steps are directed by the LORD." How have you seen this in your own life? Give specific examples of times when God seemed to be leading you in a particular direction.

3. We learn that Sophia wore lines from the "Serenity Prayer" on a chain around her neck. What does this tell us about Sophia? Does what we wear and what items we have in our homes give others an indication of our faith walk? Why or why not?

4. Before Henry is arrested, he reads from Isaiah 14. Read back over these words, beginning in verse 24. "Surely, as I have planned, so it will be." How do these words comfort you?

5. We have a strange collection of friends in this story: Emma, Henry, Tess, Grayson, and others. Do you think it's possible to have friends from such different backgrounds? Why or why not? Explain your answer.

6. Maggie's Diner manager Julie Hobbs tells Henry, Emma, and Tess she believes Henry is innocent. What reason does she

give? What is her personal experience with the local Amish population? As Christians, how we conduct ourselves and interact with our neighbors says a lot about our faith. Give one example from your town where people of faith reached out to the broader community.

7. Henry has a dream about his mother urging him to hurry, but cautiously. He doesn't completely understand the dream, but the memory of it stays with him as he rushes to aid Emma. Do you believe God sometimes sends us dreams? Or do you believe all dreams are merely creations of our subconscious? Dreams are mentioned often in the Old Testament. A few examples are Job 4:13-16, 1 Samuel 3:2-15, and Daniel 2:19.

8. Henry gives a birdhouse to Leroy and his wife to remind them that God cares and is watching over them. Matthew 10:29-31 reads, "Are not two sparrows sold for a penny? Yet not one of them will fall to the ground outside your Father's care. And even the very hairs of your head are all numbered. So don't be afraid; you are worth more than many sparrows." How do these verses encourage you at this time in your life?

9. At the end of the story, we're given the impression that the tragedy of Sophia's death led Tess to explore a life of faith. Have you known anyone who turned to Christ after going through a difficult time? How can we help others when they are making this journey?

10. One of my favorite aspects of this story is the developing relationship between Emma and Henry. Do you think it's possible for someone to find love at their age? Why or why not?

Glossary

Ausbund	Amish hymnal
Bruder	brother
Danki	thank you
Dat	father
Englischer	non-Amish person
Freind(en)	friend(s)
Gem gschehne	you're welcome
Gotte	God
Gotte's wille	God's will
Grandkinner	grandchildren
Gudemariye	good morning
Gut	good
Kapp	prayer covering
Loblied	hymn of praise
Mamm/Mammi	mom/grandmother
Nein	no
Ordnung	the unwritten set of rules and regulations that guide everyday Amish life
Rumspringa	Running-around years
Schweschder	sister
Wunderbaar	wonderful
Ya	yes
Youngie/Youngies	young adult/adults

Recipes

Breakfast Casserole

8 slices white or wheat bread, crumbled
6 eggs
2 cups milk
½ onion, diced
½ tsp. salt
½ tsp. dry mustard
1 lb. fried sausage or bacon, crumbled and drained
1 lb. Colby cheese, grated
¼ cup margarine or butter

Preheat the oven to 325°. Spread the bread across the bottom of a greased 9 x 13-inch baking dish. In a separate bowl, beat the eggs and then add the milk, onion, salt, and mustard. Sprinkle meat and cheese over the bread. Dot the margarine or butter over the cheese and pour the egg mixture over all. Bake for 45 minutes to 1 hour, until golden brown.

Recipe from Elizabeth Coblentz with Kevin Williams, The Amish Cook

Cheese Soup

¼ cup butter
¼ cup onion, finely chopped
¼ cup flour
4 cups milk
⅛ tsp. salt
1 cup cheddar cheese, grated
2 cups fresh or frozen vegetables (corn, diced carrots, peas, celery, etc.)

Melt the butter in a saucepan over medium-high heat. Add the onion and sauté. Remove the pan from heat. Add flour, milk, and salt. Return the saucepan to the heat and cook until thick, stirring constantly. Add the cheese and stir until melted. Add the vegetables. Let simmer for 30 minutes over low heat.

Recipe from Elizabeth Coblentz with Kevin Williams, The Amish Cook

Potato Casserole

---

2 lbs. potatoes, peeled and thinly sliced
2½ cups cream of chicken soup (or 1 10¾-ounce can condensed cream of chicken soup plus 1 can water)
½ cup butter, melted
2 cups cheese, grated
1 tsp. salt
2 cups sour cream
½ cup onion, chopped
4 oz. crackers, crushed

Preheat the oven to 350º. Combine the potatoes, soup, butter, cheese, salt, sour cream, and onion in a large bowl. Spoon the mixture into a 2-quart casserole dish. Sprinkle the cracker crumbs over the top and bake for 45 minutes, until the top is golden brown.

Recipe from Elizabeth Coblentz with Kevin Williams, The Amish Cook

Shoo-Fly Pie

1 unbaked piecrust (8 inches)
⅓ cup molasses
¼ cup boiling water
¼ tsp. baking soda
1 cup all-purpose flour
⅓ cup sugar
¼ cup shortening
Pinch of salt

Preheat the oven to 350°. Mix together the molasses, water, and baking soda in a small bowl and then pour into the unbaked pie shell. In a separate bowl, combine the flour, sugar, shortening, and salt. Mix until crumbly. Pour into pie shell on top of molasses mixture. Bake for 40 minutes, until the molasses mixture seeps through the top and the top is dark brown.

Recipe from Elizabeth Coblentz with Kevin Williams, The Amish Cook

Ginger Crisps

¾ cup shortening
1 cup sugar
¼ cup molasses
1 egg
2½ cups flour
¼ tsp. baking soda
2½ tsp. baking powder
1 tsp. cinnamon
½ tsp. ginger

Cream together the shortening and sugar until light and fluffy. Add the molasses and egg and mix well. Sift in the dry ingredients and mix thoroughly. Chill for 2 hours. Form into 1-inch balls and then roll in granulated sugar. Bake on cookie sheet at 375° 10 to 12 minutes.

Recipe from Sallie Y. Lapp, Amish Treats from My Kitchen

Ham Salad Spread

1 pound cooked ham, coarsely chopped
3 small stalks celery, finely diced
1 large dill pickle, finely diced
1¼ tsp. dry mustard
¼ tsp. onion powder
½ cup mayonnaise
½ tsp. salt
1 T. lemon juice

Mix together the ham, celery, and pickle. In a separate bowl, combine the mustard, onion powder, mayonnaise, salt, and lemon juice. Stir together and then stir this mixture into the ham. Spread on sandwich bread or crackers.

Recipe from Elizabeth Coblentz with Kevin Williams, The Amish Cook

Potato Salad

3 hard-boiled eggs, cooled
3 cups potatoes with skins on, cooked, diced, and chilled
¾ cup salad dressing or Miracle Whip
1½ tsp. yellow prepared mustard
2 T. apple cider vinegar
¼ small onion, chopped fine
¾ cup sugar
1 tsp. salt
½ cup chopped celery
2 T. milk

Peel the eggs and mash them with a potato masher in a large bowl. Add the potatoes, salad dressing or Miracle Whip, mustard, vinegar, onion, sugar, salt, celery, and milk. Mix well. The salad will be moist.

Recipe from Elizabeth Coblentz with Kevin Williams, The Amish Cook

Mashed Potato Rolls

2¼ tsp. (1 package) active dry yeast
¼ cup warm water (about 110°)
1¾ cups warm milk (about 110°)
¼ cup oil
6 T. sugar
1 egg

½ cup mashed potatoes
 (see note at end of recipe)
1½ tsp. salt
1 tsp. baking powder
½ tsp. baking soda
6 cups all-purpose flour
Melted butter (optional)

In a large bowl, dissolve the yeast in warm water. Add the milk, oil, sugar, egg, and mashed potatoes and mix well. Stir in the salt, baking powder, baking soda, and half of the flour. Mix either by hand using a large wooden spoon or with a mixer, gradually adding more flour until a soft dough is formed.

Turn out the dough onto a floured surface and knead for about 8 minutes. Place dough in a large greased bowl and turn so all surfaces of the dough are greased. Cover and let rise until double, about 1½ hours.

Punch down the dough. Turn out onto a lightly floured surface and shape small amounts of dough into approximately 32 round balls. Place the balls 2 inches apart on greased baking sheets. Cover and let rise until double, about 30 to 45 minutes.

Bake in a preheated 375° oven for 15 to 18 minutes or until done and the tops are golden. Remove from the oven and, if desired, immediately brush tops with melted butter. Set on racks to cool.

Note: If you don't have any leftover mashed potatoes and you're in a hurry, you can use dehydrated mashed potatoes. Just mix according to the package directions and use in place of fresh mashed potatoes.

Recipe from Georgia Varozza, 99 Favorite Amish Breads, Rolls, & Muffins

Blueberry Oatmeal Muffins

1 cup all-purpose flour
2 tsp. baking powder
½ tsp. salt
½ tsp. cinnamon
½ cup brown sugar
¾ cup rolled oats
1 egg
1 cup milk
¼ cup butter, melted
¾ cup blueberries, fresh or frozen
Sugar or cinnamon sugar for sprinkling

Whisk together the flour, baking powder, salt, and cinnamon. Add the sugar and rolled oats and mix well.

In a large bowl, beat together the egg, milk, and melted butter. Add the dry ingredients and stir just until blended. Do not overmix. Fold in the blueberries.

Fill muffin cups ⅔ full and sprinkle some sugar or cinnamon sugar on top of each muffin. Bake in a preheated 375° oven for 20 minutes or until done.

Recipe from Georgia Varozza, 99 Favorite Amish Breads, Rolls, & Muffins

Chocolate Zucchini Bread

3 eggs, beaten
1 cup oil
1¾ cups sugar
1 T. vanilla
2 cups zucchini, grated
3 cups all-purpose flour (or use half whole wheat and half all-purpose)
1 tsp. salt
1 tsp. baking soda
1 tsp. baking powder
½ cup unsweetened cocoa
½ cup chopped walnuts or pecans (optional)

In a large bowl, combine the eggs, oil, sugar, and vanilla. Add the zucchini and stir.

In a separate bowl, mix together the flour, salt, baking soda, baking powder, and cocoa. Add flour mixture to the zucchini mixture and blend well. Add nuts if using and stir again.

Grease and flour 2 loaf pans. Pour in the batter. Bake in a preheated 350° oven for 45 minutes. Cool in pans for 10 to 15 minutes before removing bread to a wire rack to finish cooling.

Recipe from Georgia Varozza, 99 Favorite Amish Breads, Rolls, & Muffins

AUTHOR'S NOTE

The Monte Vista National Wildlife Refuge was established in 1953 and is in the San Luis Valley. Composed of 14,800 acres, it may be viewed by a four-mile auto tour. Each year 20,000 cranes pass through in both the spring and the fall to rest and refuel before continuing their migration. The refuge is also home to endangered whooping cranes as well as several hundred elk.

The first Amish families settled in Colorado in the early 1900s. As of 2010, the state was home to four Amish communities, with a combined population of under 100 families. In the San Luis Valley, farming has proven to be a challenge for the Amish, as the area receives an average of only seven inches of rain annually. The growing season is approximately 90 days. Many families in the area have opened small businesses to provide an additional source of income.

Accidental/acquired savant syndrome is a condition where dormant savant skills emerge after a brain injury or disease. Although it is quite rare, researchers in 2010 identified 32 individuals who displayed unusual skills in one or more of five major areas: art, musical abilities, calendar calculation, arithmetic, and spatial skills. Males with savant syndrome outnumber females by roughly six to one.

Cell phones can be tracked via their access to local service towers or software downloaded to the phone. According to Digital Trends, simply putting your phone into airplane mode or removing the SIM card will not keep it from being tracked. Removing the battery is effective. However, most newer models of cell phones no longer allow this.

Crops for Cranes is a joint project between the Colorado Parks & Wildlife, U.S. Fish & Wildlife, and other organizations, which began in the fall of 2014. Their goal is to ensure an adequate food supply for cranes. One way they do so is by entering into agreements with local farmers to purchase a certain number of acres of their crops. The grain is left unharvested to provide forage for the cranes.

Cranes have been coming to the San Luis Valley and other parts of

Colorado since 1940, but the area has changed in recent years, putting in jeopardy the abundance of habitat the cranes require. In particular, in the Yampa Valley, agricultural trends have undergone a significant change because of economic factors. The production of local grain crops such as wheat and oats has decreased from approximately 85,000 acres in the 1940s to only 10,000 acres currently. This decrease in grain crop production has the potential to adversely impact the cranes.

I did much research on, and had the pleasure of visiting, both the Monte Vista National Wildlife Refuge and the Great Sand Dunes National Park and Preserve. I took the liberty of rearranging sections of the park to facilitate the actions of and cause trouble for my characters. Any discrepancies in the description of the park were the result of intentional dramatic license.

About the Author

 **VANNETTA CHAPMAN** writes inspirational fiction full of grace. She is the author of several novels, including the Plain and Simple Miracles series and the Pebble Creek Amish series. Vannetta is a Carol Award winner and has also received more than two dozen awards from Romance Writers of America chapter groups. She was a teacher for fifteen years and currently resides in the Texas hill country. For more information, visit her at www.VannettaChapman.com.

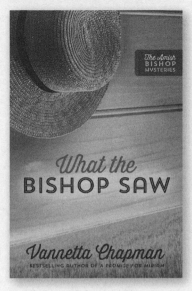

Somewhere in the Embers Lies the Truth

A fire blazes out of control in the San Luis Valley of Colorado, leaving an elderly Amish bachelor dead. Bishop Henry Lapp rushes to the scene, and he learns the fire was no accident. Someone intended to kill Vernon Frey. But who would want to kill him? Well, practically everyone—Amish and *Englisch* alike.

When the police point the finger at a suspect Henry knows is innocent, the bishop must decide whether or not to use his mysterious, God-given gift— one he's tried desperately to ignore all these years—to try and set the record straight. His close friend and neighbor, Emma Fisher, encourages Henry to follow God's leading.

Could the clue to solving the case be locked somewhere deep in Henry's memory? Will he find the courage to move forward in faith and put the right person behind bars? Is his friendship with Emma becoming something more?

What the Bishop Saw is a story of extraordinary talent, the bonds of love and friendship, and the unfailing grace of God.

A Promise for Miriam

Amish schoolteacher Miriam King loves her students. At 26, she hasn't yet met anyone who can convince her to give up the Plain school at Pebble Creek. Then newcomer Gabriel Miller steps into her life, bringing his daughter, an air of mystery, and challenges Miriam has never faced before.

A Home for Lydia

Lovely Lydia Fisher may be an outspoken Amish woman, but she also desperately needs her job at the Plain Cabins at Pebble Creek. Though sparks fly at first between her and her new boss, when the cabins are robbed, nothing is more important to Aaron than making sure Lydia is safe.

A Wedding for Julia

Julia Beechy's dream of opening a café is shattered when her mother says she must choose a husband or move to live with distant family upon her mother's imminent death. Caleb Zook thought he would never marry, but can he help this beautiful, sad woman? Is this God's plan for his future?

Anna's Healing

When a tornado strikes, Anna Schwartz's life is changed forever. She suffers a spinal cord injury and finds herself learning to live as a paraplegic. But then a miracle happens, and the world's attention is drawn to this young Amish girl who has experienced the unexplainable.

Joshua's Mission

Amish farmer Joshua Kline travels to Texas to offer aid to an *Englisch* town after a category 4 hurricane has ravaged the area. What will he find when he arrives there? A budding romance? A call from God? A possible healing of his relationship with his brother? Certainly, God's grace.

Sarah's Orphans

Through a series of tragic events, Sarah Yoder becomes the sole provider for her five younger siblings. Then two more orphans steal her heart—along with Paul Byler, the Amish man who moves in next door hoping for calm but finding God's calling instead.